Future Homes

The Adventures of John Grey
Book Ten

Future Homes

The Adventures of John Grey
Book Ten

Frederick A. Read

A *Guaranteed* Book

First Published in 2012 by
Guaranteed Books

an imprint of The Guaranteed Partnership
Po Box 12, Maesteg, Mid Glamorgan, South Wales, CF34 0XG, UK

FT
Pbk

ISBN 978 1 906864 34 7

Typeset by Christopher Teague

Printed and Bound in Wales by
MWL Digital Print, Pontypool

www.theguaranteedpartnership.com

Chapters

Foreword

The aim of the ISDM College is to provide a series of new ship concepts which would become projects to be built, and eventually the seafarers FUTUTRE HOMES.

John enters the prestigious ISDM. College only to have one of his fellow project workers steal John's conceptual model ship designs, and patent them as his own.

John and his team build his designer ship, only to be faced with the threat of court action by the thief for 'plagiarism' and patent theft by that person.

Chapter I

Under Starters Orders

"Here's a big letter for you John. You must have forgotten to tell them our new address."

"By the look of it, it's been in the sorting office for a little while too. Look at the original postmark Ma, that's almost 3 weeks ago." John replied, tearing open the large brown envelope for the contents to spill onto the table where he sat.

Looking quickly through the documents and the covering letter until John saw a telephone number he was to use and decided to phone from the comfort of his own home, instead of climbing the hill to the bus stop where he used to phone from, now some 2 miles away.

"I wish to speak to a Mr Martins. What? Oh, my name is John Grey." he said evenly, then waited until he was connected to the man.

"Hello Martins! No, I only got your package just now, because it was sent to my old address some weeks ago. Our new address is 36 Beatty Park Central, Dunmurry. I have taken time off to do a favour for a friend of mine, being free from any known contract. What's that? A new contract on offer you say from the ISDM? That sounds a fair offer which suits me fine, and I thank you for that, but give me a couple of days to get organised and I'll see you, say next Monday afternoon, as soon as I arrive. Yes, thanks! I've given you my new address, so all should be fine your end. Oh, before you go, is there a Mr McPhee there with you? Yes, that's him! It's a long story but we go way back some 16 years and more. Tell him I'll call into his office after seeing you. Yes, I'll read your instructions and act accordingly, goodbye and thanks!" he concluded, putting the phone back onto its cradle again.

"Looks as if I'm off on my jaunts again Ma! I'll be catching the Sunday night Heysham ferry, as I've got to report to that

ISDM college in Southampton I was telling you about. Look! They've sent me my boat and train tickets and a nice little cheque to cover my travel expenses. Pretty generous too."

"Maybe I can have some of it to get a new mattress, John?"

"Certainly! How much do you need?"

"I saw one in the big Co-Op in Lisburn when I went to visit Nancy and Arthur. The one I liked was only £4.15 shillings and half a crown for delivery, so it was."

"Right you are Ma; I think I can spare a fiver for you." John stated, rising up from the table with his hands full of documents and bits of paper.

"I'll get out of your way so you can get on. I'm off to my room to study this lot."

"I'll call you down for dinner, but its rabbit stew again."

"Never mind, when I come back from the village I'll bring back a nice piece of boiling ham or even tongue for supper." He said, pecking his mother on her cheek with a kiss before climbing up the stairs to his room to read his mail.

"Hmmm! They're asking a lot from me, as I'm only an Engineer not a ship designer!

Maybe I'll get to design the engine room or something like the 'Tsun Wan'." he said quietly to himself, reading on, and on and on, until he heard his mother calls him for dinner.*

"Phew Ma! You should see what they want off me! I'm only a ships engineer not a ruddy scientist. Mind you though, the terms and conditions look very favourable, and I get to travel buckshee, as Kim Soon would have said." he announced, sitting down at the table to eat his food.

Mother and son talked for a little while discussing her lonely existence in her new house, although she admitted grudgingly that it was much cosier than the draughty old cottage.

"You've got Norah and Billy just down the street from you, and you've got some friendly neighbours too. Think of it this

---

* See *Perfumed Dragons*.

2

way Ma! Unlike the old house which was built at the bottom of a hill, this is a brand new one at the top of one. So you won't have the annual flooding to put up with, or for it to almost fall down around your ears with subsidence. Besides you're only a quarter of a mile away from the Co-Op and the other shops in the village, now." John comforted.

"I suppose you're right, but I don't like that nosey biddy on the corner. She's always gossiping in the street keeping you ages talking about everything and nothing."

"Maybe she's lonely too Ma!"

"What, with a house full of grown up kids always trudging the garden path?"

"Well, whatever. Anyway, I'm off now to get that mattress money you want, before I finish off what I was doing upstairs." John said, leaving the table to walk out into the hallway.

"John! Will you bring home some shillings for the gas and electric, and get another cob, some soda farls and a wheaten bap for your tea, and a half pint of buttermilk! Your woman next door is poorly at the moment, so pop in and sees if she needs some messages as well." she called out.

"Okay! I'll pop next door to see her. Now let's see! You want some shillings, a cob, soda farls, wheaten baps, some meat and a pint of buttermilk, is that all? What meat is it you want, brawn, ham or tongue? Do you want some black puddin' too?" he asked, having rattled off the verbal shopping list.

"I'll leave it up to you!" she replied as John shut the door quietly behind him and visited his next-door neighbour, before sauntering down the street to the village shops of Dunmurry.

A couple of days later when John prepared to leave home once again, he kissed his mother in both cheeks saying,

"I'm off now Ma! Billy's giving me a lift down to the docks just now. Look after yourself and keep well. I'll write to you when I get there."

"I wished you'd give up the sea now John, but you've got to

do what you've set out to do. Come home soon." she said dolefully but waved him goodbye.

"I'm catching the Heysham ferry, sailing in 1hours time, Billy." John informed, for the two to chat all the way down to the docks.

"I'll be back in around 9 months or so. Thanks for the lift." John said, then shaking Billy's hand stepped onto the gangway of the ferry.

"Have a good trip John! Give us a bell when you've arrived." Billy called to the departing John.

"Tell Ma to look under her new mattress, I've left a little surprise for her." John responded with a wave and a smile before he boarded the ship to have his boarding ticket checked.

"Your cabin is B8 on the starboard side above the saloon, just follow the signs." the deck officer stated, clipping John's boarding pass, then pointed to a half-glass, double door which led through to the saloon.

When he arrived into his cabin, John looked out of the window to see the night-lights of Belfast twinkling at him. The city had virtually gone to sleep now, for it was a normal quiet Sunday night, and everybody needed their rest before the start of another hectic week ahead of them. Unlike the British mainland, the drink laws in Ulster banned pubs and clubs from opening on the Sunday. Apart from the local paper shop who was allowed a couple of hours in the morning to sell their wares, no shop or public building was open for trade.

Happily for the army of pub and club users, the rest of the weekdays enjoyed an Irish 20hour opening time, (from 10 in the morning till 10 at night that is).

I think I'll go on deck for the transit down the Lough, as I haven't done that for years now.' he thought, locking his cabin door behind him to make his way to the now very crowded saloon full of fellow travellers, awaiting for the ship to make her voyage.

John managed to find an empty chair and sat down to enjoy a cigarette when he felt a heavy hand thumping him on his shoulder.

"Hey you! That's my seat. I only went to get a mug of tea! Now unless you shift your scrawny arse, you'll get this tea all over you!" a gruff threatening voice said from behind him.

The people nearest him held their breath to see what John would do and say against this obvious bully of a man.
John stood up quietly then turned to the man said.

"Sorry and all that, only I didn't see any persons name on it. Here take it." he invited, seeing the obvious delight on the man's face.

"That's better. You know it makes sense to give up your seat to somebody better than you." he said with satisfaction then went to sit down.

As he did so, John whipped the chair from under him, shouting 'Ole!' then walked away carrying the chair with him.

"You can have the deck space as long as you want, but I'm having the seat." John said quietly to the shocked, dazed man lying on the deck, covered in his own tea.

The other passengers laughed at the fallen man clapping John for his neat response, to make another case of *Schadenfreude* at its best, before they went back to their own little world.

The bully got up and stormed towards John, uttering threats of what he was going to do him.

John managed to see a scruffy uniform under the man's now very wet overcoat, and saw he was in fact a 4th deck officer. Taking off his coat he showed his own 'badge of office' which was 4 solid gold rings with the coloured diamond in the middle to indicate to the bully John was in fact at the top of his profession, that of a Chief Engineer.

This recognition by the bully changed him into an apologetic creep which almost made John sick.

"Sorry, er Chief! Didn't mean to upset you, but you've got to show these people just who runs the show around here." was the meek utterance.

"Unless you are part of the ship's crew, which would mean you should be out on deck, then you are just a passenger like me.

I don't know what line you're off but I suggest you get yourself some manners and think about the welfare of others on board. For you could be called upon to help out should anything happen between leaving Belfast and arriving at Heysham. Now push off and find somewhere else to park your body. I understand there's room up on the boat deck, go try up there, or better still get below to your cabin." John snarled, turning his back on the man to conclude the incident.

'It appears there are plenty more McCluskeys around needing a few pegs taken off them.' he thought, sitting down to enjoy a cigarette before abandoning the chair, to take a stroll along the weather deck.

With fresh sea air back into his lungs again and the movement of the ship, gave John a welcome tonic to sleep soundly in his bunk as the ship sailed over the choppy Irish Sea, arriving with a slight bump as the ship hit the Heysham jetty.

A steward knocked on his cabin door announcing he had a breakfast tray for him and that he had precisely half an hour to get ashore and board the boat train for London.

John leapt out of his bunk tot the steward into the cabin, then got himself dressed again.

Thanks steward! I could do with a cuppa." he said, and commenced to have his hurried breakfast, whilst the steward busied himself making the cabin tidy for the next occupants.

ohn managed to board the train and find his 'reserved' seat before the guard waved his flag, blowing his whistle for the train driver to get moving.

When he arrived at Southampton's station, he got a cab which took him out of the city and into the countryside to a small village standing on the banks of a small meandering river.

The taxi passed between twin cottages marking the gateway of a winding approach road, leading to a very large ornate building that was an erstwhile aristocrat's house from years gone by. He marvelled at the neatly trimmed lawns, the various types of trees which he could identify from his travels around the world. There was a large marble statue of a naked lady placed in the middle of a white water fountain, with other smaller statuettes dotted around the neatly laid out formal gardens at the front and sides of the main building. He saw some smaller outbuildings looking comparably more modern in their construction, guessing these were probably the model rooms or the instructional areas where he would be attending.

Paying the taxi driver, he thanked him and stepped into a slowly revolving door to enter a large hallway with ornately carved wood panels, the like you would expect from such a grand and major building.

A tall slender looking man appeared to inform John he was the porter and that he was to accompany him to be shown his quarters.

He followed the porter along the third floor corridor to one wing of the main building, finally arriving at his room, which had a magnificent view of the river and the countryside surrounding this sumptuous place.

"Here you are Mr Grey. Just phone the reception desk if you need anything. I understand that you are to meet Mr Martins. His office is behind the reception façade you saw when you came in. You are to present yourself to him by 1630."

John, looking at his watch, decided he didn't have time for a wash and brush up so told the porter he would go immediately.

"Very good Mr Grey. I'll tell him you're on your way." the porter replied with a slight bow of his head and left the room, leaving John to his own devices.

"Good afternoon Mr Grey. Have a good journey? My Name is Kenneth Martins, the college Co-ordinator." Martins greeted John warmly, shaking his hand to welcome him into his office.

"Good afternoon, er, Ken! Yes thanks, but the long train journey was somewhat a bit tiresome after a night being tossed around the seas for seven hours. Still, here I am and all in one piece."

"Good, that's the spirit, now to business." Martins said with a smile, commencing to give John a rundown of the place, who did what, where, why, and when.

It took Martins over an hour to do this, but kept handing John various booklets and other instruction leaflets.

"In short, this place is just one big college and you're the hotel manager. I'm about to undertake some classroom training but am required to give a massive input to the continued success of the college. That Mr McPhee is the Head of the department I am joining who will be my mentor." John stated.

"That's about it. There are three final but major points though. One. Until such times as you finally get to the point of being offered a project placement, you will only get paid a retainer commensurate with your calibre of project, shall we say. That also includes free board and lodgings. Once graduated, if I may use the phrase, you will be given a salary until you return with the results of your project. Two. Any patents and ideas emanating from this college concerning your project work will be placed at the colleges' usage only. Three. We have very high security awareness around the grounds of this college, so it is in your own interest to get to know of it and the consequences if you are caught in breach of this or any other rules and regulations which I've discussed and the leaflets I have given you. That is the end of my briefing, so I hope that you will enjoy your stay here and get to know the other college inhabitants. Oh! And just a final thought. Decorum at all times if you please, because we do have a lot of V.I.P's from all over the world coming and going all the time and don't want to give them a bad image of this college or even from the staff."

"I'm a fishing and golfing person, so you won't get any trouble from me."

"Glad to hear it. Then you'll be interested to know we organise such events you've just mentioned, so if you decide to join in, then you'll be among good company."

"I'm at home already then Ken."

"Good! Then I bid you good day, as I've got two more arrivals to see before even I can relax for the day." Martins said, holding out his hand to shake John's goodbye.

'It's just like being back in the Engineering Academy, only with a lot more swank to it all. Now that I'm under starters orders, I'd better make myself known to Fergus.' he thought, retracing his steps back to his room.

Chapter II

Some Old Friends

"**G**ood morning gentlemen, welcome our new lecture auditorium. We appear to have a few fresh faces in our midst, so for your benefit, I live by my name of William Clutterbuck. I can't stand clutter around the place so you are required to keep the place shipshape and Bristol fashion, so if anything untoward happens within this college the buck stops at my desk. Apart from that I am for my sins, the Deputy Head of the UK operations for the ISDM. We have a close link with the Royal Naval Institute for Naval Architecture (RNINA) up at Greenwich along with other august bodies, but our main work is carried out in various shipyards both here and abroad." Clutterbuck stated, then went on to deliver a one-hour lecture on what everybody was about to be employed in doing.

After his initial speech and a brief recess for refreshment, Clutterbuck introduced several men of high standing within the shipbuilding industry, including a couple of blue- suited Royal Navy Admirals, and someone who brought a smile to John's face; Fergus McPhee.

Each man delivered a small speech on the projects they were involved in, before the audience was assigned to their new Project Managers, for the lecture session to be concluded.

"Looks like we're all going to be busy Fergus! Am I the only one in your team or have you got a workhouse full of slaves tucked away somewhere?" John asked, greeting McPhee with a handshake.

"I now have three teams of engineers. I've just sent out the last one on their first assigned project, and another team of five are ready to come back with their project findings. Each project will go to a suitable project monitor or provider be it a shipyard or whatever. If you complete your studies including the theoretical side of your workload over the next three months or so, then you will also be sent out to prove them for real. So John, in this instance you're lucky to have me all to yourself for that time. Come! Let's get to my office to introduce you to some old friends of yours." McPhee said with a glint in his eye.

"Just as long as it's not Cresswell and his ilk. But lead on Fergus!" John retorted, following McPhee up to his office.

John looked around it, stating that it was not as grandiose as the one he had out in Singapore, before sitting down in a very large leather armchair.

McPhee didn't answer, but went to a large cupboard built into the wall, and started to operate the lock combination before he was able to swing the heavy door open, to reveal several rolls of paper, reams of documents, diagrams and drawings.

McPhee mumbled to himself, selecting various parchments, rolls and other items then returned to his desk to dump them onto it.

"Here we are young John! Here are some of your old friends I was talking about. They represent just some of the work you've done in the past and have given me to look after, but I've put them into a recognised order as a pointer to the best way to tackle your studies." he said with delight, fetching all the rest from the large cupboard before shutting it again.

John took hold of some of the rolls and unfurled them to see what was what.

He studied the first one carefully before putting it down to read another one for a few minutes, whilst McPhee sat in his own chair and watching the surprises and expressions on Johns face.

"I did all this Fergus? Phew, I must have been on the whiskey or something. What are you planning for them? What are...?" John started to ask in quick succession, before McPhee stopped him.

"Now, now John! Calm down! Those represent your passport into this place I intend for you to re-create them here, then eventually for real on some ship that we'll get constructed. This place has top-notch designers, draftsmen, model builders and even the best technical library in the whole country at our disposal.

Take for instance, your false deck arrangement you created on the *Inverlaggan* and the *Tsun Wan*. Then the internal skin for your last ship, er the *Winnipeg* I think it was. Both ideas worked well as temporary arrangements for those ships, but I feel that we can develop these ideas into something more permanent. All of which will be your own personal projects, starting with the *Winnipeg*, John." McPhee stated, offering John a cigar.

John took the cigar, lit it and sat down to think things over.

"Before you start panicking or whatever, you'll be joining a team of ship designers who will help you with your technical problems and the like. All you've got to do is see that your plans and designs are carried out and make them work. We know they work, so at least you've got half the battle done." McPhee offered, sitting back to enjoy his own cigar.

"If the ship design is being done by others, how long have I got to deliver all this wizardry Fergus? I mean what type of ship would they make, such as freighters just like the *Winnipeg*?"

"It is obvious that you are not sure about all this John. I tell you what. After lunch, we'll take a stroll around the workshops to help you familiarise yourself." McPhee suggested.

"It's not so much that Fergus, as I'm fairly familiar with ship construction, at least to a certain degree, but I'd much prefer re-designing the engine rooms or other machinery on board these perhaps weird and wonderful ships which may be destined for the scrap yard even before they've sailed.

Having said all that, I certainly welcome your conducted tour of this place, as it should be interesting if not instructive."

"Good, then that's settled. I'll see you after lunch in the foyer, but mind you don't get caught stubbing your cigarette ends onto the porter's nicely polished floor, as he'd go daft and hit you with his broomstick." McPhee warned, stubbing the last remains of his cigar into a very ornate glass ashtray.

"The last person who tried to hit me with his stick lived to regret it, but point taken Fergus." John replied, stubbing his finished cigar into the tray.

"We normally have a 2 hour break on the first day back, but I'll see you and another project worker around the 1430 mark." McPhee advised as they got up to leave the office.

John left McPhee and went into his dining room to the table allocated for him and three others that he still had not met.

"Just like the *Brooklea* and the others, only this time I'm Mr John Grey with the title of Chief Marine Engineer." he observed from the small place names set out in front of him, and sat down to be waited upon.

"Do I hear mutterings in the ranks? Speaking from a Jacks point of view, the King had better get used to it then." a voice whispered into his ear.

John stood up quickly to face whoever crept up on him and saw Ben Ford standing there.

"Ben! Why it's great to see you again. What the devil are you doing in this part of the world? How's the gang over there? Colin and family okay?" John asked in complete surprise, first embracing then shaking hands with Ford.

"I'm right behind you Chief!" another voice said from behind him.

John spun round and found that Crabbe was also looking at him.

"Colin! You too? This is a lovely surprise. Sit down here, never mind the place names." John said with great delight at meeting up with a pair of good friends from way back.

"We only just arrived, and these are our place settings too. This is the work of a certain Scottish gentleman by the name of McPhee, I believe. He said something about old friends." Crabbe said with a big smile. embracing John in the same manner[*].

"I think this calls for a celebratory drink." Ford suggested, but it was decided to have it in the evening after supper.

They talked freely and excitedly all the way through lunch, to the extent that the waitresses had to ask them on several

---

[*] See *Fresh Water*.

13

occasions to keep the noise down as they were annoying the other diners.

John sitting facing them felt a kindred spirit with these two men who he had grown very fond of, but decided he'd much prefer his other, dearer friends as the bond was much deeper and more profound.

Crabbe saw a brief faraway look in John's face and deducing correctly that he was missing his other original friends Larter and Sinclair, told him so.

"I think we all have experienced the absence of dear friends, but at least for those of us who are here now, we can celebrate the good fortune of meeting up again. I for one am glad to have done so." Crabbe said softly, holding out his hand and shaking John's again.

"Forgive my moment of relapse gentlemen, and I offer my deepest apologies to you both if I have offended you. Yes Ben! The dining room would be too full if we had all our friends around us again. It would be like an Irish Parliament, everybody talking but nobody listening." John concluded, hearing the big grandfather clock in the hallway strike the hour.

He looked at his watch then told them he had to meet his Project Manager, and who it was.

"McPhee? Why that crafty old..." Crabbe was about to say when McPhee was seen to appear at their table.

"Thank you for recommendation Mr Crabbe, take a 100 lines to say 'I must buy my Project Manager a whiskey every day." McPhee chuckled, placing his hands gently onto John's shoulders to prevent him from standing up

"C'mon John its two o'clock and these two reprobates have their induction to see to. You and I have a tour to conduct. I'll see you two in the bar around six'ish, before dinner." McPhee prompted.

"Yes, see you both later." John responded, smiled at them before leaving with McPhee.

"You crafty devil Fergus! I don't know how you got to get

14

Ben and Colin, stuck way out there in Port Arthur, but I'm thankful that you've brought them here at the same time as me. Then again, why Ben Ford? I mean he's ex army and only has a ship repair-cum-salvage yard, whilst Colin is only a normal run of the mill Sea Captain?"

"There you go again John, giving me not just one simple question but a rapid fire of them in one go. Just enjoy your tour, everything will be revealed when we all meet up in the morning for our Project meeting." McPhee chuckled, as the two men commenced their tour.

John had his notebook and pen at the ready.

"Just like my very first trip around the *Brooklea* with my then 2nd Engineer Happy Day, Fergus!" he said with a big grin, remembering the occasion.

"Speaking of which, I think he's due back soon from his second project at the Barrow-in-Furness yard, but would more than likely be after you've taken up your first. And anyway, he's got a different project manager who is also away with him."

"Well, whatever you've got lined up for me, as long as I've got 2 of my friends to work with, then you've got a deal Fergus."

"Yes! If I remember correctly, I'm still the Ace in the pack John. Now here's the tank that tests the scale models sea worthiness before they get built for real." McPhee stated, entering a very long room which had a long glass container full of water, and a model ship being pushed along it by a mechanical device attached to the top of the tank.

Chapter III

Upstarts

John arrived back into his room, and put his notes and summations onto a fairly large table in the middle of his room. Then with a light heart he gave himself a welcome shower and a shave, put on his 'evening wear' that befits the strict dress code for such a posh place and generally prepared himself for his celebratory drink with his good re-united friends.

When he arrived into the cocktail bar, one corner of it was occupied by a group of pinstripe suited men accompanied by several elegantly dressed women, dripping in jewels, with some even wrapped in fur coats, all talking '*la de dah*' and sipping from long glasses. From the popping of corks he heard going off he deduced it was champagne, and the smell from the cigars suggested 'Havana' with a touch of Sobrani Black Russian cigarettes from the long handled cigarette holders the women were brandishing.

"Good evening sir, what can I get you?" the barman asked with a plummy voice.

"I'm expecting my friends to arrive, so I'll wait until they do, thanks" John replied.

"In that case sir, be kind enough to take advantage of our comfortable armchairs as we don't like people hanging around the bar. We have a waitress service for your convenience otherwise."

"Thanks!" John said curtly, moving slowly over to an empty corner of the room where some plush corner seats were situated. He collected a couple of ashtrays from other tables and placed them onto the highly polished table in front of him and started to smoke one of his own 'Havana's' as if to mark his own little territory like the snooty party on the opposite corner.

"Evening John! Waiting long?" Ford asked, as he and Crabbe arrived at the table.

"Just arrived. Have a seat because there's no standing at the bar, not even to order your ruddy drink."

Crabbe attracted a waitress over who took their order, with a somewhat surprised look on her face.

"Did you say Moet Chandon? But that's over £10 a bottle, and you want 4 of them?" she gasped in disbelief.

"Don't forget the 4 double whiskeys for our starters. Oh and by the way, we'll have 4 Churchill's while you're at it. If not them then a Rhodesian will do." Crabbe directed.

She had only gone a few moments when a tall swarthy man appeared speaking in a French accent, who was the Maitre 'D'.

"Excuse me gentlemen, but we only serve expensive champagne and the special cigars such as you requested to our special guests such as you see over there. So be good enough to give me a different order, apart from the whiskey that is. Better still, take yourselves off and use the Tavern at the back." he demanded, pointing to the rear of the main building.

All three of them took a sharp intake of breath, but it was Crabbe who jumped up first, grabbing hold of the waiter by his coat lapels.

"Now look here you pompous part time Frog! Just who the hell are you? Who do you think you are talking to? Do you know who we are, and I'm not talking as a resident here either?" Crabbe snarled into the man's face, which seemed to put him on his back foot. But as if to re establish his status within the establishment he gave his own riposte.

"Obviously you and your friends are upstarts who are beneath the standard required to enter this place, so I'm asking you all to leave before I call the security." came the trite reply.

"Let me put you into the Rembrandt even a Constable take your soddin' pick! I own a shipping company and have been invited here under the auspices of the ISDM, who by the way are your employers not mine." Crabbe growled then threw the man away from him in disdain.

"I, as it happens am the owner of a large shipyard business in the Canadian lakes." Ford snarled.

"And I am a Marine Chief Engineer with the same invite. In other words, asshole! We can pay for our rounds unlike of those freeloading spongers over there who're getting it for free judging by the amount being tipped down their throats. Now just get our drinks before our guest Mr McPhee arrives." John ordered.

The maitre' d looked at each of the friends in total amazement when they spoke, but it was the approaching bulk of McPhee that finally convinced him to beat a hasty retreat to fetch the order.

The rest of the occupants of the lounge bar had fallen silent to witness this altercation, and gave a polite applause, only to return to their own conversations when they saw the big frame of McPhee coming through the doorway.

"Good evening gentlemen! Nice to see you all! Now where's the 'hospitality' John?" McPhee said, shaking hands with Crabbe and Ford, unaware of the ruckus his team had caused.

"There will be a slight delay on account we've just put down a mutiny in the ranks." Ford replied with a grin, sitting down again.

Within moments two waitresses arrived carrying the drinks and ice buckets with champagne in them, much to the delight of McPhee.

They apologised for any inconvenience before disappearing as fast as they arrived.

"Now that's what I call hospitality. Cigars as well!" McPhee said with a big smile as he was given a large cigar.

"Nothing but the best for the best! That's what our motto is out in the lakes, Fergus McPhee. And especially because thanks to you, despite impossible odds, we three meet up again." Crabbe replied with a grin, holding up his whiskey glass to give a toast to 'bygone days of yore'.

The four men sat and whiled away the evening until the dinner gong reverberated throughout the large, empty hallway.

"Suppose we'd better go and eat. We can always come back and take up where we left off." Crabbe suggested, which was promptly agreed upon.

* * *

The evening was almost at a close when the barman shouted last orders, to find it was only the four friends still in the bar.

They had told of their recent past so as to bring the others up to date in their own lives, and had mutually agreed to honour their contract with ISDM.

It was discovered there were two flies in the proverbial ointment. That McPhee was due to retire at the end of his own contracted Project, and the imminent review talks about the fragmentation of ISDM.

"So it looks as if this could be the last set of projects for us all then Fergus?" John asked.

"Something like that John. Before I send you off to your project assignment, you'd best get some feelers out for the prospect of future employment. You two are lucky to have your own business concerns to keep you going. As for me, apart from my golden handshake from ISDM, I have a very nice government pension due. I intend to retire and spend it in some nice little tax haven somewhere. Probably Gib, even Singapore, being the cheapest places to live."

"Well, at least whilst we're here on this side of the pond, we intend enjoying ourselves. We're hoping to take as much trade knowledge back with us as possible, and maybe with luck we'll have a place like this to develop our own ideas." Ford said stoically.

"Well anyway. That's for the future gentlemen. I'm ready for turning in. I can hear room 208 calling me." John said lazily, standing up and stretching himself.

"Yes that's a good idea. See you all in the morning after breakfast, around 0900 in the lecture auditorium. We've got an awful lot of planning to be sorted before we can commence the triple project I've got in mind. So I'll bid you all goodnight, and thanks for a good evening. It was much appreciated." McPhee said with a yawn, as all four finally left the now empty bottles and full ashtrays for the cleaners to tidy up.

Chapter IV

Different Animals

The next two weeks was full of lectures, film shows, introductory ship building and other mind blowing subjects, which polarised the three friend's way of thinking.

At the end of the third week when everybody got together to put something tangible on the table, so McPhee could make his final decision on which projects they would be put on, he found his three 'charges' were showing signs of discord.

He asked them to his office to discuss things to see what was what.

Ford was totally wrapped up in everything he had seen and couldn't take enough notes, for he was only a ship repairer to contemplate diversifying into ship-building.

Crabbe was interested in the design applications purely on ship safety and actual handling at sea, whereas John was only interested in the new type of engines and the different layouts of the engine spaces etc on board which other project groups were developing.

"Well gentlemen, you certainly have disappointed me. I thought we could at least produce something worthy of your proven abilities to adapt, and design a decent workable craft which I could say with hand on my heart, it was my final intake who did it." McPhee said glumly.

"As I told you long ago Fergus, I'm a Marine Engineer not a ship designer. Yes, I can appreciate the need for adaptations to suit the occasion as you well know, but from everything I've seen over the last fortnight or so, designing is way over the top for me. Maybe I can help in someway to improve the life of a ship, but it would all be down to the man who actually designs the stresses and strains of the metals that are used in a ships design." John stated, calmly shutting his notepad and laying it onto the table in front of him.

"I'm purely a Sea Captain, but some of the knowledge I've gained so far should stand me in good stead. However, my mind would only be on the capability of the ship and the safety of my passengers and crew. Like John, I can offer minor adjustments to the deck layouts etc but it would be the actual designer who dictates where ideas of mine went." Crabbe stated.

"What about you Ben?" McPhee asked softly.

"This has been an eye opener for me, and I can't seem to absorb enough info to cope with my ideas. I'm hoping I can come away with at least one design I can deliver to the shipping fraternity up in the lakes, but again, I would have to rely on Colin and John to give me a decent input as to the overall shape of the vessel. I mean, its one thing for a ship to be repaired, but it's a totally different animal in actual ship design. What if something should befall the ship at sea when the design fault was suspect? Somehow I don't think I could handle such a catastrophe." Ford commented.

McPhee sat there thinking for a moment before he made his deliberations known.

"On the balance of probability, you three could produce something making it worth our while coming here, even if this turns out to be my last shout here. I had such high hopes for you three and a few projects you all had a big say in. If not then we'll call it quits and you to return home none the wiser." McPhee said sadly.

"I tell you what Fergus. Let the three of us stay over this holiday period, to see if we can give you something for your efforts in securing our place in this auspicious college. If whatever we come up with when you get back off your leave, tickles your fancy and you deem it worth a try, then we'll take it from there." John said softly to his old mentor.

"You mean that?" McPhee asked with hope in his voice.

"So lets deal, to coin a phrase. John's the King, I'm the Jack, and Colin can be whatever. When you, as the Ace come back off your weekend, maybe you can give us a solid 10!" Ford said with a big grin.

McPhee's face visibly shone with surprise and delight, as he snapped back into his old self and started to shake their hands.

"It's a deal! All of a sudden, you've made a very tired old man very happy. I'll see any facility you need will be available for you." He replied delightedly.

"Ahem Fergus! It's your turn for the beers tonight." John reminded him gently, but with a grin.

"Just put it on my tally John. Now we're back on terra firma again, you lot can bugger off so that I can get ready for my lift to town. See you all bright an early Wednesday morning at 0900, and don't be…"

"Adrift!" all three said in unison, filing out of McPhee's office.

"Poor Fergus! He must have thought his retirement date was earlier than he anticipated and his world had collapsed. Still, it was very diplomatic and thoughtful of you to remind him of my 'card trick' on the *Inverlaggan,* Ben. I for one vote we get down to some serious brain storming. Maybe in the reference library after supper." John suggested and got a willing answer back from the other two.

The friends made arrangements with the Librarian, who let them have the keys telling them to hand them back at the end of each session, but to the night receptionist.

They pulled out several reference books, drawings and other indicative reading material, even though they had their own sets of material with them, and commenced a long session of swapping ideas and thoughts in a deep and meaningful discussion.

It was the night porter who showed up around midnight reminding them of the time and asked them if they had homes to go to, as he was going to shut down the heating and lighting.

"You carry on. We're just finishing off anyway, so we'll lock up and return the key to the reception." Crabbe replied, which seemed to please the man.

"Very well. But kindly return all literature to wherever they belong, as there's nobody to clean here over the weekend. Make sure all lights are switched off too." he said gruffly and left the room after his tasks

"Right then gentlemen, I think we've got it. We'll look through some of the technical drawings to see if we can come up with something 'off the peg' rather than creating a new model. Maybe we could use the *Winnipeg* as the guinea pig instead." Ford suggested, which was readily agreed by the other two.

"But there's one thing that puzzles me about the hybrid we're about to create. Why are we concentrating just on freighters and not tankers or other types of ships?" John asked, as they went quietly into the lift to take them to their rooms.

"If we concentrate on just the one type to satisfy Fergus, then perhaps we would be able to develop it further, using say, tankers." Ford responded with a yawn.

"Anyway! We'll sort that out when we come to it. Bearing in mind that our overall problem is the weight and carrying capacity." Crabbe stated.

"Whatever!" John answered, entering his room, locking the door behind him.

'We must come up with a bloody good project for Fergus. He's been good to us, certainly me, and doubtless many others before us, so it would be a shame for him to retire on a downer.' he thought, rapidly lapsing into the land of nod.

Chapter V

Cuckoo Land

"**W**e're in luck gentlemen! I've just managed to speak to Halford the Chief Draftsman who has turned up and given us half an hour slot with him. Says to see him at 1000 in the technical office. So we'd better get our notes." John informed the other two.

Retrieving the notes they made last night along with other useful information they walked into the technical office where they saw a short grey bearded man sitting at a large drawing board.

"Morning gentlemen, what can I do for you?" Halford asked politely.

John spoke for the three of them giving a brief synopsis of what they were looking for and what they were trying to do.

"Hmmm! Yes I remember the *Winnipeg*. She was built at the Yarrow shipyard who gave her the new type of variable pitch propellers and a new set of turbines, along with an extended hull design. One of my best freighter designs she was." Halford said proudly, remembering the ship.

"Well I've given her a second hull if you like, but it was only quarter inch tinplating and welded to her transverse ribs." John informed, showing the man his original drawings, who looked it at for several moments.

"What are these cross bulkheads in the holds for?"

"I am the Captain of that ship, which carried mainly bulk grain of 2 different types; 2 for'ard and 2 aft. These bulkheads also made of tinplate, turn the ship into a multi grain carrier with up to 6 different grains. I can therefore satisfy different customers in just one voyage." Crabbe stated.

"There is another major item dealing with the ship's safety and handling whilst at sea, which you will probably know of. I call it the 'slosh' or 'slop' factor, which helps to stabilise the cargo during rough weather should the vessel be less than a 95% load capacity of either cargo or water used as ballast." John stated.

"Hmmm! I can understand, it's something most erstwhile ship designers seem to be ignorant of, but the question is why the second hull which would increase the deadweight of the ship in detriment to the capability of a full paying cargo load?"

"This ship was converted to a carrier whose grain is kept contained within a clean hold and is easier to unload or to clean out rather than having to sweep each nook and cranny from the skin, as before. Besides, it protects the ships hull from grain rot. This was as direct idea from a tanker that I was once on, called the '*Repulse Bay*.'" John replied.

"I see. But what is it you need off me?"

"Due to the slightly reduced hold capacity, to the tune of around 1000 tons between all the holds, is there any part of the ship we can use or shift to recoup that tonnage?" Crabbe asked.

"Nothing I can spot offhand. I'll get the ship's layout drawings and look at them for you, but you'll have to wait until Monday. Is there anything else I can help you with?"

"Yes. Here's a modification of a ship I had devised to be able to carry the vehicles and equipment of an army unit. It shows the positioning of temporary bulkheads and stanchions to prop up false deck heads. Notice the easy assembly and rigidity of it.
In fact I've created a little area of containership for each truck and their stores." John informed, unfurling his drawings onto Halford's large table.

Halford took down the various measurements and made a rough drawing of what he gleaned, but left the ships hull off the drawing to see how the whole thing looked like as if on dry land.

"You seem to have made a set of interconnecting boxes placed layer upon layer. So these end struts must take the weight of each layer up to deck level. Presumably if they are also interlinked, you could take a deck cargo as well, using the same method. Also by the look of it, you've managed to create a self-locking cargo holding device which would prevent any deck cargo from being lost overboard. Maybe a few securing lines on deck ring bolts would supplement the integrity." Halford observed, then went swiftly over to a cupboard and took out a large drawing.

"This is a concept ship currently in the model stage which is about to be tested in the tank. Each model is given a design number; this one has F196, as Freighter design no 196. Let's add this design to it and see if the ship is still seaworthy, stable, and not prone to capsizing that is. Mind you, we'd have to make a few adjustments to the cargo holds." Halford said quickly, superimposing his drawing onto that of the new ship.

"Incidentally! How did you unload all this? Ship borne derrick or dockside crane?"

"We had each strut of the top containers removed and put aside, then had a dockside crane lift the vehicles with four hooks which were built onto the ring bolts of the pallets they were on. A net was unsuitable and we couldn't guarantee a store of palettes available dockside. Some of these vehicles were loaded directly onto waiting flat wagons of a train moving along as each wagon got loaded. If the crane was able to move then the train could easy stand and wait until all its carriages were loaded before it pulled away." John stated.

"It looks as if you've stumbled onto an answer we've been trying to solve for a little while now. You see! This vessel is going to be some sort of a general 'box' or container cargo, but we haven't figured out how to maintain a secure load. Up to now that is." Halford said with excitement creeping into his voice.

"In fact I would go so far as to say, this is what we've been looking for. Let's hope the model trials are successful, that's all. Even if you're a bit out on your figures, we can alter them to fit properly." Halford added, pouring over John's original drawings, checking the accuracy of the figures.

"Let's put it this way. It certainly did the trick for Mr Ford here, as he was the Senior Mechanical Engineer of the army unit I was talking about." John confirmed.

"But isn't Mr Ford a shipbuilder?" Halford questioned, looking at Ford.

"It's a long story believe you me Halford. Sufficient to say he delivered my armoured unit safely and soundly from Halifax Nova Scotia all the way down the Atlantic to British Guiana. Shame about the ship otherwise." Ford said proudly.

"I think you can converse with our project manager McPhee about this when he comes back on Wednesday, but as we've now taken up too much of your time I think we'd better move on to the tank." John said, gathering up his drawings.

"No that's alright. In fact I'll come with you and show you the model F196 I mentioned."

"We welcome this opportunity Halford, and like to see just how these things get tested" Crabbe said quickly, watching John furl his drawings back up again.

"So kindly lead on." Ford responded, following the others out of the office and towards the long narrow building that housed the 'Model' tank.

They entered the long building and were met by the test engineer.

"Gentlemen, meet Professor Lloyd." Halford said, introducing the friends to a tall matchstick thin man smoking a very large pipe.

"Good morning gentlemen, welcome to the world of sunken dreams and erstwhile ship designers. This is where we give any future ships the chance to see if they are worthy of joining all the others sailing around the world." Lloyd announced, inviting them all to go down to the other end of the glass sided tank

"Here we are. As you can see, we've already got a model of a tanker attached to the slide which moves it down the tank. We have a small paddle making the waves which moves down the tank, thus creating a mock- up of a real ship moving through the seas. We have sensors on the model that makes traces on rolls of paper, which will tell us its behaviour in different wave heights and the like. Here I'll show you."

Lloyd tripped a few switches, pulled a few string cords, pressed a few buttons, which started the whole tank into its operational capacity.

They watched the wooden model move slowly down the tank with the wave paddle creating little waves for it to bob over until it reached the far end of the tank. Someone appeared through a side door to turn the model around before it was brought back again but with the waves a little more pronounced.

"As you can see gentlemen, this model is starting to yaw and duck its bow into the waves, which means it is top heavy, and hasn't got the right see-saw balance required for such a large ship. But we can examine the tracings to see if there was any interference from the wind factor which we also create above the model. However, once we've identified and corrected the problem we make a further model and take it to our special lake for further testing a ship's captain would do when sailing a real one." Lloyd explained, as the model bumped heavily into the top of the tank.

The model started to list to one side with its bow getting lower into the water, before Lloyd reached over to retrieve it before it finally sank.

Bringing the dripping model out to look at it he discovered there was a hole in the bow where it bumped against the side of the immersed housing of the mechanisms.

"Excuse me Professor, from what we've seen these models are hollow and not a solid design. If that was a tanker, then the hole it sustained would release an oil slick several miles long and perhaps spread across a wide area. Just think what it would do in a busy port.

If that was my freighter then I'd split into two like a pea-pod when the water expanded the cargo of grain I'd be carrying." Crabbe observed.

"Not really Colin. You'd have the protection of the inner skin. A flimsy one granted, but at least one that would protect you from a reasonable bump, none the less." John replied, showing the professor his *'Winnipeg'* drawings.

The professor looked at the drawings and examined the model for a moment before he called the person at the other end to come to them.

The man appeared swiftly and grabbing hold of the model started to moan about his little creation, until the Professor told him to stop whining and be thankful someone had just saved the day for him.

"The sketches you are about to see Pritchard, I admit are a bit basic, but I think even you would be able to grasp their significance." Lloyd said coldly, handing over the drawings and other details.

Pritchard put his model gently onto a table and grabbed hold of the offered drawings to examine them.

After a little while, he handed them back with a pompous attitude.

"These drawings must have been made by a drunkard. I see nothing that would enhance my efforts to produce, what is after all, a remarkable change in the way ships are designed these days. Any ship built must really be worth its construction, to incorporate what I've just seen to build a ship really must be worth its construction. If I were to incorporate from what I've just seen and the main idea behind it, would increase the cost of such a ship, making it too expensive to build. Besides which, the figures don't add up, it is therefore a totally useless waste of effort." the man said offhandedly, dismissing the whole idea as an insult to his intelligence.

"Then it appears this man is an imbecile or living on cloud cuckoo land. For these plans have already been implemented on other, albeit much older ships, and have proved totally in keeping with the cargo requirements needed at the time of usage." Crabbe growled, turning his head in disgust, away from the man.

John was not taking a direct part in all this heated discussion, as he was looking closely at the model, and even picked it up to examine it more closely.

29

He spotted the model had several components which went into the actual make up of it. He saw the basic shape of a three castle ship, as would be normal to a freighter, but the main bridge superstructure in the middle of the ship was too big, thus making it too unstable and perhaps too top heavy. He remembered seeing the strange designs from the Lake ships he had seen, where the bridge superstructure was almost on the bows with the main propulsion unit was right aft.

The model must have been still too wet for him to hold onto, for it slipped out of his hands. His reaction was swift as he managed to hold onto the bridge section to try and prevent it from smashing onto the floor. Instead, he was left standing holding the bridge section in his hands with the rest of the model lying broken on the floor.

The noise was enough for the rest of them to turn round to see what had happened, which made the creator of this hapless model go absolutely crazy.

"Why you fuckin' stupid cack-handed bastard! Look what you've done to my ship! It took me weeks to prepare it for the test, yet you come along and within minutes you've already sent it to the scrap yard." Pritchard screamed, rushing forward to assault John.

"You lay one finger on me pal and you'll be wearing the rest as a collar." John advised, squaring up to meet his assailant.

Ford and Crabbe jumped in between them, with Ford pushing Pritchard away telling him that he'd better calm down or he would end up just like his model.

John bent down and picked up the model starting to straighten it up again, then placed the bridge sectional piece on the top next to the after superstructure that had the funnel section.

"My apologies Pritchard. But as you're about to re-construct it with a double hull, maybe you can borrow my drawings to help you, so we'll call it quits. Yes?" John suggested.

Pritchard was still mad demanding compensation, but Lloyd

intervened telling him that although he was still an idiot, he'd better accept the offer as his only salvation to be kept on at the Faculty. He also reminded Pritchard of his earlier failures saying this one would have represented the final nail in his coffin to be recognised as a ship designer.

Pritchard managed to calm himself down reluctantly accepting the 'olive branch' and John's apology, then gathering up his model walked away from them.

John managed a last look at the model with its bridge section still where he had put it, before Pritchard snatched it up to rush out of the building, muttering and swearing to himself.

"I think we've had enough excitement for today gentlemen. Maybe if you come back again sometime next week I'll get F196 set up for you. In the meantime forget about Pritchard, he's been a pain in the neck since he joined us during the last session. As far as you're concerned, if he does adopt the second hull idea as a safety feature over the loss of valuable cargo, then he'll be back crowing about his new discovery and his latest invention."

"He can't do that Professor! That is my patent not his." John said with astonishment.

"That's as it may be Grey, but I suggest you refer the matter to your project manager, er, McPhee, and if you wish to take matters further then you would be advised to seek a consultation with our head of operations, Mr Clutterbuck." Lloyd said abruptly, ushering everybody out of the building before locking it up for the day.

"It's time for lunch gentlemen. I'm off duty now, so unless you've got anything else for me I bid you good day." Halford said cheerfully, turning on his heel and left the three friends to their own devices.

"Just as well we haven't!" Crabbe muttered, watching the rapidly departing Halford.

"As it happens, it's our lunch time too gentlemen. We can always re- convene afterward in the bar, to talk things over." John suggested, looking at his watch.

The suggestion was agreed unanimously so all three made their way to the dining hall to take their repast.

After lunch they went to take up their now 'reserved' seats in the lounge, but as it was a Saturday, there was hardly anybody there to disturb them.

"Okay then gentlemen. We are now in session, and we've still got a long way to go." John said amiably, as the waitress brought their round of drinks.

They recapped what had transpired during the morning and concluded that only now were they starting to wake up to the commitment needed from them to fulfil the requirements asked by their generous patrons.

The afternoon slowly ticked by as the three friends worked methodically through various subjects, putting 'meat onto the bones' of their ideas and thoughts.

"We need to see Pritchard about the double hull, because if it proves to be a goer with the Ministry for shipping, and especially the Lloyds shipping insurance people, it would mean the saving of several ships let alone the impact an oil spill from a tanker has on the marine environment.

Mind you though, perhaps the international insurance people would enforce such a change not only for tankers but for all 'deep sea' going ships." Crabbe opined, with the conversation and topics flowing gently back and fore all afternoon.

The dinner gong reverberated throughout the building causing the three friends to gather their things and trudge their way to the dining room.

On their way in they met Pritchard, who seemed to hurry past them as if trying to avoid them.

"Pritchard! One moment if you please! I need to have another look at your model, only there's something that is bothering me and I don't quite know what it is until I see it. So if you're free some time tomorrow morning, perhaps we can meet up." John said civilly.

"You stay away from my model. I spent ages making it, and now I'm forced to make a new one to be a tanker this time." Pritchard replied nastily.

"Look Pritchard! It was a pure accident I can assure you, but we really need to co-operate for all our benefits. All I need is a good look at your model, yet you'll need all my drawings and suchlike to implement your own ideas, and I'm talking about a double hull for all bulk grain ships and tankers." John replied candidly.

Pritchard looked at the friends for a moment with indecision.

"Okay then, tomorrow morning around 1100. I'm in room 240, which is in the south wing next to the utilities room." Pritchard replied sulkily.

"Better still, how about in the reference library around 1000. We can dig out any technical matters if we get stuck on anything." Ford offered.

"1000 in the library. That'll suit me. See you then." Pritchard sniffed, striding away from the friends to sit alone at his own table which was set for 10 people.

Chapter VI

Cracked It

"**M**orning Pritchard, glad you brought your model with you. Maybe we can put our heads together and come up with a joint plan that will suit both our projects." John greeted, as Pritchard huffed and puffed his way into the library with his broken model.

Pritchard walked slowly over to a large empty table and put his model onto it, carefully placing the loose bridge section onto where it should be on the model.

Crabbe started to explain to Pritchard about the second internal hull John had built onto his ship, and expounded its merits and usefulness. Ford explained how it was done, using John's drawings, and explained how the ship would earn itself more, due to the prevention of metal corrosion and the like.

Pritchard was asked to strip down the model so they could see the 'hollow' insides and he could explain what compartment was to be used and where.

John listened quietly to all of this, still trying to fathom out what was annoying his active mind.

He explained to Pritchard that he was a ship's Chief Engineer with several years experience on tankers and quoting the *Repulse Bay* among others, before he started to ask his famous rapid fire questions.

"What engines would you have fitted. What deck machinery would you recommend on this futuristic ship? And how would you clean the tanks? Have you ever thought about a multi fuel tanker?" John asked for starters, which seemed to overwhelm Pritchard.

"Kindly ask me one question at a time so that I can give you a concise answer to them. Now please start again." Pritchard said in dismay.

"Okay. What type of engines would you have fitted on board?"

"Diesel, why?"

34

"What would you use to make steam then?"

"What would I need steam for?"

"Okay then, what deck machinery would you install to operate the tank top valves, capstans tank pumps and the like on a tanker carrying refined fuel such as petrol or aircraft fuel?"

"All electrical. Just push a button in the bridge control panel. That way you would save on manual labour to operate the mechanical ones."

"Now I know you're an idiot Pritchard. Just one spark from an electrical gadget, even from the plug connecting the machinery, would blow the ship sky high.

The reason why I asked you about steam is that it's an inert gas which means it is quite safe to operate your deck machinery. What about tank cleansing prior to reloading?"

"Just pump water into the tanks until the tanks overflow and wash the residue fuel overboard."

"Wrong again Pritchard. Each tank would need a steam hose played into the hold with detergents to wash the tanks clean. If you start pumping the resulting liquid overboard, then not only are you leaving a very long oil slick in your wake, but you'd also lose some very valuable 'waste' oil that could otherwise be sold. Maybe a submersible pump to drain the tanks, but certainly via a Ventura system to separate the fuel from the water. That way only the water gets pumped overboard. It happens as a standard practice all the time in diesel ships when the fuel goes through the separator system before it gets sent to the engines."

John asked a few more questions but by now, Pritchard was all worked up and starting to get grumpy with John's grilling.

Ford intervened with a few less direct questions as did Crabbe, trying to keep the man under a more even temperament. All the while John was looking at the model with the bridge still placed on the rear of the ship.

Ford saw the look on Johns face and recognised there was something cooking in John's mind, so asked everybody to stop talking.

"I think I've found the answer to your increase of cargo capacity. Ben, maybe you can help me develop what I've got in mind. As for you Pritchard, it's your lucky day, so everybody listen up and hear what I've just thought of and see what you can do to help." John said quietly, moving slowly over to the model and taking hold of the wayward bridge section.

"Okay then here's what I've got in mind. Due to the Lake Waterways and Canal systems, all ships using or transiting through it have their size and draught governed by it. So to maximise the cargo carrying capacity the lake ships have a bridge right forward, almost on the bows of the ship, with the propulsion unit right aft, like this. This method reduces the ship from a three castle to a two castle, and gives a little more carrying capacity. My idea is based on, which if I can remember from what I have seen earlier and judging by the strange shape of the ships involved, this. " John stated, moving the bridge section up the model to show what he was saying.

"What I saw out here on the lakes were several 'Lake ships' having their bridges right for'ard almost onto their bows, with her stern area which obviously had her propulsion area and her crew quarters, thus making her a 'two castle' ship. So what say we merge the bridge section with the after section to make it one unit. That way the ship can have a cargo capacity from here right up to the bows. In other words, just the one castle." he said, showing again what he meant.

"A freighter has a long prop shaft because the engine room is mid-ships, yet any tanker has its engine room aft, therefore a shorter prop shaft. Shorter prop shaft equals more kinetic energy from the engines to the shaft. More energy equals more power to the propeller, yet less energy expended by the engines, therefore less fuel used. The ship then becomes just the one 'castle', which in itself creates more room for more cargo without increasing the overall size of the vessel. This extra room would more than compensate for the loss of cargo space created by the double hull.

Because of a much larger cargo hold, the ship could also be given false transverse bulkheads to be able to split the cargos up, if necessary, into different kinds just like the *Winnipeg* and the *Repulse Bay*." John said slowly and as carefully as he could trying not to confuse Pritchard any further.

The two friends sat there for a moment to think over what John had said, and even had a go with the model bridge section themselves to help understand the statement.

Pritchard went over to his model and broke off the front of the after section and placed the bridge there. He looked around the new design, making several calculations with his ever-present slide rule before he decided to speak.

"So if I was to trim down the size of the original bridge and have it as part of the after section, I'd have to work out the weight distribution of the vessel from that point onwards." he muttered, starting to draw furiously a new ship design on a large piece of paper.

When he was done, he showed them his 'artist impression ' of what the new design would look like, but it was patently obvious to the three friends by looking at the model before them, what it looked like for real.

"Bloody hell John! I think we've cracked it. Not only have we got our ideas ready for F196, we've also gone and designed a brand new type of ship." Crabbe whispered as the magnitude of this discovery started to sink in.

Pritchard was mumbling to himself, seeming to be in a little world of his own, scribbling all sorts of formulae and notes onto his now very full page.

"I think you've saved the 'Ace' from his early retirement John. Bloody hell man! What an astute discovery you've come across. It could revolutionise the ship-building industry, perhaps even increase the size and shape of ships both freighter and tanker."

"All I did was apply a little basic science to improve the performance of the engines, be they turbine or diesel. Still, now that we've all got something for Fergus to look at, perhaps he might give us all a 10." John replied, drawing on his fast burning cigarette.

"I think this calls for a celebration gentlemen. The champagne is on me!" Pritchard whooped as the penny finally sank in and he appreciated what an 'Eureka' moment it was.

"Now, now then Pritchard, keep your hair on. We'll leave the model building to you, but let us sort out the propulsion and deck arrangements. In the meantime just a little word of advice into your shell like ear hole. Don't ever breathe a word to anyone, not even to Mr Clutterbuck. From now on, you'll be part of our group, and it will be us who will decide on when the word gets out, not you." John advised.

"My lips are sealed. In fact I want to see if my model of F196 can be adapted in the same way. Mind you it will take a lot of working out to be able to get the right balance. I mean, if the ship is going to have all its unloaded weight on one end with the metal stress and the likes." Pritchard agreed with a nod.

"Right then gentlemen, time for lunch. Maybe we can finalise the details of what we've been through this evening, and all tomorrow if necessary. Fergus is back on Wednesday morning so let's get everything ready for him. Plans, notes, perhaps a revised model from you Pritchard, but if not then give us some artistic sketches to show him. " John announced, gathering up their belongings and locking the library up. Pritchard was seen scurrying towards the lift to deposit his toy back into his room, as the friends made their way to the dining hall.

Once they had their lunch, they decided that a few hours contemplation would benefit them and help ready them for their final big session in the morning.

'Must get the balance right. If this is going to be the way of it in future, then much bigger ships could be on the way. What about the actual construction of these giants? What about construction yards or even the docking and the like?' he thought, relaxing on his bed before he finally drifted off into oblivion.

38

Chapter VII

Something Different

"**H**ello you three? Suddenly I've got four of you now." McPhee greeted them jovially.

"Well never mind, I'm back now after a well deserved weekend, it appears once my back was turned, you lot have been burning the midnight oil, and are found guilty of pestering the senior staff to boot. Now, unless I'm mistaken, it seems its all down to you John Grey!" he stated with an ominous look.

"Actually we are all to blame Fergus! Mind you though, it was a fortuous yet careless moment with another person, who has decided to join our team and is the one who gave us the inspiration to continue with our experiments. Fergus, meet the current model maker George Pritchard." Crabbe stated boldly, introducing the new member to McPhee.

McPhee gave a sideways look at his four charges, as if he somehow detected some sort of scam or cover up, then commenced looking through the reams of paper work they had put together over the weekend.

"Hmmm! I see, and welcome to the project Pritchard. I know enough of your work to take you on board, so to speak. So the four of you have discovered a new type of ship that could revolutionise the entire shipping industry?" McPhee asked after a little while, as he returned his attention to them.

"I will not say yeah nor nay to all of this until I see a scale model of this craft in working order. For you to produce an animal such as this, we need to see if it will relate to proper conditions as per scale. By that I mean, it will have to stand the rigours of our test tank and model trials on the special lake we have here."

"Thanks to George here, we have a ready made model Fergus. But we estimate a 2 week period for its new shape and construction plus maybe a further 2 weeks to carry out any unforeseen works or designs needed. At the end of the day, if it works then we're in clover. Or in Monopoly terms, we all go to jail without passing GO and without picking up our two million dollars." Ford stated.

"How about you John, you seem pretty quiet in all this?" McPhee challenged.

"Me Fergus? I'm just an Engineer, maybe with a flair on seeing something different to the norm. All I did was to spot an idea without putting it down on paper, in case somebody pinched my ideas again. Take my Ice Docking idea for instance." John said quietly, drawing the response of "hear hear" from the other two.

McPhee gave a little smile, which grew into a big smile that gave way to a burst of laughter which caught the four off their guard.

"Now, that to me was the perfect answer I was looking for. You four will do just fine in my books, but we must be careful of the Patent protocols of this august establishment." McPhee managed to say, after his brief fit of laughter subsided, then added.

"Never mind the patenting and all the proper technical drawings etc, you've just cut your stay here down to a good half. So with luck I'll be able to send you off to a placement area early, to help you with your new way of radical thinking, shall we say."

It was several weeks before the 'project team' got the nod to be put on placement, with McPhee completing their last week of instructions and lectures.

"It appears this project team has created a certain buzz around the place, whereby the other project classes are now happy to share in their own discoveries. At the very least it has opened up cross project discussions, which started a very busy exchange of ideas and the like which this establishment has needed for some time. From what Mr Clutterbuck tells me, your amended F196 design will now be taken as a bench-mark for other would-be designers, who will probably investigate the expertise needed to build others much larger than yours. A much bigger builder's yard would be needed to cope with the sizes about to be launched." McPhee stated, then went on to inform them as to where they were going and their exact briefing of their imminent project work.

This briefing took up the entire week, with reams of paperwork given out to the team, who merely packed it all into boxes and sent it all away as 'forward baggage'.

"This is it team, and I'm happy to say I'm confident in your results and look forward to your return. In fact, for the moment, you will leave the college for a well- earned weekend and come back next Monday by 1100 where I'll have all your documentation and travel plans ready for you. Congratulations to you four at providing us with a very uplifting time. And it's all down to you I have now been offered a Directorship role within the college." McPhee said, clapping his hands to applaud his project team.

"Before you leave, see Mr Martins for an advance of your retainer. He normally doesn't give one, but tell him it's to pay your hefty bar bill he's getting anxious about." McPhee added with a smile and a knowing wink.

"Pay our bill? Pay your bill more like! We think it should be your privilege Fergus, after all, it was you doing all the slurping whilst we were doing all the slogging." John quipped.

"That dear John is what we call in the business, perks of the trade. Call it your investment for the future." McPhee chuckled, then putting his hand into his inside coat pocket pulled out his wallet.

"But seeing as it's you four reprobates of the first water, I'll make allowances just this once. Here's something towards it, and never say Scotsmen are skinflints either." he added, handing John a £20 note.

John held it up to the light, to check it was a real one.

"Can't take that Fergus! It's a Scottish note that's not legal tender down south of the border." John responded quickly and pretended to give it back, but swiftly handed it over to Pritchard.

"Here George, you're the pound stretcher among us! Let's see our pseudo froggy, the Maitre 'D's face when you slap it on his bar."

"Thanks for the gift Fergus! Each of us will match it then squander anything left over." Crabbe said quietly, which drew an excited nod and a big grin from Pritchard.

Shaking their hands in farewell, McPhee reminded them to be back for 1100 on Monday, and not to be…

"ADRIFT!" the team replied aloud in unison

"That's the word I was looking for, as I've got my beady eye on you lot." McPhee responded swiftly, making John laugh at the gentle reminder of his erstwhile Chief Mel 'Spanners' Jones.

The friends left the lecture room and made their way to their 'reserved seats' in the bar to enjoy an aperitif before lunch.

"If we've got to vacate our rooms for the weekend then just where do you suppose we could go? I mean, I live over in Belfast, George lives up somewhere around Hull and you two live away over the other side of Canada. Apart from George, it's pretty too damn far to commute just for one weekend." John asked, handing out the cigarettes.

There was a small pregnant pause as the friends thought over their dilemma, then Pritchard spoke up.

"I have an Uncle and Aunt living at a place called Cowes on the Isle of Wight, which is not too far from here. My family often go to visit them and they have an estate with a large house with plenty of spare rooms, so that's not a problem. I have my saloon car in the garage, so we can drive over to Portsmouth and go over on the car ferry if you like. We'd be home in time for tea." he suggested, the other three looked at each other for a moment as if to weigh up the possibilities.

"That's a fair offer, just as long as your relatives don't mind that is." John said evenly, lifting his glass as a sign of acceptance. The other two responded in kind thanking Pritchard for his kindness.

"Not at all. I've already told them about you three, in fact my uncle will be pleased to meet you all as he shares the same interests as us. In fact that's why he is the permanent 2nd Sea Lord at the Admiralty, you know. So I'll make a quick phone call to let them know to expect us." Pritchard bragged, but gave them all a big smile to seal the promise.

A deep 'bong' from the large round gong announced once more it was time for their repast.

"Well gentlemen. Let's eat then go and pack for our weekend retreat." John announced, stubbing the last of his cigar out into the half full ashtray, then leading the way to the dining hall.

Chapter VIII

The Raving C

"**H**ere we are then. This is where my Uncle and Aunt live." Pritchard announced, pulling up at a large gateway and tooting his horn.

A man appeared from the gateway lodge and looked to see who it was, before opening the ornate wrought iron gate with an archway, which displayed a coat of arms.

"Hello Harris! Is the Admiral at home today?" Pritchard asked civilly.

"He's out on the gun deck with some guests and will be until 1700. As the garage forecourt is full, you'll have to park down by the boat yard. The Admiral's Shipwright and Engineer by the name of Roy Ward is there, so see him before you park up." came the prompt reply.

"Thank you Harris, I'll do just that. Toodle pip!" Pritchard said jovially then beeped his horn once more before driving slowly down a straight but secluded driveway which branched off from a curved balustrade flanked driveway leading eventually to the big house.

It was a rectangular three-storied house with rounded towers on each corner fronted by a very large neatly trimmed lawn with islands of tall pampas grass growing on them. The house and gardens were shielded from prying eyes by a high stone wall that formed the perimeter of the extensive property.

'Shades of the Barbados Yacht club. This time, let's hope I'm not mistaken for somebody else again.' John mused*.

The car slithered to a stop, sending stone chippings flying everywhere as a large built man appeared, wiping his hands on a piece of rag.

"Hello Ward! Just parking the car up until the garage is clear again.

---

* See *A Fatal Encounter.*

These are three friends of mine from the ISDM college come to stay for the weekend." Pritchard explained, as Ward came up to them.

"Good afternoon George. Better park your car over to the side of the boathouse as I've got to move the Admirals barge further up the slipway, so I'll have to open these back doors of the boathouse." he instructed, which Pritchard immediately did. Once done so, he handed over the keys saying.

"Here you are! Kindly get it moved over to the garage forecourt as soon as it's available will you." Then leaving Ward, told the friends to follow him.

The four men walked round the side of the large boathouse to see a small inland waterway crammed full of small yachts and motor launches. Some were on small slipways with others still moored in the small bay.

Pritchard pointed at a vessel half in and half out of the large boat-house, explaining it is now the Admirals private motor yacht, reprieved from the scrap yard. Also by virtue of the fact it was one of a number of the Admirals ideas whereby this particular vessel was the first warship ever to be fitted with a gas turbine on the centre shaft of three propellers, and was able to do over 40 knots. For the last year or so it was being done up for official business, although it will be used a lot for private pleasure trips around the Channel and the Scilly Isles.

"Maybe that is why the Admiral is hosting a large number of visitors today, in preparation for the big launch in the morning. Knowing the score, they'll all be back if only to quaff the large numbers of bubbly bottles being handed around. It is going to be a grand occasion, but I shall not be there to enjoy the occasion, as I've got other engagements to fulfil in the afternoon." he surmised, leading the party along the shoreline towards the front of the house.

"Hello Aunt Phoebe. These are the friends I was telling you about." Pritchard greeted, kissing his aunt on her cheek before introducing them to her.

"The Admiral will be finished with his business soon, to see you. So why not take your friends and show them their quarters. I'll have a glass of sherry waiting in about half an hour. I'll get Boulston to carry your luggage." she advised, pointing towards a highly polished revolving door leading off from the large cavernous hallway.

"C'mon gentlemen, welcome to the 'RAVING C' he announced.

"We're on the East wing, second floor, but we'll use the lift instead of clunking all the way up these wooden stairs. Make such a noise so it does." Pritchard suggested, and led the friends over to a small lift, leaving Boulston to follow on behind with the luggage.

John looked out of the bay window to see a panoramic view of the Solent, and down to the where he saw a group of people sitting on deck chairs arranged in a semi circle. He saw a large flagpole placed in the middle of a concrete square, which had four outfacing naval cannons, seemingly to protect the naval ensign that flew at the masthead.

In front of it was a wide concrete pathway forming a private landing jetty which had a chain-link fence strung between bollards all along either side of a wide set of steps leading down to a pontoon.

He noticed a smaller cannon set on its own and a smaller flagpole flying a pennant flying. The letters R A V Y C on the pennant made John thought it stood for the local yacht club.

'The Admiral is probably the local Commodore of the club too.' he guessed, spotting a white clapboard building hiding under the trees to the right of the jetty with its own little slipway down to the waters edge.

A knock on the door interrupted his thoughts as Pritchard entered.

"Pretty handsome sight John. Hope you find the room comfy enough. Better than the stuffy college. Come, the others are

46

waiting in the corridor, so we'll go down and sample the delicious sherry Aunt Phoebe told us about." he said amiably.

John needed no further prompting, gathering up his smokes and other personal items he followed, shutting the ornately panelled door of his room quietly behind him.

The other two friends were swapping notes about their rooms with each other, as Pritchard led them down to the ground floor again.

"Ah George. Just in time! The Admiral will receive you in the drawing room shortly just as soon as he sees off his last remaining guests. They're going back in their motor launch, so we won't be in the way." Phoebe announced.

"Come, the stewardess Clarke will serve you with your sherry in there." she added, and left the friends to their own devices.

"Bloody hell George! The Admiral lives well doesn't he? How many servants have has he got to look after them and this place?" Ford asked.

"This is the family ancestral home, with the Admiral head of the entire family. Look, there is the family coat of arms. I told you he was a Sea Lord. Not only is he a Naval Sea Lord but also a real live Lord of the realm. This estate was given to the family way back in the 1700's and used up as a royal retreat whenever the monarch or other royals decide to take the waters of the Solent.

In fact, senior members of the royalty stayed here to conduct the Spithead review on the occasion of the Queens coronation. But she stayed in the big house on the next estate along the coastline. It's that tall towering building you can see in among the trees from your bedroom windows. In case you have not spotted the pennant on the smaller flag pole, it is the pennant of the Royal Albert and Victoria Yacht club, hence the initials. That's why it is called the Raving Cee!

The Admiral combines business with pleasure, which is why he allowed the Yacht Clubhouse to be built on the right end of the jetty. We used to use the big jetty from the big house on the next estate, but it got demolished when the estate became part of the public domain some 10 years ago now.

The Admiral has about 40 staff to do most of the looking after around the place mostly from the Naval Barracks, but he also has 10 civilian office staff to take care of the naval business side of things." He explained, as a pretty stewardess came through the door bearing their drinks.

"Hello Edna! These are my friends from the ISDM. Haven't seen you for a while, how have you been?" Pritchard asked cordially, taking his own glass from the offered tray.

"Fine thank you George. We, my husband and I that is, look forward to be racing against you tomorrow in the second round robin." she replied with a smile.

"Married? Oh yes, I forgot. Silly me to let you go, but that's just great. Congratulations to you, if that's in order. Do I know him?" Pritchard asked with genuine surprise and pleasure.

"Come on now George you know his name is Ted, he's the Chairman of the Yacht club now. He owns the 'Sea sprite' now, which is on the slipway next to your decrepit old thing. We're sailing against you tomorrow and we'll pinch your wind again, ha ha!" she laughed.

"I'll wager a magnum of bubbly on that dear girl." he responded.

"You're on George! It'll be like taking candy from a baby. I'd better make sure I've got a spare corkscrew then, 'cause we Clarkes eat such like you for breakfast." she said with relish, leaving the friends to their drinks.

"From what I can gather, she's an ex-girlfriend of yours and I take it we're all going sailing tomorrow, George?" Crabbe asked with raised eyebrows.

"Only if you want to, but I've already got my regular crew coming along tomorrow morning. You can always give us a hand to get us under way if you like. Having said that, it is all down to the Admiral and his plans."

48

The friends had finished a second drink when a tall slender man wearing an immaculate dark blue suit came into the room.

John looked at the neatly trimmed silver beard and saw the man had very piercing blue eyes which flashed around him and his friends.

"Good evening Uncle! These are my friends I was telling you about." Pritchard stated, going through the ritual of introducing the friends to him.

The Admiral spoke with a deep but polished voice and posed a few questions to each person as he was introduced.

"Ah yes, John Grey! I've heard a lot about you from the ISDM, although I haven't had the time to meet you up to now." the Admiral stated, causing John to look at him with a questioning expression, which the Admiral saw and continued.

"In case you're wondering, I'm head of the ISDM as part of my duties within the Admiralty.

I make it my business to know about all the projects undertaken there and sanction those I think will be of benefit to maritime navies be it merchant or royal." he explained, then went on to show them some of the things he had managed to create or come up with during his own time as a young engineer.

The friends were fascinated by what he revealed to them, except Pritchard, who although pretending to be interested, was in fact yawning behind his hand as he'd probably heard it so many times before.

The Admiral told them many things, the revelation that George was his protégé and if he did well at the ISDM he would be earmarked for a top job within the ship design unit at Whitehall. But Pritchard mildly protested his innocence of any knowledge of this information.

"Oh well, there you go George! It appears you have been blessed with the same streak of family genius as the Admiral here. Maybe if you play your cards right you too will become a lord and set up business next door." Ford said with a big smile and a slap on Pritchard's back to emphasise it.

A steward arrived to announce that dinner was ready to be served and for them to make their way into the large dining room.

After their meal, the Admiral asked the friends to rejoin him in the library, as he wanted to investigate their imminent project, singling John out to be their spokesman.

"Delighted you chose me Admiral, but I think you'd better get George to do that' John replied.

The Admiral leant over, then whispered in Johns ear, that compared to the rest of them, George, as far as he was concerned, couldn't quite 'cut the mustard' enough to shine a Snotties boots let alone an Admiral's

This sudden burst of candour made John take note to prepare for whatever the Admiral was to throw his way.

"I'm only a Marine Engineer Admiral. George is the ship designer between us, so it would be unfair not to let him have his glory." John said aside.

"Be that as it may, it is obvious you and the other two seem to know what its all about and able to hold your corner. Maybe this is what George needs, to help set himself up. So take this on and I'll be grateful to you."

"Very well Admiral, just this once, considering this was supposed to be a weekend off from our long ISDM course, but don't forget, each of us has a function to perform in the team. 'Team Play' so to speak. Perhaps our mentor Mr McPhee would agree with me on that."

"Ah yes! Old Fergus McPhee would too, but then he and I go a long way back together, so whatever he has said or has instructed you on, or what to do, you can take it also came from me."

"Very well Admiral lets start the ball rolling. You can be our moderator, adjudicator or whatever. But keep in mind all this is strictly off the record, as it would be deemed to be unfair to all other project teams at the college."

"That's the spirit George lacks. Maybe at the end of your project, he'll come back a whole new person with a backbone willing to take up his family responsibilities, instead of the precocious 'Snotty' he has been up to now."

'I'm used to being part of a baton relay team imparting my knowledge to up-and-coming engineers who show some guts and a willingness to learn. But I'm blowed if I'll start spoon-feeding a 'Lordy' when he's no better than the rest of us.' John mused, leaving the Admiral and gathering the friends around him in the large study room which was crammed full of half breadth models, drawings and paintings of different types of ships and other craft*.

During this impromptu lecture and presentation of the teams project work, John noticed a few more people had arrived and made themselves comfortable whilst John was delivering his talk.

One face he spotted gave him a niggling idea he knew the person but couldn't pin him down as to how, where or when.

When the exercise was finished, some two hours later, John received a hearty clap and a cheer from those who somehow got the word and to come along to listen.

It was Aunt Phoebe who came up and whispered into his ear what had happened.

"It appears you've just presented your project to some of the Admirals top brains to see if you really do' cut the mustard' as he puts it. Let me be the first to congratulate you young man, as the Admiral seems very pleased with your friends and especially your good self.

Now you've passed his 'muster' you can relax and enjoy the rest of your stay here at the castle." she purred.

"Why thank you Phoebe! I didn't realise I had to sing for my supper as well. But I've already told the Admiral we're an integral team that has strength as one unit and not as individuals as he tries to impose upon George."

---

* 'Half breadth' means just one side of the model or drawing is made, given that it mirrors the missing opposite side.

"Maybe it's why he told me that just possibly George will make it through at last on his own merit instead of the Admiral continuing to wet nurse him. Anyway, well done! Must go now and let the Admiral take charge, as always." she breathed.

"Before you go, there's one man in the room I fancy I've seen before." John said quietly, discreetly pointing to the man in question.

"Why that's Captain Richardson from the Portsmouth Dockyard. Why do you ask?"

"It's a long story Phoebe, but I must go over and say hello." John said absentmindedly excusing himself from the front of the audience.

"Hello Richardson, how are you these days?" John asked, holding out his hand to greet the man.

"Why of course, Its John Grey from the SFDs going down to the Falklands! I wasn't sure it was you, but by golly, put it there old man!" Richardson said with pleasure, standing up and shaking hands with John.

Richardson gave a brief explanation to all the surprised onlookers as to why he was shaking hands with John, who had simply returned the compliments.

Standing up, the Admiral clapped his hands in appreciation to the spontaneous greeting then declared the evening was now at a close and for everybody to enjoy the brandy and cigars being handed out by a couple of stewards.

"It seems we have a rough diamond amongst us. No airs or graces, but then who needs it when you're a pioneer to the craft of making ships for a nation of islanders." he announced, then came over to shake Johns hand in appreciation of his project presentation.

"Don't worry John Grey! I get to know all what goes on in the ISDM. You and your team, despite me having a nephew in it, have just vindicated my decision to continue with the college for a further tenure of 10 years. Maybe our mutual friend Fergus McPhee will be able to breathe more easily now, allowing him to slowly sail away into retirement a happy man."

"Fergus was always my adopted guardian ever since I first met him as the Bermuda dockyard superintendent over some fifteen years ago. I have been fortunate to be able to count other good engineer officers among my friends, which happily far outweigh my foes and no-gooders." John stated candidly.

"Well young man, if you play your cards right, and especially if George plays his full part, I can definitely see a golden future fore you within the Admiralty at Whitehall, or if all goes well certainly as an understudy to old Fergus when he retires."

John's past life passed swiftly before him, until he had the sense to reply he was just a marine engineer and not a magician or wizard which is what was needed in the college, and certainly not good enough to fill Fergus's boots.

"Well said that man! It's refreshing to hear an honest mans word for once and not those yes men I'm surrounded by." the Admiral said.

"Tomorrow I'm going to launch my barge and take it for a short voyage around the island. Make sure you get yourself on board John. See my private secretary Richardson over there who will fill you in with the details. Must go now and speak to the other guests otherwise they'll think I've forgotten them." he added with a wink then left John to join his friends.

Chapter IX

Grunts

John was woken by a knock on the door of his room before a steward entered, carrying a large silver tray with foods and drink on it.

"Morning Mr Grey. I've taken the liberty of giving you an early call with breakfast in your room, as the place will be heaving with other guests milling around the dining room or whatever.

I've brought you a full English breakfast, but eat only what you fancy. Just leave the tray on the table and I'll pick it up later."

"Thanks steward, I'm feeling rather ravenous this morning and could eat a scabby horse between two slices of mouldy bread."

"No need for that Mr Grey, its all fresh food on your plate." Getting out of bed John took his breakfast whilst the steward fussed around the room.

"Any idea what sort of Itinery I am supposed to observe today?"

"From what I know as far as you're concerned, you're to meet the Admirals nephew down at the slipway at around 0830. Your other two friends will be joining you as well. As for the rest of the day, it's pretty much in the lap of the Gods considering sea fog has blanketed the waters." he replied, finally drawing back the heavy curtains of the bay windows to reveal a silver sheen on the window-panes.

"That explains the grunts during the night. What of the Admiral's re-launch then?"[•]

"Oh it can still go ahead, but unless the fog clears for the afternoon, then it looks as if me and the rest of the staff will be

---

[•] A nickname used to describe the Diaphones, otherwise known as a foghorn on hazard buoys and lightships.

required to stay on. I was hoping to slide away early as it's the wife's birthday and I was planning to go over to the mainland to give her a treat around the Pompey shopping centre."

"Never mind steward, you can always take her out to a candle-lit supper in some carvery or wherever." John replied sympathetically, as the steward left the room shutting the door quietly behind him.

John found and joined his other three friends in the long sun lounge attached to the back of the main building.

"Morning John, hope you slept well?" Pritchard greeted.

"Yes thanks George!" John responded, nodding his recognition to the other two.

"George has told us two of his crew haven't turned up, and is asking us to man it for him." Crabbe informed.

"Yes John, how about lending a hand on board? The sea-fog will lift in time for the big race this afternoon." Pritchard asked hopefully.

"I've already been seconded to the Admirals barge today George. And anyway, I prefer an engine to a sail any day of the week. Sorry and all that but sailing is just not my scene. I had enough sailing in a lifeboat to last me a lifetime, thanks all the same." John replied civilly.•

"That goes for me too, George! I'd rather stick around the Admirals barge or even on your cousin's speed-boat, if it's all the same to you." Ford said swiftly.

"Well you can certainly count me in George. I'll be part of your crew." Crabbe said.

"Thanks Colin! It appears we have two for sailing and two against. Oh well! Never mind Colin, that's more bubbly to drink from the cup we're going to win. Providing the ruddy fog buggers off." Pritchard said with a grin.

"This now leaves John and me to enjoy the dash of a speed-

• See *Fresh Water*.

boat under our feet, without straining a muscle to get around on deck." Ford quipped, splitting them up into two factions.

Richardson appeared amongst them to inform them a small crowd was gathering at the boathouse and those who were joining the Admiral should accompany him there.

"It's just Ben and me, so lead on." John responded waving 'so long' to the other two.

"Make sure you salute the Admiral when you get on board." Pritchard called out to the departing friends.

The sea-fog was starting to thin as the friends walked through it to meet Ward in the boathouse, with John pointing out to Ford the other large motor launches which were now tied up alongside the concrete jetty.

"It appears the Admiral has a lot of guests along today. Not all of us can get aboard it surely?" Ford asked.

"The barge can accommodate up to 15 passengers on a long voyage, or about 40 on a day trip. The rest will be on board other craft which will follow on behind like a small armada. If all goes well we will sail round the island to see the Needles before we have a champagne lunch at the 'Smugglers Inn' at Freshwater Cove. Then make our way around the other half of the island and be home for around tea-time. It's all organised, subject to the weather conditions naturally." Richardson informed them, as the trio approached an empty spot at the side of the boathouse.

"See that Ben? The barge must be a good 100 feet long, with its bow almost touching the water and her stern poking out the back of the boathouse. Either the vessel is too long, or the boathouse needs to be extended further back to fit the entire vessel in it." John observed.

"It looks like the boathouse was built for a much smaller vessel, but certainly there's enough deck-head room." Ford replied, poking his head into the dark space of the boathouse.

"Let's see the stern end Ben."

The two friends examined the stern end for a while before they made their way slowly along the length of the vessel until they arrived out the other end of the boathouse to the bows end.

"She's a good looking vessel even if I say so myself. Still as lively as the day she was launched." Ward opined joining the friends.

"What is her profile, er, engine capabilities etc, er Ward?" Ford asked hesitatingly, sliding his hand along the smooth hull.

"Just call me Roy! I joined this ship as a young Artificer when she was first launched, and know every inch of her. She's been modified somewhat from her wartime existence, and has even got a brand new set of engines. She is now 120 feet long with a 35 foot beam, and a displacement of 250 tons fully loaded. She has twin Deltic diesel engines but her speed is now strictly academic, she can only do around the 20knot mark. She used to have a crew of 12, but there's just the five of us now, with me as the only Engineer cum Shipwright." came the informative reply.

"Wouldn't mind taking a look at her engine room if it's possible, erm Roy! May we?" John asked.

"It's just a compartment with the twin engines and other machinery in it. There's nothing to get excited about, so you might be more interested in the cabin space areas instead."

"On the contrary, I'm a Chief Engineer and my friend here owns a ship repair yard over on the other side of the Canadian lakes. We're about to complete our ISDM course and are guests of the Admirals nephew." John said, pointing to Ford.

"Oh well then, that makes all the difference. Here's me thinking you were two landlubbers trying to be weekend sailors like the rest of the rabble in the creek." Ward said cheerfully, leading the men on board.

"We'd better be quick, it's nearly time for the launch ceremony and the Admiral is a stickler for punctuality and correct procedures." Ward urged, looking at his wrist-watch.

The two friends looked over the engines and their controls quickly before they were satisfied with what they saw.

"I'd say around 8,000hp, Ben!" John concluded, which Ford agreed with before they joined Ward again.

"Yes, you're spot on. Mind you, although she's had a good refit, I've had to re-fit the propellers, and sort out the engines 'revs per knot' timing plus the out-dated steering gear." Ward admitted, climbing out and off the vessel.

"Maybe if you fit variable pitch propellers you wouldn't need any 'wrong way' devices fitted. Merely keep the engine running but simply reverse the blades." John advised, which made Ward give him a quick look of astonishment then a nod of understanding what he said.

"No sooner said than done, but we must let the Admiral have his day first. Perhaps next week when he's away up the big smoke. I'll get it back onto the slipway and have them fitted before he gets to know about it." Ward stated, leading the way to the waiting gaggle of elegantly dressed women accompanying the gold braid and brass buttoned blazers of their men folk.

The onshore sea fog started to thin enough for everybody to be able to see the spectacle of the vessel slide her way down the concrete slipway to splash gently into the water.

The re-launch of the vessel was a huge success for the Admiral as everybody clapped and cheered when the vessel was finally secured alongside the private jetty. A marquee was erected to provide a reception area for the guests, who, after a swift look around the vessel, decided the hospitality in the marquee was the place to be and listen to all the speeches and mutual ego massaging. All except John, Ben and Ward that is, who decided to ensconce themselves down in the refurbished engine room.

"I can't stand all that arse licking and brown nosing going on as I've definitely had enough on my first ship the *Brooklea*. Much prefer to sit and smell the newness of engines and the like." John said quietly, holding out a glass Ward had produced and who started to fill them with champagne.

"And me! We don't stand on such palavers out where I come from. Anyway, tell us more about this vessel." Ford said with a smile, as all three men raised their glasses and gave a toast to the future of this re-born vessel.

They talked and supped for a while until one of the stewards entered the engine room and found them talking shop, as they would, being engineers.

"There you two are. The Admiral was looking for you to show your faces in the marquee. But as he and the guests are on their way here, it would be prudent for you both to be on deck when they arrive." he advised them.

"We're on our way steward. Tell the Admiral we'll see him on the bridge." John responded, which made the steward visibly shrink from such a remark.

"I'll do no such thing. If the Admiral says you're to show your face, then that's just what's expected of you."

"Better do as he says, or the Admiral will have his guts for garters for not carrying out his orders." Ward said swiftly.

"He obviously shoots the messengers then! Let's go John, don't want the steward to be strung up on the nearest yardarm now do we." Ford said, to receive a grateful look from the man.

"See you later then Roy! We'll try and visit you in your engine room later, if we can get away from buggering around the ocean with a load of piss artists." John said, following him out of the engine room onto the main deck.

The sea fog had cleared a little, enough to be able to see a short distance from the end of the private landing jetty, but looked decidedly too thick for any trips around the bay let alone around the island. This however did not deter the Admiral who scoffed at anybody who railed about sailing into the thick 'pea souper'.

He relented slightly and suggesting any of the guests not wishing to make the sea trip, should make their own way over to the other side of the island. Soon there were just a paltry few left, who for one reason or other, decided to stay with the Admiral.

"I suppose we'd better stay on board Ben, or we'll be accused of being lily-livered or whatever, and probably be keel-hauled for our troubles." John whispered, suppressing his urge to escape with the others.

"Aye, I suppose so John! See if we can get down into the engine room to help Ward, for it looks as if he'll be on his own. Besides, the Admiral has enough know-it-alls around him on the bridge to handle the ship."

"I've already seen the Needles from sea-ward Ben, if you want to stay on deck to see it too."

"Maybe I'll pop my head over the engine room canopy to have a look, but I think I've seen enough chunks of rocks to last me a lifetime." Ben responded with a smile, as they made their way up and into the already crowded bridge.

"Ah! The two engineers I was telling you about. Come onto the bridge Grey, and you Ford." the Admiral stated to his guests who made way for the two friends to meet the Admiral.

The snooty onlookers gave them a casual once-over look before they turned away with disinterest and disdain.

The Admiral almost demanded they tell his guests about their theories, but John told the Admiral it would be best coming from him, as he knew both their college portfolios anyway.

There was a sharp intake of breath from most of the so-called disinterested guests, for they knew what to expect from the Admiral.

The Admiral looked at them with total disbelief, then recovered quickly enough to start chuckling to himself.

"Quite right too Grey, by damn! Not just a simpleton to perform like an organ-grinders monkey what! Pity you're not on my staff as I could do with men with spunk!" he declared, giving a withering look to those around him.

"Anyway, let's get this vessel out into the roads and see what she's made of. Have the crew mustered on the foredeck Coxswain, and get me the Signalman!" the Admiral ordered, before turning to his guests.

"Gentlemen, kindly go and join your ladies and take your seats in the passengers lounge if you please. As for you two engineers, you may go down to the engine room to give my engineer officer a hand if you please. This part of the ship is for the captain and his crew only, so be off with you." he added.

"He must have read our minds John! Still, an order is an order which must be obeyed." Ford whispered aside to John, making their quick exit off the now almost empty bridge.

"Actually Ben, its best if we stayed on deck until we're well and truly going the right way. I don't really fancy going hell for leather right into a dirty great fog bank."

"Should be okay John, look! The radar is operating and should keep us out of trouble."

John looked up to the radar, which was on top of the bridge, to see it spinning slowly round making the ship look like a clockwork toy.

"It's just as well I've been, shall we say, educated enough by my old friend Bruce Larter, to be able to tell you it's only a short range radar. I don't suppose you remember him, but he was the Radio Officer on the *Inverlaggan* with us. This fog bank will be like a snow-storm on the radar screen, therefore useless to see your way clear through it." John remarked.

"Yes I remember him. My old regiment could have done with a few of his ilk in our ranks. So if what you say is correct, then we'd better alert Roy, in case he meets trouble."

"Yes Ben! You do that, and I'll stay up here to keep watch on our backs." John replied before Ford left him to go below to the engine room.

John climbed back up the short flight of steel steps and onto the bridge, where he saw the Admiral leaning over the chart table talking to a second man. The Coxswain was at the helm with another man who John took to be the signalman.

"Port 20. Half astern port full ahead starboard. Signalman, get in contact with harbour control and advise them of our departure." The Admiral ordered calmly, looking up to see John standing on the port wing of the bridge looking over the side.

"Water passing forward to port!" John advised.

"Very good that man! Stop together! Midships. Slow ahead together. Starboard 10 and steer a course of 045." The Admiral ordered in rapid commands, which the Coxswain repeated and carried out given orders. Once done and on course the Coxswain reported all commands carried out.

The vessel crept slowly away from the land heading straight for the fog bank, but the Admiral decided he would skirt around it by coming closer inshore, and switched on the echo sounder which gave the depth of water under the ships keel.

"The Almanac states the tide will be full at this time, so we can go out and around that point before coming back into the other bay. As long as we remain outside the 2 fathom line we're okay."

"Two fathoms? According to the sounder trace we're on that now. Maybe if we go out a few more chains then we'd meet the 10 fathom line and use that." the other man stated.

"Sounds reasonable enough Pilot. Starboard 15! Half ahead together, steer a course of 075." The Admiral ordered, bringing his vessel almost within the all-encompassing fog bank.

John stood looking at the island slip slowly by him and spotted a few sailing yachts would pass across their bows.

"Signalman, look! Some small yachts up ahead of us." John prompted, showing the signalman where to look.

"Thank you sir! I'll inform the captain." the signalman responded.

"Captain! Can't raise the radio station and there's a few small sailing yachts about to cross our bows." he reported in a booming voice.

"Keep trying signalman. Coxswain! Stop starboard, slow ahead port. Use your helm to remain on course."

"Aye sir!" both men replied doing as ordered.

"Pilot, have you got that infernal radar going properly now?"

"No sir. It's just one snow shower on it. Can't even tell where those yachts are who we know are ahead of us about 5 cables away."

"Grey! As you're on the bridge you can act as a spare lookout.

Keep your eyes on those yachts and let me know if they change course or not."

"If you wish Admiral, but there's more coming out of the inlet, and the outer ones are turning to go the same way as us." John reported.

"Let's hope Colin isn't with them, the mad bastards!" John muttered to himself, then heard the Admiral give out more orders.

"We'll go around this lot by going mid channel. Starboard 10, full ahead together, come round to a course of 100." he ordered.

The vessel seemed to leap into full speed and skim across the water, as John heard the roar of the engines being put through their paces.

"Grey! Our log has not been fixed to be streamed. Get down to the engine room and find out what speed we're doing. Coxswain! Starboard 10, and steer 090!"

John left the bridge going swiftly down to the engine room to see just how these engines really performed.

He stood alongside Ward who had a big smile on his face as he showed John how well his engines were going.

"Little does the Admiral know, but we are able to do a good 25 knots now, thanks to your friend here. He's shown me how to develop more power yet using less fuel. Glad you both came aboard. We're almost on full power now at around 22knots, but give it another ten minutes and we'll be up to around the 25 knots."

"The Admiral wants to know our present speed, so perhaps you can shout it up to him via the voice pipe."

"The vessel is starting to rock and roll now with the increase of speed which means he won't be able to hear me unless he puts his ear to the pipe. So tell him around the 22 knot mark."

John nodded and waved to them as he made his way back to the bridge to make the report.

"Ah good! We can swing back around those yachts and resume our old course again. Port 10. come round and steer

230." the Admiral ordered with relief in his voice.

The fog must have shifted in one big swirl to rapidly engulf the vessel, leaving them in a white out situation.

The Admiral went over to the big chart and studied it for a moment.

"We should be on this track for about another 15 minutes, before we alter course to starboard.

According to my dead reckoning we should be well to port of the Solent lightship. Signalman! Keep a sharp lookout to starboard. Let me know when you see the lightship and the marker buoys."

"If it were me Admiral, I'd slow right down in case you bump into this lightship. I mean, look ahead of us. There's definitely some sort of a light flickering across our bows." John stated, looking intently into the fog.

The Admiral and the Pilot looked carefully out ahead and saw the faint glow of light sweeping across them.

"Bloody hell! It's that ruddy lightship! It must have moved or something. Port 20! Slow ahead together." he ordered swiftly.

One of the passengers from the saloon came up into the bridge asking why they were racing around the Solent in a thick fog bank.

"We're conducting engine and radar trials. The engines are working perfectly and according to the radar our course is clear. So tell everybody all is well, and that we'll be on the other side of the island within the hour." he lied, but with a deceptively calm voice.

"The echo sounder is showing 3 fathoms and getting shallower. Sir!" the Pilot informed, going back to the chart again.

"Look sir! If this particular light ship is the one shown on the chart then we're above the Hambleton sandbank, which is above water at low tide. This is the middle lane separation zone. Incoming ships stay to port, outgoing to our starboard. The shipping lanes from Southampton don't come down this far as they turn left and pass through the gap to join the channel sea lanes."

The Admiral leant over to see for himself when the vessel gave a mighty lurch before stopping dead.

"Bloody hell Pilot! We're aground, and in the middle of a ruddy great fog bank. Signalman! Try to get hold of the skipper of the lightship for me." the Admiral groaned.

"As it happens, we're quite safe now, and hopefully we'll be able to float off when the tide is full again." the Admiral added having got over his initial surprise, then went over to the side of the bridge to see for himself.

Several passengers came running up onto the deck and some straight to the bridge.

"What's happened Admiral? Have we hit another ship, are we about to sink?" one irate man asked with slurred speech.

"It appears you've had too much ice in your whiskey sir. Better get yourself and the rest of the passengers below where it is warm and safe. We've only hit a sandbar so will be able to float off when the tide turns again."

"You sir are a complete and utter fool to try to sail through a sea fog and I shall be making my report accordingly." the pompous person snarled, before he started to tell everybody the ship was hit and starting to sink.

John witnessing everything the man said, gasped at the preposterous claims and accusations made by the drunkard.

Typical pressmen. Tell the world anything but the truth!' he thought, casting his mind back to the numerous other occasions where pressmen were involved.

Ford and Ward came up into the bridge to see the Admiral, but he was too busy to listen to them.

Seeing John on the port side of the bridge Ford came over to speak to him.

"It's okay Ben! We've just ran out of water below us. We're stuck on some sandbank, so we'll have to wait until the tide floats us off again."

"Better come below John and give us a hand, we're starting to ship water starboard side. Our fuel pipe has been ruptured, just to start with." Ford whispered, as Ward gave up trying to talk to the Admiral let alone the Coxswain.

As they arrived, John quickly saw a large dent with a crack from which water was spurting everywhere over the starboard engine.

Smelling fuel he saw the engine room bilges were starting to fill up with escaping fuel which was now mixing with the incoming water, took immediate charge of the situation.

"Roy! Get some rags and stuff them into the crack then with a large hammer or whatever you can find knock the bulge back out again. It will stop most of the water coming in for the pumps to work.

Ben! Get one of those empty beer cans and open it up to form a collar around the broken fuel pipe. Secure it down with a jubilee clip or tie a strap around it which should arrest the fuel leak. I'll get the main lights back on and the bilge pump on the go to clear the bilges. Give the fuel tank a dip to see how much we've got in case we have to siphon some of this spilt fuel and put it through the separator." John ordered swiftly.

The banging and noises from the engine room was enough for some of the 'know it all' passengers to come down to see what was going on, offering advice of various kinds instead of helping out.

Standing at the engine room hatchway John told them in no uncertain terms to either roll their sleeves up and help to repair the damage, or to clear off and leave them alone.

One passenger got very shirty at John's suggestion who tried to come the 'I'm more qualified and know better than you' attitude. John grabbed hold of him, stripped him of his expensive coat, and shoved him so hard into the engine room he ended up in the oily bilges.

"There Mr 'know it all'! Show me just how it's done! Ben! Roy! Stop all work! Let's watch how this man tackles our problems for us!" John shouted to the other two, whilst he threw a wheel spanner towards the man.

"Well come on then 'Know it all'! What are you going to do first Mr expert? Come on! Show me!" John raged, trying to goad the man into action.

The man just stood looking down at his now very oily suit and grease smudged shirt which was originally spotlessly white. His mouth opened and shut but no sound came from it, then he threw the spanner back to John before clambering out of the bilges to squelch his way past the amazed onlookers.

"Who else among you experts wants a go? Got any more bright ideas shoved up your arses have we?" John taunted. Within moments, the so-called do-gooder experts were suddenly conspicuous by their absence, which left the three engineers to carry on where they left off.

"'Bout time some of them were put in their places John. I've been plagued by most of them for the last 10 years, so maybe I'll get some peace and quiet to get on with my job. If I'm still hired by the Admiral that is." Ward chuckled.

"You'll be okay Chief! They'll just blame John that's all. Maybe he won't be asked back for another party after this, not that John cares, I feel sure." Ford said comfortingly, and with a big smile.

"Bloody hell John! Just like McCluskey that was! Thank God you're on our side." he added, before continuing his tasks.

It took them a good two hours before they were satisfied with their efforts, and able to go up on deck to have a breath of fresh air and a smoke.

"That big dent in the side must have been made by the marker buoy which is still attached. Better tell the Admiral to get somebody over the side and get it removed before the tide covers the bank again." John observed, then flicking his dog end over the side went forward to the bridge.

He found the Admiral talking to somebody over the radio so waited until he was finished before speaking to him about what they had found and what they had done about it.

"Yes Grey! I've been advised about your conduct towards one of my V.I.P. guests. I can see you won't be getting very far in the college because of it." He complained.

"Oh well then Admiral! If that's all you're concerned about then we three engineers can just unfix your vessel so you can sink under the tide when it turns again. An Admiral putting several important guests at peril by putting to sea in a pea-souper, then finding himself aground in the middle of a busy sea lane would go down very well with the press. If you're lucky you might get away with only having to offer your resignation to go quietly with your super gold lined pension intact. At worst, you will be ridiculed and vilified mercilessly then sacked from the Admiralty without any compensation. We three engineers are the ones who saved your vessel from being sunk and your passengers from drowning. What about the souvenir you've picked up? Perhaps the Trinity Lighthouses people will want to know how and why you damaged one of their warning marker buoys. And as far as your college is concerned, I couldn't care less about it. I'm an engineer not a ship designer." John snarled, before he left to go back to the other two.

The Admiral bellowed a command for him to come back, but John took no notice and arrived back to tell the other two what had been said.

"I'll be glad to get back to Canada John! I've got a thriving business to see to rather than faff around in some grace and favour college run by a bunch of self gratifying ponces. McPhee being the only exception!" Ford muttered, offering John another cigarette.

"As far as I'm concerned Ben, I will do this project work if only for your sake, and that of McPhee and Colin. So whilst we've got George with us, it will be up to you and Colin to pick his brains for your own ends until he is no longer with us. He might be a wizard at ship design but he sure is no engineer. What do you say Ward?"

"You're almost right there. He's not as clever at ship design as you think. He pinches the ideas or uses the works of others who work within the Admirals vast empire, and claims it for himself. Copying others work is one thing but he's something else."

"Patent stealing is rife these days and I should know as I'm always being fleeced by my shipping bosses through it. You stay a mechanic and out of the politics of that college, as one day the shit will hit the fan and people will lose their livelihoods because of it."

"It's getting to look that way now, and as it happens you're on your way out of it. Do your project but try not to come back to get your paltry piece of paper saying you've done it.

As my old chief instructor used to say, if you know it works, you don't need a piece of paper to say it does." Ward replied sombrely, as all three got up and went back down into the engine room again.

As the vessel started to lift gently up from the sand-bar, the three engineers guessed correctly they were now afloat again, and began to prepare the engines for re-starting again.

"Lets hope those stern glands hold, or we'll be needing more than the ballast pump let alone the bilge pump to keep us afloat. We're a good three hours behind schedule, which means by the time we get to the pub all the greedy bastards already there will have scoffed the lot." Ward shouted, starting up one of the main engines.

It spluttered into life, settling into a healthy rhythm before Ward started up the second one. When both of them were ticking over nicely Ward gave the other two the thumbs up before shutting them down again.

"We're back in business gentlemen, but I fancy it will be just a sedate 15 knots. We've managed to salvage enough fuel to get this trip completed. This will be its last 'jolly' trip for a long time, until I get it all returned to normal once more." Ward said with a smile.

"No offence and all that gentlemen, we've only done first aid and the Admiral will want it all repaired on a more permanent basis." he added.

"No worries Roy! We're glad to have been of some help to you, engineer to engineer if you like." John said breezily, then leaving the other two went up to the bridge again.

"You've got main engines again Admiral. We've salvaged enough fuel to complete your trip to the other side of the island. But suggest you take the shortest route back as we've still got flooding problems with the stern glands, and the split in your port side just below the water line is only sticky plaster to keep the flood to a small trickle." John reported aloud.

"Thank you for your report Grey! We've decided to terminate this trip and return to the slipway. Just make sure we don't sink on the way back that's all." the Admiral replied gruffly, before turning back to the chart table to work out his route back.

The fog had lifted enough for the radar to work properly again, for the water under the keel to become deeper for them to move. John managed to catch a glimpse of the lightship, which was almost right alongside them.

'Just as well we never struck that, or we'd be stranded on it until some passing ship came along to rescue us. Thankful for small mercies in the shape of a warning buoy.' he thought, as the Admiral had the engines start up and headed the ship back to the jetty again.

There was a crowd of concerned guests waiting for them at the jetty when the ship tied up securely alongside.

The Admiral made a laugh and joke out of it pretending it was all planned to see how well the hull would survive a collision, for future references. Most of the guests agreed with him and laughed just as much, whereas some of them simply shook their heads, took their leave from their host and left post-haste.

John and Ford were about to leave Ward in the engine room when the man he had humiliated came in with two policemen, and pointed to John.

"That is the man who accosted me officer! I want him arrested for assaulting a member of Her Majesty's Government." he demanded.

One of the policeman came over to John and asked him if it was true.

"Yes! I threw the man into these bilges you are standing over, for the simple reason he was hampering an emergency rescue operation currently in progress." John stated firmly while the other policeman prepared to handcuff him.

"What rescue?" the man shouted.

"There was no rescue on board this vessel. He's making it up!" he challenged.

Ward grabbed the man by the throat and literally threw him against the damaged hull of the vessel.

"Here you useless tub of shit. Take a good look at that and tell everybody what you see." he roared into the man's face.

The man started to squeal like a stuffed pig demanding Ward was also arrested, without noticing the big scar along the side of the hull.

The second policeman moved swiftly over to take a look for himself and saw the damage demanding to know what had happened for the vessel to get like that.

"I think you'd better ask the Admiral about that, it's his ship!" Ford snorted.

"Both myself and Grey here were passengers on this vessel, but we happened to be in the engine room at the time of the collision and running aground on some sand-bar or whatever." he added swiftly.

"Yes! We were trying to prevent further damage and get the engines going again when this tub of shit decided he knew what was best and basically tried to teach his granny how to suck eggs. In fact he was totally incapable of doing anything to help but was preventing us from concentrating on what we were about. And by the way, I'm the official Engineer of this vessel and it's thanks to these two passengers we were able to leave the sandbank and return to shore again." Ward stated matter-of-factly.

The first policeman asked the man if this was true, but he denied it and demanding all of them should be locked up.

The second policeman merely sighed, then shook his head, telling his companion he had seen enough and as they were wasting their time they should report to their duty Sergeant on return to the station again.

"But! But! You can't do that!" the man stuttered, threatening the policemen with sacking or other punishments for not carrying out the wishes of an important man.

The two policemen looked at each other, then in one swift movement grabbed the man roughly, pinned his arms behind his back and handcuffed him before they read him his rights saying he was being nicked for wasting police time, and threatening two police officers in the course of their duties.

They bundled the protesting man out of the engine room, followed by several onlookers who had come to see what the altercation was all about.

One onlooker stated if the three engineers wanted legal representation because of all this then he would be only too happy to oblige, offering Ford his business card.

"Yes! We'll all stand by you if that arse'ole pipes up again. That's the least we can do for getting us going again." Another man stated, who was joined by the rest in their appreciation to the three engineers.

When the last onlooker had left, Ford showed the other two the card he was given.

"The Honourable Judge Anderson.Q.C. Lincoln Inns London. Bloody hell! Can't get much higher than that!" Ward whispered, reading the card out aloud.

"Well whoever he is, he'll be required to give evidence at some sort of inquiry over this, if the word gets out about it. Anyway, I've had enough of playing sailors to last me a long time. Who's coming ashore?" John asked, leaving the engine room with the others following closely behind him.

Trooping over the gangway they made their way towards the main building, where they met Crabbe and Pritchard.

"Now what have you two been up to while my back was turned?" Crabbe asked, handing out a bottle of beer each.

"Don't ask me, I'm only here for the beer!" Ford stated, taking a swig from his bottle, whilst Ward downed his full bottle in one go, before wiping his lips with a sigh.

"I was glad of that! Maybe we can get a refill at the bar with some real stuff, or do we have to go over to the clubhouse and join the rest of the riff-raff?" he asked.

"Actually Ward, the Admiral insists all the crew are to stay and enjoy the party if they want to, especially you three. So come on and make merry." Pritchard revealed, prompting them to follow him into the throng that was already enjoying the plentiful bounty the Admiral had laid on for his guests.

"Must be careful not to upset anybody else now, John! Or we'll be leaving here sooner than we had anticipated." Ford whispered.

"I'll be glad to get back to the college instead of staying at this menagerie!" Crabbe opined, marching swiftly after Pritchard.

Chapter X

Fix It

The chiming of the local church bells, declaring it was a Sunday for all those faithful followers to hurry along and partake in their holy worship, woke John with a start.

John looked at his watch, and noticed that whilst it was only nine o'clock he had probably missed breakfast. A knock on his door prior to it being opened, revealed a steward bearing a tray of victuals.

"Morning Mr Grey! Mr Pritchard sent me with this tray seeing you missed the breakfast table. Don't worry on that score as your other two friends have done the same. The Admiral and his lady are off to St Peters just down the road there, and won't be back much before lunch time. It is a lovely sunny morning for a nice stroll around the gardens if you wish to relax until he returns."

"Thank you Steward. Can't fault your room service. I'm hoping to have a look around the island today, providing the Admiral doesn't have any other plans for me. The side of the jetty nearest the slipway looks a good spot for fishing, any idea about that?"

"No Mr Grey! I like fishing but don't have the time, duty and all that!"

"Oh yes, I remember. Did you have time to take your wife out on her birthday treat after steward?"

"Yes thanks! Managed to slide away during the upheaval of splitting the guests into the road party and those going on board. Mind you though, I missed all the fun when you lot finally returned. Gather there were a few upset egos and tarnished images around. Ward told me a few things but said he was under orders not to say anything to anybody nor reveal just what went wrong with the Admiral's trip. Maybe you can let on?"

"Sorry and all that steward, but I was only a passenger on board, nothing to do with me." John lied, starting to tuck into his breakfast.

"Well, whatever happened will certainly be hushed up and swept under the proverbial carpet."

"Oh? Then just how will the Admiral explain away his damaged vessel needing another dockyard repair job?"

"Simple Mr Grey! He will explain it had a mishap during its re-launch, and he only needs a few items to get it repaired."

"Maybe Ward will have a say in all that, if justice is seen to be done."

"Ward? He might be a good engineer, but he really needs a good shipwright to be able to repair the hull damage and such like. The Admiral has him working on it even as we speak.
I can't see him having much shore time until he has sorted out the major damage and repairs, other than what is needed on the hull. At least that is what he's managed to tell me."

"Then it looks as if he needs the cavalry to come and rescue him. Pity really, when the collision and subsequent running aground was the Admirals fault." John murmured.

"Collided and ran aground? So that's what it was! Thanks Mr Grey! I knew it was something like that. The pilot has been blamed for everything, so he could be short of a future with the Admiral for his troubles."

"No steward! The Admiral took sole command of the vessel therefore it is he who should shoulder his responsibility and not pile it onto some other poor sod."

"Sorry and all that, but that's the way of the Navy. Someone else always gets the blame, even if it's just some poor sod walking along the beach minding his own business. No! The Admiral will get off scot-free if there really was an inquiry. But then as he's the Admiral, and the head of any such enquiries, so it will be swept under the carpet, as I said. You just watch!" the steward said, opening the big bay window curtains before gathering up the breakfast tray leaving John to his devices.

"And here's me thinking all that only happened in the Merchant navy. Still, power always corrupts those who have it, and bloody well look out those who don't" John said softly, preparing himself for the day.

John was taking a stroll along the side pathway towards the jetty when he met up with Ford and Crabbe.

"Morning gentlemen! According to what the steward said to me this morning, it appears Ward is in need of our help. Care to join me?" he greeted them.

"You bet your life we will. It's about time I got back to basics. Ship repair is my bread and butter, after all." Ford said, flicking his cigarette butt away.

"I won't be much use to you, but at least I can add a few pounds of muscle if you need it." Crabbe volunteered, as they strolled over to the slipway to find Ward in the process of having the ship winched up the ramp.

"Morning Chief! Need a hand?" Ford asked.

Ward looked up to see them taking off their jackets and rolling up their sleeves.

"Ah, just the very men I need to see! Yes! I need to get her up onto the stocks so I can see to her intake and discharge ports. If one of you takes charge of this winch, and the others help me with the cradles, then we'll have her sitting pretty sooner than later." Ward replied gratefully, as they gathered around him to do his bidding.

When the launch was finally resting on its cradle, they saw with amazement how large the concave dent and crack in the side of the hull was.

"If you've got any welding or cutting gear, Chief, then I'll get the bow section and the starboard side of the hull sorted for you. It looks bad but it's really a doddle to fix." Ford stated, examining the damage.

"And if you've got any extraction gear or blocks and tackles, then we can extract the prop shafts and re-mount new stern glands." John added.

"I've got the welding gear, and other bits and pieces, but no replacement glands until I get into the dockyard stores tomorrow.

I have some spare pipes and such like to replace the broken fuel pipes though." Ward answered with enthusiasm.

"Right then Roy! As this is now your show, we'll do as you ask." John said quietly, looking at a buckled propeller.

Ward saw him looking at it and said it needed replacing as well.

"Not really! I'm a fitter and turner by trade apart from being a Chief Marine Engineer. If you've got some spare metal lying around and a lathe, I'll fix it for you in about an hour."

Ward looked at them for a moment and decided to take up their challenge.

"Right then men! Put these spare overalls on and lets do it!" he whooped, handing out the overalls and the necessary equipment for them to do the required tasks.

Crabbe took charge of the winch, John started to remove the buckled propeller, whilst Ford donned a welder's helmet and gloves and prepared himself for a session of welding.

Ward stated what he wanted done, so they began, asked Crabbe, as the non-technical person between them to be the fetcher and carrier of whatever was needed.

After a couple of hours hard work, Crabbe called them to down tools and come into the boat-house for a well earned cup of tea, which was received with thanks.

Ward asked John and Ford how they were getting on so he could see what else needed to be done, then summed it all up by saying.

"So, the new propeller has been fitted. The ships hull is back in shape, with a spot of welding and the fuel pipes replaced. The bilges scrubbed out and the fuel system is back on line. All it needs now are the new glands, and maybe a paint brush over the repaired section of the hull. That's a bit of good work gentlemen."

"To be perfectly honest Roy! We're glad to be of assistance and at the same time get our hands onto something we know all about and earn a living by. The college is not for the likes of

Marine Engineers, let alone Ships Captains." John responded with a grin.

"Yes Chief! Speaking of which, that's the first piece of ship repair I've done in ages, and a damn fine job I've done too, even if I do say so." Ford said with pride.

"I can weld but it's obvious to me, you are way ahead of my expertise. A very fine job it is, and thank you very much. " Ward insisted, peering closely at the results.

"We've got as far as we can for now, so we might as well pack it in for the day and go for some lunch in the galley." Ward announced, taking off of his dirty overalls in company with the others.

"Pity really! 'Cause I was beginning to feel at home in this boiler suit, even though it was a bit on the large size for me. Reminds me of the good old days, Roy." John said, as the friends finally divested themselves from them, and started to leave the boat house.

John took one last look at the vessel sticking out the back of the boathouse, and at the way the she was still on the slipway with her bows almost touching the waterline.

He called Ford over and showed him this apparent common sight, asking him to take a closer look.

As Ward came over to see what they were looking at, John fired a few rapid fire questions at him.

Ward did well to answer them in order, but was confused as to why all the questions.

Crabbe, who was beginning to see the reasons why John was asking questions, started to chuckle to himself for the others to ask why he found things funny.

"I think John has got one of his so called 'light bulb' moments again, and if I'm not mistaken, it's all to do with our project. Am I right John?"

"You're on the right track Colin, but I still haven't quite fathomed out what it is. Maybe it will come to me later, but for now, I'm ruddy starving and could do with a pint." John countered, which was the signal for them all to make their way back to the big house again.

Chapter XI

Hop It

John and his two pals, deciding to take advantage of the fine weather, asked Pritchard to take them on a whistle stop tour around the island.

"Certainly! I'll get my car brought around the front and we'll go over to the other side of Cowes on our way to Sandown."

"Sandown? Isn't that a big national race course George?" John asked.

"No! This place is only a small town on the south coast of the island and for my money will be destined to be a good holiday resort within the next decade or so. I've got some friends down there who I need to see before we leave tomorrow." Pritchard replied smoothly.

"Friends as in yachting, or old school tie network?" Crabbe asked with intrigue.

"None of either! Actually, they are business partners of mine who'll get things organised for when we go on our assignment, wherever that may be."

John looked at Ford at this revelation who gave a nod in accord with what they were both thinking, just as Pritchard let slip that he was going to get these friends to make provisions for patenting and such like when the project was completed and declared a success.

Crabbe saw the look the two gave each other, and was quick on the uptake as to what Pritchard had said.

John whispered aside what the Admiral had told him, and what Ward had said to confirm it all, and the three of them to made mental note of all this for future considerations.

Ford attempted to draw Pritchard out on a couple of items, but he was not forthcoming in providing anything further, but simply gave a running narrative on the local places of interest as they passed by.

Arriving at a narrow street that seemed to run out of land, they discovered it was a local ferry crossing.

John got out of the car watching as an approaching ferry arrived which started to disgorge its small quota of vehicles and foot passengers.

"I've never seen this sort of a ferry before George, can you explain its function and its propulsion unit for me." John asked with intrigue.

"Yes George! I haven't seen the likes of it before either, tell us exactly what sort of craft is it?" Crabbe joined in swiftly.

"It's called a chain ferry. The craft has a small engine to pull it across the river by feeding links of chain on both sides of the vessel through a cog-like apparatus, which in turn pulls the vessel along it to the other side. It's a perfect mode of transport across a river and you don't even have to worry if there's a fog bank between one side of the river and the other, as the chain keeps you on course."

John watched as the vehicles drove off the craft until it was empty then the vehicles and foot passengers waiting to cross over to the opposite side drove and walked onto it. He stood there for a moment then asked a few more of his rapid fire questions, while Crabbe turned to Ford and told him John was having yet another 'Eureka' moment.

They watched John closely whilst Pritchard babbled on about the local scenery, going up to him and asking what he was thinking about that seemed to hold his entire attention.

"I'm thinking of the car ferry we came over to the island on. It is totally different to this one. Can't work out exactly what it is, but you'll know as soon as I find out." John whispered in confidence.

"Say no more John. And by the way, this is the second time you've seen something we haven't. But we'll keep 'mum' from Pritchard for when you do tell us." Ford replied softly, with a nod from Crabbe to confirm their little secrecy plot from Pritchard.

Pritchard took the three friends around to the other side of the island from where they were staying, and down to a place which would perhaps enjoy a future with holiday makers, as there was a lovely sandy beach with a proud pier straddling it, poking its nose out into the depths of the English Channel.

"This is where I do my other hobby gentlemen!" Pritchard announced, parking his car in a small car park next to a local yacht club.

"Sailing again are we George!" Crabbe asked groaning at the sight of the little sailing vessels beached onto a small slipway.

"No! We're going to meet my girlfriend who is an archaeologist, she will take us on a brief walk along a very historic part of the island. Apparently, there are lots of old fossils from the dinosaur age which can be found and can be sold on to the National Museum."

"Oh? But we already met quite a few old fossils during our ordeal on the Admiral's ship yesterday. What makes this so special it takes you away from your imminent project?" John asked peevishly on finding out the real reason for their visit.

"This is my second interest as it helps me concentrate on my development work within the ship designing period at college. But to put it more clearly, the fossils we find are catalogued and entered into a record, and at the same time we try to see what fossil actually looked like. I mean, if the creature lived so long ago, with its own unique shape and mode of moving about the place, it helps me to work out how or why they were able to do so. In turn, this helps me devise models of ships which would, or at least in theory, given the same application, in turn helping the model to be made into a living ship to sail the world over." he explained at length.

"So in other words, you try to apply nature's way with the help of modern technology, you are able to come up with some fantastic ship designs?" Ford asked with amazement.

"Yes but…" Pritchard started to reply but was interrupted by John.

"I can understand the study of flight to help an aircraft designer, but it must be some special creature you're looking for to design ships?" John asked, totally unconvinced by what Pritchard had told them.

"Okay then George! Let's meet your lady friend, to see if you can find this so-called wonder model-making animal." Crabbe suggested, totally unconvinced.

Pritchard looked behind the three friends who were standing in front of him and waved to a young woman walking steadily towards them.

When she arrived, the men drew the conclusion whilst she was scruffily dressed, she was also some beauty.

Gathering the girl up in his arms, Pritchard kissed her before introducing them to her.

"This is my Julie from the National Archaeologists Centre in Southampton. Julie, meet my project team mates I've told you about." Pritchard announced, as she shook hands with them.

"I've heard a lot about you three, and it seems quite a strange union you've got going to be in the same project team with my George. But lets get on whilst the tide is out, or we could be stuck on some rocks or other and away from safety." she said with a melodious voice and a smile.

"I'm all for it. Let's go!" Pritchard said with enthusiasm, as the others followed on behind them.

"I don't know about you two, but I can think of a million other things to do on this very fine day. Go golfing, fishing, or even just sit on the beach for a while." John muttered to the other two as they lagged way behind Pritchard and his girlfriend.

Just then, ford slipped and fell towards them, shouting he had twisted his ankle. With that, Ford shouted out to fall towards them, stating he had just twisted his ankle.

Crabbe called to Pritchard, but he obviously did not hear him, marching his own way forward with his girlfriend.

"Sod him! Better get me back to the pier to see the St John's Ambulance people." Ford suggested, wincing with the pain.

"We'll give him a fireman's chair lift John." Crabbe suggested, showing John just how they would carry Ford.

They took no time to arrive at the St John's Ambulance hut where Ford was attended to, while the others sat enjoying the cool of the hut.

Ford, with his foot bandaged up asked the other two to act as his props or he'd be forced to hop on one foot for a while. This they did, as the three made their way back to Pritchard's car where they sat for a while, waiting for him to return.

A good while passed, and as the sun was going down the three to decided they waited long enough.

"We'll take his car and drive back on our own. His girlfriend Julie arrived by car, so I expect she will bring him back. But we must report this to somebody in case we have the police onto us for car theft." Ford suggested.

"I'll go and tell the ambulance man what we're going to do, and ask him to look out for Pritchard when he arrives back." Crabbe volunteered, going swiftly back to the hut.

When he arrived back he told them although that they were about to shut shop for the night, they had promised to tell the local bobbies for them.

"Let's go then! I'm standing on my tongue and dying for a ruddy drink!" Ford prompted, as Crabbe opened the car for everybody to climb in.

"Give me the starting handle Colin and I'll crank her over to start her up." John said.

Within a few moments they were off making their way back to the Admiral's mansion, via the chain ferry, simply following the way they came.

Getting back into the grounds of the mansion was also a bit tricky, but when Crabbe told the gateman Harris what was what, he let them through, telling them Pritchard was always a strange person, and his little car was well known to the local bobbies because it was always being returned without him.

Crabbe thanked the man then drove off down the driveway to find the boathouse again to park it the way it was when they arrived.

"Better leave Roy a note about this, so he can park the car where it is supposed to be." John suggested, as Ford hopped his way in between his two supporters towards the mansion.

They were greeted by Phoebe, who was naturally concerned about Ford's injury, yet didn't seem to be put out by the absence of Pritchard.

"I expect he'll stay the night at his girlfriend's house then make his usual appearance some time tomorrow. In the meantime, I expect you are thirsty after being out in that hot sun today. I'll get the Sickbay Orderly to see to your ankle Ben, but I'll have some cold beer sent to you if you wait in the study." she said quietly.

"Thank you Phoebe! We're definitely parched more than anything else." Crabbe responded in the same manner.

When she had gone, Ford turned to the other two saying, "Let's go gentlemen, I've got a mouth like a wrestler's jock strap. Starving too!" walking quite the thing towards the study, while the other two looking on in bemusement.

"Well Ben! I see you will definitely be on the top of the list for an Oscar nomination for that performance you gave us!" John said with a chuckle, hurrying to catch up with the supposedly injured Ben.

John and Crabbe had their own back on Ford, when the Sickbay Orderly came and bandaged Ford's foot.

"Yes Doc! He's been in so much pain you'll probably have to put a splint on it and wrap it up extra thick too." Crabbe suggested, managing to give him a sly wink and a nod Ford did not see.

"Yes! I can see it has been badly sprained. I've got a bag of ice as a cold compress. I'll also give him a splint and put an extra strength bandage around it for him. Maybe a tetanus injection with my extra long needle into his arse! Yes, that should do the trick!" the orderly said with a straight face and administered the

84

treatment, then brought out a very large syringe needle which he held menacingly at Ford's bum.

"Now for the antidote to treat shirkerism!" the orderly said with relish giving the others a sly wink.

"No that's okay Doc! Just the bandages will do thanks!" Ford said, shying away from the needle.

Ford's foot was bandaged so well and tightly he was not able to stand properly, let alone put even double the size of his shoe back on again.

"Okay then, you can take the bandage off in around two days. Mind you though, the melting ice will make it a bit soggy for you, so keep your foot off the ground in case you leave a trail of water for you to slip on, especially over these polished floors." he said, then giving the other two a smile and a nod left them.

"All shipshape and Ford fashion Ben! That is definitely the best bandaging and strapping I've ever seen on a foot. Mind you don't stub a toe or whatever, because it gets very painful in that strapping." Crabbe chortled.

"Yes! Maybe a crutch under your arm. A parrot on your shoulder and you just might pass as Long Ben Silver!" John quipped.

"Har Har me lads! Shiver me timbers! And pieces of eight!" Crabbe said, pretending to be an old pirate.

"Ha Ha Ha! And here's me trying to get us out of a dead boring outing!" Ford said sarcastically then giving them a withering look started to quaff his beer again.

Chapter XII

Suspended

Yet another foggy morning greeted the awaking residents of the Admiral's mansion, except for John, who was down by the boat-house waiting for Ward to turn up.

He sat by the private pier head and watched the tide lap gently upon the slipway of the boat- house where the Admirals motor yacht had been winched back up upon returning from its disastrous launch over the weekend. He had already had his favourite breakfast, and was now enjoying his cigarette in the quiet of the morning, as four swans floated majestically pass him in an almost perfect 'V' formation. He watched with marvel at these serene wild birds until they almost reached the slipway when he noticed several young cygnets who had appeared from under their folded wings to slide down the back of the mother swan until they landed with a plop into the sea, where they paddled along until they too formed their own little 'v' flotilla formation behind their parents.

Something must have scared them, as they all suddenly scrambled onto the back of their mothers again to be hidden under the large protective wings for a while before they hesitatingly decided it was safe, sliding down the back of their mother and re-entering the water with another little plop.

"Isn't life simple for them! Just slide down a little ramp to launch themselves into the sea and merely climb back on again as and when" he said, watching the little cygnets darting about in the water trying to catch whatever it was floating their way.

"Hello John! Got a habit of talking to yourself just like me?" Ward asked suddenly appearing alongside John.

"Morning Roy! Didn't see you. All set to take the Admiral back to Portsmouth for him to catch his train up to London?" John replied with a counter question.

"No! This vessel is going nowhere until she is repaired again.

He's got a dockyard launch arriving soon to take him over. And because George has still not arrived back, you and your friends will be going over with him so you can catch the Southampton train from the Harbour station " Ward answered breezily.

"Oh? But we're due back in the college by 1100."

"The Admiral is angry over this, and has sent a special message to the college for you three to go on wherever it may be without him.

"If the Admiral doesn't know then we certainly don't. It could be anywhere between here and Timbuktu as far as I'm concerned. But never mind Roy, we'll survive from his loss somehow." John said with a smile.

"Well said that man! He's a well-known waster and a snide who seems to get by on other peoples endeavours. Can't prove it mind, but from the mess-deck buzz, he's just patented the new ship design which you three have been telling me about."

"He can't do that under the rules governing the college. Maybe seeing as he is kin to the Admiral, maybe that's how the Admiral became one, and head of the college to boot. Like Uncle like nephew and all that goes with it."

"No John! The Admiral is a genuine innovator as his motor yacht proves, pity about his memory on navigation though."

"I suppose you're right Roy. Anyway, I must be off and warn the others. I don't suppose I'll see you again, but thanks for your hospitality over the weekend. I'm sure I speak for my friends, when we wish you good luck and bid you good bye." John said, shaking Wards hand in farewell.

"Thanks John! Good luck on your project. If all goes well and I'm still around when you come back, you know where to find me." Ward said in return, watching John walk back to the main building.

"Morning Admiral! There's just the three of us for college today. We're getting our papers to go off to some ship builders God knows where, but we are certainly looking forward to it."

John greeted, seeing the Admiral preparing to board the harbour launch.

"Morning everybody!" the Admiral greeted frostily.

"Yes, I've decided that you three would best be serving the college from where you all came, namely Canada. That way you can prove your project without prompting from young George's idea of his ship design you will be working on. He will remain behind to start further ship designs from the patented drawings, so at least you have had the benefit of his input whilst he was with you at the college. Anyway gentlemen, time to cast off and get to our place of muster.

I'm off to the Admiralty for the week, but I hope you arrive safely to those outreaches of Canada." he explained then motioned the three friends to get on board so he was by tradition, the 'last one to board'.

Ford and Crabbe went to say something to the Admiral, but John shaking his head whispered to them just to board the launch and get below into the forward cabin as used by 'others' whilst the Admiral went below into the 'officers' cabin in the stern of the launch.

"So Pritchard has stolen our prototype design! Just wait until I get my hands on him, his life won't be worth living when I'm finished with him." Ford growled angrily.

"As far as I'm concerned, I shall be reporting this to Clutterbuck and handing in my notice. I don't need their charity and can afford my own fare back home." Crabbe snorted.

"Fergus will definitely have something to say about this too once we tell him. As for me, I'm quite happy to go back to Canada with the two of you to see if we can bring off this ship design concept. There are a few niggling things that need changing, which we can alter on the drawings, so if our design is of a superior quality and works out better than his, then you Ben, as the ship builder will get all the glory and not him or whomever he decides to give the first build contract to. However, we must be first off the blocks to have the vessel constructed, which means we need to have to get our skates on." John said at length, which went a long way towards abating the men's anger.

"You're on John! You can stay with us as long as you want. We'll show Pritchard up for what he really is, a thieving conniving bastard." Ford said with vehemence, which drew a nod of agreement from Crabbe.

"Okay John! We'll use the college tickets to get us back home for you to return if only to give Fergus the project reports and findings."

"Well then gentlemen, it looks as if I've got another gentleman's deal and agreement to honour, just like Bruce Larter and Andy Sinclair did with me way back to the first time I went to sea on the *Brooklea*." John grinned, shaking hands on this new partnership deal.

The train and taxi back to the college seemed to take ages as the three friends were eager to see McPhee and get their tickets out of the college for the next year or so.

"So Pritchard has struck again! This I must report to Clutterbuck in case your project is now in doubt." McPhee said gravely. then spoke to Clutterbuck over the phone.

Clutterbuck arrived with his secretary within minutes, demanding to know exactly what had happened, and asking other more in depth project questions.

John spoke of all that went on, how far the drawings were developed, for them to conduct the project. He also mentioned what the Admiral had told them, and where they were now being sent to.

"It appears the Admiral has ridden rough-shod over this college one time too many Fergus! We are committed to send them on this project, but take it from me Pritchard is now suspended from the college, whether the Admiral likes it or not." Clutterbuck stated with equal anger.

"Never mind the college, he needs suspending by his nuts, the way I see it, it is a classic case of industrial espionage, full stop." Ford said coldly.

"Come back Trewarthy and Cresswell, all is almost forgiven!" John moaned.

Clutterbuck and McPhee talked animatedly for a short while before Clutterbuck turned round to speak to the three friends.

"Unless you three are prepared to honour your college project as one unit then I am of the opinion it is now history. That is to say, you Grey can go back home without any stain on your excellent engineering career, and you other two can return to your own business in the same manner."

"As it happens, and maybe Fergus will agree with us, we have already agreed to finish off what we came here to do, which is to build a ship to our own designs. I say this because Pritchard has absconded with only half of what my final design is about, simply because I've only just finally formulated the specs for the build. If he takes what I've put down as gospel and gets it wrong then any ship John designs and builds are doomed to failure, with God forbid, the loss of the crews on board those vessels." John responded quietly.

"In that case, you had better furnish us with your final designs and specs so we can register them and compare them with what Pritchard has submitted." Clutterbuck advised.

McPhee looked at the three friends with great relief and thanked them gratefully for their support.

"The thing Pritchard has forgotten in seemingly stealing our project designs and other notations, is the fact we've already built a ship almost to those specs and details, but as I said, they need certain major adjustments to make the vessel safe and fit for purpose. So unless Pritchard can prove he designed and built the *Winnipeg,* then he is already on a sticky wicket and will be found out. Not even the Admiral will stick up for him in an industrial espionage tribunal especially when he is the leading light on fighting such crimes." Ford stated evenly, making Clutterbuck and McPhee gasp in surprise at such a revelation.

"Why that's right! My ship the *Winnipeg* and the other two Ben here converted for me are trading quite the thing up in the lakes." Crabbe announced.

"Hang on though! It is my idea and invention of the single castle that is at stake here gentlemen. To make this type of ship of any decent size then you would require a very large slipway to build it on. And it's this very problem that I only just managed to solve over the weekend, but have not put down on paper as yet. It will take this second idea to make it worth the while of any big shipbuilders with that sort of capacity as I've just mentioned."

"In the meantime, maybe if we contact the QC, er Anderson, whomever, he could help us deal with Pritchard. Show Fergus the card you got Ben!" John added swiftly.

Ford fished out the card from his wallet showing it to McPhee and Clutterbuck, explaining briefly how they got to meet the man.

"We already have a team of lawyers working for the college, but perhaps this gentleman in his lofty position can help us with a raft of other problems we've got." Clutterbuck said, showing the card to his secretary who made a note of the details before handing it back to Ford.

"Well whatever the other problems are, we must concentrate on your project anyway. You will need to overcome them to make the whole ship design workable. Under the special circumstances, I for one will sanction your decision, and come to see how you're getting on McPhee.

However, as you will only be allowed two such visits as project manager and moderator, it will be up to the project team to keep us informed of each development so we can judge for ourselves."

"I'll accept your two visits Clutterbuck, but I will certainly pay for one or two of my own, subject to the Itinery laid down for the other three projects currently under scrutiny." McPhee declared with an exaggerated nod towards the three friends.

"Right then, that's settled. Get your project team out and on their way McPhee! When they've gone, report back to my office after lunch for us to make the necessary adjustments to our college protocol. As for you three, get to it and I wish you all the best. I shall keep a keen interest on your development and try to keep things under control from here despite you working in

91

another country, Commonwealth or not." Clutterbuck concluded, taking his time to bid them farewell, before leaving.

"Right then team! Lets deal!" McPhee enthused, starting to hand out their travel tickets, passports, money and other items required for the journey.

"I have already sent your father a large package of instructions Ford, so here are the rest of them for you to take. Guard them with your life, as they are the only ones in existence. That also applies to you other two, and I need your monikers put into this ledger to say you've been issued with them." McPhee stated, thrusting several packages and leaflets into their hands.

"I shall be coming with you to the railway station as it's my car you'll be travelling in. Get it all loaded up first then we'll have a swift coffee before we leave." he concluded.

"Flippin' heck Fergus! We'd need a stacker truck to load all this into your car. Maybe we could put it all into a trunk as luggage..." Crabbe started to say before McPhee answered swiftly.

"You can leave your luggage wherever you want, but you will need every package on you when you leave here. It would be like leaving your passport or your wallet behind if you don't."

"Well at least let us have some sort of a holdall each, seeing we're dragging all our luggage as well Fergus." John appealed.

McPhee smiled at the struggling men before he relented and going over to a large cupboard brought out just what John had wished for.

"Was saving them for a rainy day gentlemen, but seeing as it's you three reprobates who've paid for my beer bill these months I decided you deserved something back in return. Mind you though, I'll need a receipt for them."

"Who said the Scots were skinflints!" Ford quipped, throwing an armful of bundles into his holdall before zipping it up.

"Some say 'good old Fergus' but others tell the truth!" John added, with his load going the same way as Fords'.

"There you are gentlemen. Mine's a whiskey in my coffee and don't forget the cigar!" McPhee chortled, leading the three friends out of his office.

Chapter XIII

Time Travellers

The trip to the railway station was a silent one, with the friends looking out of the windows of the car wrapped up in their thoughts, McPhee was really talking to himself.

"Here we are team! You've got about ten minutes to grab a paper and get your luggage stowed aboard your train already standing at platform 4." McPhee announced.

The friends clambered out of the car and piled their luggage onto a nearby luggage cart.

"This is it then Fergus! Thanks for everything. We'll do our best for you." John stated, holding out his hand to shake farewell to McPhee.

"One last order for you all! John has been delegated as your team leader, to make out your reports and the like. But it's definitely a team effort needed to pull this off, so work as one like you did in the college. I'll be coming to cast my beady eye over you lot in 3 months or so. Any project problems or technical details needed, then here's an address to contact. The person named was a project manager just like me, but has now recently retired from the college and is helping the Canadian Navy with their own ship designs. He's also an old friend of mine from the Halifax shipyard and I've told him about you three so expect him to look you up soon." McPhee advised, handing John a business card with the details.

The friends took a few moments to say farewell and shake hands with McPhee before they hurried to board their train.

"Give me a bell when you've arrived, John!" McPhee called, and got a wave back in response.

The friends dumped their luggage into the guard's compartment before locating their seats in the first class carriage. Within moments of the train puffing its way out of the station a smartly dressed man appeared next to them.

"Tickets please!"

John handed him the tickets and asked about the journey details.

"Oh! Just the one ticket for the three of you? London Airport?" The ticket inspector discovered before handing the ticket back.

"There is a trolley service that will be around shortly, the dining car, which is just behind you is now open for late lunch if you care to use it. The toilets are situated to the front of this carriage.

We should arrive in Waterloo in two hours where a courier will be there to meet you and take you to the air terminal. Have a pleasant journey!" the man stated civilly and was thanked by John before he walked away to see to the other passengers in the carriage.

"We've got a long day ahead of us. According to the Itinery Fergus has given us, our flight is not due until 2100. And by the look of it, we've got three of them before we arrive in Port Arthur. Look!" John invited, discovering and reading red folder marked, 'Travel Instructions' then handing it over to the others to read.

Ford read it through briefly before handing it to Crabbe who started to read it more thoroughly.

"It says here that if we wished to, we could go either via Toronto and have an overnight stay before catching the Vancouver Pullman express train. Or go via a Chicago flight to Duluth to catch the train up from there. If I remember correctly, the *Maple Woods* should be docked in Chicago around that time, and ready to be on its way back to Port Arthur if we want to sail home again. I'll give her a radio call and see when we arrive in New York." Crabbe mentioned.

"Sail back home? That sounds nice!" Ford opined.

"Is she one of your bulk grain freighters like the *Oak Woods* you mentioned the other day?" John asked.

"No! She is now a bulk ore carrier with a 10 passenger permit.

The *Oak Woods* is more or less the same as the *Winnipeg* although a little smaller, but still a multi cargo grain carrier."

"Perhaps it would be more prudent to catch the train in Toronto, as it seems to be just as broad as it's long. " Ford suggested, prompting a three way discussion to settle the matter.

In the end they settled for the overland train journey from Toronto, while John took the rest of their present train ride up to London, to tell them about his Pan American train journey with Bruce Larter and Andy Sinclair. It whiled away the time for them, so it really didn't matter John was not able to finish the tale by the time the train pulled to a stop in London.

"Look out for a young lady…" John was about to say, when the other two interrupted him.

"Now then John! Stop giving us ideas, we happen to be married men you know!" they chuckled.

John smiled at the apparent suggestion, then saw a pretty young woman in a blue uniform holding a card up asking for Mr Grey and party.

"There she is! She's even inviting us to a party too. Single men first!" John responded, pushing the other two aside for him to walk towards her.

"Down Rover!" Crabbe called as he and Ford piled their baggage onto an abandoned baggage trolley.

The young woman greeted them explaining there was a coach to take them to the air terminal, where their flight details and suchlike were dealt with. She handed them some vouchers which would entitle them to a meal and other refreshments, whilst waiting to board their plane. Crabbe asked a few questions about the flight but was told that once they got on board they would receive their brochures with all the information they needed to know.

Thanking her politely they followed her to the coach being filled with other would be passengers.

They arrived shortly afterwards at the terminal which was bustling with people coming and going from here to there and seemingly everywhere.

"Seems a busy place Ben! Just like a boat deck after a lifeboat drill." Crabbe observed.

John indicated they had to check in their baggage then see to the customs and other protocols before they were able to sample the delights of the cafeteria and licensed bar.

"Better stock up with the fags and all that John, because our flight over to join the ISDM was rather short of any decent brands, unless of course you like the Yanks Lucky Strike, or their Marlboro, which taste like camel dung."

"Not being an army man like you to go around tasting camel dung Ben I couldn't say, but I will certainly make sure my decent cigars aren't made from it." John breezed.

"You'd smoke anything after one of those long flights believe you me John." Crabbe answered, receiving a gentle elbow dig in the ribs for his remark from Ford.

The friends went through the lengthy process of customs and baggage checks and other pre flight hurdles all would be air passengers are subjected to, they finally got through to the departure lounge and settled down for a long wait until they could board their plane.

John was no stranger to flying but it was still a novel thing for Ford and Crabbe, even though they had both made the flight over to Great Britain.

"How is it we're flying BOAC to New York and not Trans World Airways? I mean, TWA seems to have three times more flights than ours yet we've got to wait for them." Crabbe asked from a long inspection of the flight arrivals and departures.

"Maybe it's because BOAC have a mutual agreement with the Canadian Airlines to take us to Toronto as our opted route. Had we gone via Chicago and Duluth then it would have been TWA or even via the PAN-AM Airways if you see the other departure board for the U.S." John stated, only to be asked to explain several other such ponderables from Crabbe.

Ford started to chuckle at all the questions but threw Crabbe a brochure which described all the air routes each air company operated in.

"Here Colin! Take this home as a souvenir. Maybe you'll be all the wiser when your make your return trans Atlantic flight back to the ISDM."

Crabbe stuffed the brochure into his holdall but stated he would definitely not be coming back.

"But aren't you originally from Carlisle or somewhere in the north of England?" John asked.

"Yes! Penrith actually. But I'm now a Canadian National, just like Ben's family several years before me." Crabbe stated proudly.

"Good for you Colin! Probably Canada suits you, as some people are suited to Oz land, or other such far flung places they emigrate to. Anyway, time for that next year." John said cheerfully, looking around the crowded place.

"I don't know about you two but I'm rather peckish. Let's go and sample some of that lovely grub they're serving over there." he suggested.

"Lead on John! You're the one with the meal tickets." Ford enthused as leaving the bar area they sought out some nourishment.

While they were enjoying an after meal cigar and a drink they heard the announcement for them to proceed to the departure gate also to have their boarding passes ready.

"That's us! Gob your drinks and go!" Crabbe said swiftly, emptying his almost full glass of beer down in one go. The others followed suit, then carrying their holdalls made their way over to the departure gate.

Walking through the gate they boarded a coach which took them out to the plane, and within moments they were stepping off it to climb the steep ladders into their silver bird which would take them several thousand miles across the sea scape of the Atlantic.

The smell of eau de cologne greeted their nostrils as they

found their allocated seats bathed in blue lighting and settled down to be whisked away up into the night sky.

Looking at his watch Ford told them when they arrived in New York it would be the same time as now when they were about to take off.

"Yes! You put your clocks back around 8 hours before we land. When I flew to Singapore, it was eight hours in front, but it took me a good 14 hours to get there." John confirmed.

"So we're time travellers as well as Seafarers!" Crabbe laughed.

"Fasten your seatbelts gentlemen. No smoking until you see the light above you say otherwise, and here's a sweet to suck to help your ears cope with the different air pressures." A young stewardess announced, as she suddenly appeared next to them."

"Be good boys now and do what Miss tells you!" John teased, but smiling took his boiled sweet from her.

"Please miss! On my ship, I give out lifebelts, do you issue parachutes on yours?" Crabbe asked pretending to be a schoolboy.

The stewardess smiled and told him that if anything happened during the flight she would come and hold his hand for him.

"But only if you're a good boy!" she giggled, before moving off to the next row of seats.

"Some blokes get all the luck around here!" Ford sighed, frapping Crabbe across the head with the in flight magazine.

Their flight was filled with incidents as the aircraft hit several turbulent patches causing concern and nervousness amongst some of the passengers.

The captain announced he would descend a few thousand feet to escape the upper wind patterns, which he did but was told almost an hour landing that the plane had to climb to avoid the stacking system the New York airport had developed.

As John had the window seat he pointed out to the others that they must be circling unless New York had more than one Statue of Liberty.

The overhead warning light to fasten safety belts as they were due to land was met with a muffled cheer, and it wasn't long before the passengers disembarked into a very dark and rainy night.

The three friends were instructed to wait in the transit lounge until they were told to board their second flight for Toronto.

"Must contact base to let them know where we are, in case there's a ship we can use instead of the train." Crabbe announced, going over to a battery of telephones.

"I wouldn't bother Colin! It'll take us about three days to arrive by train, but probably a week by sea. We'll let them know we're on our way when we arrive at Toronto." Ford called, making Crabbe retrace his steps back to them.

"This is our short hop flight. No wonder we've been down graded from a jet liner to a turbo prop. Still as long as the engines work in unison we're okay." John stated, climbing up the aluminium ladders into the more cramped body of the aircraft.

Yet again the plane bucked and shook as they went through a lengthy turbulent patch for the pilot to be able to level the plane off and settle down into to a much smoother flight.

He apologised for the inconvenience informing them they were now at their cruising speed and height for their 3 hour hop to Toronto, and wished everybody a pleasant flight.

A stewardess came around with a trolley offering drinks and snacks to those who wished to partake, which was seized upon by the friends.

They joked and chatted to her for a while until she made her way back down the gangway again to see to the other passengers. The time seemed to be spirited away for the pilot to announce their imminent arrival then thanked everybody for travelling with his airline.

Their taxi sped through the streets of down town Toronto to the railway station where they saw a massive steam engine standing at the buffers at the very end of the track huffing and puffing to itself.

'What a magnificent engine. I'd love to get onto its footplate and look around.' John thought, as they walked swiftly down the long line of carriages until they finally identified the carriage they were to occupy for the last part of their journey.

The train and platform were almost in darkness, save for the odd lamp suspended over the train to offering some illumination.

"We had better find the supervisors cabin before we start picking a compartment that's not ours." Ford suggested.

"If it's run like the US then it will be between this carriage and the sleeper. It's only 5 in the morning so I expect he's still asleep." John said, pointing to a small window with its blinds drawn.

Crabbe went into the carriage and knocked firmly but quietly on the door, to be rewarded by a face poking out of the half open door.

"Who are you? What the hell do you want?" the man asked angrily.

Crabbe explained the three of them had just arrived from New York and were on their way to Port Arthur, then showed the man his ticket and travel itinerary.

"This is the Vancouver Pullman that's just arrived. We're not due out until 1600 hrs, but you'd have to get off at Sundbury and catch the one going via Nipogon.

The train you want is the 0630 from platform 6, but you'd better hurry, as my mate Theo the Chief Guard is getting ready for his departure."

"If we use that train would our tickets still be valid?"

"If that one is a Pullman then it will be okay. If not then whilst the tickets will be valid you'd have to wait until the conductor could allocate you seats."

"Who cares as long as we get on board and back home again." Crabbe sighed.

"Sorry to have bothered you. Platform six at 0630." he added, as the man slammed his cabin door shut again.

"You heard the man! Platform 6 and we've got about fifteen minutes to catch it." Crabbe said swiftly, for them to hurry back down the long platform to find their train.

"I see platform 5 but not 6. Where the hell is it?" Ford shouted, looking around the almost empty station.

"Over there! There's the guard standing at the end of the train with his signal lamp. Better get there before they disappear." Crabbe said hurriedly, running towards the man and shouting to him to wait.

The guard saw them rushing towards him and decided to wait until they arrived.

"If you're name is Theo, then we were told to catch this train by your mate off the Vancouver express on platform 4, as we're trying to get to Port Arthur." Crabbe explained, breathing heavily with his exertions.

"Joshua? Good! He's arrived safely then. Yes, this will be your last train to Port Arthur for two days or so due to problems on the line north of Sundbury, so better climb aboard then I can sort you out a cabin." the guard said, waving his flag and blowing his whistle for the train driver seemingly miles away down the platform to leave.

They bundled their luggage into the guards van and jumped on board with relief, as the train strained and pulled its heavy charge of carriages along at an accelerating speed.

"Thanks for waiting conductor! Don't fancy walking there this time of the morning." John said gratefully, handing over their tickets.

The guard examined them and told them they were in luck as the majority of the passengers would not be boarding until they got to Sundbury and even then most of them were not advance bookings. He also said that whilst the train was not a Pullman it still gave a first-class service with well appointed carriages for them to enjoy.

Escorting them to their compartment he introduced them their own carriage steward who helped them get settled with an early serving of coffee and rolls.

"This is our home for the next couple of days, so we might as well get some kip until lunch time. Kindly give us a knock for then if you please." John instructed the steward when he came back for the empty crockery.

"Yes! That's when we reach Sundbury. The dining car is two up from yours but if you wish a beer then the saloon is up one from it. See you then." the steward said evenly and slid the compartment door quietly behind him.

'Just like the journey across the States, but I've got a nagging doubt about this one.' he thought, lying down on his bunk to let the motion of the train send him off to sleep.

Chapter XIV

The Last Segment

An insistent knocking on the compartment door woke John up with a start but he was quick as a flash to answer whomever it was disturbing them.

"Mr Grey! We're about to serve the evening meal before we reach Missanbie and the Magpie River junction. I tried to wake you for lunch when we got to Sundbury, but decided to let you sleep considering you've had a long trip over from the U.K." he said anxiously.

"Evening meal steward? What time is it?" he asked, looking at his watch.

"Nearly 6 o'clock!"

"Hmm, must have forgotten to alter my watch!" he declared altering his watch accordingly.

"There is a problem west of here so we might have to take a detour up to Hearst before we can rejoin our route back down to Nipigon. The train splits up at the junction anyway, so it will be for the passengers to decide which alternative route they wish to make and for me to alter their tickets accordingly."

"Many thanks for that information steward. I will let my friends know, but we'll definitely be taking our seats in the diner as soon as we're compis mentis again." John said quietly, as the steward made his way along the corridor of the carriage.

"What? Who was that John?" Crabbe asked, climbing down from his upper bunk looking bleary- eyed at his watch.

"I make it 1200 for lunch time!" he said, yawning then stretching his lanky body as if to iron out the creases in it.

Ford was rising from his bunk too and swore, as he noticed the time on his wrist-watch.

"Bloody hell! It's nearly 1800! What happened to dinner?" he asked incredulously.

John explained to them what the steward had said and for

them to hurry to partake in their first decent meal of the day, albeit some 12 hours later.

While John was waiting for the others to ready themselves, he opened the Venetian blinds of the compartment and looked out at the scenery slowly passing him by.

"Look at this would you!" he gasped in amazement, looking down the back end of the train towards the front of it.

"I've seen long trains in the States, as I've already told you, but look! This seems to be four trains in the one long link, and by the look of it we're in the last segment." he added.

The other two looked out just as the train was halfway across a steel bridge spanning a deep ravine which seemed to be the mid point of a large horse-shoe pass crossing a raging river a long way below them. They saw each side of this pass had several high snow capped peaks but was also cloaked in green forestry.

"Look there're the two lead engines, with two in the next section, one in the section in front and two on ours, but why the two on the end? I count 90 carriages and what looks like 8 goods wagons at the end of each one. Lets see! I would make it around the two mile long mark!" John breathed, making a brief mental calculation.

"Yes, about right! And as we're supposed to be the last to be unhitched that's why we're 'Tail end Charlie' bringing up the rear. The third section with only one engine has a fairly flat section to cross, whereas the rest of us need the two rear engines as a banker to climb up the steep gradients along this section. Mind you, some of them would need a further one at the end to give a big shove as well." Ford explained.

"I wonder what the problem is for a change of course though?" Crabbe asked when they made their way to the dining table.

"Whatever it is, we'll soon find out, that's for dead certain!" Let's eat and find out later!" John quipped, as they were shown to their 'reserved' table.

* * *

They enjoyed their meal although it was described in French, it was in fact a dish John had enjoyed in the early mornings in the streets of Hong Kong as cooked by the local Chinese inhabitants.

"Didn't know you were a chopstick wallah, John?" Ford asked.

"Well certainly! If you can recall me telling you about the *Tsun Wan* and Kim Soon, then you should remember some of the things he'd taught me." John replied with a grin, reaching out with his chopsticks to pick off a grain of rice from Ford's chin.

"It appears you have seconds Ben! Here's what you forgot to eat." John replied, placing the wayward grain of rice onto Ford's plate.

"Smart arse! I only use the standard British utensils such as knives and forks!" Crabbe joked.

"Ahem! You're now a suspect Canadian, and I emphasise the word 'Suspect' Colin. Maybe the dual identities of being between a French Colonial and a British Subject has yet to affect you." John chuckled, holding up his glass of wine offering them a toast.

A tall 'bean pole' of a man appeared calling the packed diner carriage to listen to him.

"This train will be separating into their own units when we arrive at the Crows Nest junction of the Magpie river. Due to the continued storm damage to the line between here and Marathon, any passengers wishing to take the alternative route via Olba and Longtown to continue their journey to Port Arthur and Duluth can do so, but you have exactly half an hour to transfer to the next train up from this one."

"Exactly what is the problem for us to transfer?" a man wearing a dog collar asked.

"Storm damage to the signalling system and parts of the permanent way is the answer. But to you reverend, it means a long wait until the railroad is deemed safe to travel on."

Another man stood up to ask if the company would compensate him if he missed his connecting air ferry from Nipogon to Fort Francis, while a third man asked a similar question about arriving late to catch his river ferry to Kasbatown.

"Far from me to tell you what to do, but I would suggest when we get to the cross junction, you contact those persons whom you have arranged to meet, and tell them of this delay. The railroad company will not be deemed liable for any personal loss, given the delay is caused by natural causes. If you have taken the time to read the brochures freely available throughout the train, then you will have read, we the train operator, will not be liable for any personal or company loss, inconvenience or whatever. I simply to state it is up to you to decide which route you now take to complete your journey." The man said calmly which quelled any further irate questioning from other passengers in the carriage.

The dining room went quiet for a moment before people started to leave hurriedly to make use of the time left to them to change trains.

"As far as we're concerned gentlemen, our tickets states we're going via Marathon to Nipogon to Port Arthur, and that's exactly what we're going to do. I state this because the small print in our travel insurance insists we must stick to the planned route." John said quietly.

"As long as we get a telephone link up with our families to let them know of our delay then it suits us just fine John. The thing is, it's the time of year when the rail companies get hit with all sorts of problems as you already experienced the last time you were over here. So we might as well stay aboard here and take what's coming to us." Ford said stoically, which was echoed by Crabbe.

"In that case, we can spend this spare time going over some of our plans which still needs sorting out before we decide to implement them. Maybe if we ask the chief barman to let us have a crate of ale and a few bottles of wine to take to our cabin, and the steward to provide some sarnies later on, we can remain there until we do arrive in Port Arthur." John conceded.

Chapter XV

Collateral Damage

The friends were busy discussing their project when the steward interrupted them.

"Sorry to disturb you gentlemen, but this is as far as we can proceed in safety. If you care to look out of your window, you will see what the hold up is and appreciate the danger we are now in. Sufficient to inform you, we've run into an area that is now in the middle of a very nasty storm. The railway cutting we've just passed through has been sealed off due to a local landslide."

"Bloody hell! I heard some noise but put it down to entering a tunnel or maybe some sudden waterfall onto the track. Filled in did you say? What's ahead of us to prevent us from carrying on?" Ford asked with surprise.

"I'm not prepared to state one way or other, but it is my duty to ask you all to accompany me to the front of the train where the Chief Engineer will let you know of the situation as it stands now and if it's possible for us to continue our journey." he announced quietly, so as not to set his passengers into a panic or a major drama stress situation.

Looking out of the carriage window they saw the train was on a tight curve and standing on the approaches of a dam head, with the engine almost on the dam itself. In the poor lighting across the site, which was itself flashing off and on, with sparks flying from the overhead cables, they were able to see water leaking from the massive concave shaped dam wall standing several hundred feet above the valley below it. The torrential rain lashed down with intermittent flashes of lightning followed immediately by thunder rolling over their heads.

There must have been an unstable mountain nearby which started shedding great lumps of rocks into the lake, adding to the overspill on the dam.

"Bloody hell! The dam doesn't stand a chance! If it gives way, then anybody in the valley can look out! The dam wall looks a good 350 feet high and forms the header of a lake some ten miles long by four miles wide back from it." Ford whistled.

"From what I can see, the dam is still safe to cross, but only in dribs and drabs." John said calmly, offering his initial appraisal of the scene.

"Then you'd better tell that to the Engineer. He's been driving this train over this route for the past forty odd years now and knows his stuff." the steward replied with disdain.

"Lets get our stuff, and go up front to find out what the real story is gentlemen." John urged, grabbing his notes and other personal effects and stuffed them into his hold-all to lead the way.

The train was a long one, yet there were very few passengers to warrant such a train, as everybody turned up to meet the engine driver.

The engine driver waited until he saw there were no stragglers still making their way to see him, before he started to give his considered opinion as to what was what, so they could make their own decisions as to what they considered would be safest to do and enable them to finish their journey.

There were several concerned passengers all voicing their opinions or making different suggestions which only added to the mayhem and discontentment.

The engineer and the train supervisor tried to allay the fears and disquiet from these increasingly disgruntled passengers, when Ford made his way to the front of the circle of passengers, flanked by the other two.

Introducing himself along with the other two he started to offer some alternative solutions to their problems, but did so in a calm and civil manner.

John explained how the three of them friends had been in a similar dangerous situation before. How they had successfully managed to get an entire train, with several hundred passengers, safely across a booby trapped by terrorists with tons of dynamite and ready to blow.* *

There was a Supervisor of the Dam crew present who had stopped the train in the first place. He stated the chief electrician and the manager had gone off for a few days leave only that morning, not wanting to be delayed or caught on site when the storms hit them.

It was his stupid but truthful statement which tipped the balance of patience and reasonability among the passengers, turning them into a baying mob, looking for someone of account to be set upon. A lot of the passengers decided they had heard enough and determined to head towards the station offices, shouting for whomever was in charge for them to confront.

The few remaining passengers had accepted the basic principle of how to get across until someone asked where the Hydro-electric dam manager was to help them.

A burly man with a pointed beard with a French accent introduced himself as a national newspaper reporter. He asked the Dam Supervisor who the Hydro electric and the dam managers were, and what contingency plan did they have to cope with such emergencies.

"My name is McDuff, the head men are Messieurs Du Blanc and <u>Fabré</u> in that order. They are the top managers who hold the controlling shares of the entire hydro scheme in this province. They come and go as they please, with nobody to give account to, apart from the Prime Minister up in Ottawa. I was due to go home having completed my month on shift, but when the storms started to break over us, they told me to take over for a while, as part of their staff appraisal and promotion scheme they are implementing at the moment." he stated tersely.

"So in other words, they've buggered off and left you to hold the baby, so to speak!" Crabbe said vehemently.

McDuff merely nodded, telling them this was not the first

---

* See *Ice Mountains.*

time he was bounced for such a task, and nothing beneficial had come from his last attempt in taking charge in such perilous conditions.

"It seems these two are enjoying a very high salary paid out by the government, yet when it comes to doing the necessary, they pull rank and disappear until any problems were solved for them to show their faces and take over again. What did you say your name was again?" the reporter snarled, finishing writing down what was said.

"In the meantime gentlemen, we've got half a train-load of people to get across. Maybe if we can have a closer inspection of the dam to assess our chances before it's too late." John urged.

"It looks as if some of the passengers are in no mood for reason and might start to wreck the place even before Mother Nature does. So better we start now." John said hurriedly, walking swiftly towards the dam head.

"Okay McDuff! From what I can deduce, for every spout of water coming from the wall, you've got a turbine which generates the electricity directly onto your grid. Correct?"

"Yes! We have all turbine and emergency sluices open to take the sudden surge of water coming down from the feeder lake above us. It became overpowered and collapsed due to an earthquake causing an avalanche which half filled it a few hours ago, apart from the rain adding to it.

Our dam has a 5 fathom safety margin before we open our top sluices, but they are being overwhelmed by the sheer volume of water which hit us like a tidal wave. The weight on the wall has increased several fold and almost to the limit of the design specs.

The top feeder dam holds half a million tons of water, but this one on a regular basis holds 20 million tons. The inference being that the top dam has a water pressure of only 200 tons per square feet of dam, with ours being able to contain 900 tons per square feet. The top dam has overloaded us to critical level but what with the extra rain fall and natural feeder streams, the water has starting to come over the top of the wall, filling up the railroad channel, making the tonnage per square feet over the 1,000 ton mark. In other words the dam is doomed to fail at any time now." he explained.

"Are your turbines on full power onto the grid? What happens to an overload from them?" John asked quickly, seeing the solid jets of water coming from the turbine discharge holes, the sparks flying off the ground installation equipment several sparks coming off the overhead pylons.

"This is the Amber Dam project the government stated would be their new flagship in hydro- electric power stations, in their attempt to get rid of some of the old coal powered ones.

Most of our battery of turbines are located in the lower dam section are old, which should have been replaced by the new super models the government has already bought and paid for, but none have been installed as far as I am aware. For instance, just before you arrived, two of the generators exploded through being overloaded, and I've had to shut down a further four as the water was too powerful for them. We've already got two out of commission for maintenance. So out of our battery of twelve we've only got four left supplying the grid. Even they are over their generating safety limits and I don't know how long they can cope before they too melt down." McDuff explained.

"The only thing you can do now, is to shut them all down but open their bypass valves to keep their sluice gates open easing the pressure on the dam wall. If you've got any emergency back up such as an emergency generator or dynamo, keep it going if only for lighting and personnel safety." John responded.

John turned to the engine driver and told him to get his train staff to uncouple each carriage, and have the two engines separated, one at the front and one at the rear. He explained that one would push from the rear end while the front one with a winch would pull the carriages across once the rear engine had disengaged itself.

"The thing is Chief! The railway cutting we just came through has collapsed which means we cannot reverse back down the track beyond the tunnel to the last junction signal box, so all we can do is to try and cross the dam to the other side and connect up with the next junction box signalling section. We can get the train across bit by bit, so to speak." John explained at length.

"We'll have to sort out the tracking system first though, as there's no cross line junctions!" came the reply.

This reply left John stuck for an answer for a moment until Crabbe came up with the suggestion that as long as an engine which was about twice the weight of a carriage got across, then if everybody was put into one carriage, and that carriage dragged across by a winch, then all would be fine.

One of the train staff also chipped in with the idea of putting a suitable road vehicle onto the track to ferry people over in batches, never mind the train. At least the dam would be crossed on a lighter vehicle, and all the passengers need do was to wait until a relief train came to pick them up from the other side.

They all agreed this was the simplest and best solution, providing the rest of the passengers would calm down and undertake this very dangerous short trip across a very dodgy dam. It took both the friends and the train crew to finally get the rest of the passengers gathered together, so they could explain what was going to happen, and tell everybody to prepare themselves.

Some passengers finally decided on staying behind in the safety of the train or even in the power station offices, but the rest decided as they were wanting to get home, they'd rather risk crossing in the very light truck now waiting on the line crossing over in the train.

The friends had three of the train crew volunteer to make the crossing, with the train supervisor leading in the first group

"As a ships captain, and given the same dilemma, I would recommend we send the passengers over in batches of ten, and forget the ruddy luggage. Get the passengers into family groups and let's see how many trips it would take to get across. I reckon on about 10 crossings taking about 3 minutes per trip. If that's okay with you train supervisor?" Crabbe declared.

"Yes, it sounds okay with me. I've got the passenger list to be able to account for each one." the man answered promptly, and pulling out a long sheet of names started to call out their name.

"We've no time for all that, just get on with it!" Crabbe snorted, starting to help the first group of passengers onto the converted truck.

"Ben! This is your forte so to speak. Will you drive the vehicle as a shuttle?" John asked aside.

"Piece of cake John! But I've a feeling this dam is ripe for destruction sooner than later. If only I could get to a radio telephone, I'd have my rescue team up here long before the government decides to act."

"I'm keeping my eye on the slow deterioration of the dam wall, but perhaps we can make it if you can speed things up on the other end. That is to say, never mind helping people to climb down, just throw them off and get back full speed. You'll probably need to remove the tyres off the vehicle so it can run on the rails, so get men to strip them off, whilst we sort the passengers out into their groups." John stated, going over to speak to McDuff.

"Can you give us a swift account on what the collateral damage would be if the dam does fail? I mean, if we land on the other promontory would we be safe from the drag factor of the escaping water?" John asked hurriedly, surprising the man.

He gave a slow look around the dam site, pointing to all areas which could collapse and be affected, before commenting.

"This side of the site will be destroyed including the train on the apron of the dam. The other end has a tunnel about one hundred yards from the dam head, so if everybody is there then they should be okay. I have already instructed the shift manager to get the men out, but most of their escape routes have been destroyed. Their only hope is to try and use the old rung ladder up the sides of the rock faces to higher and more solid parts of the mountain side. But they've not been used for a very long time now, so I don't know if they are safe to use or not. This disaster which is about to happen was predicted only a few years ago by the Hydro Safety Management team from Ottawa." McDuff said almost absentmindedly, looking around the site in total disbelief.

"Poor bastards! Maybe if you can get some of your men up onto the ramparts and join the train passengers, we could save them too. But they had better be quick about it." John countered.

"I'll try and get somebody to answer me on my mobile radio phone, but can't guarantee anything." McDuff stated, pulling out his hand held radio telephone.

"Okay then. We can only take ten passengers at a time, but if the worst comes to the worst, we can try crawling across under the lip of the dam I can see." John stated, pointing to a curled overhang of concrete the water was splashing over like a waterfall.

"Worth a try, but just get those passengers across, as they're not part of the station insurance policy. Which is to say, no liability and all?"

"Bloody hell! If that's the case, then you'd better make certain you get across with us if only to sort out the aftermath of all this." John concluded, running back to tell the others.

The storm seemed to be at its height as the water was driven in waves over the dam, drenching the truck rushing back and fore.

"How goes it Ben?" John asked, when a large wave almost washed the empty truck off its rails.

"Bloody hell John! Glad I was a soldier not one of you boys. This is my last trip John, so better get McDuff and hop on board as best you can."

"McDuff told me he's got some men coming over. Get across yourself, but send the truck back on its own. We'll run it back on our own."

114

"I'll put it in slow reverse, so you can jump on it to operate the brake lever. It's this one here John." Ford explained, tapping the big brake lever.

"Get going Ben! Here, take our holdalls with you in case we can't get the passengers luggage over as well. You will need them for the project even if I happen to be absent at the time." John shouted over the noise of the storm, throwing the three holdalls at him.

"I'll be back, so don't go wandering off now!" Ford shouted, revving the vehicle off and into the black watery evening.

A group of passengers turned up telling John they changed their minds and decided to cross over the dam anyway, demanding to be taken across.

John counted the number, stating the truck could only take ten at a time so they would have to split into two lots, but families first. This caused a furore within the group, with a self appointed spokesperson shouting the odds at John.

"Just who the hell are you to tell us what to do. You're just a nobody passenger. Get the hell from here and let me decide. We go over in one lot or not at all!" the loud-mouthed person stormed, pushing John aside.

McDuff arrived with a group of shift workers, asking John when the next truck was due over.

"Here it comes now, but somebody needs to jump onto it to stop it as there is no driver on it." John shouted over to McDuff.

"Du Voir! Jump into the truck and stop it, quickly!" McDuff shouted to the nearest worker.

But the worker must not have heard him or was not quick enough to jump onto the passing truck, as it sped past them only to crash into the train some yards behind them.

"You stupid bastard! Why didn't you stop it? Now what are we going to do." the loudmouth passenger railed to the worker.

"But M'sieur, I didn't hear what was said! How was I to know to stop it?" the worker asked, holding out his arms shrugging his shoulders in total innocence.

"Typical Frog bastards! Too fucking lazy to understand the Queens English!" he growled and spat at the man.

This was an incident that had not McDuff stepped in to nip the animosity in the bud then there would have been a mini riot on top of the highly dangerous situation everybody found themselves in.

"I suggest you shut your mouth and help us get out of here or you leave us and go back to the hole you've just crawled out of." he said vehemently, which drew a cheer from most of the others.

"That's just typical! Here I am trying to save us all from disaster and this is all I get!" the man said in disgust then sloped off from the group and was last seen heading towards the train.

"Good riddance too!" a woman shrieked, clutching her two small children.

A big flash of lightning and a loud roll of thunder seem to herald a number of splashes and the dam head to tremble under their feet.

This made some of the remaining passengers shout with panic and fear, for the dam was now visibly starting to vibrate more.

"What about us? You promised us you'd get us over!" an irate man shouted into John's face.

"Save your breath for crossing if I were you. You're a big man, so you can help the women and children." John hissed, going over to McDuff.

"Get some rope and tie it around each person and in four strings. You will lead the first string, but place your men in between say two passengers for each string. I will follow in the fourth string, but I will be the last man off." John dictated without waiting for any argument from him.

McDuff carried out his instructions and had everybody ready for the off.

"Listen up everyone! There is a narrow inspection footpath with a handrail running under the lip of the overhang of the concrete dam which we can use to cross. Just keep one hand on the rail and one onto your rope. The lip of the dam will protect you from most of the overflow of the water, but whatever you do, don't stop."

John had everybody lined up and tied together like a string of sausages, putting one dam worker in between each passenger

You men will keep your eyes on the person in front and be ready to grab anybody who might get caught in a downpour. All small children are to be carried, and again, should anybody trip or fall then they will be picked up and carried if necessary. Two of you will carry the lady with the crutches over, using her crutches as a makeshift stretcher, or she'll never make it. It is only about two hundred yards from here to the other side, so start off in step and make your way across. String No 1 are you ready?" John shouted over the rumble of thunder.

McDuff waved his hand and commenced to lead his string across, followed quickly by strings two and three.

John looked at the progress of the leading strings, which were stumbling and faltering in an agonisingly slow transit as each big wave cascaded over the dam. It seemed to him that as each string traversed the dam, it was getting more and more fragile and almost ready to burst.

He actually saw cracks starting to appear on the upper half of the dam wall, with water beginning to trickle from them and the top lip of the dam was breaking into big lumps and falling over the precipice.

"Okay then everybody, it's our turn now. We've only got about four hundred steps to get to the other side. Keep as close to the dam wall as you can. I need somebody to count those steps, but let's cross in style" John cheered.

He supervised the line of people and told them to march in step like the army boys do, and for everybody to keep in step.

"Okay everybody. Put your left foot out and start marching. Left, right, left, right, left!" John shouted.

"C'mon you lot, Let me hear you shout. Left, right, left right." John cajoled, managing to get the string of passengers to shout their steps in unison.

"That man in front! Hey Daddy-long-legs! Think of us short-arsed people coming behind you, take shorter strides for heavens sake. As for the rest of you, never mind the water, some of you need a bath anyway. Don't look down unless you've got a parachute on your back." John joked, which brought a nervous giggle from the rest of them.

"C'mon! Keep it going! Left, right, left, right. It's a long way to Tipperary!" John started to sing and some of those who knew the words joined in, as they marched swiftly over to the other side.

When John finally stepped off the end of the dam onto solid rock again, the others were laughing and crying in a mixture of emotions when they realised they had literally marched through their ordeal and survived.

He stood there for a moment to reflect on what had taken place when he felt somebody tugging at his hand.

Looking down he saw a little blue-eyed blond girl with a freckly face looking up at him, so he hunkered down to make his face the same level as hers.

"I counted hundreds and hundreds of paces that my daddy took when he was carrying me all the way, and I don't know who Dippy Mary is, but my daddy said I was the sweetest girl he knew. And my mother too he said. Mmm Hmm!" she declared proudly with a pronounced nod of her head.

"That's a clever little girl who can count that many! I wish I had a pretty girl like you! " John replied softly with a big smile, giving her a gentle hug.

Her mother came over swiftly, picking her up saying,

"Daddy is lucky he has pretty girls like us!" gasping, hugging and kissing her little girl joyfully.

"Thank you mister whoever you are. We'll not forget what you've done for all of us." she said tearfully, walking back to join her husband and all the others.

John looked at the extremely relieved people who managed to cross a very dangerous place.

"Okay then, hands up who's missing?" John joked to his string of people who were only now getting themselves untied.

"Only those gutless passengers who decided to stay behind." said one very happy man, hugging his wife.

His words were drowned by a series of loud cracking noises, as the air seem to vibrate around them. The natural thunder and lightning was of little consequence, neither was the heavy downpour of rain compared with the body shaking noise as the dam finally burst, releasing a cascading wave of water down the ravine to create death and destruction for all in its path.

John looked first at the office buildings to see they were starting to peel off the side of the mountain, then to the other side where the apron the train was standing on was also swept away, taking the entire train with it into the rapidly disappearing water, to be swept over the precipice and follow the rest of the debris into the ravine to sweep away the already destroyed pumping sheds and other buildings at the bottom of the dam.

"Bloody hell! Those passengers who went there to wait will certainly get there before us now, look!" a man cried, pointing to the train which fell into the deluge of water and over the precipice of the broken dam.

It took twenty minutes of ear-splitting noise for the totally destroyed hydro electric station to be demolished and millions of tons of water to disappear, as everybody stood in awe at such a devastatingly powerful phenomena unfolding in front of their very eyes.

Once the noise had died down and the water finally stopped flowing, McDuff took off his hard hat and bowed his head, weeping silently to himself.

This seemed to be the trigger for the others to weep openly, but not John and his two friends, as they had witnessed other such catastrophes during their travels. But they guessed they wept not only for their own survival, but also for all those innocent people who would find themselves in the path of a monster hurtling towards them.

"That ravine seems to twist and turn but what's down stream of it?" John asked aside to Ford as the three men stood transfixed watching the sight of the mighty power and devastation the sheer wall of water was leaving in its wake.

"The Condor lake is the nearest, about ten miles or so. The river follows a deep ravine most of the way, but has a facing bank of mountains on the other side of the lake, so it will stop there. Those on the lake will get flooded but at least won't have the wall of water hitting them." Ford responded with a whisper, seeing the now empty reservoir to reveal the extent of the damage.

"Somebody is in for it when the Mounties come to investigate this lot. Let's hope McDuff is not the only senior survivor of the station, or he'll end up dead in some woods if he starts to go it alone and point the finger of blame towards his boss and his side kick, Blanc whomever." Crabbe breathed, as McDuff came over to them.

"I've just been in contact with some of the shift workers who were due to go off shift. They say twenty of them perished when their bus got buried under an avalanche. The other thirty stayed in the safety area of the railway tunnel and will remain on site to see what help they can offer. Most of the train passengers were lost too, with only four of them found alive. I don't know how many passengers there were, but I reckon there's about 90 people lost." he said, holding up his hand-held radio set.

"Glad you've got one of those! If you radio my outfit in Port Arthur, I can have a rescue team up here within a day or so. But you'd be advised to contact the Mounties and tell them to come and get us." Ford suggested.

The engine driver came to them to explain there was a junction signal box about two miles away who would be alerted to something happening to the line as his signal lines would be cut.

"It also means as we're late, and have not crossed his signalling area he will be alerting the railroad company. We should have a recce train arriving soon to see what is what, so at least we can be taken on to the next recognised railroad station for onward dispatch." he stated, looking at his pocket watch, mentally working out the time it would take for it to arrive.

"Yes! He'll be here in about thirty minutes." He concluded, dropping his watch back into his waistcoat pocket.

"What I can't understand is why such a large and high dam? I mean, it's not as if you're short of fresh water to conserve it." John asked McDuff.

"This was only half the size up to ten years ago, when they decided to upgrade the turbines and raise the level of the water. The lake was only averaging about 10 fathoms, but nearer 50 at the dam head. We allow flooding of up to a further 10 fathoms, with as I've said a further 5 fathom safety margin on top. The thing is, most of the lake gets frozen solid and up to a good 2 fathoms thick, but this dam can still provide electricity from the lower turbines at all times, all year round, whereas all the other hydros get frozen solid. This station is linked with two more like it that produces a good 70% of the electricity to the Province network, and a good 30% for the national grid. You're talking about the capability of providing three cities the size of Toronto at one flick of a switch." he explained.

"What now?" Crabbe asked.

"The dam should not have gone like that as there are, or at least were, several of the larger sluice gates opened to relieve the pressure. But I should imagine the actual overflow of water created by the failure of the feeder dam at the other end of the lake, and perhaps the effects of the earthquake starting several avalanches to swell the lake anyway, is the answer to it all." McDuff spoke almost to himself for he was slowly looking around at the scars on the sides of the mountains and the newly formed islands in the middle of the lake.

"If this place is not only earthquake but also avalanche prone, then why build the dam here in the first place?" John asked.

"A natural catchment area of water was all the boffins were interested in. Plus the fact that the railroad company needed a good solid crossing point in this area. Now it seems they'll be forced to build a bridge like they should have done in the first place when they found the span was too wide for them, so Lord only knows."

"Supervisor! My two mates and me were sent down to the bottom inspection tunnel and found most of the sluice gates were still shut! We checked each control mechanism and saw where it indicated open, in fact they were shut. We tried to open them by hand, but we snapped the heavy duty wheel-spanner on the first one. It was as if something was jamming the works up." a large man informed him.

"Bloody hell Pearson! What with the lack of maintenance and now this! Where's your wheel spanner now? What sluice numbers were they and can you make some sort of a drawing as to what you found?" McDuff shouted angrily.

"We can do better than that supervisor! We found all the sluices on the bottom two layers of the inspection tunnels which had the main sluices 1 through 8, plus two turbines were still intact as the dam didn't crack all the way down or break cleanly from the sides, and there's about 5 fathoms of water still left behind the wall." Pearson stated, pointing to where the concrete wall had broken away from a very large hole carved out of the dam revealing some of the sluice mechanisms.

McDuff and the three friends looked over the parapet of the safety wall and peered into the lightning lit dark abyss that was once a magnificent dam.

"Pearson! You and your two friends will join the train passengers and stay with them until help arrives. Then I want you to go home and stay there and say absolutely nothing about this. If you do, then you might find yourselves waking up with a knife in your back. Stay at home and shut up!" McDuff warned ominously.

"Actually, there's no need for all that McDuff! No matter how you try to conceal the facts, it's the wreckage and what's remaining of the dam which will reveal all the investigators will want to know. Pearson, just keep hold of your wheel-spanner, and pretend it's a souvenir until that team finally interviews you. There'll be too many witnesses to tell what happened for you to be harmed. My name is John Grey and I'm a Marine Chief Engineer and Ben Ford here is a Ship repairer, so between the two of us, we would be able to see for ourselves if what you've just told us is true or not." John interrupted quickly.

McDuff took a swift intake of breath and declared he somehow knew the three friends were not just any run of the mill train passengers.

"You never know who you deal with on trains McDuff, so on this occasion we'll certainly support you when the time comes." Crabbe said with a grin.

"Okay Pearson. Do as they say, but keep your head down just in case, as our two absent managers will try and manipulate things to get themselves out of this pile of shit." McDuff conceded, as Pearson nodded and left to join his mates.

The friends decided to follow Pearson and join up with the rest of the survivors as a small diesel engine pulling some carriages emerged slowly from the tunnel where everybody was sheltering in from the storm.

The two engine drivers spoke at length to each other before the rescue train driver stood up and spoke loudly to them all.

"Everyone is to climb on board. There's a set of small steps at the end of each carriage to use to help you. You'll just have to make room for everybody, as I didn't know how many of you there would be. Once we get to the next signal box junction there'll be a relief train to take you on to the next stop. There's only light refreshments available on board, but once we get you to Coalston we'll have proper facilities available for you, on the house so to speak, but have your tickets available for inspection!"

"Tickets? He's asking for tickets!" a man exploded, and went to grab the train driver.

Crabbe, who was nearest to the driver stood in the man's way,

"What's the matter with you pal? He's only pulling your leg. If it wasn't for the fact you had a ticket to board the original train, then you wouldn't be here in the first place. Now get going!" he snarled, pushing the man away.

This remark seemed to have let the steam out of the situation as the people swiftly climbed into the warm and dry carriages and out of the cold dampness of the tunnel.

Chapter XVI

Vindicated

The train took an hour journeying through the stormy night to reach the next halt on the line, where several newspaper reporters and an army of helpers met them.

"Look out Ben! Colin and I know what's coming from the pack of paparazzi and newshounds over there, so keep close and tight-lipped. For what it's worth, any nonsense from them, then a good kick in their balls should deter any further pestering. Remember coming back from the *Inverlaggan* Colin?" John whispered to the other two as the 'I've got the 'God given' right to ask you anything and for you to tell us all we want to know' mob of photographers and interviewers who surrounded them in their droves.

A few apparently highbrow officials from the Electricity and Railroad concerns greeted the two engine drivers, asking McDuff along with some of his men to give a first hand account as to what had happened. A female radio reporter who was with them declared over 90 people had perished in the accidental disaster, and asked the officials what they were going to do to recompense all those involved, dead or alive.

As the three friends were standing close to this initial interview, they were totally vindicated in their belief that no straight answers would be given by those men. Nor would they commit themselves to any decent response to any other questions the reporters put to them.

"See what I mean Ben! They've just committed the rest of us poor people to be hounded from pillar to post by those pack of jackals in their quest to get some sort of a story back to their editors. It will be anything but the truth, because they don't let the truth or reality spoil a good lucrative story." John whispered, pushing them away from the increasing number of cameras which were flashing like the lightning the storm had created over the dam.

Managing to get away from the baying crowd of photographers and interviewers, they sought shelter on the train which would take them away, to their final destination.

"It looks like we're the only ones with luggage, so we'd better hide them in case some bigmouth comes along asking why he hasn't got his too." Crabbe suggested, picking out the best compartment for themselves.

"Ben! See if you can secure the door for us, as we need to show our faces in the reception hut on the end of the platform. I feel sure you two are starving just like me, and from what I can smell, there's a veritable feast waiting for us there." Crabbe continued, for them to make their way back off the train and along the platform to the brightly lit building.

Many of the passengers were already inside, eating hungrily from the plates of food they were given. They saw some of the very young children who had already been fed, were being wrapped up in woolly blankets to help them sleep.

Several helpers were walking round handing out various bits of clothing and 'creature comforts' while the older children were very quite and reserved.

Finding an empty table the friends were given food and blankets, and offered them other welcome items. After a few bottles of wine they decided it was time to sneak back to their compartment to get their heads down, declining the offer of a nice hot shower or bath from their hosts.

When they got back into their compartment they put a 'do not disturb' notice on the door before securing it from the inside to finally relax on their respective bunks.

"I managed to purloin a couple bottles of wine, and some smokes for us." Crabbe whispered, hearing other people finally boarding the train.

"I've collected some chicken and a few rolls as well. It will keep us happy until we reach Manathon, at least." John added.

"Now we're self sufficient until then." Ford yawned.

"It's three in the morning. Arrival time at Manathon should be in about four hours time, providing there're no further delays." He added, rolling over and switching off his bunk light to fall fast asleep.

"Bloody hell Colin! All those deaths and the seriously injured, the powers that be will be in big trouble over that, I should imagine. I know the skipper of the *Inverlaggan* got the fault for us being blown up, but as he was dead the company got off Scot free." John whispered.

"That's not the half of it John, believe you me. Sufficient to tell you we're both free men without a blemish on our careers, or more importantly, on our characters." Crabbe yawned, then farted loudly, before he too rolled over and went to sleep.

The smell from Crabbe was so bad, forcing John to get up and slide open the small window at the top of the large plate glass one, to breathe in some fresh air.

He managed to see the new train was now ready to pull away with a powerful diesel engine at the front, while a throng of people surrounded the hapless officials of the dam and train company.

An insistent knocking on the door told John it was perhaps a member of the train crew wanting to check up on them.

"Hello inspector! We've got our tickets, but grabbed this compartment so as not to disturb any of the other passengers." John said quietly.

The man who had a piece of paper in his hand, asked who he and the other occupants in the compartment were so that he could keep a tab on those still trying to get to Fort George and all points south of it. Telling him what he wanted to know John and asked if this train would be theirs for the rest of their journey.

The man told John they had been classed as missing, so he was thankful they were on board to be found again. Also the train would take a few hours due to severe storms with a delay in Manathon to take on a proper manifest and further passengers.

"So my friends and I can have a decent sleep. What about the rest of the passengers, they okay now?"

"We've had to send a few to hospital due to being traumatised, but the rest will be okay once they've had a few days rest. By the way, I've got this card from a gentleman who asked me to give it to you, if and when you were found again. He is one of the passengers who wishes to speak with you."

John took the business card and read the print on it, then thanked the inspector for giving it to him. The inspector simply nodded his head, concluding by telling John about the scheduled breakfast stop at Manathon, with lunch in Nipogon if all goes well.

"Thanks inspector! We'll be there. One last thing before you go. My friends and I wish to offer you and your train crew our deep condolences on the loss of some of your members. I hope your rail company will be forthcoming in offering suitable insurance compensations to the families they left behind."

"Thank you Mr Grey! I will tell them know of your kind wishes. You are the first of the passengers to wish us such sympathy, for they are too wrapped up in their own thoughts to do so. It is kind of you. Good night, or at least what's left of it." the inspector whispered, sliding the door shut leaving John to secure it again from unwanted guests.

Chapter XVII

A Great Start

It was the lack of noises and movement from the train which woke them up almost simultaneously.

Crabbe leaned over and peeked behind the curtain to see what was going on, to be faced with a large sign declaring the place was Manathon, and the clouds were trying to scurry away to shed some light on the place.

Ford checked his watch, stating it was 0700, just as he had of predicted.

"As a matter of fact gentlemen, we'd better get ourselves into the diner carriage, because we've got a free breakfast to sample." John announced, then told the others of his conversation with the inspector.

"In that case, let's go! We'll keep the rolls in case we get hungry again." Crabbe suggested, leaving their compartment locked they made their way to the first of the two diner carriages.

During their meal, John showed them the card he was given, which prompted a round of guessing games until a fairly tall, stout man made his way over to them and introduced himself as the person on the card.

"Hello Mr Ward! " John said, getting up to introduce the other two to him, what is it that we can do for you?" he asked politely.

Ward explained briefly that he already knew of Ford's ship repair business and outlined what he wanted to see them about, which came as something of a surprise and bit of a bombshell for the three friends.

"We three, who should be four, are on a special project which involves building some Future Homes for the sailors of the world over, providing of course all works out. The fourth element of our project team will not now be joining us, but we have our project manager to come and oversee our work. If you wish to offer us a contract Mr Ward, then I'm sure we can come up with something suitable." John confided.

"Yes Mr Ward! I have a small fleet of ships operating within the Lakes called the 'Leaf Line', with the *SS Winnipeg* as my flagship. Our home port is Port Arthur and is under a repair and maintenance contract with Mr Ford here, who as you know is part of the new shipyard complex up there. If you want us to repair your existing fleet of coalers and ore ships then it will be up to him. However, as you state you wish to increase your output of coal, or maybe grain from your small harbour outlets then I will be more than glad to help out." Crabbe stated civilly, with Ward nodding his head in agreement.

"What about you Mr Grey?" Ward asked directly.

"I'm a Chief Marine Engineer, to see the ship gets a decent propulsion unit and make sure all machinery on board works the way it should. Amongst other things as well, mind you." John replied.

"Then if I was to fund the entire cost of building two new ships, how soon can you deliver them?" Ward asked slowly, looking closely at them to gauge their reactions.

"We'd have to start from scratch, but what size are you thinking of?" Ford asked sharply.

"Oh! About the 450-550 foot mark! Don't forget some of my vessels have to transit the canal waterways, whereas the others can be as big as you like as they're only sail the Superior, from Dean Harbour to Hitchcock Bay."

"Hmm! I've got a 600foot dry dock Which is earmarked for the *Winnipeg's* next docking down, two floating docks that can take up to 200feet, and a 250foot wide by 320 foot long slipway for any other smaller vessels requiring to be taken out at once. If you provide the materials, shipped by Captain Crabbe's vessels, then I reckon on about ten months for such a vessel. Mind you Ward, what we've got in mind will knock your socks off and you probably won't want anything bigger." Ford said after a little while thinking about it.

"Hmm, it sounds fair enough to me, but I suppose during to the winter months you will not be able to do much building, so as long as I can have the first one in time for my next consignment in August next year, then it will do."

"Something like that yes, but we'll have to get the supplies in first before the lake freezes over." Ford responded.

"In which case gentlemen, I'll get some of my lawyers onto making out this contract as soon as we arrive at Nipogon where my headquarters are. I have several private jetties and own a couple of small loading ports around the place, but we'll use your docking facilities seeing as you're only down the road at Port Arthur." Ward concluded, standing up to shake their hands in a sort of a gentleman's agreement.

"We'll be pretty busy from the moment we arrive in Port Arthur, so give us a couple of months before you to come down to take a look at our place." Ford offered.

"That's a good idea. Make sure Mr Grey is among you when I arrive, probably by seaplane. It's in for repair which is why I had to travel in this infernal contraption, even though it's probably built with the steel I cart around the ruddy lakes." This revelation took them by surprise, with Crabbe asking the key question.

"How did he come to offer them this lucrative offer?"

"It was Mr Grey here who made us cross the dam and arrive safely on the other side." he admitted.

"It was my little Granddaughter Caroline who came and spoke to you Mr Grey. I will always be grateful to you for saving all our lives, just as what my daughter told you." Ward added softly, shaking John's hand gratefully.

"Just doing something which needed to be done as did my two friends here. For it was Ben who used the truck to shuttle back and fore getting everybody over, and Colin here who kept everybody calm whilst they were waiting. Don't forget the train crew either!" John insisted, trying to shift the limelight away from himself.

"Maybe so, but who the hell is Dippy Mary she is now singing about?" Ward asked.

John thought for a moment then laughed and told him it was supposed to be the place in Ireland called Tipperary. Ward stopped for a moment as the penny dropped then started to laugh.

"Well whatever, Grey! You three will never be forgotten in a hurry that's for sure." he stated, then waving his hand left their table.

"Flippin' heck John! If that's all it takes to secure a bloody great start to our project, then I'm all for looking around for more suspect dams to swing across!" Ford said with incredulity, joined swiftly by Crabbe.

"I think the Yanks call it Serendipity, but I call it just sheer coincidence. Besides, don't forget your own heroics gentlemen. Anyway, I'm off doing that kind of stuff for a while, as even the Gods need a rest!" John retorted, fishing out a fresh packet of cigarettes from his pocket to offer them a smoke.

"The news of the dam will not have reached Fort George just yet, so if we've got time before the train leaves, I'll phone home to let Glenda know we're okay and on our way, somewhat late." Crabbe announced, which was greeted with a nod from the other two.

"How come it will take that long Colin? I mean, those reporters had all the radio gear and suchlike to be able to tell the whole nation!" John asked with surprise.

"It's something to do with inter-Province communications, and the Government's crackdown on any sensational reporting that would alarm everybody. Sometimes, and depending on the story, it could take up to a week before people in say Halifax to read all about it at their breakfast table. It's the thousands of miles and a good 5 time zones probably." Ford explained.

"Back in Blighty, if a man is caught pinching a bottle of milk off a doorstep in Scotland, it would be all over the rest of the country by the evening stop-press. 'Man deported to Australia for stealing milk' sort of." John sighed, as the three left their table and sauntered back to their compartment, with Crabbe stating he was going to find a phone booth.

"You'd better hurry up Colin! We've only got about another 10 minutes or so." Ford prompted, as Crabbe ran off the train and towards the station's passenger facilities.

When he came back he told them what he had said to his wife and that they would be expecting a nice welcome when they arrived home, as the news had just been announced a few minutes before he rang her.

"Oh well then. A few beers and a knees-up will just round it all up nicely. Here, sup some if this in the meantime." Ford said happily, handing out the bottles of wine.

Chapter XVIII

Getting Organised

They left Nipogon on their last leg of their long journey, with a fresh briefcase of paperwork for the m to wade through before they arrived home.

"He wants a 450 and a 500 footer. The dry dock is already spoken for, and the floating docks would be too small. Anyway they will be icebound during the winter months. The yard and the slipway is only 400feet long, even taking the workshops into consideration. " Ford said, shaking his head at the dimensions required for the ships.

"How far out into the lake does your concrete apron go. I mean to what depth?" John asked, glancing over the drawings.

"It's solid rock on a 10degree downward slope for about 100 yards up to the depth of 3 fathoms before dropping beyond the 10 fathom mark. I get the vessels secured onto my mobile underwater cradles before they are winched up out of the water and onto the land cradles. But the longest vessel we could land would be around the 370foot mark with a maximum draught of also around the 10 feet mark. On re-launch, we let the vessel slip off its land cradle to settle down onto the submerged one, when we tow it and the vessel out far enough for it to float off on its own." Ford answered with deliberation.

"So you have two cradles, which will be fine. But what beam can they handle?"

"What is the reason for these questions John? Is this something to do with what you saw back at the Admirals place?" Crabbe asked with increasing intrigue.

"Yes it has Colin! We'll build those ships to our design, providing you widen your cradles to take around an 80 foot beam. We would need two sets of cradles in parallel, but as Ben has only got the one then we can only build one ship at a time." John responded quickly.

"Two cradles long? But one cradle is submerged!" Ford asked with surprise.

"Ah Ben, that's just it! The Yanks built prefabricated ships called 'Liberty Ships' to cope with the shipping demands of the last war, which were welded together and they had several launched within a few months. We on the other hand rivet our ships, taking much longer as we need to ensure our vessels have a decent rigid hull to cope with the sheer weight of any cargo being carried. What I have in mind is; We'll build one half of the vessel on the first cradle, then slide it down the ramp onto the second one until we build the other half onto the end. Those prefabricated ships constructed during the war, were made in two halves, or even sometimes in 4 pieces were then joined together. Don't forget, we're going to build a one-castle ship not three or even two. So we can build the stern first, shove it down into the water with the propellers fully immersed in the water, so when we come to launch the ship she can pull herself off using her own power. That way, we get to test the engines at the same time too. And if she doesn't float on her own, then we can tow her out with a harbour tug until she does float on her own." John revealed.

Ford and Crabbe looked at each other for a moment trying to take in this new and radical idea of ship building, before they started to speak at once.

"Whoa hold on you two! I can handle several questions at a time but not two voices. Now who's first?" John chuckled.

Ford asked several questions John was able to answer and some he wasn't able to without the full project diagrams and suchlike.

Crabbe asked his myriad of questions before they were both satisfied all would be okay, subject to rescrutiny of the drawings, but they all agreed they needed to get some sort of answers from the ISDM or at least for McPhee to come and give them an earlier visit than previously planned.

Crabbe began smiling at John, which made him curious as to what was going on.

"It's something Ben has said, that's taken my fancy." Crabbe replied with a bigger grin, and whispered aside to Ford, who nodded his head and started to grin too.

"Yes! You have now been dubbed Long John!" Ford said with amusement.

"But without the parrot or the wooden leg to make your surname Silver!" Crabbe added, leaving made John non-plussed as to what they were talking about.

"Whatever it is you decide, just as long as I get to name you two reprobates something." he said with mock disapproval.

"What a way to spend a train journey!" John added with a sigh, and threw a half eaten roll at the two of them.

"We have a lot to consider, perhaps my father and his partnership can come up with something to help us. If only that idiot Pritchard had been halfway decent, he would be here to help us out. We will be hard pressed to make ward his first rowing boat let alone a 450 foot ship. And that is only from my end of the team spectrum so to speak." Ford stated softly.

"It will take a good couple of weeks to get the paperwork and the small print sorted out on his contract. In the meanwhile, we can start preparing your slipways for 'Long John' here, so we can build a ship almost twice as long as your existing facility. What we must do is make a decent start with what we've got. If the first ship to be built in this manner is a headline grabber, even from those very intrusive and insensitive newsmen and women we met earlier, then it may give us a financial boost towards making an even bigger slipway for even bigger vessels. If not, then we'll have to get the financial backing from the government to have a ship building yard out on the St Lawrence to be able to take the super versions of the ships we've got in our drawings." Crabbe opined.

"Yes that sounds a good idea. However, what I've told you is an idealistic solution to the existing set-up. If it turns out to be a winner, then we'd be looking for a much bigger workforce, with at least a 100% increase of facilities needing to be built to cope with the demands. I welcome this challenge, but I certainly issue a big note of caution, as we've not got the expertise of even the likes of Pritchard to sort out our field of metal stresses and suchlike, to be able to predict such a marvel of engineering, safe for any mariner to use, on the tame lakes of Canada, let alone the hurricane alley of the mid Atlantic, or the typhoons out in the China seas." John contributed.

The discussions went on for a while until they were interrupted by the inspector who informed them they were about to enter the signal controlled area of Port Arthur shortly, and they should start getting organised to disembark within the hour.

"At long last! This has been one hell of a journey inspector, let alone losing our valuable luggage." John commented.

"As you are among the group of survivors from the dam disaster there will be a welcoming committee waiting for you. The remaining few passengers going on to Duluth will be kept on board until their turn. But this won't happen until the RCMP have removed the large gang of men expecting the arrival of their union boss, as they are still not aware their leader and his bodyguards perished at the dam. He, by the way, was the one with the big mouth who tried to lay down the law to everybody. From what I've heard through the grapevine, he was always stirring up strikes and other troubles just when everybody could have done without it. He definitely was the national Mr Trouble, with a capital 'T', and good riddance to the double-dealing conniving bastard, I say. Anyway, as I've being trying to tell you, you are advised to wait until you see one of the guards passing along with a white flag held up, for you to finally disembark. The sooner these men are dispersed, the sooner you will be able to join your families waiting for you at the ticket barriers." the inspector advised, before making his way along the train again.

"There you have it gentlemen! Yet another delay. It seems that the last mile of our journey is the longest." John moaned, then shutting the door sat down with the others to gather up their belongings.

Chapter XIX

A Vast Improvement

Before the train had time to shudder to a stop, a large mob carrying banners and slogans could be heard telling the world what they were all complaining about.

The chants of strike, fair wages and fair deals were loud and vociferous as was the name of their leader who they were waiting upon to emerge from the train and pontificate their wishes to have their strike to consume this part of the province, let alone the entire nation.

The appearance of several mounted police accompanied by a platoon of Mounties in riot gear, and an armoured vehicle took them all by surprise, as three Mounties hustled a small group of people off the train. The smallest of them who seemed to be the main person to be detained shouted various slogans telling the men as best he could that they were taken against their wishes and against the national protocols of the union movements.

This started a mini riot, which the mounted police managed to quell at the rear while their counterparts dressed in riot gear at the front grabbed and took away the struggling union rioters.

This lasted for a good half an hour before all went quiet, so the peaceful elements of the township could come to greet the survivors of the dam disaster.

"A time in history with two opposing halves of the human spectrum!" Crabbe whispered, as the happier side of the events took over to wipe away the bad taste of the erstwhile strikers.

Ford and Crabbe had a joyful reunion when they met their wives and children, with John feeling like the proverbial gooseberry, until Big Mac arrived to literally pick John up bodily in a bear hug as he greeted his return.

"John Grey! Let these married men enjoy family life so's you and me can enjoy the delights of my new hostel. All free and gratis!" Mackintosh cheered, putting the gasping John gently back onto his feet again.

"Why you great lummox! How the devil are you? I'll certainly take you up on your offer but say my hello's first!" John gasped, still struggling to regain his breath.

John briefly greeted Ford's wife Susan and his two children then Crabbe's wife Glenda and their little child before acknowledging it was quality time for the married men to enjoy, he agreed to meet up with them at the shipyard tomorrow afternoon.

"Okay then! See you around 1400 and don't be…"

"Adrift!" John shouted back as the other two friends left in the world of their own.

"C'mon Big Mac! We've got some serious catching up to do." John whooped, as Mackintosh led him to his jeep and roared away from the railway station.

When John arrived at Mackintosh's newly enlarged hostel, he found it much more of a homely place. And instead of pictures of almost virtually naked ladies adorning each wall, there were pictures of some rustic locations showing it was the idyllic place to visit and enjoy.

He looked around and saw instead of sawdust and spittoons covering the wooden floors, there were animal skins of all kinds, and hunting trophies hung in various places. The main thing which caught his eye was a large axe embedded into a round piece of wood.

Mackintosh saw him looking at it and chuckled.

"That's the very axe McClusky threw at you and your friends that night. I took the legs off the table and mounted the top onto the wall. There's another board next to it for the woodsmen to throw their hunting knives at, before they start drinking. In other words, any knife missing from it when the owner's still here drinking, then they will not get the blame if somebody is found to be stabbed or whatever. The same goes for their guns. They get handed over the bar as soon as they enter this place." Mackintosh explained.

"Sounds a good policy Big Mac. I'm sure your local constables appreciate such good citizenship."

"Actually, this hostel belongs to my new missus Joanna, whom I think you already met last time around. And if you're thinking of the cat house, then it is back at the old part of place where she has banned me from going anywhere near it. But I'd be glad to escort you there for your night time pleasures in case somebody decides to play rough with you." Mackintosh said hopefully, before Joanna came along and greeted them.

"Hello Mr Grey! Glad you came back to see us all again. Do you like my new home? Nice and gentle it is, with plenty of families patronising the place." she greeted pecking him on both cheeks.

"Well it certainly is a vast improvement I will say that. But what about ..." John started to say, before he was interrupted.

"You men! That's all you men can think of!" she admonished gently, motioning two very nubile girls over to her.

"We have a hostess service here instead of the cat house. You can have what you want, but you've got to take the girls off to the annex for your business, as I won't have nobody but myself performing in this building." she said lewdly, while the two young girls giggled and stood either side of John.

"Thank you kindly for this hospitality Joanna, but for the moment I would much prefer a few beers with Big Mac. Maybe later on ?" John enthused, as the girls left looking glum faced.

"In that case, come and sit awhile. Bring us some ale dear wench!" Mackintosh said delightedly, leading John to a secluded part of the large saloon bar.

They talked for quite a while whilst quaffing several drinks, before John started to feel the strain.

"Must get turned in Big Mac. What room have you got for me?" he asked.

Mackintosh must have beckoned the two girls John had met earlier, and instructed them to look after him for the night, so John left the hostel with them fussing around him.

140

"S'funny how you can remember where things fit into!' he thought, when he watched one of the naked girls impale herself onto his equally naked body.

Chapter XX

The First Phase

"**A**fternoon John, glad you could make it!" Ken Ford greeted, as John walked into the main offices of the shipyard.

"Hello Ken! Nice to see you again." John responded with a warm hand shake.

"The other two are down in the yard at the moment. Coffee?" Ford offered.

"Yes please. White, one sugar please. So how's business out in this neck of the woods Ken?" John asked politely.

"Since you left, we've managed to gain a good forty percent of the ship repair business up in the lakes, and Ben has obtained the main contract rights from the government for the supply and maintenance of heavy plant machinery necessary to keep the road and rail haulage going throughout the entire province and beyond." Ken stated candidly, handing John his coffee and very large cigar.

"So if we can pull this new shipbuilding venture off, you will have the edge on most of the companies operating the lakes. I mean, especially if you're already in partnership with Colin Crabbe and his operations."

"As far as I'm concerned John, ship repairs is one animal I know inside out, whereas shipbuilding is a totally different one that I don't. Ben has been sending me loads of manuscripts and drawings which make some sense, but the bottom line of it is I'm not too sure about the metallurgy of it all. Maybe if we get down to the nitty gritty and actually build a ship from scratch, then perhaps I'll understand a whole lot more."

"We've managed to bring all our drawings and notes from the ISDM, but we've got a couple of contacts in case we run into some technical detail we cannot solve here. Especially the planned visit by our project overseer Fergus McPhee, due to visit us in a couple of months. But the difference between our project and the others set by the ISDM is that you, being our placement provider and therefore the company to fund it, you have now got a subscriber who has offered the full funding of the project, at least to the tune of two large sized ships. Which means you will have little to worry about financially, so you will be able to concentrate on getting a decent, dare I say, strike free work force to perform for us for at least the next year whilst this project is under scrutiny. " John informed Ken giving him the business cards of the people he referred to.

Ford looked at the cards and raised an eyebrow on reading one of them.

"Ward? I know him! Big man with a big business, shame about the crippling strikes he had to put up with." he exclaimed, handing back the cards.

"I've got a couple of contacts of my own. This one in particular is down in Chicago who just might want some of the action, but as it's the three of you whose show it is, only you can say yes or no to him. Here's his business card." Ford offered giving John a card, as the other two breezed into the office to greet them in turn. From their countenance and manner, it was obvious both men had been re-united with their wives enjoying their conjugal pleasures after several months of being away.

The four men sat around a large table discussing the format or the shape of the project facing them, and decided Ken would lead the team as the outsider from the ISDM project.

They made outline plans for all sorts of tasks and events which would take place, with regular reviews and planning stages as they went along.

Crabbe was given the job of designing the main superstructure quarters and other compartments on board, plus fetching and carrying the materials or other items needed for a ship.

John was given the job of selecting and installing the propulsion and other ship borne machinery. Ben Ford was to work alongside Lawson to get the building yard set up, whilst

Ken Ford would act as the 'site co-ordinator 'and to see to the workforce, or other background support needed by the others.

This initial but crucial meeting lasted well into the evening, until they all decided they'd done enough for one day and would start the ball rolling in the morning.

"Before we wrap it up gentlemen. I know we've got a long road ahead of us, but I would request we have a daily meeting and preferably at the end of the day. This is designed so that we can mark down the daily progress and iron out any problems we come across in doing our jobs. I ask this as I've experienced first hand how valuable these meetings can be. Letting the left hand know what the right hand one is doing, so to speak. Maybe when we have our site inspection tomorrow we can use what's left of the day and the rest of the week to get the 'irons into the fire' if you like. Ken! We need a communal office with all our individual diagrams and other plans pinned to the wall so when we do have our daily meetings, we know exactly what each of us has been talking about. I am asking this of you gentlemen, as I've already tried and tested this type of management system, and have found it the only way we can produce the goods for our first sponsor Ward. Incidentally and according to his word, he will be contacting us shortly to have a look round.

If all goes well, he will be the biggest piece of good luck and the major factor in the fortunes of our project, and as such, represents our first patron who is going to provide our first big contract. If he comes to see us, then at least when he comes into our joint office he will see we are not only above-board on how his money is to be spent, but also to prove to him we are a top line set up as opposed to the cowboys he has been dealing with lately. And before I conclude Ken, we had better get a work force not influenced by any unions. By that I mean, we need to run our own lives rather than have the likes of the Union brethren of know-alls try and dictate otherwise. Finally gentlemen, I wish to formally dub this new project as 'FUTURE HOMES'." John insisted, which drew a cheer and a standing ovation from the rest of them.

Ken Ford thanked the friends for placing the top honours onto his shoulders, declaring he would use his extensive set of contacts to make certain the FUTURE HOMES project will succeed, especially for the benefit of everybody who chooses to throw their lot into it.

Next day a clear but very cold morning greeted the project team, who had gathered in the new offices allocated for their HQ.

Ken Ford explained the presence of several people who would act as secretaries, aides and other such go betweens, telling the team they were to provide a succession of charts, drawings, and any other items which would be beneficial to plan through each stage of the project.

John produced a Project Cycle Chart which highlighted the target dates on what should be happening when and by whom, with the estimated time for completion of just one of Ward's ships. His brief explanation to this new and valuable piece of wall-chart, helped cut short the time needed to answer several lengthy questions..

After a quick coffee, they all trooped out into the cold, made their way over to the main slipway which would represent the engraving dock for the first ship ever to be built on the Canadian side of the Great lakes.

"As you can see gentlemen, this slipway is ideal for medium sized vessels to be brought ashore and serviced when the floating or dry docks are still in use. We already have a support warehouse at the end of it, but even if we use that, it will still be too short for us to build anything over the 400 feet Ward is asking off us. I have provided for the track based goalpost cranes and others for the overhead heavy lifting and so on, and built several types of buildings to store our ship making stuff, if necessary we could convert the smaller slipway to house the foundries and other important warehouses needed for the build.

As this represents our first phase of preparation for

shipbuilding, we need to get the right length and the proper back up for our first ship which is quoted at around the 500 foot mark. What a pity though, because ideally speaking we could really do with a large dry dock instead. " Ken directed, while the rest of the group looked around them.

"I think this is where you come into the equation John! You mentioned something on the train about all this." Ben quipped.

John, busy looking around him was caught out by this statement.

"Hmm! Train?" he replied almost absentmindedly.

"Oh yes! It was just an idea from an earlier situation I had come across, but would probably not work given this set up." John inferred, looking at the sea of questioning faces.

"Let's know what you've got in mind Mr Grey! Maybe we can adapt it to fit, so to speak!" one of the designated shipwright supervisors asked swiftly.

John explained a situation he had seen whilst staying at the Admirals place, and thought perhaps it would work here, but for everybody to see just what was what, they needed to examine the new ship design and how he thought it could be done.

"The basic idea being, we build the stern section first, then slide it down the ramp so we can build the next section onto it. Once the entire hull has been completed, the ship could use its own engines to pull itself off the ramp and be put alongside for its finishing touches and suchlike!" John concluded.

For several minutes, there was total silence from everybody, including his other two friends who had heard of his idea in the first place.

"So you see gentlemen, it was only an idea which has taken me several days to iron out the niggling details in my head before I could try to put some sort of configuration to it." John prompted.

"As your host provider for this project John, I will get the groundwork team started as of today. Let's return to the office now, to go over this new design and see what we can do to make this idea work." Ken beamed, leading the group of men back into the warmth of the big office.

The large wall diagram of the design was unfurled and pinned to the wall for everybody to see. The first gasp of surprise was because the ship had only one castle, which was followed up by other innovations John had drawn onto the original shape, earmarked for further developments.

It took several minutes before somebody spoke up, starting a flood of questions which made John and his two friends sit up and try to answer as best they could.

After a while, John stood and told everybody that any ship designed in this fashion would be totally seaworthy and functional to any shipping lines wishing to buy one, but the building of such vessels would depend on several factors, not least the space needed for its construction.

As in any meeting which has several different mindsets, there is always a doubter or sceptic who will try to undermine or pooh-pooh the ideas put forward and change the minds of those who subscribe to them. and so it was, as a man stood and asked a leading question which he put to John to answer.

"You're project planning and time schedules are geared for European climates. If as you suggest the stern section of this vessel is built now, then just how are you going to shift it out into the bay when there's a good 2 fathoms of solid ice holding it back? Unless of course, you wait until the following thaw to continue the build?"

Acknowledging the question was a good one, John asked what had prompted the man to ask.

"It's like this! We're ice bound for at least a good 4 months this far up in the northern hemisphere. Any prospective buyers would be out of their minds to have one built as it would not only take too long to construct but also increase the costing of the ship."

John thought for a moment, and asked the man for his name before he gave his answer.

"Mr Morris, I have to thank you for your astuteness and forethought. As someone who has gained knowledge of how ice and cold water behaves, I am able to offer you the following two solutions, but it would depend on the actual size of the slipways and the area we have to build on.

One: We build the ship sideways along the shoreline, and launch it 'broadside'.

Or two: When we've built the stern superstructure, we use thermal lances to cut out a space in the ice big enough for the stern section to be slotted into whilst we build the remaining bow sections. If that's the case, then once the ice starts to melt, the stern section will merely float, kept in check on the lower cradle until we've finished the rest of the ship. Then when we're ready, all we do is flash up the engines for it to pull herself off the launch pad to float freely by itself. Would that do you Mr Morris?"

There was a deafening silence for a moment while everybody took in what John had said, before they all realised the truth of what could be achieved.

Morris looked at the swift drawings John had made to emphasise his points, scratching his head in bemusement, seemingly too speechless to answer back.

"The thing is gentlemen, for this to work I will need someone with the knowledge to be able to tell me how far out into the lake I can go. That is to say, I need to know the depth of ice and how far out I can go without the risk of flooding." John emphasised, filling the silent vacuum.

"Depending on the climatic conditions for the winter months, the water can freeze up to the ten foot mark, but around here its usually on the twelve foot mark. Therefore we can pinch up to a good 180 feet of lake bottom. That being the case, the entire lower cradle would be uncovered for the vessel to be built upon, and whilst it is still out of water we could take the opportunity to have it serviced and suchlike." Morris answered, holding up an ordinance survey map of the area.

Ken Ford took the map and looked carefully at it for a moment before commenting.

"If we decide to build stern first then we only need 150 feet of lake space. Otherwise we'd need to clear a further two hundred foot space along the shoreline. Apart from the logistical side of things, such as clearing everything away and making a larger cradle etc, it would also mean we'd have run out of the bedrock apron." he stated, holding it up for everybody to see.

"The thing is gentlemen, our customer, who is paying for all this, is due to visit us soon and will be looking for us to give him his new ships sooner rather than later. He won't be concerned as to which way we have to build it, as long as she floats and actually does what she has been built for." Crabbe announced over the hubbub of the meeting.

This settled the meeting down again, and everybody began to realise they were about to create something no other company had ever tried before, which was to build a ship longer than the yard is, and especially over winter when the rest of the country would be under several feet of snow and ice.

"So I take it then, we're all in the same frame of mind to go for it. We're about to build a ship nobody has ever seen before, against all the odds in an icebound part of the world, and all within one year?" John asked in an upbeat manner.

Everybody looked at each other with surprise and in wonderment at the idea of such an undertaking but declared loudly in unison their approval and vowed to make it happen.

This then was the new resolve of the workforce and for the project team to start the work without further ado.

The meeting broke up with everybody feeling in a euphoric mood, all except Morris, who stayed behind to speak to the team.

"I don't know where you get your fancy notions about cutting ice out of the lake to make room for the ship, but it's impossible for a start. Just how are you going to control the flooding? I mean, ice melts from underneath not from the surface. And just how are you going to cut through several feet of ice?" he snapped.

John looked at this irate man for a moment then asked him.

"Have you ever seen a ship as big as the *Winnipeg* weighing some 15,000 tons parked on top of an iceberg for the crew to fix a hole in her hull? Do you know what a thermal lance is or how it works?"[*]

Morris shook his head on both occasions but declared the ice would have snapped under the weight of the ship, and that nothing could cut through a 2 fathom thick block of ice.

"It is obvious to me you are one of the doubting Thomases, Mr Morris. When the time comes, I will be glad to demonstrate our secret weapon. In the meantime I suggest you either join in with the rest of the workforce or keep away from hindering us." John sighed, before he made his excuses and left to join the others.

---

[*] See *Ice Mountains.*

Chapter XXI

The Price Tag

The new shipbuilding yard had been more or less completed ready for the next phase of the project to be conducted. Due to the very tall trees surrounding the area, there were no outward signs of such activity, apart from the waterfront where a steady procession of ships were arriving loaded with vital equipment, and pieces of metal of all shapes and sizes. But what was apparent to everybody, was that word had got around about a new shipyard starting up, resulting in a large influx of new workers of all kinds of trades to swell the inhabitants of both Port Arthur and Fort George. This was a welcome boost for the local economy even though everybody knew it was started on a wing-and-a-prayer for such a ship to be build so far north, which would be ice-bound for months on end. This fact lent to a fear that because of the weather intervention there would be no work, therefore no money to spend. But unbeknown to them the project team had their secret weapon to use to counteract it.

It was during the first month of construction when the team got word that their customer Mr Ward was coming to visit them to see how his 'investment' was coming along.

"Hello Ward! Come to see the impossible being done using a few miracles?" John asked, meeting and greeting him with a handshake.

"Hello Grey! Yes! I've brought my legal advisers and accountant teams along with me to see what is what." he said pleasantly, as both men introduced each other's key men involved with the project.

We have a large room we will use for the meeting. It is full of relevant details pinned to the wall for your team to look at. Maybe help them to speed their deliberations up somewhat." Ben Ford stated, leading the way.

They arrived into the main 'planning room' where all sorts of

151

plans, diagrams, drawings, and project development schemes were pinned around the wooden walls of the building.

Ward and his retinue were amazed at such a display and stated they were pleased to find somebody at last, who would perhaps make things happen the way things should.

Ward and his aide Wilding went around the room looking at the display until they were satisfied by what they saw.

"All looks fine to me Grey! But there's something that's not quite right. If your slipway is only 300 feet long, just how the blazes are you going to build one over 450 feet long on it?" Wilding asked, scratching his head in bewilderment.

"Apart from that, your diagrams show only the stern part of the ship. What about the bridge and everything?" Ward asked in equal bemusement.

"It seems you have not had the time to view our artists' impression of how your ship will look like." Crabbe said, placing an artist's impression painting of the ship on the table.

Ward and the others gathered around and whistled at the very sleek vessel the team was about to build.

"But she's only got the one castle!" One of the visitors declared.

"That's right! The bridge and the propulsion unit is all aft, so as to give the cargo holds a bigger area and therefore a larger carrying capacity for the same size of ship." Crabbe stated.

"In engineering terms, the shorter the prop shaft, the more power gained from the engine to propel the ship. More power, less fuel. Less fuel therefore more economic. At least that is the theory behind such a design." John declared.

"Yes but what about the length problem I asked about?" Wilding prompted.

"It's quite simple. The ship will be built in two or three segments. We build the stern end first, then the middle section before we slide it down the ramp so we can build the bows onto it. Then when the ship's hull is complete, we simply flash up the engines for her to pull herself off the ramp. We get to test the engines as well in doing so." John quipped.

152

Ward and his team were impressed by the idea and the whole concept of such a good-looking ship, which made the rest of the meeting glide along smoothly.

The meeting was a formal one, with legal representation and accountants from both sides locked into negotiations which went well into overtime.

Ward and his team talked about the costs involved, and had decided as they had sufficient scrap material and even ships engines to put into this new one, they could be generous by offering the project team a decent price of around the $2million price tag.

John stood up declaring that although as this was a concept ship with no guarantees at the end of being able to produce her, she would be built from scratch using brand new materials.

Ken Ford backed John's thrust of building from new, stating if the shipbuilder spies were anything to go by, then the word would soon get around the entire lake waterways of this new fanciful ship.

"Also given that fact, which would be others wanting a piece of the action and be prepared to offer items for building that would stake their claims for them to have such a ship built for them.

Especially the U.S. side of the divide, when they find out about our new containership vessel we also intend to build. In other words gentlemen, you will have to up your price tag to at least double if only to keep out any outside interference, so to speak. I would suggest you think in pounds Sterling, and a starting price of £1 million." he concluded.

"Never mind the outside interference Ford! I'm talking about the here and now, with a handsome $2 million." Ward scoffed, starting a further round of 'horse trading' which was definitely beyond John's expertise so he left it to the rest of his team to sort out the argument and the final score.

The sticking point was when Ward's team raised the winter freeze question which would hold up the production, despite the ship being assembled as a prefabricated vessel in the first place.

153

"What you must understand Ward, is that we're too far north to be able to guarantee a firm date for delivery. Whilst we can make internal progress on the ship, we'd have to allow a further four months or so until the ice melts for us to get the second part of the ship built, off cradle and alongside for its finishing touches. Then of course, you will have to come along and see she conducts the standard engine and sea trials before you finally accept her into your company." Ben stated.

"Have you set a launch date yet? How long will it take you to build this ship of mine?"

"Sooner than you think Ward!" Ken said with confidence.

"You seem quite sure of yourselves. But I like that in a person who has the courage of their own convictions." Ward grunted, then leant over to speak to Wilding and another person next to him for a while before making his answer.

"In view of your forthright manner and honest approach to things, which I like in a man, I shall provide you with a £1 million Sterling purse up front to build my ship, but paid in 3 stages and in Canadian Dollars. Providing you can have my ship ready for her trials to send on her first voyage around the time of next years grain harvest. If you were to succeed in having an early launch and acceptance trials by then, then you can have a special completion bonus of a further $1 million. The down side to that is, if you fail to do any of this or the ship is a total waste of money then I shall be seeking suitable recompense for my troubles." Ward insisted.

John and his friends looked around at each other speaking in hushed voices discussing this new but better deal.

After a little while, John stood up pointing out to Ward and his team that they were the ones who made the initial statement offering the project team a build of not one but two ships, so he could not understand why he and his team were placed under such crippling demands. He stated the project team would much rather just build one ship in their own time, which incidentally would be financed by the Canadian Federal Bank. Then if the worst came to the worst and the ship failed her myriad of trials and was deemed only fit for scrap, the project team would not be out of pocket, etc. He a reminded them the entire shipbuilding world would be looking on with more than a keen interest into their affairs as well, and what they were planning to do would be of the highest quality and order they could produce.

"In other words gentlemen, our ship although conceptual in design, will definitely change the construction and shape of the Merchantile shipping fleets the world over. Not to make too finer a point of it, this ship design will rank just as important as the steamship was to sailing vessels, and that I can assure you of. At the end of the day, if this ship was built anywhere else the price tag for all this would be in the region of 3-5 million pounds sterling. This way you'll be getting a brand new type of ship at a good discount. Remember though, it is still a conceptual design and where your gamble, or your money, will be spent." he stated with confidence.

Ward and his team made another huddle and whispered in hurried response to what John had told them.

"It appears you've done your sums Grey, and yes I was the one to suggest such a venture. Whilst the government will finance this trial ship, they need a buyer to prove its viability for them to sink their money into this venture in the first place. I am prepared to offer some extra funding to it, if only to guarantee my own company will be the first to own such a ship. Also, if this trial ship is what you say, then I will commission your team to build a couple of the same for me, although $3 million each would be a bit steep even for my pockets. Mind you, I would ask you to keep my company as the 'exclusive and preferred first buyer', in return for your guaranteed wage packets when the winter months has shut you down for months on end. What do you say to this arrangement?" Ward stated in a booming voice.

Ken Ford stood up and stated as it was his ship repair company which stood to gain or even lose heavily for entering into shi building as well, he had the final say in all these

155

negotiations, although a nod and a wink would still be needed from the government agency involved as well.

"That's fine by me Ford! If you agree in principle to my statement of intent, then we'll get a document written up for us all to sign up to it. The sooner you get on with the ship's building, the sooner she can be out in open waters earning her keep, preferably mine."

Ken Ford looked at the team seeing them nod their heads in agreement told Ward an acceptable mutual charter could be set up within the week.

"Good! Then that is all I need for now. I will have one of my legal team stay behind for a few days to work with yours, so we can set up a working arrangement where I am able to come along from time to time to view the work in progress, so to speak.

I am well-known in Government circles for square dealing and above-board company affairs, not like the trash who operated the erstwhile Lake Line Shipping Company which went belly up in spectacular fashion recently."

"Yes, quite! I too run a genuine and reputable company Ward, so hopefully we can keep the con artists and riff-raff out of it all and make a good living out of what is in fact one fantastic ship in the making." Ken agreed, as the shook hand to cement a gentleman's agreement.

"Mr Wilding is my legal hound who will help you with your paperwork, but if you need help from other highly qualified members of staff, such as a construction site engineer or whatever, then I'll be more than happy for them to come along. Free of charge of course. In the meantime, my sources tell me you have shall we say, a small cash flow problem in getting your yard ready, which the government will not cover as it's part of your 'Tender to contract' with them.

I am in need of some good ships sooner rather than later, and if what I've seen of your newfangled ship, she will more than recoup my money within two years of her being in service. So in that respect, I am able to offer you an advance of $200,000, duly declared to the government agencies and all above-board, if you wish to take advantage of it. " Ward insisted.

"I thank you for your kindness Ward, but as it happens I'm okay for the moment. Perhaps later on in the programme, say around October time, when the snows start drifting in. However, we do need several highly skilled workers, especially metallurgists and some slide-rule boffins for my management team. If you can send me what I need, and pay their wages, accommodation and suchlike for me, then that would be more practical for me to manage." Ken Ford admitted

"I'll get Mr Brady onto it for you, he's my chief 'Head hunter' who finds me my top men. Each one has so far proved to be a real credit to my company. In case you're not aware of it, I have coalmines, several grain silo and granary depots, plus an oil terminal. They all have a loading wharf, for the several ships I also own. I export mostly to the Yanks across the lakes, but I have a couple of ships taking grain out to Nova Scotia for our Trans Atlantic crossings. The only shipping company that can out carry my fleet now is Crabbe's, as the Lake Line fleet has been scuttled and the company now defunct, over here at least."

"Yes Ward, I knew who you were when John and his project team told me about you. We both might just come up smelling of roses after this first ship launch. But at the end of it, all I want to do to be able to keep my ship repair yard going as the best one this side of the St Laurence waterway."

"Maybe someday we can come to some mutual trading on that. Anyway Ford, time to leave as I must dash now! The Government agency will be descending on you within the week, but I'll leave Wilding here on loan to you to help with the reams of red tape and bumf they usually like to go through even if it is only tends up as bonfire material." Ward offered, bidding Ken and the team farewell before walking swiftly to his waiting seaplane.

Chapter XXII

New Deal

The newly emerging ship-building yard manifested itself on the local environment, so much so it looked like an ants' nest as everybody took care of their own little end of the building process. The word had got around about the new yard, attracting new workers from all types of trades, even from as far away as the big cities such as Chicago on the U.S. side of the lakes, they were arriving daily, thus swelling the local communities almost to bursting point.

Things seemed ideal for a while, until the spectre of unionism raised its ugly head starting to sour the up to then, good relationship between the workers and the management.

A group of workers claiming they should be the only ones to run the yard, so anybody who didn't belong to their Brotherhood would face the consequences if they did not join, called for a general strike.

John was in the main office solving a problem with the large seam-welding equipment prefabricating the large pieces of sheet steel together for final welding on to the ship's ribs.

"It appears our ex-colonial cousins are stirring up trouble for us, and have commenced their Yank ways of trying to run the yard instead of us. And just guess where it all stems from?" Ben announced, walking quickly into the room.

John and the others around him groaned aloud, but it was Collins who asked just who these men were to come here and try to take over.

"Apparently, this is the work of that short-arsed runt the Mounties dragged from the train. It appears he is the sidekick of that big-mouth up at the dam, who was a big union baron who gained some support from a Yank engineering union which has a large network of Canadian followers to draw upon this side of the national borders. Not sure of the mouthpiece out there, but perhaps we'd better go out and confront this pest in case he shuts down the entire yard." Ben suggested.

"Colin, look out of that window to where these men are 'holding court' so to speak, I need to have a close look at them if you care to pass me your binoculars." John directed, then looked at the assembled men, three were standing on some makeshift platform out in front of them shouting and directing the show.

"Hmmm! I somehow recognise the big man doing all the ranting and shouting, although I can't remember his name. Who is he, anybody know?" John asked.

Crabbe looked through the glasses too before going over to a large steel locker extracting a file from it.

"According to the personnel file, he is one of the foremen in charge of the yard security but also an active union man. Fred Gleave by name." Crabbe offered.

John watched the man for little while, before turning and asking to dig out his special trophy case for him, which he did.

Opening the special case that held a replica of his solid gold wheel-spanner and solid silver Stilson wrench, both of which represented his 'Badge of Office', he picked out the oversized wheel-spanner and slipped it up his jacket sleeve so it would not be seen, then asked the others to accompany him to this wild-cat strike meeting.

The full project team approached the side of the meeting which was gathering momentum as those on the platform were goading the men into a fevered pitch.

There was a short silence in the rantings and ravings, enough for John to approach the dais and ask if he could speak to them.

John's appearance onto the stage was greeted with cat-calls and heckling as the three ringleaders passed sneering remarks about him.

John went right up to Gleave and looked him square in the face before he swiftly producing his large wheel-spanner, then with an upward swing he gave the man a blow between his legs, causing Gleave to instantly crumple down onto his knees, gasping in pain whilst holding onto his genitals.

The sight of their union boss being struck down drew gasps of disbelief from the large crowd that had gathered, which silenced them as they waited to hear what the outcome of this incident would bring.

"Goddam-it! That's the second time someone has done this to me." he screamed through his pain.

John stood over Gleave waving the wheel-spanner in his face. "Hello Sergeant! Remember me? Fancy you forgetting your friend who visited you on the *Tsun Wan* out in your Indo China mission." John whispered in his ear.• *

The man took a little time to finally recognise John, then immediately changed his demeanour towards him.

"Bloody hell Limey! Where the hell have you sprung from? Don't tell me you're the one in charge of this cock-a-mamie outfit?" he asked between bouts of searing pain.

"It's like this sergeant! I'm here to help build a brand new type of ship which already has its own set of major problems without the likes of you coming along and upsetting everybody.

Now clear off and take your cronies with you. In fact you can tell your big chief I will sue the both of you and all your kind for the millions that you don't own, and I mean in terms of pounds Sterling not Yankee monopoly money. The alternative is for you to come and speak to the management team in a proper military fashion to discuss matters tomorrow morning when you're feeling better. The choice is all down to you, but whatever your choice of words are to this meeting, you had better get these men back to work as of ten minutes ago or you'll be joining your leader in jail for a few years." John commanded.

"But what can we say to undo the call to strike action?" one of Gleave's henchmen begged.

"Simple! Just tell your men, a new deal will be negotiated tomorrow morning, but for now everybody is to get back to

---

• See *Perfumed Dragons.*

160

work, without further union action taken by them." Crabbe replied loudly.

The buzz of a 'new deal' went through the massed ranks of the workers like wildfire, which seemed to appease them enough to encourage them to pick up their tools again.

"There you are sergeant! Unlike the military where you are told what to say, think and do, the workers have already made up their own minds and voted with their feet. Perimeter secured as you might say! Now get yourself to the medics and have your wounds seen to, then come and see us tomorrow morning around 0900." John breezed, helping Gleave back onto his feet.

Gleave merely nodded his head and directed his side-kicks to do what was suggested, before they climbed down off the makeshift dais.

"Before you go Gleave! Make that your last trick or performance in this yard. This is a government run show, so be warned that in future, I will have the military in here to forcibly remove any person who tries strike action again, and that's a promise." Ben announced, leaving the now deserted scene.

"What's this new deal John? Something I know about?" Ken asked with concern.

"Yes Ken! They get the same deal as what I offered the ship repair dockyard over in Belfast. Either they work for their pay or get sacked without one. I have it all written down in a special pamphlet for your perusal. The system works a treat, and one which our increasing workforce numbers should accept without a problem. Basically it's the old proverbial stick and carrot routine, which prevents or at least excludes any bother from the Union brethren we have met up with today."

"Yes, I've managed to read some of it, and it looks good. I would suggest we give Gleave and his cronies the job of implementing such a scheme. He's an ex Marine Sergeant, so he'll move hell and high water to do his best for it to work for us." Crabbe suggested.

"We'll know in the morning. In the meantime gentlemen, we've still got our daily meeting to get through." Ben stated as a gentle reminder.

Chapter XXIII

Those in Favour

The management team had assembled in the big office in time to receive Gleave and his team of five others.

It was Lawson who opened the meeting, by giving Gleave and his party copies of the pamphlet John had made, and they all went through it page by page.

There were many questions asked and problems raised by Gleave, who had simple and logical answers offered to him; all of which were accepted in good faith by the rest of them. This meeting took several hours with cups of coffee and short breaks along the way, until finally there was a general consensus and agreement from all concerned.

"To make things easy for you and your team Gleave, we will make you the prime mover in all this.

If you accept the challenges we have laid down before you, then we will provide you with your own office and facilities to run it. You will become our Personnel Director and see to it the yard and all personnel are in good shape and fully functional. For that, you and your team will cease to be union men and will encourage a decent work ethic within the yard. There will be more than enough work available for those who wish to earn a decent days wage without any interference from the Union Brethren. In fact, as this yard is a private concern, it will be part of your job to see all union practices are stopped, as of today. That is the deal." John explained at length.

"We will need to have a general meeting of all union members to put your proposals to the vote." Said one of them.

"You obviously have not listened or understood a word spoken here today. This is a private yard which is outside union controls. You will either change your tack to become a regular worker like the other non-unionist workers or every last one of you will be escorted off our premises by the military. I don't care which way you play it, but there are thousands of local non-union men just waiting to take your places. You will work our way or not at all." John hissed.

"Hold on a cotton pickin' minute! I'm the spokesman for us all, and what I say goes. It appears we have a golden opportunity to make a decent workforce here, and I'll kick asses to see it does just that. What he means is we do need a meeting of the entire workforce, if only to explain the new deal you promised them yesterday. The way I see it, we're all onto a winner for as long as there's work to be had long term." Gleave shouted as if on a parade ground giving orders to his men.

"In that case, you will hold your meeting this afternoon on the launch slipway. Because tomorrow is Sunday, the workforce will have the day off to reflect their future. With full pay I might add. For Monday will be the day we impose the new routines. Make no mistake about this gentlemen, but those who refuse to co-operate as of Monday will be sacked on the spot." Ken advised.

Gleave and his team left the main office for the management team to mull over the outcome of the protracted meeting.

"I think Gleave will pull this off for us, if only for the first launch." Lawson opined.

"The thing is gentlemen, if this workforce grasps the same nettle as the workers in Belfast did, then they'll all want to work with pride and commitment. Woe betide any shirkers or men not pulling their weight, as the others will get shot of them even before we have the chance to sack them ourselves. Just leave the workforce to sort themselves out, and I feel sure our Sergeant Gleave will 'kick their asses' to see they comply with our plans. This yard is destined for great things you just watch." John insisted.

Gleave stood up on the dais in front of the crowd of workers and waving the pamphlet he was given earlier explained briefly to them what it contained and what was said at their meeting with the management. John and the rest of the management team were at hand in case Gleave needed clarification on certain items, but he had done extremely well to provide the right answers to the myriad of questions the crowd posed.

By the time Gleave and his aides, were finished, the men were eagerly devouring each morsel of information, which was apparent by their body language and voices.

"Talk about eating out of his hand!" John whispered aside to Crabbe and the others.

Gleave kept the best to last when he told them that Sunday would be a day off with pay, and everybody should report for work first thing Monday morning providing they caught the free transport which would pick them up en route to the yard. Also that everybody would be allocated their new shift system and work areas.

"This is the last time a union meeting will be conducted at this yard. So for the last time, I need a show of hands to accept this new deal. Those in favour raise their right hand." Gleave shouted over the excited hubbub of the men.

From where John was standing he saw a forest of arms held aloft.

"Those against this new deal?" he invited.

Not one hand was raised, which was quickly realised by the men as they gave a huge cheer and clapped Gleave and his aides on the dais.

John raced quickly onto the dais before the men started to leave, and introduced himself to them.

"As the Chief Engineer of this yard, and I speak for the rest of the management, we thank you all for your enthusiastic support to this new deal which I personally introduced over in the U.K in Belfast some time ago.

The system works a treat as long as you are prepared to earn your daily bread. There is one bit of news Gleave did not tell you, and that is." John said, pausing to see all the men were still looking and listening to him.

"We have a deadline to meet next year. If you have this vessel launched before that deadline and have her fitted out ready for her first voyage, then each man still with us, will receive a production bonus worth around a good months wages. On the other hand, any day over that date then we'll incur penalties of the same order. Last but by no means least, once we've got everybody sorted out into their shift patterns, and have you all working as a team, we the management will guarantee a decent increase in your weekly wage packet, which includes shift bonuses. But for that you really must want to earn it." John concluded, which gave rise to an even bigger cheer, as the men left in their droves to make their way home.

Gleave and his five aides came over to John and the management team, shaking hands to cement the new beginning.

"Well done Gleave! You will have your new office and department in the admin building. You get to keep your five aides as your personnel team and move in there tomorrow. We will provide you with your list of duties which you will perform on our behalf, and we expect you and your team to be on call 24/7 just like we senior management are.

Like us you will be paid monthly, but we'll need a bank account number or a Post Office account number for a direct transfer. Anyway, if you all come to my office in the morning, we'll make out your new work contracts." Lawson stated with a smile, as Gleave grinned broadly to acknowledge his instructions.

"You have been given a field commission of a General now Sergeant! Not bad for a day's work!" John rejoined with a big smile.

"My dad said I was officer material, but I only managed to make 'Top Sergeant' with the Marine Corps. Maybe now I have the chance to prove him right. I'll have our perimeter secured quicker than a broad can drop her knickers on pay night." he drawled.

"Make it so General!" Ken Ford quipped, as Gleave and his team left the room.

"Time for our supper gentlemen! Last one out switches off the light!" Ken announced, for the room to fall silent and into pitch blackness.

Chapter XXIV

Strategic Discussions

The first few weeks under the new regime melted away as the workforce began to dovetail themselves into their shift patterns, so much so each shift were having a friendly banter as to who was the best shift to work for. They even formed their own departmental sports teams with the management sponsoring the cups and prizes they were to compete for.

Over the weeks which seemed to merge into one blur, the keel had been laid down with the prefabrication teams assembling the lumps of steel to make the ships hull and superstructure. Fortunately the weather was kind to the workers as they managed to install the large and very heavy engine along with the short prop shaft awaiting its special five blade variable pitch propeller which would drive the ship through the lakes. Once the profile of the superstructure was completed they were ready to start on the middle part of the ship that had the main cargo area, creating a pause in the momentum of things.

This moment in time co-incided with a national holiday, so John and his management team decided everybody was to have a few well-earned days off, with pay, then come back to complete the second half of this ship which was starting to tower above the tall trees of the forest surrounding the yard.

During the past few months, Ken Ford had adopted the working routine of the building yard to his ship repair yard just down a little way on the lake shore line, and was glad of the full order books to be able to continue with subsidising the high cost incurred by the building yard.

"Gentlemen, we're getting near to the freeze point, which means we may have to lay off workers for the duration Our workforce have proved themselves to be beyond doubt the pride of the whole lake, and I for one should hate to face them with such a crippling blow especially as most of them have now taken up residence in the twin communities. If we cut short the workforce, then the local economy will suffer, and in turn, the way human nature is, our workforce would be earmarked for abuse and threatening behaviour." He announced at the daily planning meeting.

This announcement raised the spectre of doom and gloom on what was, up to now, a very good period of prosperity for all, making each of them think seriously on how to deal with this alarming state of affairs.

Crabbe stood up from the general discussion, went over to a filing cabinet and pulled out a small dossier.

"If I remember rightly, the last time John was staying here, we had a good liaison with a certain reporter, who has not shown his face since we started up this project. We've already had Ward and his top men come to help out, even some of the top Government advisors to put us wise to certain matters. Whilst we have been given monies as part of the ongoing building grant, we've not had word from them about this big barrier we are about to face. Maybe because since the government has seen the repair yard has more or less kept us solvent, they perhaps deem we do not need their extra help in keeping our workforce on. I mean, it is as if because of the big freeze nothing gets done, therefore nobody is working therefore nobody gets paid. At the end of the day gentlemen, unless we can keep our yard in full production, then we'll end up with nothing bu a bankruptcy hearing with the local magistrates." Crabbe offered.

"Then why don't we approach, er Winstanley or even his editor, what's his name, erm Boyes or whatever, to highlight our problem. I mean, we were their darlings during the Whately scam, so at least they could perhaps drum up some support from the Ministry of Employment or whatever it is in this part of the world." John suggested with enthusiasm.

"The thing is John, whilst we can make an overhead shelter for both yards to work under during the blizzards, nobody would gamble on your secret weapon to work. We would be greeted with total scorn and disbelief, to the point whereby any sane person would give us a wide berth from then onwards. I.e., brand us as a bunch of nutcases, stop any further funding and take us to the cleaners just like Whateley." Ken Ford advised.

"How long have we got before all this happens?" John asked sharply.

"With luck about 5 weeks." Ken Ford responded.

"Then I suggest I get in contact with some old friends, Fergus McPhee for a start, maybe a couple of top scientists such as Lovatt, and Van Hayden. In the meantime we get Winstanley over a.s.a.p to give him the low-down as to what we are planning. If they can't persuade the powers that be to give us money to tide us over the winter freeze then nobody can. My simple plan will work for this one time only. If proven correct, then the government might just give us a further grant to build onto our launch site and create what the ice dam did for us. Not to put a finer point on things, it would be cheaper for the government to step in with the necessary funding rather than face the prospect of paying several millions over the odds in social welfare benefits. On the other hand, if despite all our efforts everything goes pear shaped, we'll be facing definite ruin, with over a thousand men plus two local communities after our blood."

"You have a point there John, but I am in favour of doing just that." Crabbe stated sombrely.

"Gleave has been our motivator and prime mover with the workforce in both yards. But I feel we must keep this strategic discussion and outcome to ourselves for now. Keep it under wraps until it's necessary for the workforce to be told, via him that is." Lawson observed.

"Yes, he's certainly earned his spurs. But as you say, we'll maintain a need to know basis for now." Ken agreed.

The others nodded in favour agreeing that this decision would be kept under wraps until the last moment.

***

The workforce arrived back off their holidays and set about their work with renewed strength and dedication.

As the first two thirds of the ship had been built, the workers not involved with fitting the superstructure with its vital equipment, such as radio, radar, fridges, accommodation furniture, galley and suchlike, were employed in clearing up the yards, building up the steel stocks or other jobs, preparing for the big freeze. The welders were kept busy in the prefabrication of the ship's plates that were going to be used on the final third part of the ship. In all, they were kept busy right up to the first big blizzard, which somehow seemed to burst their bubble of happy days of plenty.

Gleave sensed their change of mood which was just as chilled as the snow, so he went over to the planning office to speak to the management team.

"Hello Gleave! Glad you've come, as we've been expecting you these last few days." Lawson stated as Gleave made himself at home by the big roaring fire.

"We have two visitors with us today you might wish to know about. Mr Winstanley from the National Broadcasting Corporation, and a Mr Hewer from the Government Social Welfare Department," he added, moving on to give a brief outline why these men were there.

Gleave listened attentively to all that was put to him, then was given a moment to think things over before commenting.

He asked a few pertinent questions before making his deliberations.

"The way I see it is this. We can either wrap it in now so the men can receive their severance pay and claim national assistance for the few months over the winter period, and incidentally each man must be re-employed afterward. Or keep working on reduced man hours, say 20 hours per week, but they must be on a guaranteed wage for those hours. Obviously there will be no overtime, but each man will share the workload whether he be used as a labourer or as a welder. This is what a union chief would insist upon, so at least it is a viable option if you wish to take it."

"We have a third option for you Gleave, and it's this." John stated calmly, pinning a couple of large drawings onto the wooden walls of the office for everybody to see.

John explained the basic concept of his idea and plan, backing it up with a couple of letters which were sent by the scientists John had contacted weeks ago.

Both Gleave and Winstanley looked in total amazement at these drawings, but voiced their doubts as to whether it would work.

"Sorry and all that Grey, but I'm not prepared to offer pie in the sky hopes to my workforce. They deserve better than that!" Gleave scoffed.

"As for me, I'm quite prepared to stay around to see it work. If it does, then this yard will become famous overnight. But I demand exclusivity on the entire coverage of such a plan given the backing of some of the finest scientific minds living today." Winstanley stated in a trance whilst still looking at the drawings.

"Okay then Gleave! We'll agree on a compromise. If this plan works, then everybody will be in full production of the second half of the ship. We'll have the entire yard cocooned in heavy tarpaulins to protect the workers, but they will need to put up with the cold. Perhaps scatter a few braziers around to help them. If it doesn't, then we go onto a guaranteed working hours and pay week of 15 hours per man with 15 hours basic pay. They will work Monday through Friday no overtime or shift premiums. Subsidised meals and free transport still applies." Ken Ford offered.

Winstanley turned to Gleave and told him the latter was the finest offer he had heard from an employer for some time, and he'd be a fool not to take it.

"We are not Union affiliated Winstanley, so the men would have to take it or leave it. But we can guarantee them full employment again in the spring." Crabbe advised.

"If it is of any value to you, should you implement this temporary employment scheme, then I see no reason why you cannot qualify for a special one-off grant towards helping those family men over the winter period. Judging by your total work force eligible for this payment, then it should realise the sum in the region of $1million over that period." Hewer offered in a quietly spoken manner.

Gleave took time to take stock of what was said and nodded his head in agreement to the temporary pay deal, but stated it was all down to the men if they wished to turn up for work or not. As there were no union involvement the only way to know would be the numbers turning up for shift.

"The way I see it Gleave, if the men decide not to work over the winter period, then we've all lost out on our completion bonus, and would perhaps spell the end of what is turning out to be a brilliant team of men who can turn their hand to anything we give then. Shame to lose it all over a few feet of snow. On the bright side, if the men keep working even at a reduced capacity, and get to take home at least some wage then when the good weather comes along it's a laugh all the way to the bank." Ken concluded.

Gleave thanked the management team for their candid remarks and told them he would call the work force to a special meeting within the hour, but it was for them to inform the men and not him.

"You tell them, and I'll do the rest." Gleave advised, leaving the warmth of the room.

"There you have it gentlemen. Gleave has underlined the non-unionism factor of this company, so it will be all down to us to help them make the right choice, as far as we're concerned." Lawson stated, as they all got ready for the meeting.

The meeting was a low key affair, with Winstanley flitting around taking pictures of the men and the half finished ship towering above them.

John stated exactly what was to happen just as he did at the beginning of their new deal, and was heartened by the fact Hewer endorsed his words with the promise of the state funding.

After the usual questions and answers, John deemed it time to ask for their response, with a show of hands.

To a man they all raised their hands high declaring that as the management and the company was a good one to work for then they would stick it out albeit on a reduced working week and wages.

"In that case gentlemen, we can now prepare the circus tent to be rigged and get on with our work. We the management team wish to thank you all for your support during this crisis, but it will be worth it especially if we can get our ship down that launch ramp on time." John concluded, as the management team gave the men a hearty applause in appreciation.

"Well Gleave! It's all down to you again to secure our perimeter. Keep up the good work, but don't kick asses too hard this time." Ken said, shaking Leave's hand before leaving with the rest of the team.

Chapter XXV

A Fighting Chance

The crisis had been averted, so the workforce knuckled down to their task of working under canvas whilst the blizzards raged overhead.

"Right then gentlemen, it's Showtime now. Ben, have you brought the thermal lances from the repair yard?"

"They're on the starboard side of the launch ramp!"

"Okay! Colin, phone Gleave and have him stand by there with his team of men. Then tell Winstanley to get here within the hour." John directed, and donned his heavy overcoat to protect him from the cold.

The team made their way over to the large tent covering the exposed front end of the ship to find Gleave waiting for them,

"Okay gather round everybody. Here's what I intend doing. Are you watching and paying attention Mr Morris. This is for your benefit too!" John commanded, drawing a rough sketch of the stern end of the ship in the snow covered ground.

One of the men who must have been kin to the natives up in the northern territories, interrupted John by telling him how ice should be cut, and even stacked.

John thanked the man and started to show them how the thermal lances worked and for them to follow him to the frozen edge of the very large lake.

Crabbe was already out on the ice, using red paint to mark out the area to be cut.

"Don't forget men, keep your nozzles pointing into the hole you have made, and use it just like a welder would his torch. Slow and easy! Cut a square yard of ice from the top down before moving down onto the next section. You men shifting the blocks can stack them along the perimeter. Remember, if any of you feel that you're cracking the ice or start to sink, then climb down off the surface. The chill factor in the wind should help to freeze that patch solid again for you to go back to it. But so as not to tempt fate, I have set up a series of fans that will blow cold air laced with co2, which will maintain the freeze temperature and also give us a few more feet of ice to cut through, so the ship can have water under her for her launch. " John instructed.

It took both teams several hours to cut away the iced water leaving a bed of seaweed-covered rock exposed to the elements. As the cutters got further out, the wall of ice became higher until they reached the end of the cutting zone, which was around the twelve-foot mark.

John was happy with the result as Winstanley went around taking photographs of the event. The men were almost exhausted but were amazed at their handiwork, as was everybody else who came to look at this phenomenon.

"See Winstanley! This is one little trick I learned some years ago. My Ice Docking theory in reverse if you like. Even the boffins could not have wished for a better result.

Better take as many photos as you can and give some to me so I can send them on to those scientists I know." John said with a big grin.

Once John made his all round inspection and patted the stern of the ship waiting to be moved he called everybody back onto the shoreline again.

"The natural elements and the blowers will sustain the wall of ice for the next few months or so, until it starts to melt from the bottom up. In the meantime, to take advantage of the empty space, we will have a second construction site on the go, to provide a proper stone wall some twelve feet thick and some ten feet above the high-water mark around the ship, thus making a proper dry dock, with a hinged wooden gate on the end. We'll need several pumps to flood or empty the 'dock' as and when it's required. Once the ship has been floated out of the dock, any future extensions or constructions added to it can be done at leisure. The next step is to ensure the lower cradle is working properly, before we slide the ship down and it takes up this part of the lake-bed. Step three is when we have built the final front section. Once the ice melts, the weight of the water will hold the 'gate' shut. All we've got to do then is when the ship is ready for her launch out of the dock, we equalise the pressure on both sides of the gate by pumping water into the dock for the ship to float off her cradles. Her keel depth will be around the 10 feet mark, so she will have plenty of water under her propeller for her to move herself away and out of the dock. If this works, then a proper dock bottom cradle can be constructed ready for the next 'build'." John explained to the gawping workmen around him.

One big burly man came over and gave John a gentle bear hug as he was lifted right off the snow covered ground, before putting him gently back down again.

"We never thought it would work, but you have now given us a fighting chance to earn our money over the winter. From now on Chief Engineer, you will be the toast of all us in this workforce. My missus and kids will have a nice Christmas this year, for the first time in many." the man said in a deep gravely voice.

John took a few moments to catch his breath again before answering.

"The battle is not yet won matey! We've still got the small matter of building the bow section." again."

"You've done your bit Chief, now let us do ours. That ship will be sailing long before you know it, just watch!" another man offered, which was echoed by all the others before they gave John three cheers.

Crabbe appeared next to him as did the Fords, receiving an equally loud cheer before the men started to drift away.

Winstanley had this phenomenon spread across the front pages of his newspaper, which resulted in several plane-loads of sightseers come along to see it. A television crew came from Ottawa to film this strange ship and how it was being built.

"Never has anything like this been seen before, which proves the indomitable spirit of a workforce who refuses to yield to the forces of the big freeze." The T.V. Announcer stated, as he sought out any of the workers who had the remotest connection with it, but found there was nobody from the management team available for comment.

The novelty of a half-built ship nestled in a dry dock being ready for moving into a dock made from walls of ice, soon wore off for the workers, as they started to build the framework for the second section of the ship with a vengeance. For the workers, the gloom and doom of being laid off or put on half pay been spirited away, instead, the men had been given new heart and hope for the future. This new breath of life had its own casualty in the almost redundant 'kicking of asses' by Gleave and his team, so much so he actually came and complained to John about it.

"Don't be too hard on yourself Gleave. It means you have it easy for a while, so just relax and enjoy the ride. If you want something to do in the meantime, how about setting up a new recruitment drive in the spring. If all goes well, we'll need a back up team to work the two new ships we intend building side by side, let alone the extra 'Days only' workers to cope with the increase in the yard logistics. If that happens, then you should be able to get back into kicking ass mode again sergeant." John breezed, offering Gleave a cigar

"Putting it like that suits me just dandy, and thanks for the cigar Chief. Must go now and get my team on duty again." Gleave said gratefully, leaving the office in a cloud of cigar smoke.

"Come to think of it John, we need to find a decent calibre for a Captain and his crew to be able to manage the new innovations this vessel has been fitted with. " Crabbe declared.

"As it happens Colin! This is your forte in all this, but I have already got my eye on a couple of engineers within your fleet, who came forward to help out during the engine installation and subsequent build up of the other machinery on board. However that will be all down to Ward and his team, as it is up to them to install their own crew. As far as I'm concerned, once this vessel is deemed seaworthy and has completed her trials successfully, we move on to the next vessel to be built. Don't forget, we only have to build just the one vessel as our profile more or less dictates, and for it to be floating around the place in good order, then our project is at an end. If however, Ward or anybody else out there wishes to have a similar build but adapted to suit their own needs, then we can add each type to our patent claims accordingly. And I say this with confidence despite that rat Pritchard who thinks he's got it all to himself."

Ken came over and joined the conversation saying, whilst the statement about just needing the one build to prove the vessel design works, thus ending their project in the eyes of the ISDM wad correct; they still had a legal duty not only to the Government but to the workforce in developing the site into a more permanent shipbuilders yard. He added once the word got around the globe about this new type of vessel everyone would want to build them in their own countries, without the partners rights to their building plans or rights of patents.

"Then the only thing we can do is to try and get the Government to grant us sole rights to building such vessels, and in doing so, perhaps encourage them to provide a better launch facility. Possibly build a new launching berth with concrete walls instead of relying on ice walls. The other side of the coin is to allocate us with enough land to have a self contained area which will provide a beam launch instead of the traditional bow or stern launch. It might take a few years, but at least it would fall into the realms of creating a healthier local economic stability within the province if not the well-being of the entire country." Lawson expanded.

"If what you say stands true, then we could look for a rock solid contract with the government to provide their shipping needs, military or otherwise." Ken responded almost off-handedly.

"Then if that's the case, we will be given millions worth of contracts, which means my company could become the leading shipping line this side of the great pond let alone north of the US borders." Crabbe added with a sense of glee.

John listened to the gradual build up of euphoria and well-being among the team and decided that he had to speak up.

As he stood up, he rapped the big table with his big wheel spanner calling for their attention.

"Excuse me gentlemen! If you climb down off your clouds and stow the wacky baccy you lot must be smoking, there is one thing you all have forgotten." he announced, which hushed the others down to whispers.

"Whilst I appreciate a moment of day-dreaming and pie in the sky talk about all the fleets you seem to be building, but you forget we still have just the one ship to complete under the most difficult circumstances. The way I see it, is we must keep focus on the here and now and let the future take care of itself." he suggested.

His words brought them down to earth, as they realised the truth of what was said.

It took several moments for the others to gather their rational thoughts back into play then Lawson commented on the cold logic of what John had said and telling him that it was just as well someone had their feet still on solid ground.

John smiled at their collective candour, told them he was just as excited as them especially as the ICE DOCK had proved itself to be a world-beater on its own let alone the ship they were trying to build.

Gleave burst through the door in a flurry of snow, slamming it shut to keep out the winter, before shaking off his heavy overcoat.

"Do come in Gleave, is there something we can help you with?" Crabbe asked pleasantly.

"Afternoon gentlemen! Glad you are all here as I've come to see about the Christmas routine which seems to be a bit vague according to your instructions." he said swiftly before going over to the big belly stove and helping himself to a hot cup of coffee.

179

Ken went over to a filing cabinet and taking out a large folder opened it up and put it onto the big table.

"What seems to be the trouble? But take a moment to warm yourself up. " he asked.

Gleave took a little while to answer as he was trying to heat himself up in front of the stove and drink the obviously hot coffee.

"Christmas week is the time I wish to refer to. According to planned working hours, you have given the shift crews Christmas Eve through to the day after Boxing day off, but only the days regular crew are required to work on Christmas Eve. As Christmas Eve falls on a Monday this year, and given that the shift teams would have to struggle through this bad weather just for one day, I would suggest they should stay at home. Therefore once the day workers have completed their tasks on the Saturday and not the Sunday, they too can have the Christmas Eve off. The long and short of it all is, the entire shift crews can have a long weekend off from the Saturday mid-day until the following Wednesday. It would give those living away the time to go home to stay with their families over this period." Gleave suggested in his own fashion which sounded as if he was giving orders on the parade ground.

Crabbe took up the suggestion then asked if the same set up would be required for the New Years celebrations, which Gleave had obviously not thought about, and started to um and er over.

"How about this Gleave! Excluding the Safety and Security Team, what if we shut down the yard from the end of the day shift on the Saturday to cover the entire period, say from then right through to the day shift starting on Tuesday the 2nd Jan?" Lawson asked, giving a brief look over the files Ford had produced

"Yea? What's the catch? I sense a sting in this generosity." Gleave drawled as if unimpressed.

Crabbe, quick on the uptake as to what Lawson was thinking, replied.

"The workers will be entitled to full wages for their public holiday periods but will only get half pay for the rest of the time they are off. We are still under the spotlight from the Government on how we spend our money, and it is all we can afford this time round. Besides, call it a gesture of goodwill from us as befits the season of the year."

"At least those married men living apart from their loved ones can have a longer time at home and still get some pay out of it." Ken added.

"The thing is Gleave! If the workers come back after a decent holiday, never mind coming back in this dreadful weather, then they will come back fully refreshed, and ready for the next phase of our project. Besides, almost one week of extra holidays, even with half pay is nothing to sneeze at even though you've caught the cold weather. So to be exact, we'll shut down on the Saturday the 23rd and reopen with the start up shift on Tues 2nd Jan." John chipped in.

"You will appreciate we still need a team of volunteers over that time to keep an eye on both yards, with your Safety and Security teams in overall control that is. " Ken advised.

Gleave looked at the management team and realising what they had said was genuine and above board, appreciated the situation and accepted the proposals.

"Then all that needs to be done is to put a note in each mans wage docket to tell him of this, and in plenty of time for them to make their plans accordingly. I will get the volunteer team sorted right away. As for me, I thank you all for backing my own thoughts on the matter. That's all I have come to see about so I'll be off to instruct my team about your new orders." Gleave concluded, donning his heavy overcoat and opening the door to leave.

"What you might appreciate Gleave, is that I too was a Top Sergeant. I, just like you, looked after my men, being just like a mother to them. I trained and reared them up from a green rookie into a formidable fighting force. When the going was tough, they were the tough men who got going, looking after one another just like a small band of brothers. So it is with you and our workforce. We give you the orders as our Shifts Manager but it is you who gets them to carry out those orders. They were facing very tough times recently and have proved they were up to the challenge. So now is our chance through you, to show our appreciation in this way and as best we can by offering this holiday period we spoke about." Ben said, holding the door open for him.

Gleave shook Ben Ford's hand and thanked him for his kind words before disappearing into the blinding snow blizzard.

"Blimey! I didn't realise Christmas was just around the corner. Before we all know it, it will be time to complete phase three, with the prospect of McPhee and his pal coming to knock on our door." John stated in amazement, looking at the calendar pinned to the wall

"Not only that, my rescue team have now started up their operations, so it will mean our big tractors will be needed to keep the roads clear to provide the transport for those workers who were living out in the snow covered forests." Ben said with a frown.

"We'll do what I've had to do. Let your top Anchormen and senior supervisors take charge. It's about time they were given their head anyway. This shipbuilding project has taken over all our lives and until such times as we have a result, none of us can take our eyes off the ball so to speak. Just give the usual pep talk and only poke your nose in when it's needed. It is a very hard thing to do, but taking one step back from the front line gives you a much bigger picture to look over. Only that way can you see your way forward to be able to command the troop wisely instead of rushing around like a chicken with its head chopped off." Ken advised.

John agreed with the analogy, as did Crabbe for Ben to acquiesce to the suggestion.

"Now we've sorted the world out, it's time for the duty manager to have some hush around here. So thin out and clear off gentlemen, I've got a lot of work to go through before the sandman hits me across the head." Crabbe ordered, gathering up a pile of documents and dumping them onto the table.

"Okay Massa boss! We's on our way Massa Mmm Hmm!." the Fords said in unison pretending to be black slaves, as they tugged their forelocks and donned their heavy winter gear.

"C'mon John, we'll give you a lift down to Big Mac's. See you in the morning cap'n." Ken Ford offered, and leaving Crabbe to his own devices they made their way through the snowstorm before roaring off in their powerful land rover.

Chapter XXVI

Finely Balanced

Two weeks before the run up to the Christmas shut down period, John and his project team gathered to take stock of how things were progressing. They needed to make a general inspection of the half built vessel, before starting their second phase.

As Crabbe was the duty manager he took charge of the meeting.

"Judging by the updated task board, everything seems to be on schedule. But there is something we need to tackle, which is the gradual dwindling of work being done. Whilst I cannot comment about the repair yard, I am certainly concerned about this yard. This state of affairs is nothing to do with the shift teams, but more to do with the completion of certain tasks until they start up again in Phase Three." He started, then went through several items needed to be verified.

"Most of the main departments responsible for the build are almost at a stop now, especially the seam welders on the prefab lines, that also includes the ship repair yard." Ben advised.

"Have you received the paint stores yet?" Crabbe asked Lawson.

"Came in today, along with the accommodation equipment and other initial stores." Lawson confirmed.

"Have your main engine and ancillary machinery testing teams completed their inspections John?"

"All my engineers are on top of their work, but we still have a problem with some of them. Either they are duff full stop, or we need updated manuals to test them. However, the main engine has been given its first guff of air to make sure it turned over as per manufacturers' instructions. As for the rest, an external inspection at dock bottom would suffice for now." John reported evenly.

"How goes the repair yard Ken?"

"We're slightly behind schedule due to the hold up of spares. But I'm expecting them any day now to be able to press on. Mind you, we do need some workers over from the building yard to catch up." Ken stated flatly.

Crabbe took a moment to sum up the picture painted by the team before he made his deliberations.

"Okay then gentlemen, here's what I offer to you for your consideration." Crabbe commenced, and started to reel off what he was proposing.

"That is my summation, any questions?" he asked politely.

"As far as the workforce is concerned, they would only be too happy to keep their momentum going, as they'd much rather work than loaf around. If you can spare me say 50 workers to match the list of trades I have prepared, than I'm more than happy!" Ken said, handing over a list of tradesmen needed.

"My team of engineers are self-sufficient as you know Colin, but I do need a few pairs of helping hands to lift and shift machinery to and from the test bays." John said, adding his info into the discussions.

"And I need to know how much scrap and salvaged material we've got for me to make a new inventory." Lawson added.

"I will see Gleave to get the 'spare men' issued with paint brushes and have as much internal and external painting done as is possible." Ben chipped in.

"In which case gentlemen, if we all agree to this temporary arrangement then make it so. There is one rule I must insist upon, which is the continuous Safety at Work practice. By that I mean, we need to get a team of what I would call' prodders' who will go around prodding the overhead tarpaulins and the screening canvas, to shake off the build up of snow on them. We also need extra braziers around to keep the men warmer under our tent, but not so many we set fire to the place. Most importantly, it might be prudent of us to construct a wooden fence around the ice wall as a safety measure, just in case we have some days of fine weather enough to melt a few feet of ice around us. The Government insurers are keeping a very sharp eye on our ice-dam, but as far as I'm concerned, nature will keep us safe, and we've got an excellent safety record so far, which I for one intend keeping. To conclude this session, I propose a full yard and dock bottom inspection be carried out tomorrow, so we can assess our overall progress. We will need all relevant department supervisors to attend." Crabbe concluded.

The others agreed on the impromptu inspection, as it would provide the 'yard stick' for them to plan the next phase after the Christmas lay off.

"From the planned layout of the hull, we did a half-breed, in that she is neither Transoceanic nor totally flat-bottomed for canal sailing. That is to say we're building a ship which sails in fresh water, even though the lakes are almost ocean sized. The extra bilge keels should keep her stable, and she has a false bottom where her bilge tanks are installed taking virtually the whole length of the hull." Ken stated, pointing to the fat underbelly they were standing under.

John looked at the port aft thruster engine cowling and other purpose built holes the ship needed to function, taking time over the new propeller and rudder section at the stern.

"It seems this prop is too small to give the thrust needed to sail her. I mean, the engine is powerful enough, and even though the prop is a variable pitched one, we'd need a power trial to see if it will do." John advised, peering at his set of drawings.

"It's a standard 5 blade variable pitch propeller, with an 8 .5 foot diameter as per plan. Any bigger then it will protrude below keel level John. Don't forget she will only have a 10 foot stern displacement draught, and as you know, if the prop was to feather out of the water it would cause a knock on effect on the engine to make it race faster than the engine's set rev speed." Ken commented.

"Whilst I appreciate your comment, you will have to square the equation of engine power to the ship's loaded weight ratio. As she will be around the 7,000 tonne displacement, she may be pushing a carried weight almost four times that. Therefore, if what I suspect proves correct, she will do a max of around 25 knots unladen, but fully loaded with cargo, her optimum speed for fuel consumption would only be about 16. Having said that, the speed limit through the canal waterways is only 10knots, so that doesn't matter. The point I am making is we may have to alter her fulcrum point to keep her balanced and also give the prop the extra power. " John explained slowly and carefully.

This discussion took several minutes to sort out with Ken stating this major point must be taken into consideration for the next build.

They moved slowly along the underbelly of the ship until they came to the end of the partially constructed hull.

"If you notice gentlemen, we've staggered the lengths of longitudinal ribs and the keel, so there is not what I call a 'snap off' area. That is to say, if we kept each length of steel all the way around, including the keel, then should there be a massive weight shift between the cargo section and the stern section, it would create a clean 'snap off' causing the ship to fall apart into two sections. However, if you notice each longitudinal rib sticking out has covered a good twenty feet section of the hull still to be built on.

That way we would not need expansion plates and other safety devices to protect the fabric of the hull. At least as this was my consideration, I made alterations to the main blue-print of the vessel. Not only that, there are extra transverse ribs put on with a shorter side plate on each section to help in the strengthening process, which by the way, is a mirror of what we had done to the stern section. If all goes well, then this ship will be stronger than had it have been built in one go. I mentioned the balance equation. For the ship to remain virtually on an even keel be it in ballast or fully laden, as the stern end has all the weight of say 2,000 tons, then the middle section plus the extra weight of the bow section would balance it off at around the 6th transverse bulkhead between cargo hold 5 and the superstructure. As it happens, due to the ship being almost confined to a fresh water existence, the ship would not be subjected to the sag, hogging and the shear effects she would experience with the significant swells that you would find in the three major oceans.

So the new design on the blueprint will be just like a finely balanced sword whereby all the bulk is in the handle. As long as the blade is sufficiently weighted to balance the entire length at the hilt, then you have a perfectly good balanced weapon to wield all day without tiring your sword arm."

John stated, pointing to the various lengths of steel sticking out of the proposed final cargo and bow section.

"Yes John, it is a good idea but why have you layered the thickness of the hull?" Ben asked.

John explained his findings whilst he was on the *Tsun Wan,* so had it developed so that the superstructure did not give a 'top heavy' problem.

"If you remember, this was the problem our erstwhile project partner Pritchard had with his model. In other words, he had his specs laid down for a full one and one eighth inch steel as a uniform thickness for the entire build, which caused a very high centre of gravity for it to capsize. Whereas in our case, the entire waterline of the hull gets only gets seven eights up to the load line and reduced to three quarters of an inch onto deck level. The superstructure section has a five eighth inch plating, reduced to half inch up to the bridge level. All accommodation bulkheads are only three eights including the top of the bridge and the boat deck. In fact the funnel casing is only quarter of an inch. The transverse bulkheads separating the cargo holds are only three eighths inch plates but are reinforced with a quarter inch of tin plating each side of it, as is the entire secondary skin within the cargo holds. Mind you though, the bilge deck has a full one inch plating to withstand the load so as not to crush the various bilge tanks. To put it simply, the higher you build the thinner the steel gets, which in turn reduces the 'top' weight, and in doing so, a lower centre of gravity can be achieved. At the end of the day, all the weight of the ship be it in ballast or fully laden, will be below the water line even though this ship will have a very high free board." He said evenly, then added

"But don't go thanking me for all this as it was Kim Soon's father, a bloody good ship builder in his day, who came up with the original idea. Incidentally this is an item our erstwhile friend has failed to grasp, making any ship he designs top heavy liable to capsize just like his F196 model did."

"No wonder the seam welders were taking longer than normal, to cope with the different thickness in the steel plates. But why the thick bow section John?" Ken asked.

"It will match the thicker stem post and extra fore-ribs. The bow section will have a full one and seven eighth's thickness of steel which is needed if the ship meets a section of ice it cannot get through, short of using an ice breaker that is. Incidentally, the ship should be able to cut through ice up to about a foot thick without sustaining any damage. I've already mentioned the bow section will act as the natural balancing weight which will dispense with any ballast tanks to keep the bows down whilst moving unladen." John stated pointing to the drawing again.

"If this is the case, then we'll have to put the bow spoiler lower down towards the keel more, or even have it as a solid instead of a hollow section." Crabbe responded.

"We can make that decision prior to the fabricators starting up in the New Year, but for my money we might be pushed for space on the launch cradle, unless we can create more room. We've only got about 140 feet of borrowed lake, but from the look of things we might need a further thirty." Ken added.

"We'll be okay Ken! The theory behind all this so far is; when we've completed the second section up to the bulkhead of hold number 2, we will slide the lower cradle further down into the ice dock for us to complete the bow section. As each section is added the ship gains weight accordingly, so she will hold herself still on the launch cradles until we finish. So by the time we've built the bow section, she could be floating only by her stern section, until the whole ship is built. The bigger part will still be held on the cradles by her own weight, and all it will take is for the ship to be released from her cradle for the backward momentum weight to send her afloat on her own. Maybe a few arrester wires to stop her going out too far might be needed, but that would constitute her 'launching ceremony'. That principle has been used and tested on several occasions in the past and works well, so why do something else more elaborate. Our overriding concern and the ultimate worry, is that we have to make sure the hull is completed before the ice melts." John explained to the hushed crowd of supervisors or other dockyard foremen standing around them.

"So in other words, we can built a 600 footer on this short piece of slipway?" one of the supervisors asked with incredulity.

"No! You'd need about half of the vessel's length on shore and on the cradles for it to remain stable to complete the build." John responded swiftly, which created more questions from some of the others, until Ken held his hand up, calling for them all to stop.

"All will be revealed when everybody comes back off their Christmas leave. In the meantime gentlemen, I suggest you start getting your men to tidy this place up in time for the stores and suchlike, to be ready for the start up shift when they come back." he directed, which seemed to dispatch them to all corners of the yard.

"I think we'd all better adjourn to the main planning room and get ourselves warmed up again." Crabbe suggested, as he drew his thick fur lined hood further over his head until only his nose and eyes could be seen.

Chapter XXVII

Seasonal Greetings

The week leading up to the Christmas break was a hectic time for everybody as they worked furiously to ensure a good start when they all came back again in the New Year.

Lawson had the pay office team working almost overnight to sort out the rates of pay and other anomalies which are found in a multi-skilled workforce. In the end he decided and much to the delight of the recipients, to give everybody the same so nobody could come and complain why someone got more for less and so on.

The project team stood at the main gate wishing the workers seasonal greetings and hoped they would return safely. To a man they all returned the good wishes and vowed to be back on time. When the last truck load of men and the last coach of canteen and other female staff left, Crabbe turned round and pulled the large cast-iron gates shut with a loud clang. The security men came out and padlocked the gates before they went on their rounds switching off the lights and locking doors along the way.

"Well gentlemen! Time we also went home." Ben suggested, as the made their way back to the main office to collect their personal things.

They discussed their Christmas plans and family gatherings until Crabbe remembered that John was still unattached and offered him a place at his Christmas table, with the others following in quick succession.

"Thank you all for that, but this is a family occasion, and you don't want me to untidy the place. Besides, Big Mac and a couple of the other loners staying over will keep me company. Plenty to eat, drink and be merry. Now you lot go home and I'll probably see you in town some time." John replied quietly, drinking the last of his whiskey from his glass.

The others finished off theirs too as their driver poked his head through the door.

"Ready gentlemen? The security bloke is waiting at the side entrance to lock up behind us." He announced, as the team left the now very dark building and trudged through the falling snow to their land rover to be taken home for a well earned rest.

John was the first to be dropped off and waved to the others before he went into the big saloon to sit at his usual table by the large inglenook and warmed himself by the roaring fire.

There were a lot of dockyard workers already enjoying some of their holiday pay, but didn't bother John in any way.

Soon Big Mac came over to him, slamming a very large salmon onto the table before greeting him.

"Hello John, here's something for the holiday period! Bet you can't catch whoppers like that over in your lakes! I've brought ten more like it out the back, plus half a dozen elk and several wild turkeys which I bagged yesterday. So we'll have ourselves a real feast over the next week or so." Macintosh boomed, sitting down heavily into an empty chair.

"Hello Big Mac! You certainly have been busy up country. As for me, I've brought a box of special cigars and a case of real scotch whiskey back with me to help us out as well. But first let's have a flagon to line our stomachs with." John responded, as one of the 'hostesses' came over with overflowing flagons and planked them on the table next to the extremely large fish.

"Oh look at that whopper!" she cooed suggestively.

"Take it to madam and tell her to start cooking it. Once these dockyard workers have buggered off home, there's going to be a lot of hungry and thirsty lumberjacks arriving soon. So get the girls all tarted up and ready for them." he ordered in a deep gravely voice.

The girl almost staggered under the weight of the fish as she took it away, calling it all the smelly things going.

"How come you're not winging your way back to Blighty John?"

"Too far for just a few days. Besides, our project manager is supposed to be arriving for a few weeks. In fact he should be on the last train." John stated, looking at his watch.

"That is why I came early, to see you and give you his room rent. He's here for two weeks or so. Anyway, here's a cheque to cover it, mine too." John offered.

Big Mac took the cheque and threw it into the fire, saying,

"There is no need to insult me John! You will always be a free guest in my hotel, as are your friends when they come. For without you and now the dockyard workers whom you have hired, I would be in shit-street or still up country chopping down 100 foot trees to earn a living. We in this community have long memories for what you and your friends did for us in the past, which cannot be paid in money terms. Have your friend stay here with you and if he's one of those canny Scotsmen then we'll be in for a good old traditional Hogmanay night to celebrate the New Year." Mackintosh purred, quaffing his ale in large gulps.

John merely smiled and nodded his head as he too started to down his ale, before offering the giant of a man one of his favourite cigars.

"Here, try one of these!" John said, handing the big cigar over which looked like a matchstick in the giant man's hand.

They drank their ale and enjoyed a short while in each others company, until the revellers became too noisy and boisterous.

Macintosh simply stood up and with a few strides he picked up a couple of the revellers literally threw them out the front door, where they landed heavily in the deep snow.

"Now go home to your family. Come back next year when you're sober." he growled, going back to throw a few more out in the same fashion.

John smiled at this scene, as, for all the world, it seemed as if Mackintosh was sweeping the place clean, not with a broom but with his big tree trunk like arms.

The rest of the party- goers decided they didn't want the same treatment, so drank their ale quickly and made a hasty exit before they too were forcibly ejected. When they had gone, some of the hostesses cleared and tidied the place up, generally putting the room back to normal again.

Mackintosh came sauntering over and apologised for the disturbance, but said he was glad of a little bit of peace before the real men arrived.

"Seems as if the girls are going to be busy this time round. Don't they get time off as well?" John observed.

"Yes. Today's their last day for the week, so if you need a bed warmer then I'll get madam to come and see you before they all disappear."

"Thanks but no thanks. I'm too bloody knackered for hanky-panky. Maybe when McPhee has gone back."

"Sound thinking. I've got a fresh bunch of girls arriving in two weeks, so you'll get first pick, so to speak."

"Maybe I'll do just that. In the meantime, and according to my watch, either McPhee has found a different mode of travel or his train is late."

Mackintosh looked at the big brass clock hanging above the bar declaring the train was late suggested John should take a walk down to the station to see for himself.

"If your men are on the same train then they should also be here. No sense going out into the snow storm this time of the evening, so I'll just wait until they show up."

"There's some sense in that John. Maybe the train got held up just like yours did, but let's hope it is something a little less dramatic this time." Mackintosh opined as they supped yet another ale.

The big wooden door was flung wide open with a flurry of snow flakes and a big draught of cold wind, as several large men trudged into the warmth of the building.

"Give us several large flagons of ale and a plate full of makings, wenches!" One large man boomed, then first taking aim he threw his large wooden handled axe towards a round piece of wood nailed to one of the walls, looking almost like a giant dart board.

John watched as the axe twirled through the air and literally 'thwacked' into the centre of its target.

"That's Henry McDougal, the Lumberjack foreman from the northern forest, and these are his team. The others behind are from the western forests. This is when they divest themselves of their weapons as I told you about." Big Mac whispered, as several other lumberjacks threw their axes in the same direction. Others merely flicked their knives, but those with guns, just dumped them onto a waiting table. As each axe or knife landed in the coloured parts of the targets there were laughs or jeers at those who 'scored' the most or least 'points' the board had painted on it.

John watched as the men took off their big and seemingly clumsy drab outer garments to reveal each one wore very colourful clothing. The 'Western' gang were now being distinguished by the cowboy hats which were produced almost by magic. Once they had all sat down and started to drink their ale, John's attention was drawn to another very large man who had entered the place.

The spectacle of seeing a true Scotsman in his full regalia standing there caused the lumberjacks to whistle and shout ribald remarks at him.

"I'm looking for a ships engineer by the name of John Grey! If any of you fancy a knuckle sandwich for supper then step forward, five at a time." came a deep booming voice over the cat-calls and ribald remarks.

Big Mac walked slowly over to this man introducing himself as the proprietor told him that John Grey had been expecting him, then invited him to come and join him over by the large inglenook.

"Aye, I've heard of ye Big Mac. I'll no need of the fire, but could do with yon bottle of whiskey you've got stacked at the back of your bar there." McPhee announced, pointing to the bottle in question.

This statement made most of the lumberjacks quieten down in recognition this person was just as good a whiskey drinker as they were.

Macintosh led McPhee through the crowded saloon until they met up with John.

"Fergus McPhee in person no less! Come and have a few bevvies!" John greeted, standing up to shake hands with McPhee.

"Good journey McPhee, erm Fergus?" Macintosh asked politely, as they all sat down again, while the rest of the occupants got back to their own conversations.

"Came up by plane from Duluth. Landed next to a very strange looking ship by all accounts. Now knowing John, I guess that would be his doing.. The ship that is."

"How long do you intend staying Fergus? Only if you need a good bed warmer then you'd better book her now before she goes home for the weekend." John asked.

"Bed warmer? Haven't had one of them in years. Wouldn't know what to stick into where these days. Now a good bottle of whiskey would be a different story. Anyway, to answer your question, I'm here for two weeks to assess your project. Having said that, from what we've been reading in the newspapers back home, I might have to stay here until a certain, shall we say, problem, has been solved."

"You can stay here for as long as you wish Fergus McPhee. Your board, lodgings and beer are free, but you must pay for your bed warmer each time." Macintosh informed.

"Many thanks for your generous offer, erm Big Mac. I think I'm going to like it here, despite the noisy neighbours." McPhee said with a grin, nodding his head to the noisy crowd of men at the next table.

Joanne came over to be introduced to McPhee, and stayed a little while whilst the rest of the occupants of the saloon were making merry.

"By the looks of you Fergus, you need something to cheer yourself up and I don't mean a bottle of whiskey either. I tell you what, I'll go to get one of my, shall we say, mature girls to keep you company." she said, then disappeared to return shortly with a strikingly good looking mature woman, and introduced her to him.

McPhee went red as a beetroot, but stood up and shaking hands with her asked her to sit down, ordering a drink for her from a passing hostess.

"Now then Fergus! Can't beat this cosiness can you?" John asked, as McPhee became engrossed in a conversation with the woman.

Macintosh and his wife smiled at John, who whispered to him.

"Poor man! It definitely looks as though it's been such a long time since he's had a good woman that he's so rusty he doesn't know what to say or do next. But don't worry as Claire will be kind and gentle with him and look after him if he'll let her."

"Can't think of a better Christmas present than that. He's a good man and deserves something more than a handshake and a bottle of whiskey." John conceded.

"Morning Fergus! It's a clear morning, fancy a stroll after your breakfast?" John asked cheerfully as McPhee strolled into the saloon-cum-dining area.

"Morning John! What's for breakfast, I'm bloody well starving!" McPhee greeted him sleepily.

"Whatever you fancy Fergus. We might be in Canada, but I'm certainly enjoying my Australian breakfast. I've got venison steak, eggs, mushrooms, French fries and a couple of fresh rolls with my mug of tea."

"Sounds great to me, so I'll have the same." McPhee stated as one of the hostesses came over to take his order.

"Sleep well Fergus?"

"Let's put it this way, I must have done a good impression of Rip Van Winkle, as I've only now got up."

"I've been staying here since day one on account this was my first place to visit when I first came to this part of the world. The place has grown much bigger and gone up market since then, despite the rough and tumble patronage of the lumberjacks littering the floor spaces" John said, pointing to several sleeping bodies lying around.

"I've been to Canada several times before, but not at this time of the year and not this far over. I'm supposed to be on my way back during the third week of January, providing the weather is kind to us. But I've a feeling my stay will be a couple of weeks longer, and I hope to be an advisor to you if or when a certain problem crops up over in Blighty." McPhee started to say but got interrupted by the hostess who laid his large platter of sizzling food in front of him.

"But we'll talk about that as and when the time comes. In the meantime, let's get my belly sorted out just like the rest of my anatomy was, last night." McPhee concluded, tucking into his large meal.

John sat there quietly, smoking his after breakfast cigarette until McPhee had finished and joined him with a cigar and some coffee.

"That's better! Can face the world now John!" he said, giving a loud belch and patting his stomach.

"When you're ready Fergus, we'll get Big Mac to drive us into town to see the Christmas lights and have a bit of fresh air before the Christmas Eve party mood starts to take over." John announced.

As John got up to put his large overcoat on, Gleave came racing through the door and saw him.

"Chief! Glad to find you here! There's been an accident down at the yard! You'll need to come and see for yourself!" Gleave said in bursts, trying to gather his breath from his exertions.

Big Mac had appeared and hearing Gleave, started to rouse the sleeping lumberjacks telling them there'd been an accident at the shipyard and the Chief Engineer needed their help.

It took only a few minutes until big Mac had a crowd of half sober but willing men ready to come along.

"Wilder! Here! Get the truck from out the back and bring the men over to the shipbuilding yard as quick as you can. We'll be going by land rover!" Big Mac ordered, tossing a set of keys over to the man.

"On my way Big Mac!" the man responded and went through a back door in a hurry.

"C'mon Chief, we'll use my transport." Gleave urged, leading the way with John, McPhee and Big Mac following closely behind.

"What is the nature of this accident Gleave? " John asked as Gleave drove his vehicle through the heavy downfall of snow, like a man possessed, towards the shipyard.

"We were too late! There was nothing we could do to stop it either, Chief!" Gleave gasped, wrestling with his steering wheel.

The land rover slipped and slid along the axle deep snow covered road only marked by the neat clearance between the tall snow laden trees.

After the third jolt as they hit the side of a tree, did Mackintosh let his annoyance to the discomfort be known.

"Take your time Gleave, the place isn't going to run away. So slow down and let's get there in one piece." he growled.

"I'm using the trees to ricochet off to get me round the corners of this so called road."

"Just as well there is a lorry coming behind to pick up our pieces, then." McPhee quipped.

"Yes Gleave! It's no wonder you're trashing your transport. These vehicles cost plenty, so slow down." John concluded, as the vehicle rounded a bend to come to a sliding stop at the big wooden gates marking the main entrance of the yard.

Gleave sounded his horn several times before the gate was finally opened just as for the lorry arrived behind them.

"Thank God you're back boss! We've got three men buried under it, and need help." the man shouted before he saw the truck arriving.

"Hooray for the cavalry then!" he cried, letting the vehicles through.

Gleave drove along the back of two large sheds and as he turned the corner to face the side of the ship, the extent of the accident was evident for all to see.

John took immediate control of the situation, and ordered McPhee to get down aft to the superstructure and check that the ship is still safe on its cradle.

Mackintosh who had his massive axe with him went over to take charge of his own men.

"How did this happen?" John asked quickly, looking over the devastation.

"The recent snow storm since last night has kept us alert to keep a close eye on things. Then this morning during my morning inspection from aft, we heard a large ripping noise from the front of the ship. We found the middle skirt on deck had parted so we tried to seal it off again, but as the securing rope had snapped and shredded the lace holes of the canvas, we tried to make new ones whilst threading a new rope to draw it together again.

The wind was too strong for us and as it got underneath, the entire cocoon was lifted off several of the upright struts holding it off the ship. The winds forced the deck struts to give way, which caused a domino effect on some of the other upright posts, making the entire cocoon collapse. I had three volunteer prodders inside but they, as you can see, are buried under it all." Gleave reported in his usual military style.

Mackintosh had joined John and Gleave so John told him what was what, asking for the trapped men to be rescued first, before sorting out the mess.

Mackintosh issuing his own orders soon had the men start to work their way under the several tons of canvas and timber to effect the rescue. He had a couple of axe wielding men to start cutting the broken tree trunks away then to make a temporary shelter with some of the ripped canvas for everybody.

John busied himself by inspecting the recently built section of the ship to make sure there was no real damage to it, until McPhee finally joined him.

"That's a fine looking ship you've got there John. That ice dock sure lives up to its awesome name too. The ship is safe and secured well into its cradle. I'd like to take a good look at your plans and designs when we've got Hogmanay over with." McPhee stated, surveying the rest of the building yard.

"All will be 'rendered unto Caesar' in due course. In the meantime, we'd better get an ambulance here for the casualties." John replied, as Mackintosh reappeared from under the wreckage.

"How's it looking Big Mac?" John asked swiftly.

"Two dead, and one in a bad way. I'll get Wilder and another to take them to the hospital. They can use the land rover, as we won't be going anywhere until we've rebuilt this contraption again."

Gleave arrived carrying the severely injured man, followed closely by others carrying the two dead men to have them gently laid into the back of the land rover.

"These are my men chief, so I'll take them. " Gleave stated, then told Wilder to get the land rover and take them to the hospital.

"Get the men back here Gleave. Fergus, kindly stay here. Big Mac come with me if you would." John ordered as he left and made a swift recce around the area as best he could, hampered by the heavy snowfall and strong winds.

The two men skirted around the affected area, with John pointing to various items.

"I'll get Gleave to have the workers rebuild this when they come off their Christmas leave. So all we need to do is to clear up the mess and make everything safe so that nothing else will blow away." John stated.

"I suppose that's all we can do being as it's Christmas eve. Still, at least it can't fall any further now John."

"Yes, I suppose you're right. Have the men drag the canvas and tarpaulins over the new build area it was covering. Then get some cordage from that shed over there and have it all tied down. It will keep the new build area snow free, at least." John replied, pointing to a shed next to them.

When they got back, John told the men what was needed, but

for them to do it quickly so they could get back to the warmth of the bar again.

The men cheered at that, and rushed off with Mackintosh rattling out orders as they went.

"Let's hope you've got good safety regulations and a decent insurance policy to cover the casualties. How long will it take to rebuild this cocoon?" McPhee asked, looking around at the debris from under their hastily built shelter.

"As it happens, we have. It took twenty men a week to construct the entire cocoon, but I'll get as many men as I need to rebuild only the front end of it. Without the cocoon for the men to work under, the completion date could be seriously in jeopardy. The men are on a completion bonus, so they'll pull out all the stops to ensure the ship does meet its launch date."

"Now that's what I call forward planning. I'm sure I'll discover more over the coming weeks, John. In the meantime, and by the looks of it, you'll be required to foot a decent size bar bill racked up by the men here." McPhee said with a grin.

"Seeing as Big Mac refused our money for our board and lodgings, I'll use that instead of paying out of company funds. Our dockyard manager Lawson will sort it all out for me." John responded with an equally large grin.

It took the men a couple of hours to clear the place up and have everything secured for them to return to the shelter, Mackintosh being the last to arrive.

John waited until the men had quietened down before he addressed them.

"On behalf of the dockyard management team, I wish to thank you all for your response today and the good work you've done for us. In appreciation of that, I will pay your food and bar bill for today and tomorrow, seeing as its Christmas Day." he said loudly, which resulted in the men giving a rousing cheer.

"But that don't mean you lot will turn my place into a doss house. So behave yourselves or I'll start knocking a few of your coconuts together." Mackintosh added swiftly.

"Before we go Big Mac, have this shelter knocked down and stowed neatly under the ship over there and out of the way." John said, pointing to the underbelly of the ship.

John sat between Mackintosh who was the driver and McPhee in the big cabin of the lorry, as it lurched through the snow and back to the hotel.

The men gave a loud cheer and rushed through the large doorway of the hotel to belly up to the bar and start receiving their rewards.

John was sitting at his usual table next to the inglenook fireplace with McPhee and Mackintosh, enjoying a social drink together, when Gleave and Wilder came through the door, causing some of the occupants to complain about the sudden rush of cold wind and snow that covered all three of them.

"We've just come back from the hospital. Clancy, who was in my old platoon way back then, has just died. He tried to save the other two by pushing them away from a falling timber strut, but they got buried under the debris anyway. We now have three dead men to bury chief! " he said sadly.

"What a Christmas present for their wives and family." McPhee said softly, beckoning them to sit by the table as he ordered a large drink for them.

"As it happens, they were loners who opted to do the Christmas weekend watches for the married men. If I remember, Clancy has a Sister in Chicago somewhere, but I'll have to check up on the others personnel files to get their details." Gleave said, draining his large glass of whiskey straight down in one go.

"As long as you make a detailed report in the accident log and give it to Lawson, then you have satisfied the company records. Have you notified the local police chief?" He'll want a full statement off you, and don't forget to inform the local coroner. Ask the police to help you on that. It's just as well this is our very first accident of any merit, otherwise we'd all be in the mire, accident or not."

"No Chief! I've come here to let you know first hand. I have to return to the yard to get the others organised before I do anything else though."

"In that case Gleave. I'll secure your perimeter for you and inform the local authorities, if in fact the hospital hasn't already done so. Death in hospital is always expected, so no doubt we'll receive their help as well. Come back and see me again sometime tomorrow afternoon when it's all quiet. Take somebody with you as this weather can be treacherous." John said softly.

"Thanks! See you all tomorrow then!" Gleave agreed and left. Mackintosh strode over to the bar and spoke into a telephone for several minutes before returning.

"The Mounties have been informed of the three deaths, and the Major is on his way over to speak to us." Macintosh stated before turning to the men in the bar.

"Men! We've got the Major coming here soon to take statements about what we did this morning. Those of you who actually found or retrieved the bodies will definitely be required, so watch your intake of grog. And by the way, in case you didn't hear, the third man we rescued has also died. So I'll ask you all to have a whip-round for the three men. We'll get it sent to their kinsfolk." he shouted over the hubbub of the cavernous bar.

The men knew they were having free drinks, so were generous in donating by throwing fists full of coins into an empty beer keg hastily produced for the collection.

Once it was done, Wilder sat at a table with two others as helpers, and counted it all up.

After a little while he stood up with the announcement.

"Ladies and gentlemen! The collection has raised $800, and thank you all for your generous donations." he said with pride, holding up the piece of paper with the figures on it.

"There are three of them Mr Wilder. So to make it an even amount for each family, Mr McPhee and I will make it up to the $900. In case some of you blockheads are wondering, that will make it $300 each. Besides which, no doubt once the yard management team and especially the dockyard workers coming off leave get to know, they will be only too glad to contribute as well." John announced. All of which received a rousing ovation from them all, this coincided with the entrance of the Major, who thought it was for him until John told him what the score was.

"And here's me thinking the natives were appreciating all the good work I've done these last years before I retire." Richmond replied with a grin.

The Major took down all the details he elicited from them, including the statements from the men who actually retrieved the bodies, just as Mackintosh had warned them.

When he completed his lengthy statement gathering, he came back to John's table and sat down to wrap things up.

"I'll notify the Coroner, but nothing will be done until after the Christmas period. If you can provide me with the details of their kinsfolk, say on Boxing Day, then that will be that."

"Thanks for your help Major. Here's a large glass of your very favourite brandy. Cheers!" Macintosh said, offering a glass of golden liquid and raising his own glass to him.

As Richmond took it and drank it slowly to savour each mouthful, Wilder came up and asked about the collection money.

"We are not allowed to get involved with this, so as it's your pigeon Mr Grey, then you can do the honours." Richmond said civilly.

"Okay Wilder, just leave it behind the bar. Once we've notified the families, we'll send it then. Mind you though, that won't be until at least Boxing day." Mackintosh stated, as Wilder retracing his steps handed it all over to the barman.

"Well gentlemen, duty calls and all that. So I bid you good day." Richmond said as he stood up and put his Stetson on his head to let everybody know he was now back on the job.

"Before you go Major. Would you be kind enough to liaise with our dockyard manager Mr Lawson. He will get the bodies returned to their kinfolk, or at least make a suitable burial arrangement with the local clergy." John asked, standing up to shake the Major's hand in farewell.

"Yes, leave it with me Mr Grey. Merry Christmas to you." the Major said softly and left.

Once the major left the hushed bar, everything soon got back to its normal ambience of jolly revelry, as the Christmas Eve party got under way.

Chapter XXVIII

Phase Three

"**G**ood morning gentlemen, albeit yet another day of snow-storms. I hope you enjoyed your Christmas holiday despite the sad work of sorting out the funeral arrangement of our deceased workmen." John greeted, as the rest of the management team and the heads of the various departments gathered in the warmth of the main office.

"Before we begin, I'd like to introduce our Project manager Fergus McPhee who arrived from the U.K. on Christmas Eve to spend a few weeks with us. His task is to assess our project and progress so far and perhaps beyond our current status with the build. In other words, to coin the phrase of a certain late chief engineer, he's got his beady eye on all of us, so we had better be at our best so he can give us the shiny 10 we will be looking for." John announced, commencing his lengthy overture to the new start of the third phase of their project.

He used the many drawings and diagrams pinned around the room to emphasise and underline what he was talking about. Most of the team were au fait with what he said as they were virtually part of these drawings, which turned McPhee into the Devil's Advocate who questioned various points and aspects of the project, enough for Ken Ford to object to the almost constant questioning by McPhee.

Whilst John, in his capacity as the duty manager and also the spokesperson for the project, appreciated the friction building up between Ken the ship-builder and McPhee, who was still almost unknown amongst them. He asked them both the same question then sent them to the back of the room to sort out a joint answer. In doing so, he managed to conclude the rest of his delivery without any further interference.

"In short gentlemen we have reached the point of no return. If the project is to succeed, it is down to us to you to see all goes to plan se we can start the final section of the ship. The world will be watching us, so it will be up to you to see that we not a bunch of lunatics trying to outfox nature, but in fact a dedicated workforce who can produce a well made ship on time, despite the odds." John concluded, just in time for Ken and McPhee to come back to offer their joint response to his question.

McPhee spoke on their behalf, concisely and directly to the point, while the rest of the gathering to weighed up the merits of their decision, but it took John a couple of minutes to make a suitable reply.

"This is the very first time a ship has been constructed bit by bit, on the shore line to be shoved into the water to be completed due to the lack of building space.

Given the fact we have the lower mobile cradle to take up the stern section of the ship, even though the ship may be floatable making it very nearly too unstable to complete the build, the ship will hold itself steady as required, as most of the weight will still be held by the middle section of both the upper and lower cradles. Our only concern is the actual downward pressure of the ship as she gets lowered into the ice dock. Therefore, despite your constructive point of view, it will all be down to the restraining capability of the winches operating the mechanism of raising and lowering the cradles. The drawing behind me has the specifics of such a manoeuvre and should be self- explanatory to you both to see what I mean." John asserted, which seemed to satisfy both men.

When the meeting was completed and everybody had a large measure of coffee laced with brandy, McPhee called for everybody's attention.

"From what I've seen and heard so far, I am quite satisfied with this project, but I intend to ferret around the place to make sure when I submit my own report, you will be given a fair account of your efforts. You will get a copy of my report, as will other interested parties in this project. There is however, one fly in your ointment which can be of highly significant consequence, and that is the pending litigation levelled against the project team from none other than their erstwhile team mate Pritchard. For this very reason, I intend my investigations be intrusive of your paper work and at the outset, appear to be the devil incarnate just as I was during your meeting.

Just you remember, not only am I on your side but also are those at the I.S.D.M who sent you here, and as for all the others who dispute your endeavours they can to go to the devil." McPhee announced, followed by a round of applause from the meeting, with some of the heads of departments declaring he could inspect their department anytime he liked. Gleave even offered him a squad of men to escort him around the place, as did the technical drawings office manager whose department produced all the drawings and suchlike. McPhee assured them all if he wanted help then he'd ask for it, other than that he wished them just to do their allocated tasks around the dockyard as normal.

The head personnel filed out of the main office leaving the management team to complete the rest of their meetings in private.

"Once the new cocoon has been completed and the yard cleared for work, we can get down to the nitty gritty." Ken stated, taking a diagram off the wall then placing it flat onto the table that they were sitting around.

"As Ben will tell you, we've got four rack-and-pinion winches with twelve heavy arrester wires wrapped around the stern of the ship, and another four winches of the same attached onto the lower cradle. The rate of descent onto the lower cradle will be just one foot per minute with a kind of a doorstop at the stern end to prevent a 'runaway'.

The ice wall clearance between that and the ship is three feet, so if anything happens, the ship will rest on the ice to prevent her from capsizing or rolling right over. On top of that, she will have columns of ice blocks to help shore her up in a true upright position to assist the rest of the build. She will be stopped three feet from the end of the ice dock, with the log buffer to prevent her from striking the ice wall. Should this happen then the integrity of the ice wall could be breached causing a premature flooding of the entire section, all of which would bring John's theory into question without a doubt." Ken explained.

"Have we got enough grease laid down to help with the easing down of the ship? I'm talking about a good two tons of it to ease off the metal which is probably welded together by the thermal conditions even as we speak." John asked.

"No! We've only got half a ton in stores, and according to our suppliers, they won't be here until next week." Lawson stated.

"Next week? We need that grease as of yesterday. Where is your supplier situated?" John asked swiftly.

"As it happens, I've got a ton of it in the repair yard, if that's any good." Ken Ford offered.

"It'll have to do, but we'll need to play steam hoses over the cradle and the underbelly of the ship to unlock its thermal grip and help the grease melt a bit. The warmed up grease will flow easier in between the metal and cut down on any friction or sticking points along the surfaces." John said confidently, but received some doubtful looks from Crabbe, Ben Ford, and Lawson.

"Trust me gentlemen. You seem to forget I was among the cream of scientists who helped me create my iceberg docking phenomena, and the very reason as to why we've got our own ice dock some yards from here." John chuckled, as his statement seem to allay the fears of the doubters.

"So once we've got the ship secured in its lower position, we can commence with the bow section of the ship. Mind you though, we have to be ultra quick in completing it all before the ice dam melts. That includes the anchor lowering and raising tests and having the paint job completed." Ken Ford opined.

"Yes Ken. We haven't got a finishing yard nor a berth for the ship to secure the ship alongside, as all the dry docks will still be in use." Ben stated.

"The thing is gentlemen. As long as the ship is afloat and tied up onto the nearest floating dock or nearest jetty, we can always bring whatever materials we need to complete what little internal work is still to be done. I mean, any ships stores etc can be loaded in the same way. Even the fuel lighters etc can be brought alongside for the fuelling or filling up the bilge tanks etc." Crabbe added.

McPhee sat there quietly observing and recording in his notebook everything they said, making notes from the wall designs and drawings he looked at. When the team had virtually completed their meeting, he made a short announcement.

"Gentlemen! I've listened to and recorded your brainstorming session and ideas, noticing how you bounced ideas off each other. It appears your phase three is about to be implemented, and the sooner the better rather than have a mothers meeting about it. Your plans should pan out as scheduled, but you must have a contingency plan in case things go pear-shaped." he advised.

"The only other plan we've got Fergus, is to apply for a Government grant to build a proper shipbuilding yard with a proper berth for the ships, rather than rely on mother nature to hold the ice up for us each year." Lawson said with conviction.

"That will depend on the Canadian Government, but I fancy you would best be served operating on the St Lawrence seaway to build even bigger ships of this type. I mean, given the constraints of the canals and waterways."

"You forget Fergus. Our remit doesn't go beyond this ship. Once it's proved seaworthy and on its way to its commercial potential, our project is at an end. The ISDM college debriefing is subject to that rat Pritchard getting his come uppance." John retorted.

As McPhee nodded his agreement, John called the meeting to a close.

"Let's do it gentlemen!" he concluded, and wrapping up his big bundle of papers stowed them away.

Chapter XXIX

The Big Let Down

A large crowd of photographers, newspaper reporters, government officials and others had gathered to witness something no other shipyard had ever contemplated doing.

John and his team were on the observation platform above the powerful winches which would perform such a feat of engineering.

The rest of the entire dockyard workers not directly involved with the ice docking procedure, stood around, ready to give a hand if required, watching with awe the sight of a ship moving gracefully towards her natural habitat.

"Keep your eye on the starboard outer winch! Its paying out faster than the others!" Ben Ford shouted.

The winches paying out the thick steel ropes were screaming their protests as the weight of the ship started to take its toll on them. The noise was added to with screeches and groans prompting the 'grease monkeys' to slop buckets of soft soap and tubs of grease over the area thus to dampen the noise. Foot by foot the ship slithered her way down into the man made ice dock as she was let down agonisingly slowly until safely onto the lower cradle and rolled down to the bottom buffers she was finally coming to a rest.

"Take up the slack from the upper winches and secure the lower cradle winches. Make sure all sprakes are fully engaged." Ben shouted through a megaphone.

The hammering of wood and steel chocks under the ship rang out for a few minutes until the hip was declared safe with the 'all clear' hooter blasting out.

Everybody around the yard who witnessed this big let down, started to clap and cheer as they saw the empty space which was left for them to complete the last part of the ship.

The procedure had taken several nail biting hours to come to a successful completion, with the newsmen taking their photographs and finishing off their running commentary of something they would probably never witness again.

Once the team climbed down off their own platform they were almost crushed by the stampede of newsmen in their bid to be first to interview anybody and everybody.

Gleave spotted this, so sent a squad of his own men to extricate them from the melee and escort them to a more genteel crowd of well-wishers.

"Well done John! I knew when I saw your designs, the detailed drawings and especially the magnificent model of your ship the other day, your project team had all avenues covered so to speak. No doubt the Government Minister for Shipping will have a few words to say to you as indeed will other high powered people." McPhee said with a large grin, shaking each of their hands in congratulation.

A small reception was laid on in the main office for the VIPs, who bided their time, waiting for their moment to pose their own myriad of questions which the team had refused to answer from the paparazzi.

Little did John know, but Gleave had removed most of the drawings and designs adorning the main office walls, so they were conspicuous by their absence.

"What? Where're all our drawings?" Ken Ford and John asked in unison with alarm in their voices.

"Mr Crabbe's instructions! They've been stowed away safely in case some conniving thief decided to photograph them or even nick them, drawing pins and all." Gleave whispered.

This had been a good forethought by Crabbe, as indeed several cameramen pushed themselves into the office trying to photo everything in sight, until Gleave and his squad came in and literally threw them back outside again.

The champagne, canapés and other titbits were drunk and scoffed by the VIPs as fast as they were brought in, leaving little or nothing for the management team to enjoy.

After a short time, the Government minister seemingly in charge of them all, cleared his throat with another gargle of champagne, and made a small speech with the team as his recipients.

"The old adage of seeing is believing is strictly true here today. Never would I ever believe a half built ship could be manoeuvred down a slipway into a wall of ice as its dock, until today that is. If your workforce can complete the building of this ship in the same fashion as your model we can see here, before the ice melts and for my ministers to deem it seaworthy, then there would be no reason for you not to be awarded a Federal grant to build more ships in this way, but with a more substantial dockyard rather than relying on the whim of nature." he stated condescendingly, receiving a consenting nod from all the others around him.

"Yes Mr Ford. As of now your workforce can be guaranteed a wage package providing you can build similar but bigger ships in a similar dockyard in the east, maybe on the Atlantic seaboard. We need several ships of this new kind, but some even more diverse to suit our Admirals, shall we say." Hewer added.

"Who is the mastermind of this new design?" one VIP asked.

"Actually, it's a prototype being built by a project team under my tutelage as the representative of the International Ship Design Moratorium and based in Southampton, Great Britain." McPhee interjected on their behalf.

"In that case, see the appropriate department and draw what finances you need to complete your build, but I'll expect to be present when the ship is finally launched. Well done for your efforts and I commend you Mr McPhee, for taking on such a high risk project such as this in the first place.

We're off now, so keep in touch as I've told you." the Government Minister stated then gestured to the members of his retinue to leave with him.

Once the VIPs had left, the team relaxed to hold their own little party celebrating what was only the second biggest gamble of the project, after to the ice dock they had created.

214

We start tomorrow on the last 125feet of the ship Gleave, so let the workforce know they can go home for the rest of the day, but make sure all is well before they leave. Before you go, we wish to thank you for your forethought in providing the security blanket you created here to prevent prying eyes and other no-gooders taking advantage of us." Ken Ford stated, shaking Gleave's hand in gratitude.

"It's what you pay me for, but all perimeters are secured! See you all tomorrow." Gleave said with pride, leaving the office.

"He's certainly making a good name for himself with the workforce. Glad you were able to shall we say, persuade him, to change tack and join us, John." Crabbe opined.

"Yes, he's certainly the main mover in both yards, and I've already offered him the chance to understudy me with the running of the yards. He's still a bit headstrong and still lacking in diplomacy, but he sure is a good motivator nevertheless." Lawson concluded, as Mr Morris came through the door.

"Hello Mr Morris! What do we owe the pleasure of your company to then?" John asked.

"I've been monitoring the ice-field around the bay, and I predict there will be an early thaw. This normally happens around the middle of March, but on this occasion I estimate it at the end of February." He stated with conviction.

The room fell into complete silence with that bolt from the blue, before John spoke up.

"Mr Morris! You were totally sceptical about my ice dock theory, so what should make me believe you, unless you have corroborative evidence to prove you correct?" John asked warily.

Morris was not phased by John's statement, but dragged out a small roll of paper, unfurling it onto the big desk.

"As it happens Mr Grey, I was the first to concede to the marvel of your ice dock, which is why I decided to make it my business to see that with my own expertise, you would be advised about any thermal changes in the ice walls to perhaps advise you of any pending danger. This is the reason for my visit." he answered.

The team looked at the pen marks on the graphs but asked Morris to interpret them for their benefit, which he did with great delight.

When he had finished, the team were under no illusions, Morris was in fact on the ball and what he had produced did not lie to them.

This led to a swift calculation by the Fords who said they only had around 7 weeks to complete the build instead of the expected 10.

"It seems Mr Morris, you have presented a big headache to the project team, which will take a mammoth task to get round, given the material situation in both yards as it stands." McPhee stated civilly.

"Bloody hell Ken! The last consignment of steel plating has been held up, which means that if Morris's prediction comes true, we've only got enough to finish the bilge tank system and the hull plating only a few feet up from the displacement water line." Lawson said anxiously.

The instant brain storming session left Morris in awe with their discussions, so he sat down and helped himself to a drink, seemingly forgotten by the others.

After a while, Morris cleared his throat to remind them he was still there, and for them to finally remember him.

"Our apologies Mr Morris for our impoliteness! We thank you for your valuable information, and on behalf of the management team we wish you to continue to monitor the ice wall until it becomes too unstable to maintain. On top of that, as we don't have a decent advisor to the metrological equation in the nature of our building yard, we will draw up a special contract for you to fulfil this roll. You will be given any instrumentation and any helpers you need to operate this new department. You may start first thing tomorrow, but inform Gleave of this promotion of yours." Lawson said cheerfully, as Morris seemed to swell with pride in the sudden recognition of his work, by the management team.

"Why thank you Mr Lawson! You won't regret that!" he said jubilantly, shutting the door behind him on his way out.

"Okay then gentlemen! You know what this means!" McPhee opined as what was to become the obvious.

Chapter XXX

Clear the Area

"I have been here a good four weeks now, longer than anticipated, but can go back to the U.K. with the knowledge my last project team can produce something that, so far, will knock the socks off anybody else. So without further ado, I will take my leave of you hoping to return for the launch. I will keep in touch with you, but whoever is the chosen one to return to the college to offer their findings and the project dissertation, will need to be on the ball.

There is one major item I must inform you about , which is a large court case brewing up back home, instigated by the International Ship Federation over the patentcy rights of your ship designs, and until I need to say anything else about who is your contender is, it might be prudent for you to get a good defence team together, as we in the ISDM are providing for our own ends. Sufficient to tell you here and now, we shall be on the same side but will be attacking on different levels to ensure this person and his cronies are well and truly scuppered." McPhee announced as routine 'end of the day' meeting finished.

John thanked McPhee for his visit and his obvious massive support to the team's effort, then they all clapped and cheered him wishing him a safe journey back.

"I've asked Mackintosh to keep my new female friend safe for my return, as I have a strong notion I might just marry the woman and have done with my enforced bachelorhood once and for all." McPhee whispered in John's ear.

"Then let's make it a double celebration, my old friend. At long last, I'm looking forward to finally giving you away." John responded in kind and with a big smile, as McPhee waving them all goodbye climbed into his transport which roared off into the falling snow.

"Now that he's given us a qualified 'ten' and put us on the

final straight in our race against the odds, maybe we can concentrate on the finale." Crabbe stated, pinning a large list of 'jobs still outstanding' bringing everybody back to the here and now.

For the next few weeks, the mood of the workers was such they had worked themselves into a feverish pitch where nothing stood in their way to prevent them completing the build. Even the carpenters and other tradesmen working in the superstructure, creating a decent home for the comfort of the future sailors of this vessel, competed in the unwritten rules of the race to complete their sections before the others. It was a race against time and the natural elements, but it would be word of just one thing which would declare who won it, which was the state of the ice wall Morris was monitoring even more closely as the days went by.

The day finally came for him to sound the special siren warning everybody to clear the area, as the ice wall started to break in spectacular fashion.

John, Crabbe and Ken Ford were aft on the boat deck inspecting some of the deck furnishings, newly installed lifeboats and such like, when they heard the faint groans and cracking noises coming from the ice wall. Rushing over to take a look they observed the final collapse of the wall, and between them agreed it was akin to the final destruction of the dam wall.

The water swirled slowly at first around the stern end of the ship, before rushing up the slope to take its natural space onto the borrowed land.

"Well John! Morris was true to his word and even smack on the day too. Just as well we managed to compete the bow section, even though we still have to test the raising and lowering of the anchors." Crabbe said with incredulity, as the ship still remained firmly onto her lower cradle.

John noticed the subtleties between having one half a ship in the water, with the other half completely out of it.

"That, and finish off the painting and other minor works before we launch her properly. Once done, then we've got the big task of sorting out just who she belongs to, before we conduct the acceptance trials and have her certified as seaworthy." Ken Ford stated.

"I think you're right gentlemen!" John said with a big smile as they shook hands in mutual congratulations to an extremely dodgy and hair-raising project which was slated to be doomed even from the start.

Before they had gathered their wits again, they heard a big cheer from the large gathering of workers below them on the dockside as they all started to clap and dance around in the shallow waters of the shoreline.

"The men seem pleased, as they know the sooner this ship is launched, the sooner they will get started on the next one Ward said he wanted." Ken Ford remarked eagerly.

"Maybe next time they'll complete it in a much shorter time seeing as they know the score now, Ken. You might even get a Government grant to go ahead and build a proper builders yard, and maybe build much bigger ships than even the *Winnipeg*" Crabbe responded with a big smile giving Ford a gentle pat on his back.

"That or offer him a second yard on the St Laurence for much bigger ships going transoceanic. Which reminds me to alter some of the design drawings for you to use." John stated

"Come to think of it, I could do with a couple of larger vessels to use on my new Hornblende mineral shipping contract." Crabbe added.•

• Hornblende is a mineral that contains a mixture of, aluminium, magnesium, iron, sodium and calcium.

Chapter XXXI

Afloat

The big day arrived for the launch of the ship, which drew crowds of people not just from the local towns of Port Arthur and Fort George, but shipping companies from around the world, the Federal government officials, but most importantly Ward, his wife doing the honours, and McPhee with two representatives from the ISDM.

A special dais was built for the Ward's, and the project team, whilst the other VIPs sat on tiers of seats behind them. All the workers from both yards were assembled around each side of the ship, looking on with interest at those men detailed off to conduct the 'behind the scenes' work.

For it is they who actually launch the ship by releasing her from her cradle, and slacken off the huge hawse wires from the massive winches which controlled the lower cradle, allowing the ship to be lowered down until she finds her natural buoyancy to float off on her own.

The brief speeches by each of the management team and Ward were made, then his wife stepped forward to make a small speech of her own and delivered the phrase which was the cue for the men to get ready to wield their sledge hammers and knock the wedges away to allow the ship to move down and away from them.

"I name this ship the *Caroline*, and may God bless all who sail on her!"

She swung the traditional bottle of champagne towards the bow, which smashed to smithereens as the liquid splashed over the bow area, and the ship almost silently glided away from them until she finally floated off a short way until her tow ropes were gathered up and she was brought alongside a specially prepared pontoon jetty. Whilst the ship was lowered into the water, several small ships and fishing boats had gathered to welcome this newcomer, sounding their horns with four fire launches providing an arch of water from their fire hoses for her to slip under with ease.

The workforce walked swiftly down to the waters edge and saw their handiwork was floating handsomely as it was being brought alongside.

A large marquee the size of a football pitch was erected which contained the 'hospitality' for the local dignitaries and the other invited guests. Whilst the entire yard was turned into a large party area for the workers, their families and anybody else who attended. In fact it was deemed as a local holiday for everybody, with everyone making the most of such a triumphal day.

It was mid-afternoon when the VIPs started to filter away, as did most of the townsfolk and the workers with their families, leaving the management team, the Ward's and a few hangers on to conclude the days business.

"Now we're on our own so to speak, can I take it your team is ready to build another two fine ships for me?" Ward asked.

"I'm giving my building yard workforce a few days off and will start first thing next Monday to clear away and be ready for whatever you want building." Ken announced with pride.

"Don't forget we've still got the acceptance trials and the statutory examination by the Federal Ministry for Shipping to undergo. We still need two weeks to complete the ship, so it gives you time to get a crew together for those trials I spoke about." Crabbe stated.

"Crew? But it took it as read that you would provide them. I mean your own ship is still in dry dock and all that." Ward asked with alarm.

"You bought the ship, and as the owner it's up to you to provide the crew. I was part of a project which is almost at an end. Therefore once completed, I am needed to return without any further delay to attend to my own interests which is running my own shipping company."

"Where am I to get a crew this sudden?" Ward flustered.

"Ah yes! You're embroiled in a big union problem, what strikes and all that!" Gleave interjected.

"Yes, and it's going to cost me several thousands to sort out, let alone I'm about to lose a multi- million shipping contract with an American car company." he admitted sadly.

"We did away with unionism from my repair-yard a couple of years ago, and have successfully kept it from our builders yard too, mainly thanks to Mr Gleave here and his team." Lawson said with a nod towards Gleave.

This discussion went on for a while with John sitting back listening to it all.

"The way I see it Ward, is if Captain Crabbe provides a crew to man this ship from his own company, and if he was to honour your shipping contract using this and some of his own ships, then he would be entitled to some shares or equity from your company. Better still, you could concentrate on contracts ashore, while Captain Crabbe concentrates on the shipping side of things. In other words, a joint shipping line with Crabbe here in sole charge of it as he sees fit." John suggested, with a quietness in his voice which only his friends knew meant he was being deadly serious.

The enormity of what he said made Ward cough and splutter in his drink.

"Give my shipping line over? No way! It took me a long time to get it where it is now, and no Johnny-come-lately is going to take it off me. Besides, it's me who's keeping this yard going! I'm the one who can take it over if I want to." Ward gasped.

"As a matter of fact Ward, you don't and can't, the yard I mean!" Lawson asserted.

"We have been given a Government contract to build four supply ships for the Canadian Navy, and in the meantime they are drawing a contract up for a permanent builders yard to be built on or near this site. The contract will be made out to us, with no mention of a certain Mr Ward in the small print." Ken persisted.

"But… but!" Ward stammered.

"It's very simple Ward. Nobody including this ship is going anywhere until a crew is sorted. So think long and hard over my suggestion and come back to us when you're ready." John stated

"In the meanwhile, all your other ships are lying idle, strike-bound and without crews, and as each day goes by you're probably on a losing streak costing God knows what in lost contracts and the like." he added, as if to tighten the proverbial screw on Ward.

McPhee interrupted the conversation with his own thoughts.

"As an outsider to all this political and company wrangling, it would seem the obvious course is for you to allow Captain Crabbe to provide a crew for the purposes of conducting the acceptance trials. This would be a temporary arrangement between your two shipping companies until the ship has been signed over to you. Obviously, if your strike problem is still in force and starting to cripple other parts of your company, then I dare say Captain Crabbe here would be only too happy to run your shipping affairs for you, but using his own line, and duly authorised to take over your shipping contracts. On that note however, I dare say on behalf of Crabbe, he would see to it you'd get, say for the sake of argument, 10% share of the profits."

It took Ward and his entourage a few minutes to come to a joint agreement on what McPhee had suggested, and for a proper contract to be made out taking effect immediately.

This action somehow cleared the air for them all, sufficiently for the Ward entourage to leave the launch party in high spirits.

After a short while, Gleave announced the place was now going to be shut down and would everybody kindly leave the premises and go home to wherever they came from.

"It's a long way to bonnie Scotland Fergus! So I expect you'll be joining big Mac and me at the fireside again tonight." John breezed.

McPhee looked down into his empty whiskey glass and admitted it was so, as they all decided to act upon Gleave's orders.

"Secure the perimeters as usual Gleave, but don't forget the workforce is off until Monday morning. Then it's back to square one again." Lawson said quietly, as Gleave ushered them all from the marquee.

The small management party along with their wives went their separate ways, as Mackintosh arrived in his jeep to take them back to the hotel.

"That was one party I hadn't fancied but really enjoyed in the end." Mackintosh admitted.

"Yes, it's not often Fergus and me to get to attend a launching ceremony. We're usually on board watching from the other end of the telescope, so to speak."

"So what's the encore Fergus? I've heard from the grapevine you're getting shackled to some dame somewhere. Anybody I know?" Mackintosh asked with a grin and a sideways wink to John.

"Aye I am! Me'n Claire is getting wed on Saturday. Nothing fancy you understand, but I've got the local 'Sin bosun' to call by and do the honours. Claire is organising everything else, all I've got to do is turn up, and sober too."•

"Why you old scallywag! Thanks for telling me Fergus! I'll have to get an appropriate speech made out if I'm the one who's giving you away!" John said with a big grin.

"I was going to tell you only it must have slipped my mind what with all the rigmarole of the launch papers and suchlike."

"Get away! And here's me thinking you were too fond of your bed, with or without your Claire in it." Mackintosh teased.

"So we've got two days to get the haggis and whiskey organised. Wait till I tell the others Fergus, they'll be wanting to wish you well too you know."

"I think Claire has already sent out the invites and all that shenanigans. Mind you, I don't want a speech full of mumbo-jumbo from you. Just the plain truth, short and sweet."

"Now then McPhee! It's about time you listened to your students once in a while! John chided jokingly, as they arrived at the hotel again.

• Sin Bosun is Naval slang for a man of the cloth such as a Padre/Vicar.

Chapter XXXII

Still Single

"**N**ow then McPhee! Just calm down to a slight panic and concentrate on what you're about to do. It's not very often a fine looking Scottish gentleman complete in his full Clan tartan splendour gets spliced around these parts. So pay attention to the detail and it will be all over before you know it." John whispered to his very nervous friend.

McPhee looked at his watch for the umpteenth time, declaring she was adrift for the muster, and started to fidget with his full dress tartan attire.

"Come now Fergus, you know it's the right of the bride to arrive late. For the last time stop fidgeting with your sporran, you look tremendous." John chuckled quietly, smiling to the waiting throng who had crowded the bar of the hotel.

Some sailor with a squeeze box started to play 'here comes the bride' which was the cue for a tall stout man with a long but well kept beard, dressed in clergymen's clothing to appear before them, holding a large bible in his hand.*

"Just keep your eyes on me until your bride is standing next to you." The Sin Bosun whispered as the whole room cheered when the bride started to walk up towards the makeshift altar, which was in fact the large counter of the bar suitably covered in a clean white cloth and decorated with vases of flowers.

When Claire stepped alongside McPhee she took his hand and held it in hers whilst the Sin Bosun waffled on about the rites of the marriage ceremony, before asking them both to declare their vows.

The bar, full of grinning lumberjacks, all of the bar girls, some dockyard workers and their wives, a few of the local townspeople, and the others in the management team, stood hushed throughout the entire ceremony and to hear the final words

---

* Slang for a smaller version of an accordion called a ' Melodeon'.

pronouncing that Fergus McPhee and Claire Self were now man and wife.

Everybody cheered and shouted their best wishes to the happy couple with the usual queue of the single men lining up to 'kiss the bride'.

"Not before I kiss her myself!" McPhee roared, as he picked Claire up in his arms and kissed her long and passionately, before demanding only the first 5 could do so.

Claire joked she would kiss them all as a final gesture now she had been made an honest woman again. This led to whoops of laughter with men vying to be first, yet it was only a few who did so.

McPhee was surrounded by the bar girls who cheekily asked if it was true about Scotsmen and their kilts with a few slipping their hands up to give him a crafty grope.

"OOOH Claire! I wish my men were like that, you lucky woman." One declared, for Claire to come swiftly over to rescue him from their clutches.

"Hey, that's my property now girls, so hands off the merchandise. He's a married man now you know!" Claire ordered with a big grin on her face as he caught her and kissed her again.

The reception went well with everybody giving Claire little presents as wedding gifts, who thanked each and everyone for their kindness. The pile of presents was stacked high in one corner of the bar, with tables on the other side stacked high with as much food as the guests could eat.

At the end of the day, when most people had filtered away, the happy couple declared they needed to retire to enjoy the best part of the day, and any food that was left should be sent over to the orphanage and the local hospital.

John went over to the happy couple and with a big smile said,

"I give you the boy, now give me back the man. He is none other than our illustrious project manager, so be gentle with him and bring him back to us in one piece."

"Why he's nothing but a big teddy bear. Yes! I'll look after him." she giggled, slipping her hand up his kilt and asking him.

"Coming my way big boy?"

McPhee blushed bright red mumbling his thanks to everybody for being so kind and providing such a wonderful day for them both, before he gathered her up in his arms to carry her up the grand staircase leading to the 'guest' rooms.

Once the couple had gone and all the rest of the management team had finally left, the only ones left were a few lumberjack late-comers, John and Mackintosh.

"Fergus may be a fellow Scotsman, but he certainly knows how to push the boat out. He will certainly be missed when he leaves for Southampton next week." Mackintosh said unhappily.

"Yes, he's just like you. He's a big man with an even bigger heart, especially to those who treat him half decent. I too will be leaving as soon as the ship has been given the all clear by the Federal government shipping agent." John said quietly, as one of the girls came over and served them with yet another drink.

"You never did say if you were married or not. Got a missus back home?"

"No! From all the good friends I have known and teamed up with, I'm the only one who is still single. Maybe someday when I finally leave the sea, perhaps." John avowed.

"Where will you settle John? Most folk around here would like you to stay here and make this place your home. That young woman you've taken a shine to, er ,Laura, yes she would make a good wife for you just like Claire with Fergus, let alone my Joanna with me."

John looked around the almost empty bar and saw the girl in question coming towards him, and stood up to greet her.

"I've come as quick as I could John. My train got held up coming back from my Grandparents up north." she said, giving him a hug and a kiss, then started to remove her heavy overcoat.

"Better sit by the fire here Laura, and I'll have one of the girls to fix you up with some food. John, I've got some business to attend to so I'll leave you two for a while." Mackintosh insisted, leaving to speak to the bartender.

Laura told him about her visit, her awful journey back, and how she was glad he was still here.

"I was worried about you not turning up Laura. The happy couple have retired now, and sorry you missed such a wonderful occasion." John said, telling her all about it as her food and hot drink was laid in front of her.

When he had finished relating all what happened, and she just eaten her food, she looked at him tearfully and asked him to be kind to her because she has something to tell him.

John was taken by surprise, not just by her question but by the sudden realisation he harboured a deep affection towards this girl, and not from sheer lust between the sheets either, then tensed himself for what he was about to hear.

"John, you know you've been my first and only man I've been with ever since I came here. You've been very kind and generous towards me, and I've always saved myself for you. Joanna and the other girls and even Big Mac know this, that's why the other girls leave you alone, and make sure I'm off limits to all the other men who come here. The thing is, while I was away, I've met someone I knew as a school friend, who's coming here to work in the dockyard." she informed him, then went on about this young handsome man who was destined to make her a wife and mother of all the children she wanted.

He heard her voice and saw the tears rolling down her cheeks, but for him, this revelation was yet one more time fate had dealt him a cruel and savage blow to the affairs of his heart. First Helena, then Telani, then May Kwan his Singapore girl and now Laura, which finally brought home to him he was destined to always be the 'best man' never the groom.

Laura finally finished with a little sob and told him she was very sorry to do this to him.

John went very cold and quiet for a moment, before he finally found his voice again to reply as gently as he could to her despite the devastation he was feeling inside him.

"I think dear Laura, there are some things you need to know, and it appears that right now is the time to discuss it all in private. I'll have Joanna send some food and drink up to our cabin." he whispered and escorted her towards the cabins above the bar, with a brief word to Joanna before they left the hustle and bustle of the bar.

Laura was looking very pale and morose at having done this to John, but when John sat her down to and tell her more about his past loves which he had not told her before, she became even more upset.

"At the end of the day Laura, I'm a seafaring man whose home is where his hat hangs up, be it on the way to Timbuktu or this side of the Black Stump as one of my Antipodean friends would put it. All of which means, until I'm finished sailing the oceans of the world I'm no use to any girl wanting her man to come home to her every night as with a normal married couple. For you to want this and your man is probably desired from this er, boyfriend of yours is natural, who am I to deny you the kind of happiness I cannot give you, for another few years at least." he said gently, cradling her in his arms with his eyes sparkling in the dim light, fighting back his own tears.

He looked across to the small log fire burning the logs slowly away, but for a full minute or so felt as if it was giving off an enormous heat which was warming his whole body.

"Remember I told you about Helena and Telani" he whispered almost in a trance whilst stroking Laura's tear stained face.

She nodded slowly then looked in the same direction as John to see what had attracted him, but seeing nothing turned back around to see he had a little smile on his face, which disappeared as quickly as it had come.

"What was all that?" she whispered in total bewilderment.

"It's okay Laura, nothing for you to worry about. To put you at peace with yourself, Helena and Telani knew this would happen and have told me my day has still not come for a lifelong mate like you will have with this boyfriend of yours. Just remember this, you will have 5 children, first son after me, and the two girls you will have are to be named Helena and Telani May. Do this and you will live a long and happy life. Promise me you'll do this?" He whispered back slowly whilst coming out of the 'visitation' he just experienced while the warm feeling slipped away from him.

"But, but, how do you know this John?

"Trust me with your life on this one Laura. Now I've told you all this, you will not mention it ever again." he said solemnly with a nod of his head.

Laura nodded and whispered her agreement then asked,

"What happens now?"

"You can stay with me until I leave to go back to the U.K if you wish. But obviously should your boyfriend turn up before then, it would be best if you sought accommodation elsewhere. Speak to Joanna on that as she knows how to, erm, rehabilitate her bar girls. Maybe the local Woman's Guild could sort out something respectable for you if your boyfriend is unaware of your present occupation."

"I've told him I work in a local hotel as a barmaid and teased him that I was a very popular girl, so not for him to do me wrong." she smiled, wiping her face dry.

"That's the spirit Laura, now let's get some of this delicious food Joanna provided down us or we'll starve to death in the meantime!" he replied, giving her a kiss on her forehead.

Chapter XXXIII

First Run

"**N**ow that Fergus has gone back to the college with his new wife, perhaps we can get on with the business of having this ship earn its keep, sooner than later. As Fergus told you, I am now the Project Leader to conclude the business, and this is what I intend doing." John announced, for the management team to gather around the big table in the office.

He explained and expanded the outline details of what needed to be done, and the others offered questions or observations as to his overall scheme of things. The meeting lasted many hours with several ideas and items fully agreed by all concerned.

"The ship can be docked now the *Winnipeg* has sailed, which means we can have the various shipwrights and other tradesmen work on her from there. She doesn't need a full docking down, so we can put lighter barges alongside her for when she gets her fuel etc." Ken suggested.

"On the question of a crew, Ward has sent a duly signed document for me to take over the ship until their strikes are done with, but I'll need a couple of days to sort out my officers and crewmen, before I get them on board." Crabbe directed.

"As far as I'm concerned, my yard is being set up for the next build, but you are welcome to any fitter or craftsmen you need, at least for the next few weeks or so." Ken Ford offered.

"Thank you for your support gentlemen, this just about wraps up the verbals for now. The next thing is for us to conduct a full inspection of the ship, the inside of the hull that is. We can conduct it whilst the ship is moved into the dock, and I would prefer it to commence tomorrow morning with you and the appropriate supervisors available to take suitable notes etc. Kindly get it organised if you would." John concluded, rolling up the large bundle of maps, diagrams, and other project material.

The Dockyard Inspection Team roamed all over the new vessel for several hours, issuing orders to the relevant supervisor in charge of such details. When they finally arrived into the officers / passengers saloon, John decided they should have a short break for some refreshments and to recap on what had transpired during the inspection.

He looked around the enlarged saloon with puzzlement until he realised what it was.

"Colin! Was this saloon design part of our, shall we say, a Captain's input to passenger / crew comfort?" he asked politely.

"Why yes John! This and quite a few others you have seen throughout the entire accommodation areas" Crabbe stated simply, as he saw John looking around the compartment.

Crabbe saw his frown and deduced John was looking at the overlarge area in which they were all gathered.

"Oh, the dining area and saloon as one big area! Yes, a cousin of mine who was a steward in the Inver line on board the, er *Inverary*, I think it was. Well never mind, but he told me about the 2nd Engineer having to strip down the dividing bulkhead between the dining area and the saloon, and replacing it with concertina screens just as you see. The crack being that both spaces could be used as one big one to accommodate a larger number of passengers/crew, should the need arise, just like now. He apparently adopted the idea for use in the hotel he was running, and to good effect too. Hence the concertina bulkhead you now see." Crabbe explained, then saw a slow grin appearing on John's face.

"Yes Colin! I know all about it as I was that Engineer, and to be honest I'd forgotten all about it until what I saw jogged my memory." John chuckled.

"So it's true then! And all along, here's me thinking he was just a typical sailor with fancy yarns and strange ideas." Crabbe gasped.

"There you go Colin. It goes to show you never know just whom you might bump into whilst at sea. Hope he's well and enjoying his retirement in Worthing."

233

"As it happens, he's on his way out here to become the Chief Steward on board this vessel. He will be pleased you are on board if only to substantiate his wild claims of what happened on board that ship."

"Glad to be of service Colin. Now we must get on with what's left of this circus." John replied with a smile, and called everybody to commence their all important post inspection briefing.

It was a gentle bump as the ship nudged the solid stone-wall of the dry dock which told them the ship had now arrived alongside, and John bring the meeting to and end.

"Tomorrow we will get fuel on board and have the engines turned over. The side thrusters will be tested whilst we're in the dock, which gives us space to move the ship from side to side. If these engines work according to the design specs, then this ship would have no need for tug assisted docking / undocking. This however, will rely purely on the sheer expertise of a Captain who can handle his ship properly in the first place. Our Captain will no doubt take great delight in teaching those instructions accordingly. I want all the vital radio / radar and other navigational equipment installed by the weekend as I intend taking this ship out on its first run around the bay. Any internal work, such as the completion of the wooden deck-covering within the accommodation space, and the testing of the deck-mounted hoists etc can be done whilst on the lake. We have to complete everything as the government shipping team of inspectors are due in two weeks time, so be on your toes. That will be all gentlemen." John announced.

Chapter XXXIV

The Big Day

The ship had been worked upon until all the final touches were completed during the initial sea trials around the island a few miles off shore from the yard.

All went well considering some of the unexpected teething problems, especially with the thruster engines which were used to dock and undock her, yet still a big enough attraction for those dockside to witness a ship docking itself instead of by the traditional method of using tugs.

There was a bit of a panic during their full speed trials when one of the turbines propelling the ship overheated and started to knock alarmingly before it was shut down and inspected. John had his team of senior engineers replace it in case of any further mishap.

Everybody worked long and hard in readiness for the team of inspectors who were on their way to see them, impatient now the last of the ice on the lake had finally melted away and the ship was wearing her fresh coat of paint, with a handsome house flag flying at the top of the signal mast.

"The radio phone call from shore says the team will be here in the morning John!

From my inspection all seems to be in order, so I intend letting the crew get ashore for the night but I'm holding a full meeting of officers in an hour from now, as I want to give them a briefing and some sort of an idea on what to expect during the inspection, which will take place within the hour they board and we put out to sea. That however won't be until approx 0900 and should take approx 4 hours before we return alongside, when they will give us the low-down on what they found or not. Let's hope it's the latter!" Crabbe stated.

"Actually it's not all bad Colin, if the inspection is done in the same manner to what the *'Tsun Wan'* went through, despite the

Royal Navy breathing down our necks then we've got no problem."

"Hmm! Hope you're right! Must go now, see you in 1 hour!" Crabbe concluded, leaving John to go into his bridge cabin.

"Okay then gentlemen, settle down and let's have some hush around here. I've summoned you all here to give you a preview of what to expect tomorrow, although the Chief Engineer, as he has already gone through such an ordeal, will be spreading most of the good word amongst you." Crabbe started, then went through the various test requirements, conditions and suchlike from a long list of notes he had prepared earlier.

John gave a running commentary on just how to come through the very rigorous inspection any new ship is required to undergo and pass before she is given her licence to trade upon the high seas. All of which was taken in with a mixture of a gung-ho attitude and reservations by the officers who had to come to terms with the dreaded hour.

There were a few questions and problems arose which Crabbe and John answered before everybody felt confident within themselves to face the following day come what may.

Crabbe concluded the meeting by wishing everybody a good day tomorrow, with John echoing his sentiments but added the bar would be open for those staying on board to enjoy a few libations paid for by the two senior officers, the remainder were to "get ashore and buy your own drinks."

This was greeted by a cheer and a rush to the bar to inundate the steward with their drink requests, with Crabbe and John standing back smiling at them.

"If all goes well John..." Crabbe started to say, but was cut short by John.

"Oh ye of little faith Colin! Everything will be just fine, you just wait and see."

"Thank you for your kind words John. I'll be shooting ashore now until 0600, how about you and er, Laura?"

"I've still got a few niggling problems with the master blue-print drawing of the ship to sort out as I'll be needing it when I return to Southampton. You know how strict old Fergus can be let alone the Dean Mr Clutterbuck. Besides Laura has gone to visit a relative of hers over in the fort, so maybe a rest is on the cards for now." John replied swiftly dodging the question.

"See you in the morning then Colin, don't let the sand get in your pants, or in this case, the ruddy snow, because it has a habit of turning your knackers to ice cubes." John concluded and escorted Crabbe to the gangway before waving him off.

The morning was bright with a fresh breeze coming in from the lake as the ship lay resting at her berth awaited for her passengers to board, with the crew smartly dressed and quietly carrying out their duties, all awaiting their big day.

John and Crabbe stood patiently at the gangway looking around at the crew at work and engaging in good humoured banter.

"Like lambs to the slaughter Colin! This is just like passing your driving test. Do well and give the right but straight answers to their questions, and never try to flannel them. Mind you, this is a brand-new type of ship they've never come across, so they'll be more inquisitive than normal to offer credence to any of your logical answers. For me it'll be the examination of that final blue-print I took nearly all night to perfect, as the rest of my department are only running a standard diesel engine powered turbine for you."

"Hmm! Speak of the devil, here they come. Good luck John" Crabbe said, shaking John's hand, before they moved over to the brow of the gangway and greeted each of the 6 man inspection team.

"Good morning Captain Crabbe, Chief Engineer Grey. I'm Mr Reid your Chef Inspector, along with Messrs Langford and Carter, with Mr Simmonds and Walters from the Government's Maritime Ministry, and Mr Clutterbuck whom you already know of." Reid said cheerfully, casting a slow look around the ship to seem pleased by what he saw.

"It's a fine morning for a quick sail around the island and back Captain! Your ship certainly looks a fine one." Walters commented cheerfully following the entourage up onto the bridge.

"It was nice of you to come, as I wasn't expecting to see you until I came back to the college. At least you'll get a first-hand snoop of the ship but knowing you, the master blue-print of her design." John said amiably to Clutterbuck, who was looking admiringly at the neatness of the ship beneath his feet.

"I had to make this trip to confirm everything Fergus McPhee told me and all the photographs he brought back with him, let alone all the press coverage you had in her build. So far so good, but lets hope she lives up to what he's cracked her up to be." Clutterbuck replied with a big smile then stood at the back of the bridge letting Crabbe and the others crowd around the focal point of the bridge, which was the bridge control console which had a small tapper bar steering-mechanism surrounded by an array of dials, push-buttons, levers and a couple of telephones.

The bridge windows afforded a panoramic view of the entire length of the cargo deck, bow section and even right along the sides of the ship to be able to view the stern.

The spacious bridge had a chart table, radar screen, radio transceiver, tannoy system, echo sounder and a small door leading to the Captain's small bridge cabin.

Everything they saw brought gasps of amazement from the team who had never seen such a ship as this bringing a rapid fire of questions from each team member which seemed to overwhelm Crabbe, until Reid held his hand up asking them to calm down and find their own answers to the questions they had posed.

The undocking was yet another moment of magic because the team were expecting a tug to pull them off the jetty, instead, they marvelled at the ease by which the side mounted thrusters moved the ship sideways and clear of the jetty for the main engines to start up with a puff of smoke and a thrum of the propeller to move the ship right out into the lake, free from the land.

"Okay gentlemen! Now we're off shore let's get down to some inspection work. You have been split into two teams, one for the ship, and one for the engineering and machinery. You all know what to look for to make your recommendations and reports. Team 'A' will use channel A on your radio, team 'B' on C, I'll be using channel 'B' for myself. Meet back in the passengers lounge in 2 hours, good hunting!" Reid announced, before turning to Crabbe and John.

"Chief Engineer Grey, Mr Clutterbuck and I wish to see your master design blue-prints and other technical drawings if you please. We'll set them up in the main lounge for when I get the ongoing reports and comments from the teams. Captain Crabbe, you're obviously needed here on the bridge, but some of us will be poking and prodding around expecting you to provide some answers. May I ask you provide the information the teams need as and when." he requested yet in a demanding way.

"All my drawings and other ship design drawings are already on view in the lounge. If you care to come along now, you will get to meet one of our designers and the Manager of our shipbuilding team." John said civilly and had them follow him to the lounge.

The lounge had been 'opened' up to provide what John called his 'Rembrandt' gallery, displaying several technical drawings from all parts of the ship, culminating on a scale model of the ship in a glass cage.

Reid and Clutterbuck walked into the lounge with gaping mouths and wide eyes, totally amazed on how big the lounge was, to see all the drawings they would ever need to see about the ship.

"Gentlemen, may I introduce you to Mr Ben Ford who is part of our Design and Build team. The other gentleman is his father Mr Ken Ford who provided the manpower and material from his repair dockyard." John said cheerfully as they all shook hands and exchanged pleasantries.

239

"It seems as if you've read my mind Grey, for you to have exactly what I need to know, starting with this, your master blueprint. The model is a good idea for us to compare the drawings with rather than traipsing all around the vessel. The others can do all that, me, I prefer a much quieter life, if you get my drift." Reid said with a grin, relaxing from his officious 'inspection team' stance.

For a good hour the 5 men poured over most of the major plans and drawings, using the model as a reference point each time, with the Ford's and John providing answers to relevant and very technical questions, until Reid was satisfied with what he saw.

Looking at the ship's clock, then at his watch he decided it was time for a mid-morning cuppa.

He needn't have bothered, because the Chief Steward had already entered with a tray of cups and a jug of delicious smelling coffee, which he placed on a side table.

Soon the lounge took on the smell of coffee laced with cigar tobacco smoke, the steward returned to switch on the extractor fan and clear the air. Again Reid was amazed by the almost uncanny way his every move or thought was anticipated and he commented upon it.

John, taking up the remark told him he had already done a ship refit and acceptance trials out in Singapore under the very watchful eye of Mr Fergus McPhee. Clutterbuck confirmed that, and told Reid this ship was John's own creation and design as his 'test model' for acceptance into the ISDM in Southampton, England.

"Yes, I've heard all about the ISDM, which means that if this ship proves it's fit for purpose then Grey will have succeeded in such a tall order." Reid said almost magnanimously, before having them return to the business of the inspection.

Reid and the others in the inspection team had used up some 3 hours of the inspection time testing and witnessing certain 'operational' routines a ship needed to perform including a full speed trial witnessed in the spacious engine-room.

He called for the inspection to be wound up with a meeting in the lounge which was to be attended by all of the ship's officers not on watch to give his verdict as to whether the ship was 'fit for purpose' or not.

"Right settle down gentlemen. The sooner I deliver the team's verdict and get back into harbour again the sooner we can all go home." Reid announced.

He went through the various stages of the inspection involving the various departments, making comments or eliciting comments from those team members who had taken charge of them, before he came to his final verdict.

"This is where we either hit pay dirt or get sued for wasting Government's money and time." Crabbe whispered to John and the Fords.

"Actually, you've given a good show and one that we in the ISDM can build on despite what his final verdict dictates." Clutterbuck whispered aside with a knowing wink.

Reid cleared his throat and picking up a piece of paper from his pile of notes held it up for everybody to see.

"We from the Board of Maritime ship Inspectors wish to make the following announcement, and as Head of the team, I will now do so. This ship had been constructed in very demanding circumstances and despite all the odds. She represents a totally new way of ship design and also in the method in which she was constructed. There are numerous innovative gadgets and equipment on board that would be an envy of many an international shipbuilder, which could pave the way for even better and more advanced technology to incorporate on the modern ships of today which were not perhaps envisaged even 5 years ago.

This ship will stand the passage of time and become a legend in her own right, with many a budding ship designer vying to copy her meticulous design and manufacture.

We the Government's inspection team do hereby declare that this ship is fit for purpose and may she prosper in her working life. Signed by myself Mr Reid, and countersigned by the rest of the team." Reid said in a booming voice.

There was total silence in the lounge for a moment as John and the rest of his 'Management' team along with the ship's officers took time to digest such a momentous verdict.

"Quite right too! Clutterbuck shouted and stood to clap his hands which gave way to a hearty applause and cheers from everybody.

"Captain Crabbe! Kindly reverse course and get us back alongside again, as I feel you and your team will need a few days to get over this remarkable achievement which nobody back in the Capital gave you much chance of pulling off We will have the necessary paperwork and title deeds sent to you within the week, well done!" Reid said with a large grin on his face, reflected in the same manner by the rest of the inspection team.

Crabbe stood up and gave a short but succinct speech in reply, with every sentence cheered on by the rest of the ships officers.

"That's your project and your presentation dealt with John, but it will be a different matter when you get back to the college to re-present your drawings, notations and other relevant factors went into building your 'prototype'. Most only provide a scale model to be subjected for testing in the test tanks, but somehow we've not got a tank big enough to accommodate your, er, model." Clutterbuck said aside to John, who was still smiling at the accolades bestowed on him and his project team.

Ben Ford heard this remark and with a pat on John's shoulder said.

"Look's like you'll be making the trip back to the college on your own John, as Colin and I will be needed this end." Then asked Clutterbuck

"How long has John got before returning? Only we've got a ton of paperwork to get ready for him, he'll need a camel train to tote it all back with him?"

"Hmm! Probably one week to pack things up and send it by sea mail, then he'll get word on his flight home shortly after that. This, by the way, is designed to give your team enough time to prepare your deliberations on the project you've just completed, and very successfully too."

Ben, when told of this news was sad to find that the 'team' was to be split up.

"Actually Ben, you and Crabbe are required here in Canada to provide certain evidence which will be needed in a very long and expensive law suit instigated by none other than Pritchard, backed by a wealth of high calibre lawyers." Clutterbuck informed them

"Hah! Just as I thought! Just wait until I get my hands around his scrawny neck." John vowed, pretending to wring a chicken's neck.

"Actually, from the drawings he provided for examination as proof of 'patency' there is nothing in them to touch your designs, drawings, or the various innovations this ship is carrying and I mean from the keel right up to the funnel. So calm down and let's get back to the business of you being accepted within the Brethren of the ISDM. Besides, Fergus McPhee's just seen off the last of the Whateley saga for good now, and is looking forward to you taking over the mantle from him."

"Hang on now! Ben and his father Ken here are much better placed than me to do such a thing. I mean, I'm just a Marine Engineer trying to earn his salt."

"You will be needed at the college to fill in the vacuum Whateley and his cronies have left, so apart from having it all to do when you come back, you've only just begun being a so-called Chief Engineer and Ship's designer, John Grey."

John groaned at the thought and muttered he wished he'd stayed in the lowly ranks of even a 3rd engineer to enjoy the freedom such as Aussie Clarke had been enjoying for a while now.

"You can stop that right now John Grey! What would Larter and Sinclair say if they heard you now?" Crabbe admonished sharply, John looked around at the Ford's, and Crabbe, before he suddenly realised he had only 1 more week in their company before yet another close circle of friends was broken up again for him.

"Aye, suppose you're right. Let's get ashore and paint the town any damn colour we want." John sighed.

"That's the spirit John!" Crabbe said, patting John's shoulder gently.

Chapter XXXV

Wrap Up

The ship was alongside the jetty having the final 'little touches' added to her, with various work parties coming and going adding to the hustle and bustle of her first proper voyage.

John, was looking over the ship from the jetty marvelled on how she looked, and felt a great pride in the knowledge he had actually 'managed' the build, when Crabbe arrived alongside him.

"There you are John. We've just sent the last bundle of copied drawings off by rail, so all we will need is for you to take charge of the master blue-print, which Ben is wrapping up for you. We've got Ward coming to visit us shortly, and I'm hoping you'll be there if only to say goodbye."

"Hello Colin! Yes, I'm on my way. I was just taking a last close-up look of her realising what we have achieved. I don't know about you and Ben let alone Ken, but I'm still a bit awestruck over it all."

"You're right there!" Crabbe chuckled, then added

"Let's enjoy this one as maybe the next one might be an anticlimax or antidote for it. The press have already been going wild about the ship, which could mean the winning frame against that poxy bastard Pritchard."

"Amen to all that. Anyway, what's Ward visiting us for?"

"He's gone and got himself into another big strike, and wants me to 'lend' him a crew or two. At least that's what his phone call was about yesterday."

"If I remember rightly, we've had this discussion before, with the idea for you to take over his shipping business, temporarily of course, and for you to claim certain, er, 'royalties' or whatever you people call it. Either way, Colin, you're in a win win situation, especially as you're part of a new up-and-coming Shipbuilding empire with a solid and reliable workforce to back any decision you care to make."

245

Crabbe looked at John for a moment, then suddenly realising what he said was the truth smiled, rubbing his hands together.

"Come to mention it John, I can feel the cash in my hands already." he concluded, as they both walked through the dockyard and into the main office building.

"Mr Gleave! When Mr Ward arrives in his seaplane, be kind enough to transfer him to the pontoon and escort him here. Crabbe said cheerfully.

"On my way Captain. By the way, I've just had a call from a Mr Simmonds from the inspection team. He says he'll be making a two day visit as of this Saturday morning and would we make suitable arrangements for him."

"I wonder what he wants? Okay, that's fine. Make the arrangements and let's know the final details." Crabbe responded, and entered the large main 'meeting room' where all discussions and decisions were made from.

"Fred Gleave is now our Personnel Director, with one of his original team as Head Security Officer. The workforce respect him as he's their 'motivator' who would much rather give a man a 'kick up his arse' for his trouble than sack him. 'Kicking ass! as he calls it. He appears to be a kind of a reverse McCluskey, but it certainly works well and everybody is happy." Crabbe volunteered.

"Hmm! Maybe his bollocks are still troubling him since I 'knackered' him so to speak, but he was a bloody good Marine in his days. Good luck to the man, I say!" John said quietly watching Gleave leave the building in great bounding steps.

"Good afternoon Mr Ward, have yourself and your negotiating team sit down, relax and have a coffee if you wish." Crabbe invited cordially.

John was sitting at the large oak table with the Ford's and now Gleave, who represented the 'Board of Governors' for the new Shipyard.

Nodding to them in recognition, Ward took off his coat and accepted a hot cup of coffee from Gleave.

"Between us, we've come a long way and crossed many a broken dam, so to speak Ward, and you know we're here to help out as and when we can, despite you being one of my shipping competitors. What is it you wish to discuss in person for us all to be here?" Crabbe asked politely, looking around at the men who accompanied Ward, some of whom he had met before.

"As I mentioned in my phone call, the Unionist movement has blacklisted my ships, stopping me from entering or leaving my own docks and jetties all the way down to Montreal. None of my crew are willing to cross their picket lines and I've only got a few more weeks to get my ships in position to transport the annual grain harvest across to Halifax. All of which leaves me with just one ship, the *Caroline*, who is still manned by your crew members and yet to be handed over to me. Whilst I appreciate the *Caroline* has been a wonder to behold, it's not enough for me to survive and honour my contractual agreements. That's my starting point." Ward stated.

"If I remember correctly Ward, we had this discussion some time ago, and the reason why I delayed in transferring the ship to you was that had I done so, it too would have been targeted and strike bound. Your affairs with the Union appears to be a backlash from the Whateley scandal whereby he had total control of all local dock unions on both sides of the borders, so they are trying to get a similar sort of a deal like they had with him. We on the other hand have an ace up our sleeve, a man who by his own hard work has managed to steer our affairs away from the spectre of unionism, allowing us to operate freely and at will without fear of any such shenanigans from them. We have no intention of interfering with your protracted union problems save to say that our own man here Fred Gleave, is a former top Regional Negotiator whom you might wish to come to some sort of agreement with to sort your problems out, but we must concentrate solely on the good health of not only your company but the rest of the shipping companies operating these lakes. Before I continue maybe Mr Gleave here would wish to open up the subject for us to see just what we can or cannot help you with." Crabbe stated, then nodded to Gleave for him to have his say.

Gleave listened carefully for several minutes before giving his initial appraisal of the situation, while the rest of the management teams took detailed notes on everything they said.

Once Ward had agreed with Gleave's assessment of the situation it was clear to Crabbe and certainly the rest of both management teams they would open a set of lasting commitments which would not only benefit Gleave but more importantly Ward, whose other much more lucrative ventures ashore would now come good.

Thus an hour of horse trading came about, with Ward and his team agreeing to most of what was, on the face of it, a complete takeover of Ward's fleet by Crabbe, in exchange of a mutual cartel price arrangement whereby both have equal shares of the proceeds.

During this discussion, John was half listening and half deep in thought about his imminent departure. The affairs of Crabbe, Ward and the management teams were for them to sort out, not him. Despite the glorious launch of a fine vessel under such extreme conditions, he was secretly thankful to be able to leave all that grief and hard work behind.

'*After all, I'm only a Marine engineer!*' he thought.

Ben Ford saw the bored look on John's face and requested they had a refreshment break before they wrapped things up for the legal team to take over. This was accepted gratefully by all as it had been a torrid bout of deep bargaining and trading between them before they all felt comfortable with what was being proposed or other ideas being put on offer.

Crabbe came over to John and asked his opinion of the dealings so far, hoping for some sort of a response from him he had not otherwise offered as was his usual nature.

"Colin, you really don't need me to hold your hand anymore than I need yours, and as you know I've still got the small matter

248

of returning to the college to present our project for our 'graduation' if you like, despite the proof of the pudding was in our successful launch of the *Caroline*. All I can think of is, Fred Gleave should make himself known over in the Ward camp, and Ward must inform the strikers he has now sold his shipping concern, so all of them are now redundant without any compensation. After that two things could happen. 1. The workforce will realise the error of their ways, turn on their union bosses and crucify them for getting them into such a pickle, when they find out why the union bosses will get their strike pay and not the men, they will try negotiate an honourable return to work. In which case, Ward will refuse point blank due to the constant unionist actions perpetrated against him, pointing the blame directly at the union bosses who have conducted such matters for the past several years, and that he will be glad to get shot of them all. 2. If given his head for just one more time in the world of unionism, Fred Gleave may persuade a large part of the workers to join us here in Port Arthur thus giving you the crew to man the, er, surplus ships you're just about to acquire. You are in a win-win situation whereby you've doubled your fleet and in the process are about to double your wealth from the trade that will be conducted. Ward is also in a win-win situation as he will have the new freedom of concentrating on his more lucrative mining businesses which will make him a wealthier man he thought he would be in the shipping business.

In other words dear friend, you'll have filled the vacuum of which Whately and his cronies have left, and so you should spread the good word about what you have now built up here in this part of the world." John said quietly and at length, while Crabbe smiled at the truth of what he heard.

The meeting had re-convened for a further hour until everybody was in accord about what was to take place, and with everybody congratulating each other on such a good result. In short, everybody had won despite the outcome on what was about to happen.

Ward and his team were escorted back to their seaplane by Gleave, while the rest drew up a swift conclusion on the state of play, which was short and sweet, and to the tune of 'Happy days are here again'.

"Speaking of which, according to Fergus's latest letter I get to meet up with my old Chief Happy Day again. Maybe with luck I can also meet up with one of my old skippers Joe Tomlinson, who knows. But from what Fergus is saying, once we've been given our final '10', you two will be able to command the respect due you and endorse yourselves as top 'International Shipbuilders'." John said happily as Crabbe and the Ford's smiled and clapping their hands in delight.

"In that case, we'll have trial run on a bubbly bash to celebrate before you go John. We'll have it in big Mac's place say on Thursday." Crabbe said with delight.

"Yes! When you give us the word, we'll give the dockyard workers the day off and help them to celebrate in style at the good news, for if it wasn't for them all this would not have happened." Ben Ford admitted with a big grin.

"No doubt our Mr Gleave will echo these sentiments when he comes back, so for now gentlemen, we've just wrapped up our big business for today but tomorrow we've got a second round with the visit of Mr Simmonds and his tribe. The prospect there is for us to get the go ahead to build a proper builders yard with full launch facilities and a fitting out yard, all to be built on the off shore island so as not to spoil the natural habitat, according to our Mr Morris that is." Crabbe concluded, as them all left the office.

The final day for John's stay had arrived, he was feeling sad at the loss of yet another good set of friends, but needed to take a walk along the shore line to enjoy the cool breeze coming off the lake which helped clear his foggy brain from the effects of his farewell party last night. Deciding to have just one more walk around the 'launch pad' as his personal farewell to the place and to get himself ready for the long flight back to Southampton, he walked through the wrought iron gates of the dockyard making his way to the main office when a burly man with two large Alsatian dogs straining at their leashes appeared from the back of some some trees and confronted him.

"Just where do you think you're going pal! Stand still or I'll set the dogs onto you." came the rough challenge.

John stood still and waited until he could see his would-be assailants, when the 2 dogs started to snap at his legs and arms.

"If you don't get these dogs off me I'll ruddy kill them then bloody well kill you." John snarled.

"Oh! We've got a wise boy here! Who are you and what are you doing entering these premises?"

"I don't know who the hell you are but you mister are sacked. If you haven't already recognised me by now then you obviously aren't doing your job properly unable to recognise a friend from a foe." John snarled and kicking one of the dogs full on its face sent it yelping away from him, before doing the same to the other dog.

"Not only are you an intruder but you've just damaged company property. It looks as if you need a lesson pal." the man grunted, swinging a large pick handle at him.

John simply dodged out of the way, grabbed hold of the man's arm and threw him judo style some feet away from him before snatching the weapon off his attacker and clubbing him mercilessly. For each hit he made, he spelt out one letter of his name to complete it by announcing it spelt John Grey. Then told him he was the Chief Engineer and the Senior Manager of the yard.

If it wasn't for one of the Security Inspectors on his rounds coming across this fracas, John would have carried on hitting this now unconscious man.

"Stop Chief! I think he's had enough, better give me the weapon now, he won't be needing it for a while." the new arrival said quietly, taking it firmly yet gently from John, who although was not quite out of puff was glad to have been stopped anyway.

"That man is to be sacked. Get him off the yard this minute and take his mutts with him as I don't want to see his face in this yard ever again, especially as everybody knows me by sight and in daylight too." John replied angrily.

"Whatever you say Chief, but I'll have to report this incident it to our Head of Security, and have the man put into the sickbay before he is sent home."

John turned to look at his victim who had just recovered consciousness and told him that it was his duty to familiarise himself with all top personnel who own and run the yard, therefore he had failed in that duty and sacked because of it.

"Point taken Chief! Unfortunately this man only started two days ago and had already intercepted 3 men up to no good skulking around the yard. Maybe he thought you was one of them."

"As I've said. He should have been given a couple of days to get to know who his employers are and who uses these gates on a regular basis. Only that way will he'll know the goodies from the baddies before shooting first then asking questions later."

The Security Officer helped the beaten man onto his feet and told him to go back into the guard house to get first aid from the gate keeper then wait until he returned.

"If you're okay and happy to continue with your walk around then I'll see you'll not be bothered again."

"Actually Officer, this was supposed to be a quiet little walk and my last site seeing visit around the yard as I'm due to fly back to the UK in a few hours time. In view of the impromptu exercise I went through disabling my attacker, tell him he can keep his job as my going away present, but always remember who he tried to, shall we say, arrest for trespassing and up to no good. Knowing who your friends are first before tackling the foe!" John advised with a smile then turned around and went back from where he came.

Crabbe, the Ford's and Gleave, along with several other top personnel managers had gathered together, including Mackintosh with some of this men all standing in front of a large gathering of dockyard mateys who were shouting good wishes and farewells to John, walking slowly towards the pontoon jetty where a small sea-plane waited to take him on board. He was surprised to see Laura standing in among the dockyard crowd, weeping as she stood close to and held onto a very large man with a bandaged arm and a plaster on his chin.

'Sorry Laura! Maybe he'll know better next time, but good luck to you both!' he thought.

"Well John! It's time to say goodbye. Have a good trip home again and let us know you arrived safely. We here will always remember you and hope you will maybe come back to us one day." Colin said softly.

"Yes, tell Fergus he owes us a big shiny 10." Ben Ford said with a smile then started the round of hand shakings and slaps of farewell from each of his well wishers.

John went over to who was obviously Laura's boyfriend and said, "My apologies for your injuries young man, I know you were only doing your duty. You get to keep your job as my farewell present. So shake hands with me and have no hard feelings." John whispered, holding out his hand in a gesture of peace.

"As you rightly pointed out, I should have known who you were. My Laura here will see me better again." He said with a wisp of a smile and shook John's hand.

"Laura. Remember what I told you the last time we met up about Helena and Princess Telani. According to them, you will have five children and are to name them just as I have said. You'll do this for both our sakes. Your fiancé, soon to be your husband must not know of this until your dotage. Until then I wish you both well." John whispered in her ear.

Laura wiped the tears from her face with a hankie and gave John a peck on his cheek.

"Thank you for everything you've taught me, and told me about my life. Good bye John Grey." she whispered, with more tears streaming down her cheeks, John dabbed them away with his own clean hankie then left to rejoin the rest.

John made Crabbe his last person to say farewell to and came back to him.

"Take care Colin, maybe we'll see each other back in the ISDM some day but you've got your empire to run now, so keep well my friend of many a 'Sand wich'." John whispered sadly.

Crabbe understood that phrase and nodded with equal sadness to him before John waving his arm to everybody as his last gesture, disappeared into the sea-plane.

John looked out the little porthole to see a rapidly widening gap between him and the pontoon and realised now the aircraft was aloft it was the start of a very long trip back to the delights of the strike-torn inhabitants of the U.K.

'Nothing new there either, I suppose.' he thought as a pretty stewardess came and offered him a refreshment drink.

Chapter XXXVI

Haggis Yaffler

The college seemed almost deserted when John finally arrived exhausted and feeling parched, longing for the decent cool drink he knew he'd get from the bar.

Dumping his baggage in the luggage room at the side of the large foyer, he made his way to the dimly lit lounge where just a couple of people were sitting alone in their own elbow space.

"Hmm, I forgot! It's the holiday weekend with nearly everybody away. Oh well, more ale for me then!" he whispered as he approached the bar.

"Double whiskey, a large cigar of Rhodesian origin and a glass of water please." He quietly asked the barman who looked almost half asleep.

The barman either didn't hear him or chose to ignore him in the hope he'd just go away.

John repeated his order once more, still getting no response he went round the bar, opened up the flap to gain access to the bar and grabbing hold of the man by his lapels literally shouted his order into his face.

The barman managed to disengage himself from John's grip told him that students were not allowed in this bar and he should go round to the tavern at the back.

Before John could say or do anything he felt a pair of arms wrap around him holding him in a vice like grip.

"You have been warned not to come in here. Now get out of here before I get the security man to throw you out." a man with garlic breath said in a French accent.

John recognised this voice as the Maitre d', who, although seeming a foppish man had a good strength in his arms.

John let his weight drop down to the floor so he could get free, then turning round and standing he head butted the man on his large protruding nose.

"You've obviously forgotten your manners you pretentious Frog. You should know who I am as my name appears on the weekend arrival guest list. I'm Chief Engineer Grey. I've just returned from Canada with my project report and demand full respect and courtesy from not only you but everybody else in this room. Now unless you wish to wear that broomstick you're holding right up your ass, get me the order I requested not once but 3 times. So that's 3 orders if you please." John snorted then walked slowly to the other side of the bar to receive it.

The Maitre d' held his bloodstained hankie over his obviously broken nose and told the lazy barman to serve John his drinks, which he did putting each one slowly onto a tray.

John took his drinks and cigars, as the barman held out his hand for payment.

"Ask the Maitre d', he's paying for it! He already owes me a few drinks from last time!" John said calmly then walked away from the bar with the Maitre d' stuttering and bewailing his fate.

The quietness of the bar was almost depressing to John as he just sat reminiscing about the last time he was here, and the fun he had had with his now absent friends.

He decided that once he'd finished his cigars he'd go and see the porter to find which room he was to occupy, when a large man accompanied by a well-dressed woman walked slowly into the bar, then made their way to sit on a large leather sofa with the man signalling to the barman for service.

"Some hopes pal!" John said quietly as he stubbed the last of his remaining cigar into the ornate glass ashtray,

Either the barman was still acting stupid or deaf, because the man shouted loudly in a thick Scottish accent, which John instantly recognised.

"Oy, you big Haggis yaffler! Get yer own!" John shouted over, then went over to greet them.

"Is that you John? When did you arrive back to plague the place?" McPhee said aloud gleefully, as the two men met and gave a 'man's back slapping welcoming embrace.

256

John looked at the woman and recognising her bent down and pecked her on both cheeks.

"Hello Claire! It's good to see you both alive and well. Has he been behaving himself?" he asked with a nod towards McPhee.

"Aye! He's good as gold. Like me, he misses the Canadian way of life we knew when we first met. He says he wants to go back but deep down inside he's saying it just for me, the big soft lummox." she said quietly.

"I've just come back to face the music so to speak. But all I've got so far is a stupid pretend Froggie trying to throw me out of the bar. And here's me thinking decorum is the pre-requisite around here."

"So that's what the noise was when we came in. Come to think of it, Fergus told me about the first time you met the Maitre d' or Jon as he likes to be called, in fact he's really Onre Le Bonk from Guernsey, but because of his very large nose, everybody calls him 'Enery the Conk."

"Well I'll be! From now on it'll be 'Enery he'll get from me especially in front of the posh visitors who come and go." John smiled then chuckled at the devilment he'd be causing.

"So then John! What're you going to do with yourself until this holiday period finishes a week this Monday?" McPhee asked jovially as they all sipped their drinks which had finally arrived.

"If I'd known I was coming back to a holiday period here, I would have much preferred to stay with Big Mac, Colin, and the lads, let alone the lasses from the hotel. But my orders were to report here today for further briefing and instructions from Bill Clutterbuck."

"Actually, I'm the only senior staff member here doing duty over this weekend, which's why I sent for Claire to come and stay with me in the main lodgings until then. Bill Clutterbuck is still on his bike doing the rounds of the other projects due to be completed by the end of this month. So as far as I'm concerned, and as your Project Manager you can stand down until I give you the word to pipe up again. Incidentally, here's your room key, it's the same room you stayed in last time you were here." McPhee said as taking out a key from his coat pocket he slid it across the table to him.

John looked at it for a moment before he pocketed it and said, "Well it's not exactly big Mac's place but at least I've got the room all to myself this time."

Claire looking at John smiled knowingly at what he was referring to, then told him he was back in Blighty now, where according to the posh people, sex is what the coal is carried in.

They talked for quite a while until the night porter came and reminded them they had homes to go to so he could lock up.

"It's okay Jones! I'll lock up. Just go get your head down as there's a load of guests arriving early in the morning."

"Thank you Mr McPhee! Good night then!" Jones said gratefully and beat a hasty retreat in case McPhee changed his mind.

"Who's coming to visit this time Fergus? Yet another back-slapping bunch slurping all the best wine and eating us all out of house and home?"

"Now that would be telling the state secrets. Walls have ears, loose lips sink ships and anything else which springs to mind young John. You'll find out soon enough, but make sure you have an early breakfast or there'll be none left if I know this bunch of gannets." McPhee yawned then looked at his watch.

"It's his way of telling me he wants to get to bed again." Claire giggled, stroking McPhee's knee suggestively.

John smiled and told them he had had an extraordinarily tedious flight to London airport then down to here, he would be glad to get turned in for the first decent sleep since leaving Port Arthur nearly 2 days ago.

"Well good night John! After breakfast, come and see me in my study around the 10 o'clock mark if you would." McPhee said, standing up to assist Claire to her feet.

"Yes John good night! See you sometime in the morning!" she whispered, pecking his cheek and he left McPhee to lock up and secure the bar for the night, as the barman had long since gone home.

* * *

John entered his sumptuous room taking a moment to look around and re-familiarise himself with the place, then decided to take a long lazy shower before getting turned into the inviting bed in the middle of the room.

He had his shower, slipped into his blue and gold dressing gown which his Singapore girl May Kwan had given him, and deciding to take a late night cap from the 'courtesy bar' went over to the small veranda of the room to take in the night air.

On opening the curtains to step out onto the veranda he heard a loud commotion which sounded as if there was a party on the go, coming from the room below him. Whilst this did not phase him, there was one voice amongst the crowd he heard and eventually recognised. It was Pritchard's, who was crowing about his coup against a former project team member and how his Uncle, who was the Permanent 2nd Sea Lord was going to proclaim his project the winner for the year, and his position as such would be able to grant him a top position on the Board of the Grand Masters of the college. All of which received lots of cheers and hurrahs, but the muttering and oaths coming from John was unheard, who decided that he would keep a low profile until such times he met up with this thief and obvious braggart.

John, arrived late into the dining room to take his breakfast was told there was nothing left except a few slices of toast and maybe some coffee dregs, on account the German project team had already dined half an hour ago, and were now about to take over the indoor swimming pool.

"Nothing to worry about steward, my favourite breakfast is a couple of buttered rolls with slices of bacon or ham, and a big mug of tea, can do?" he said cheerfully.

"Hmm! Yes, that's okay by me, and thanks for being sympathetic towards our dilemma, as there're other guests still to arrive, notably Mr Pritchard and his distinguished guests." the steward responded with a smile and nod before leaving him.

"Er, before you go, I'll have my breakfast out in the

conservatory if you don't mind. I need a bit of fresh air to enjoy my breakfast before the bulls start to come in, as this place will be smelling full of bullshit when they arrive." John called, receiving a further nod from the steward.

His leisurely after breakfast cigarette was interrupted by McPhee and Claire who came and sat down by him only to be served with fresh hot steaming cups of coffee.

"Managed to get in before the gannets Fergus, or could it be contraband stuff from Brazil, judging by the lovely aroma?" John asked with a smile.

"I thought it was only hungry lumberjacks who could eat everything they saw on the galley range before they left to go up country again, but these Germans sure are a close run second to them. I had advised the duty chef to keep something back for the rest of the guests else they'd never want to come back again." Claire laughed, holding up her cup of coffee in a little toast to him.

"What's on the agenda Fergus, or are you keeping me waiting until I report to you in your office?"

"Change of plan. We've got a staff car on loan to us for the day so we decided to go touring up around the South Downs as far as Hambledon where the first ever cricket match was played. I understand there're plenty of local inns to keep us fed and watered so we won't be back until around tea time. You by the way are detailed off to keep us company, and as the word has it Pritchard is now on campus, I don't want you mixing with him just yet." McPhee said with a frown.

"Why is Pritchard here on campus? His famous Uncle only lives a few sea-miles from here, so why here and not there?" John asked with feigned surprise.

"Apparently, he's come here to book up the test-tank for the entire week so he can give his final demo with his latest ship model before it is taken to the test lake. That means none of the other project teams will get a look in until it's too late for them to get ready for the annual project showdown. The one with the best model and demo gets the first prize and a place on the

Management board for a period of 5 years. As one of the Faculty Head for this campus I'm already 'staff' so nobody can usurp my place despite any backing the project teams can muster." McPhee admitted with a glum face.

"He has, has he? I mean booked up the test tank? We'll certainly see about that! John exclaimed.

"If you'll excuse me for a moment, I've got to see a man about some bullshit about to be spread around here. Kindly wait here until I return Fergus." John added, leaving swiftly towards the swimming pool area.

"Good morning gentlemen! My name is John Grey, a fellow student just like yourselves, and I too am here to find out the results of my project for the grand finale next week." John announced evenly, as he came up to a six strong group of young German ship designers.

"Goot morgan mein Herr! Vat is it you vish from us?" one of the men asked as he stood up to meet John.

"We are all competitors aiming to gain the accolade we have worked long and hard for. For me it's been several years, with my last year conducting a full ship build. But I am informing you discreetly there is a person in charge of a project team who is about to requisition the test tank for the whole week which will leave us no time to set our own up for the final 'lake' test." John said evenly and with a solemn look on his face.

Another tall, blond and muscular man stood up and asked just what he was implying.

"Quite simply! There is a project team headed by a person by the name of Pritchard who is planning to start his trials as of 1200 today and for the rest of the week, so nobody else can use it. His Uncle is one of the Faculty Heads of the college, also the main judge conducting the lake trials. All of which means there could be nepotism, favouritism, or just plain double-dealings to fix it up for Pritchard."

"The schvine! I'll double-deal him." another member swore and went to get up, but was stopped by another of the team.

261

"How come you, as one of our competitors came to warn us?" the blond man asked with a sideways glance, as if he could feel a catch in what John had told them.

"I told you my name is John Grey, a Chief Engineer Officer. This man Pritchard was part of my project team until he stole my initial concept design drawing and patented it in his own name. It's his version of my model he's hoping to use to steal the very prize we've all worked towards. I don't really have to take part in these tests and trials as my model has already been built and launched, and is now sailing around the Canadian Lakes full of cargo. In other words gentlemen, I've nothing to lose except at the Patency Court of Enquiry as to just who really is the real patent owner. You have been warned, and I would suggest you warn all the others quietly, so it turns out he doesn't get to see even one wave in the test tank."

"John Grey? I've heard of that name. Aren't you the one with a ship which was built in an ice dock?" the eldest member of the group asked with wonder.

"Yes! So gentlemen, I'll leave you all now to think over what I've just said, but you've got about 1 hour to get organised. Don't forget to inform all the others and keep it quiet from Pritchard. My Project Manager is a very old friend of mine called Mr McPhee and is the duty manager for the weekend. We're about to go off for the day, so do your stuff as Pritchard won't be able to complain to McPhee until after the event, so to speak." John concluded.

The eldest of the group finally stood and coming up to John, thanked him for his typical 'British fair play' attitude then shook his hand as John left them.

John returned to the company of the McPhees with Claire noticing how pleased he seemed to be and asked him just what he was up to.

"Me? I'm just a student on campus dear Claire. What could I do to upset the decorum of this august place?" John asked innocently.

McPhee spotted the 'playing dull and innocence act' and came up with a reasonable guess as to what and where John had been and done.

"Let's put it this way dear Fergus, I'm saying nothing until we get back. That way you too will be innocent of any or all charges levelled against you by whoever is wearing a cap that fits."

Claire laughed and told them they were naughty boys up to no good, and anyway it was time they departed before all hell broke loose.

They climbed into their car and drove off into the area of the New Forest as the start of their day, with John looking back at the rapidly disappearing college, fancying he was hearing the moans, wails and complaints from the precocious brat Pritchard.

John and the McPhees arrived back into the campus around supper time, knowing full well the German team would have already cleared the larder once more, so they went into the lounge bar to have a quiet drink until it was their time at the 'trough'. The lounge was starting to fill up with several arrivals of new sets of project teams.

No sooner had they sat down, when there was a shout and a rush of irate students led by Pritchard came into the bar and directly to their table.

"You're supposed to be the duty Master! You're supposed to stay on campus to make sure all is well and not swan off apparently into the country side." screamed the irate Pritchard, shoving his red snarling face into McPhees.

McPhee simply gave him an uppercut which laid Pritchard out unconscious on the floor, then standing asked the rest of the angry project team if they wanted the same.

"I am the duty Manager and as such I represent the Faculty. None of us will ever be subjected to any of this threatening behaviour no matter who the student is, let alone use that tone of voice to me." McPhee looked belligerently around him challenging any further outburst from the other 3 members of the team.

John stood up, grabbed the soda siphon from the table to squirt it full into Pritchard's face which brought him back to life, coughing and spluttering, yet still swearing and cursing.

Reaching down, McPhee grabbed Pritchard by the scruff of the neck, threw him onto a chair and asked him in a quiet voice just what his problem was to come in here upsetting everybody. Pritchard took a few moments to gather himself together before he let rip telling everybody he had been denied the use of the test tank, and as it had been booked for the rest of the week, it was not fair he should be left out of taking turns in using it.

McPhee put a few questions to the other three members of Pritchard's team, who either declined to answer or just didn't know the answers as Pritchard was their project leader and they did what he told them to do.

John sat there quietly with a deadpan face, secretly laughing to himself at what he, after all, had instigated then asked in a quiet spoken voice one of his simple double-edged questions he was famous for.

Seeing John facing him, Pritchard went a distinctly pale colour and started to cough nervously.

"What is it so special about your model you need it testing given the fact you already know it works? Surely the final lake test will prove your ingenious and unique design to be the winner, so what had you in mind when you planned to book up the test tank for the entire week just for yourself? And I ask you this from information gained from a reliable source."

"What do you mean book the tank up all week? What are you insinuating Grey? Why are you here in the first place? How come your project has finished before mine? What...what..." Pritchard started to ask in a querulous voice but was cut short by McPhee.

"You had a party in your room last night which is against the campus decorum rules. Not only that, you and your team were heard to brag you were going to fix it so nobody else would have the chance of using the test tank during this final week. What do you say about this?" McPhee asked gruffly.

264

"I know nothing of what you say. Everybody is entitled to, in fact required to conduct 3 test runs in the tank that I know of. So far everybody has booked up leaving me no room to do my tests, and that's not fair." Pritchard moaned.

"But why test it in the first place when you already know your Uncle has fixed it so you win the competition, albeit on a stolen concept and design?" John insisted which made Pritchard squirm even more.

The room had gone totally silent witnessing this scene, learning Pritchard was using unfair and illegal means to achieve the winning design in what was supposed to be an open and fair competition to project teams coming from all corners of the world.

The other members of Pritchard's team were looking at their feet wishing a hole would open up and swallow them to take them away from such an embarrassing situation.

Pritchard didn't answer John's question but must have decided it was time he took the initiative so attacked John with a mirror image of what John had asked.

"Stolen what Grey? Do you mean the concept design you stole off me? The very one I'd already submitted into the patency courts? It's you who is the thief Grey, and I intend proving it with my drawings and the performance of my model if I can get it tested. If you're not aware of it Grey, I've already started court proceedings against you for your theft of my design. My Uncle will see to it you'll never build any kind of ship bigger than the rowing boat." Pritchard bluffed, then got up and walked away from this electrifying scene, taking his team with him.

The room remained silent for several moments until well after Pritchard had left, then everybody began start cheering and clapping for reasons John had no clue about.

McPhee stood up and advised them all as the floor show had now finished they should be quiet and just enjoy the rest of the evening.

The Maitre d' came over to their table with a tray of food and drinks then laid it down for them to help themselves.

"Sorry abut your nose Enery! You look quite different now, dare I say more handsome. Thanks for the drinks, but who ordered them?" John asked

"Complements from the German and Danish teams over in the other corner. It appears you hit the right spot, and I don't mean my ruddy nose either. Now the whole campus is alerted to one big showdown especially between you and Pritchard." he replied.

McPhee raised a glass and toasted the German and Danish groups in thanks for them, before turning to Claire.

"We believe in fair play in this country dear lass. Any man not doing so will get his come-uppance warning him not to try anything like it ever again. I mean it's 'just not cricket' so the Sassenachs keep saying. We in the north would simply give him a 'Glasgow kiss'!" he said in his broad Scottish accent, showing Claire his knuckled fist.

"Oh! Then what would you do to us 'poor wee lasses' as you call us dear Fergus?" Claire asked, fluttering her eyelashes at him which made him chuckle, but didn't answer.

John had just finished his drink and put the glass down with a thump.

"Bloody hell Fergus! Pritchard still doesn't know about the *Caroline*, or her sister ship about to be built. But how can this be when our German friends and other project teams already know about them?"

"Ah now that would be telling. Let's put it this way. I'm your Ace in the pack yes? Well I've managed to keep his project team completely in the dark by ordering them not to look over other project teams shoulders and cheat, just in case what they're copying could amount to plagiarism. Pritchard thinks he's got away with stealing your designs but little does he know his designs could not , nor would not work under normal shipping conditions, and that's just what we've seen from his project notes so far. Bill Clutterbuck and the other Faculty heads have examined your work against his and find yours is of a much

266

higher standard of design and ship innovation. Now just maybe you'll understand my stance against you out in Canada dear boy."

"Hmm! Will I have to be around for the court proceedings or can I stay on to form yet another project team for the next round of ship designs?"

McPhee gave a sigh then told him he was a glutton for punishment and should be grateful he was still able to come here given the aftermath of Whateley and his gang, and the revelation as to what they were lining up to perpetrate against me let alone the college."

John thought hard on what Fergus had said and managed to recall Whateley's words on how he was going to do mischief against Fergus and the rest of the ISDM Corporation.

"Yes Fergus! I remember what he said, and I for one am glad our friend Colin Crabbe had the balls to do what he did. The rest is history now and the reason why I'm entitled to return to find out the results."

Claire looked at the large brass clock on the wall and declared it was time for some shut-eye, so Fergus should get the bar cleared then up to bed.

McPhee started to say that he was still the duty manager until John shushed him up.

"You two carry on, I'll secure to the perimeters as Fred Gleave would say. I've still got a few bevvies to quaff before I get turned in, besides I want a quick word with the German team captain. He seems to be a good sort so I don't suppose WW3 will start up tonight." he said quietly and with a grin as they got up and left the bar.

"That's right you dear old haggis yaffler! Claire will help you make up for all your lost time as a bachelor." he muttered, watching them leave.

267

Chapter XXXVII

The Project Tests and Results

The week of trials and testing of each project teams' various ship designs or innovations was a very trying time for them all. Not one team escaped without finding some problem or other needing to be solved in time for their models to be ready for the big day, except for John who was anxiously waiting the delivery of his model.

All the test models had their plans and blue-prints kept under lock and key and only accessed by their team leader, as the stigma of plagiarism or the stealing of designs were uppermost in people's minds and accusing Pritchard as the instigator of such recent affairs.

It was late in the week when John's had finally turned up from Canada, and he kept it under wraps until the final day. Pritchard sneered at John every time they came across one another, with Pritchard boasting to everybody how his idea and his design would win the competition. All of which was wearing very thin on the patience and tolerance of the rest of the project teams, so much so Pritchard was taken to one side by his Uncle who told him in no uncertain terms to shut up, and keep his head down, now everybody had learned of their plot to fix the result in Pritchard's favour.

All the faculty heads, Project Managers, guest examiners from various international ship-building yards, and the project teams were now gathered together in what was a typical nerve wracking examination period for college students coming from all around the world.

One by one, each master blueprint was put up onto a display board for the examiners to go over in minute detail in order to asses the model's performance in the tank tests. They interviewed each project team who were required to make a presentation or an introduction to their project.

That was stage one.

Stage two was the tank test to see if the model matched the design and other 'bench mark' tests done as the forerunner to the fun and games in the test lake, where the project team leaders got to either actually ride in the models, or have them in a radio remote control set-up to show off the model's true potential.

Stage three would be the marking of the design blue-prints and then judged accordingly.

Stage four would be the final voting between the judges as to which models or innovations were the best in the 'fleet' that year. Because of the pending court case Pritchard V Grey, both sets of drawings and models were under lock and key, and kept until last for their interviews making it a special 'head to head ' winner takes all contest between them.

The panel of judges for the interviews and presentations, was made up of 4 judges and 3 Project Managers, with Clutterbuck acting as the Moderator who had to remain silent and independent from the panel. The judges were from a different nationality to the presenter, and no Project Manager was allowed to mark their own teams.

John walked into the interview room to see the main blue-print of his model was pinned to a display board, with his model placed on a long table in front of the panel of judges.

Opening his brief case he produced several photographs, newspaper cuttings and a copy of the final test certificate from the Canadian Maritime Ministry.

He introduced himself and his project by explaining each facet of his model, his blueprint and his photographs.

"My model is of the recently launched *MV Caroline* which was passed fit for purpose and given her seaworthiness certificate which you see before you. My original design was to build a multi-fuel carrying tanker, but I was requested by a sponsor to build a bulk grain-carrier, so I had it built as a bulk multi-grain carrier instead. She was built on a launch pad half her length, and under Arctic conditions for nearly 4 months. From the photographs, you will see I had a special dry dock carved out of the iced up lake so I could complete her construction. Happily all was done before the ice dock melted, allowing her to float away under her own power.

The 'single castle' idea came from what you would call an 'Eureka' moment of inspiration, which I developed from scratch considering my original drawing was stolen, therefore giving me a fresh canvas to create my 'paintings'. The 'castle' as I call it is the superstructure aft which has the bridge, accommodation area and engine room, leaving nearly four fifths of the rest her length free to carry a much bigger cargo load, calculated to be at least 2,500 tonnes more than a three or even a two castle vessel, despite her having a double hull. She has her cargo holds built into different chambers with longitudinal and even transverse bulkheads not only to separate the different grains, but as an anti 'slosh' safety measure to prevent any loose cargo movement, and help keep the vessel in trim during heavy weather. Because she has a high freeboard and therefore subject to wind pressures, I've introduced two broadside manoeuvring motors on each end to thrust her off the dockside, or conversely, help her manoeuvre alongside without tug assistance. You will notice all her various tanks, such as the lub oil, fuel, and sanitary tank are contained below the cargo hold area.

She is powered by two diesel engines which operate electric motors to turn the propeller, and due to the engine room being aft just like a traditional tanker, she has a better power to weight ratio and the extra thrust to move the vessel. They also provide all the onboard electricity supply including an electric boiler to provide hot water as required at any one time. This by the way is done via cold water passing through heated coils to produce hot water on tap. Instead of the traditional goal post or derrick configuration, she has five electrically operated cranes on deck to gain access to the different areas of the cargo hold, and even auxiliary suction pumps to unload or load up the vessel with 'loose' cargo such as barley, or wheat. Her overall dimension cannot be much more than 600 by 90 feet, with a maximum draught of 30 feet, hence her virtual flat bottom, as she will be confined to the St Laurents Seaway and the Great Lake canal system, therefore locked in to that area of waterways. All of which are a good 4,000 miles from end to end, meaning the vessel could make a decent 8,000mile round trip voyage which would be comparable to any ocean going vessels." He explained smoothly and calmly.

The panel spent a good 15 minutes asking various technical and leading questions to which he replied in a straight-forward manner, before they summed the session up.

"It appears your new concept of ship design for vessels over 200ft, and the many new innovations we have not come across before, could set the trend for ships of the future. You've got a few, and pardon the pun, grey areas which we need clarifying. It will either need you to come before us again or for us to wait until after the results of your tank tests, but you will be given an opportunity to respond. Thank you for your good presentation , you may leave now but kindly leave your paper work behind so we can continue our deliberations, and you can prepare your model for the next stage." Clutterbuck said with a smile, escorting John to the door for him to leave.

On the morning of the second day, everybody held their breaths as they gathered round the long test tank, where their models lined up side by side, were given the exact same tests. Eventually only Pritchard's and Grey's models were left, but all the other teams had stayed behind to witness this 'grudge' match.

John carried his model into the test area, putting it onto a plinth for everybody to see before the model was committed to the tank, and so the technicians could wire it up to the monitoring panel, with Pritchard sneering at the puny effort of copying his own model.

They all gasped at the one castle design, and marvelled at the two little holes front and rear of the model which, under closer inspection, they found out were broadside manoeuvring motors. Pritchard's ship had the same one castle design, but seemed big and cumbersome compared to John's model, but both models were admired by the others for they looked magnificent sitting there in the water, with John's being slightly smaller than Pritchard's.

The models went down the entire length of the tank without a hitch where the technicians turned them round ready for a return run. Pritchard's model was way down at the stern with the bows almost out of the water, yet John's was almost horizontal giving a clean profile in the tank. As the waves were made bigger, Pritchard's model was rocking and rolling all over the place while John's looked as if the water was like a mill-pond.

For the second run, each model was half-filled with water to create a cargo load and to see how the ships would perform in the 'rough seas' of the tank. Pritchard's ship was lurching from side to side and when examined as to why via the sensors on board, the cargo was sloshing and slopping from side to side causing the model to almost capsize, yet John's model just sailed on without so much as a wobble.

It was patently obvious to the examination team that Pritchard's model didn't like being half-full, so on the final run they decided to fill it up to capacity with the view of stabilising the model. John's was also filled right up carry out the same test so there could be no hint of an unfair test on Pritchard.

The waves of the tank were made to create 'heavy seas' and a deep swell to see if the models would hold their own in such conditions.

Both models were only a third of the way down the tank when Pritchard's ship suddenly snapped in two to sink with the stern end falling away from the cargo end, whereas John's model sailed to the end and back again without any bother. John's model was then brought alongside a model jetty in the tank to demonstrate a further design development of the little side thruster motors on his model. This was very much a big surprise to the spectators when they realised this vessel did not need a tug to dock or undock.

On retrieving the two parts of Pritchard's broken model they discovered the stern end had sheared off in a neat break with the corresponding break showing on the bigger part of the model.

Everybody had gasped at the sight of the ship snapping into two parts but gawped even more when they were shown how the ship's bridge and superstructure had sheared clean off.

"To think if that had been real, there'd be no survivors from it" One judge commented aloud, which made all the other project students realise that had they sailed on one of Pritchard's ships of this design then they'd have drowned without anybody knowing what had happened to them.

Pritchard, even more than his project team, looked absolutely gutted at what they'd seen but even more so when they saw John's model still running up and down the tank without any bother.

McPhee took the two pieces of the ship and tried to put them back together again but handed them over to Pritchard.

"If you are the master planner and designer of this ship and have the gall to accuse Grey of stealing your designs then how come his model is still sailing around the tank, while yours is at the bottom of the ocean in bits?" He snarled.

"He must have altered them." Pritchard mumbled.

"How can he alter your design when you had the only drawing?" McPhee persisted.

"Must have been a sheer guess!"

"A shear guess just like your model, more like Pritchard?"

Everyone sensed just what McPhee was getting at and started to ask their own questions until Clutterbuck held his hand up to remind them all they were under the trials examination rules, which quelled the near uproar the other students were creating given the stick and sarcastic comments Pritchard had given them all week.

273

"Pritchard, you have one day to repair your model for the lake test. But given the magnitude of the failure in this safety tank, I suggest you either convert it into a radio controlled model or whoever gets to ride in it is fitted with a frog suit." Clutterbuck snarled, then declaring the trials for this tank were now over suggested the judges examined the tracers and other electronic data taken to find out effects each model was subject to. They were to give special attention to the differences in the performances between the last two models, and prepare the results for future references.

"I ask this of you so you can give a fair result even though you have witnessed the reality of each model's performance." Clutterbuck concluded, which signalled to everybody it was the end of the session and they all should wrap it in for the day and prepare for the next phase.

The lounge bar was full and fired up at what they had witnessed in the test tank, with everyone talking and nobody listening, until Pritchard and his team walked into the room.

There seemed to be a sharp intake of breath by everybody and the silence became deafening for a moment until one of the other project team leaders stood up and threw his beer into Pritchard's face, almost 'glassing' him in the process. The others were also given the same treatment before they hastily retraced their steps, with ashtrays and other objects hitting them as they left the bar.

John was sitting in a corner with the German team next to their team leader enjoying a drink with them, but had observed what transpired when the man spoke to him in perfect English.

"They turned themselves into the campus pariahs and have deserved that from day one. If it's one thing I've learned from you people, nobody likes a 'smart arse'. In his case a dumkopft, as his model was as much use as a lead zeppelin."

"This exam period is but a side-show of the real thing to come soon. He's taking me to court for stealing his ship concept and design. In fact, all he got was just the concept, with no clue as to how the ship was to be built amongst other things, despite him having the only master blue-print copy." John responded quietly.

"As an engineer like you Grey, I too have my pride in what I do and make certain that whatever machine I design must be for proper usage, and more besides."

"Yes Klein, I've noticed certain features on your model which intrigue me very much. I can understand a glass-bottomed boat but yours doesn't seem to have a bottom. Is that because your design is on a ship-launched submersible, or a cable laying device to match the hole in the vessel?"

"Actually, my prototype model has a plate over a hole, and operates something like the bomb doors on a plane. That was the one I was hoping to test, but this model seems to be holding its own. The submersible factor to either one is problematic because unless we're alongside using a heavy dockyard crane, we can't lift it off its cradle to do any hull repairs or whatever."

"Hmm! How heavy are your two submersibles?"

"The robot one is only 5 tonnes, the manned one around 18 tonnes, but why do you ask?"

"It's just a thought, but given your bomb door model then you might think of this!" John said, taking a pencil from his top pocket and fishing out one of his little note pads.

"Put a goal post type of steel girder each side of your pool running fore to aft. Then put a parallel set of girders athwartships to rest on top of the goal posts so they pass over the pool. Suggest you use maybe 9 X 9 inch girders. Put an electrically operated hoist onto both girders fitted with a set of 4 wheels either side of the girders for them to traverse along the cross members to reach both sides of the pool. Do your maths but each hoist's working load should be around 20 tonnes to give plenty of lift strength. Have a cradle placed on each side for their individual submersibles, so when you lift them out you can place them exactly onto them when you bring them back on board again. Obviously, once you've 'captured' the submersibles in the pool you can shut the bottom doors again to prevent any excess water coming into the compartment. I suggest that before you pump the pool out, you send a couple of divers down to pass a belly band under each end of the submersible to hook them up onto the hoists, but make sure your divers clear the pool before you hoist away. Have a heaving line attached to the submersible to prevent it swinging too much, should the ship be in rough waters. The controls of each hoist should be on the end of a 'wandering lead' for direct control as opposed to a push button control box welded to the bulkhead. That way you can control the lift and position of them as they're being hoisted. Simply reverse the procedure for launching them. Remember, before you open your 'bomb' doors you make sure you've got enough water 'ship side' to equalise the pressure 'outside'. This will ensure no excess water will enter your compartment to cause flooding." John explained, showing Klein his drawings.

Klein looked at the drawings for a moment then showed his team mates what John had just given him.

To a man, they nodded their heads then smiling at John and asked why he as a competitor was helping them out once more.
John looked around the table of inquisitive faces, each asking questions of their own, then he answered them in one go.

"It's quite easy gentlemen. Apart from Pritchard and his team, each one of us here are first and foremost engineers. Granted each of us hold different skills and fields of expertise, but if you cannot help out a fellow engineer in a time of need, no matter what colour his skin is or what country he hails from, then you'd be a disgrace to the entire brotherhood of engineers." he said with a smile and gave Klein a nod.

The team looked at each other for a moment perhaps to understand his speech in their own language, then as each one of them gave him a polite clap and a nod of their heads, he took it they all understood his message.

"We have got our project ship already under construction on the builder's blocks in Bremerhaven, and hope for it to be ready for launch soon. The reason why we're here is because we were hoping to pick the brains of the ISDMs management team to give us some of the answers to our problems which you've apparently provided in broad terms for us. Our project was paid for by the International Scientific Research Organisation based in Basle, Switzerland, who will be looking to make the ship's first voyage up into the Arctic circle. I'm telling you this as I'd like to have you in my Experimental team for that voyage, whatever the outcome of these competition trials." Klein said slowly with the rest of his team nodding their approval at what he said.

"Many thanks for your consideration Klein, and don't think I'm casting your invitation aside without a thought. I've worked extremely hard to fight my way up through the ranks of the marine engineering officers' promotional ladder to be able gain the right of entry into this college as a Project Manager. It really is a long story I will not bore you with, but if I'm successful here this week then I intend taking up this position. Maybe if things work out whereby you need help in the future from the Faculty heads of this college, I'll certainly keep your invite in mind. You have a team to work with but I'm on my own as my team is already at work over in the Great Lakes. So I must take my leave of you and get some details ready for tomorrow's big lake test. Tell your team I wish you all the best for tomorrow Klein." John said and rose to leave.

Klein stood up and shaking John's hand warmly returned the sentiment especially against that fraud Pritchard.

All the teams had been allocated their own pontoon at the side of the fair sized, yet shallow lake which was used to demonstrate and profile each model ship designed by the teams.

They had all been there very early to be able to use every precious second of the hour they were given to prepare their demo in front of the entire examination team, a battery of cameras and photographers who profile each model as it sailed along.

The main idea of such a test is to give the prospective captain of the future ship, some idea as to how it would handle especially as he gets to steer it past the various objects and items dotted across the lake to make things a bit harder for these would be mariners. Over the years, many a model came to grief, and despite their magnificent appearances received the thumbs down, never to be built in that form ever again. The failure of their model would mean the end to any prospect of a bright engineering or shipbuilding future for each member of that team. The hopes of many had been dashed during these tests, with just the very few enjoying success in whatever country they came from.

John, representing his Canadian team was next to a Greek team whose model was a 6 masted tall ship able to turn her masts full of sail into wherever the winds blew, and propel it just as fast as some of the motorised models. The Japanese team had an extremely large tanker, which if given its full size would be over a good 1200 feet long, 250 feet wide, probably capable of carrying at least a million tons of oil. The German team had their ship with the big hole in her hull, which would demonstrate how it was able to launch and retrieve a submersible. The British team entry was a new type of cross channel ferry called a DO DO (drive on drive off vehicular ferry with multiple decks) but appeared to have dodgy bow doors. The Australian team had a new type of refrigeration ship with John having the sneaking suspicion they must have borrowed some of his Taraniti techniques to freeze such a large cargo capacity. He smiled at the automatic thought of Aussie Clarke as being the main suspect, but he didn't care and secretly wished them a good result. The South African teams model was of a very powerful tug which could pull the equivalent of a million tons, happen there was the Japanese model of a ship around to do so. The Danish team was a model of another ferry boat with a novel emergency escape over the side.

The Italians model was of a twin hulled hydrofoil that somehow flipped over and did cartwheels even in little waves.

The Norwegian team brought an impressive model of a Whale

Factory ship, which gave fuel to John's own ideas on such a ship, but to be built for military purposes instead of slaughtering the dwindling population of helpless whales.

John produced his model of the *'Caroline'* which took the breath away from most of the spectators and caused a stir among the paparazzi. Then along came Pritchard's model, stuck back together again, with one of the team sitting down inside it pretending to be the captain. The other teams just laughed at Pritchard's team shouting several colourful sarcastic remarks, which even if the spectators didn't understand the various languages they still had a good idea and a laugh.

"Pay attention everybody! When you hear the siren, you will launch your model and have it sail around the course laid out for you. Pilotage rules and navigation laws are in force, so any person deemed to have caused a collision or whatever, will have severe penalty points deducted from their marks." Clutterbuck announced over the PA system.

A deadly hush crept over the lake for a moment until the siren sounded, when the noise level increased 100 fold as each team leader shouting out their instructions and the examination team walked around observing the launches.

John untied his model from the pontoon, and with the use of his remote controls moved his vessel sideways from the pontoon for a little way, before he used his control switches again to it sail slowly and easily through the lake, negotiating each obstacle and keeping well clear of any other model posing a threat to him. All the models except one were out into the lake, which was the biggest and most cumbersome of the lot, Pritchard's. The weight of the 'captain' on the model caused it to sink almost to the main deck level, thus grounding it in the mud. So he got out, dragging the model deeper into the lake before climbing back into it again and finally sailing away in pursuit of all the others. Pritchard's model was one of four to have a 'coxswain' on board, but the only one who sailed through the 'fleet' causing mayhem to the others, as he was waving and shouting at them to move out of the way. Unknown to the teams, there were special underwater effects about to be used to provide some realistic sea conditions. First there were a few muffled explosions which suddenly produced water mushrooming up above the lake level, to effect turbulence in the water. Then two of the obstacles with large paddles started to rotate from side to side to create ringlets of large waves which swept across the lake, rocking the models in turn. The Italian model flipped and did its predicted trick of cart-wheeling before it sank. The English model's bow doors somehow opened letting the water to flood in enough to capsize it. The biggest surprise to confront the paparazzi and causing howls of laughter from all the other teams, was when Pritchard's model snapped in two, with each piece sinking rapidly to the bottom of the lake, leaving the red-faced coxswain sitting in water up to his shoulders before managing to climb out of the wreck and swim back to the lake side again. John's model did the required three laps around the course before coming neatly alongside its pontoon again, to dock perfectly without the model tug being needed.

The Admiral whose task it was to conduct this final test, stormed off angrily, stating his nephew was a total disgrace to the family name and had dishonoured him so much he would face the consequences because of it. This outburst from the Admiral opened speculation as to who would now fill the opening with the Naval Ship Design team in the Royal Dockyard of Devonport, now his nephew who was the favourite to win the competition had failed so dramatically.

The end of the demos and exams were sounded by the hooter again and Clutterbuck announced everybody was to clear away all their stuff, while the exam results would be promulgated on the main notice board in the main foyer and the prize giving ceremony would be held next Monday afternoon in the Student's assembly hall.

The Project Team Managers went swiftly towards their teams with McPhee arriving alongside John, who had somebody helping him load his model onto the back of his hand-card.

"You did well today John, well done. I feel sure the real acceptance trails and inspections are of more consequence compared with today. I say this because some models don't handle or perform as well as the real thing. Off the record, there're only 2 positions up for grabs this year, but there's a few developments in the pipeline for some of the 'also rans' if you like, so don't despair if you're not picked. So keep smiling, and if you decide to start talking to yourself again, make sure it's with a girl at the other end of your pillow." he said cheerfully, slapping John playfully on his back in a congratulatory manner.

"Thanks for your kind words Fergus! I've been here in the lions den all on my own, and if it wasn't for your unwavering support, I'd probably be a nervous wreck, a floating wreck maybe but still a wreck." he replied sincerely, basking in the warm bond made between them over the years.

McPhee chuckled at the word wreck, telling John that Pritchard's law suit was looking very dodgy especially now that his model had shown the world he's no designer except from the basic drawings he'd stolen from the genuine ones, yours included, over these past few years.

"Go and get yourself cleaned up and see me in the bar this evening, as this is the last drink most of the students will have before taking the weekend off to come back on Monday for the prize giving. " McPhee concluded and waving to John and left.

John was up very early and took a stroll out onto the front lawn to have his pre-breakfast cigarette, when he met up with Klein who must have had the same idea.

"Morning Klein! What a fine morning for an early stroll!" he greeted.

"Morning Grey! Yes, I always get up early so I can get my brain in gear for what may lay ahead of me during the day. My team are still young and just taking their showers but should be out here soon for their early morning exercises. I'm too old for such things, so I let them get on with it."

281

"Me too. As the captain of a baton race team, for the past few years I've been looking after some of up-and-coming engineers for me to hand the baton over to, I think I'm entitled to a few perks of the trade if you like."

Klein chuckled at John's remark and agreed entirely with his sentiments, they carried on with their walk around the gardens in silence for a few minutes, relaxing in each others company.

"This past week has been one hell of a time for us all, and I'm glad it's all over bar the shouting, so to speak. Whatever the outcome and the decisions made by the judges, none of us will leave here without feeling a change in our lives, some for the good some for the bad." John said quietly.

"Hmm! You're right, especially for the likes of Pritchard. It's what I would call, a crossroads in your life. Which path to tread is the big question. For me, I've still got my submersible and parent ship to get operational and ready for duties up around the Arctic. With luck it will keep me busy for a few years until I retire to a little chalet near Cologne that I've been building over the past year or so."

"Well Klein, once again, I wish you good luck on Monday and I certainly hope you will enjoy the fruits of your labours when you retire." John said quietly, holding out his hand and shaking Klein's.

"Yes Grey! I don't have the time to indulge these niceties with you, as my team's taking the weekend off back home in Germany, but good luck to you as well. Who knows, we just might be fellow Project Managers by this time Monday night." Klein concluded as the two men made their way back into the main foyer.

The weekend for John was a quiet and peaceful time as he went fishing in a local river for hours on end. He had the time to gather his thoughts and put lots of things into perspective, especially on the twin subjects of the forthcoming results day on Monday and the interviews with the legal team conducting his defence in the pending legal wrangle with Pritchard.

"Take one day at a time John" he muttered as he managed to catch a magnificent salmon, which he had earmarked for his Sunday evening supper invite at the McPhees house. Even that was a lazy slow moving night full of light hearted small talk as they dared not spoil things by the mention of the dreaded Monday everybody hates, including the examiners and staff according to Fergus.

He was driven back to the campus late on the Sunday night so he was not to be seen open a charge of favouritism with any person on the examination teams.

"See you both at the prize giving, and many thanks for your excellent hospitality, where on times I seemed to be back in big Mac's place once more." John chuckled, waving them off, and then walking through the main gates of the campus made his way back to his cabin.

It was 0900, when everybody had returned and gathered in the main foyer to read their Project comments and deliberations made by the exam judges, each with varying degrees of fortune, or in Pritchard's case, misfortune.

Looking around John saw Pritchard's project team members looking very despondent at their results, yet Pritchard was conspicuous by his absence. Everyone picked up on this and decided to take pity on them with encouraging words of 'better next time' or 'next time pick somebody worthy of Team Leader' or even 'try on your very own, you might get somewhere', all of which seemed to cheer them up to eventually and correctly lay the blame of their failure directly on Pritchard's doorstep.

Each team's project was praised on the good points with excellent constructive criticism on the bad, then give a summary verdict as to what category they were judged in and the merit table or final exam marks given.

John's eyes found the criticism his vessel did not have enough facility for the provision of fresh water or fuel on board, given that each vessel must have enough fuel and water on board for a minimum of 10 days. They were the only 'X's' in all the little 'tick boxes' on the score sheet therefore not to giving him a full 100% mark. The biggest mark and tick was for the model to be 'fit for purpose' to be able to pass the course, which his and only 3 of the others had received. The rest got a great big 'X' and the comments stating why.

"As she was purpose built to operate in the fresh water of the Great Lakes the extra water facility is therefore not needed, and it only takes 5 days to get from one end to the other therefore less is fuel needed. Her own deadweight has to be less to be able to carry the extra cargo tonnage through the canal systems." he muttered, deciding to take this up with the panel of judges who interviewed him, as a matter of principle and not one of complaint against his marks.

He went to the Adjudicator who dealt with appeals and objections from disgruntled students, and managed to meet up with Clutterbuck who happened to be in the room at the same time.

"Excuse me gentlemen, my name is John Grey, the designer and builder of the *MV Carolina*, and I have come to appeal against your decision to marking me down on two items which are not necessary on board my project vessel." John stated on entering the room.

"Good morning Mr Grey. What is your argument against such a decision?" the adjudicator asked civilly.

"The *MV Caroline* was purpose built for her life sailing in the Great Lakes of Canada, i.e. 3,000 miles of fresh water to take on board as and when needed. That being so, she does not require more than a few tons of fresh water on board. Secondly, her longest trip would be from one end of the lakes to the other taking no more than 5 days sailing, therefore she would be able to refuel before making her way back again. This provision is to take into account the extra tonnage she would be able to carry through the canal system thus gaining extra revenue for her owners." John stated calmly.

284

The adjudicator went to a storage room and brought out John's main ship's design and blue-prints to take a look at what John was talking about. It took the man several moments looking at the designs, and dialogue with Clutterbuck to make his deliberations.

"It seems you are correct in what you have told us in regard to the fresh water, so we will adjust your marking accordingly. In regard to your fuel capacity deficiency in providing extra cargo load, we uphold the decision by the judges. This is because the vessel might get delayed through storms or lack of provision of fuel at the destination port, therefore the vessel would not be able to make any further progression along her planned voyage. We can quote several such incidents of what we speak about, but you as an experienced Marine Engineer should already know, it's best to have enough fuel to get into port rather than a ship full of cargo floating helplessly in the middle of the ocean, or in your case, a lake."

John realised what he said was true given the fuel crises he'd had on the *Tsun Wan*, but decided to give one more push to win the whole argument not just half of it.

"For a vessel to be judged fit for purpose and be given a full seaworthy certificate from the Lloyds Shipping Registry as the *Caroline* was, then just who has the overall say in deciding what fuel capacity any vessel must have before putting to sea, apart from the 10 day ruling that is?"

"I will put it to you Mr Grey, the 10 day rule is an internationally recognised standard, for it to be the only factor to take into consideration for your appeal. This is my final decision on the matter, however you will consider yourself fortunate you've been able to get a second opinion winning at least half of your appeal which most students don't ever get. See you at the prize giving Mr Grey, which no doubt your Project Manager, er Mr McPhee, will be looking forward to, given he's also your 'proposer' to join our Faculty as part of the management team, providing of course you achieve the 'honours' required. Thank you for your astuteness Mr Grey, you may now leave us to listen to other such appeals. Good luck!" the chief examiner said as Clutterbuck escorted John out of the room.

"After all we've gone through to build, test and sail a ship full of cargo, it seems we've only got a 9 and a half, not quite the full deck for Fergus to give us our shiny '10'." he muttered to himself feeling quite disgruntled as if he'd personally let the team down, by what was after all a basic error.

The main hall was full of the luminaries with their guests, and a battery of flashing cameras to record the proceedings as the project teams filed in to fill up the rows of seats allocated to them.

John representing the Canadian team managed to sit next to Klein and his German team with Heemskirk the Dutch project team leader next to them waiting for the final outcome of what was to come about.

In succession to stand up and speak it was Clutterbuck, followed by the Admiral, then the Chief Examiner, and a few of the international brethren representing the ship-building fraternity, before the chief adjudicator stood up to announce what each project team member had waited so long for, the verdict.

Standing up he made a long winded speech waffling on about each project team's performance, the merits or otherwise of their model and the comments which were made to award them their marks then finally got on with the nerve-wracking results.

"From this year's crop of projects I will announce those which have made the best contribution towards this college, but in no particular order. Those not mentioned should deem themselves to have failed, and will need a further attempt to gain the accolades this college can afford them." he began.

John looked at Klein and held out his hand, "Here we go Klein! Best of luck." he whispered, as Klein returned the sentiment.

"Project team Denmark have been given a merit therefore a pass. Project team Greece also have a merit and a pass. Project team Japan have been given a distinction. The top two who gained the most votes and points are..." he said and gave a long pause to keep up the suspense.

"In second place is the Project team from Germany! Come forward and receive your £250,000 prize, your 2nd place trophy and your parchment to claim your place within this college as a Project Team Manager. " he announced with a great cheer from the hall, and much jubilation from Klein's team.

Klein's team stood up and cheered in joy as Klein approached the platform to receive his award and certificate from his Project Manager who was all smiles and full of praise for his team.

Once Klein had made his little acceptance speech and left the platform, the Adjudicator then held up his hands to name the overall winner of the year, and again with a big pregnant pause announced: "Project team Canada! Well done Canada. Come forward and receive your accolade and your prize of £500,000 plus your certificate to become one of the college's Project Managers."

Klein had just returned and slapped John's back in a joyful manner congratulating him on his win, for John to return the compliment and remind him that although he did come second, the two of them would be fellow Project Managers for the next 5 years.

On reaching the platform he was met by McPhee, who was beaming from ear to ear and gave John a great big bear hug before making a small speech, John breathless after the hug, felt his mind racing as to what to say in his acceptance speech.

John held up his 'winning' trophy which was a large lead crystal bowl filled to the brim with champagne for him and his team to quaff. As he was on his own, he gave it a good slurp before offering it to McPhee to drink the rest, while he pocketed his cheque whilst clutching his coveted certificate. The rest of the teams were chanting for him to give his speech, he obliged whilst being held in a one armed hug by McPhee who was almost twice his size.

"Honoured guests, venerable judges, college management, and fellow project team members. It gives me great pleasure to receive this award on behalf of my fellow team members who are out in Canada building a sister ship to my model even as I stand here. I have to thank my guide and definitely my mentor Fergus McPhee here, who, for his sins, took me under his wing and has nurtured me along the way for over a good 15 years now. For it has been a very long and hard journey through the ranks of the Marine Engineering Officer's code of practice to be able to stand here in front of you. We are all fellow project team members, each with our own ideas and inspirations, and I take this opportunity to salute each and every one of you who has made it to these hallowed buildings to be able to compete on a level playing field despite the tank water being a big rough on times. I mean, that tank test is enough to crack and sink anybody let alone their model." he added as a jibe towards Pritchard who was sitting at the back of the room, causing much laughter from the assembly as they knew just what he was referring to, and much to the chagrin of Pritchard.

"Finally, I congratulate Mr Klein and his German team for their success for being able to join me here as our certificate dictates, the next wave of chosen Project Managers." he said with aplomb, but with a grin from ear to ear. The response to his speech was a standing ovation, and cheers from everybody in the room, including Pritchard's team members, despite the scowls and black looks coming from Pritchard himself, who was seen to slink out of the room some seconds later.

The big day had come to its finale and everybody gathered in the main lounge for the end of course and finals do enjoying it with their chosen guests for the day. This was a farewell party for all to remember their 'Finals' in the college, as they would depart for good in the morning, some never to meet up again.

John caught up with the McPhee's who were sitting at the back of the lounge in company with a few of the other Project

Managers and invited him to join them.

"Well done Grey! We hope you will kick-start this Scotch Haggis into staying for a further few years." one of them said holding out a hand to shake his in congratulations, with most of his companions agreeing.

"I still need a shiny '10' from my Ace to be able to report back to my team out in Port Arthur, which incidentally is soon to be called 'Thunder bay'." John replied, feeling much more relaxed now.

Clutterbuck, who was with his wife, nodded to John and took time to mention he was to have a few days off at home before reporting back to take up his duties, but he'd need to prepare himself for the pending imposition of a litigation against him and the college, all thanks to you know who, and who was also challenging their decision on choosing John's project for the college's top award instead of it going to him.

McPhee looked a bit concerned about this but John put him at ease with a succinct observation which made everybody take notice.

"What Pritchard stole was a concept drawing of a ship in two parts. On one side as a separate drawing was the superstructure aft, complete with engine room, bridge and accommodation for the entire crew plus a few passengers. On the other side was a drawing consisting of just the cargo hold area. If his model snapped clean off at a particular join, then I suspect all he did was to build both sections separately then merely bolt them both together to make the ship a whole one. Unfortunately for him that's all he had. The concept is fine for prefabrication especially if you've got less launch pad footage to build the vessel on just like I had. If he'd done the decent thing and came with the rest of the team, then he'd have found out the ship needed the type of construction my master blue-print clearly shows, to be able to withstand all the load the hull would have sustain during any heavy weather. Hence his model snapping neatly in two even in a measly test tank, all of this, which even a blind man would spot, was the

289

real difference between his concept for this type of ship and mine. His uncle the Admiral knows he doesn't stand a chance of winning this argument, but then I'm no legal expert on these matters. My project team's final master blueprint I used to demonstrate our model will be the deciding factor, that I feel sure of."

"Well said John!" a voice said quietly from behind him yet in his ear.

John turned around to see the figure of Happy Day looking down at him with a big smile on his face.

"Happy! By God, it's nice to see you again! When did you arrive, as I didn't see you in the assembly today." John said, shaking Day's hand so vigorously he had to tell John jokingly he'd better watch in case his arm dropped off.

"I joined the management team last year just after you'd left for Canada. So by all accounts from what I've gathered here today, you've finally made the grade and will be joining the rest of us as a new Project Manager. Congratulations John! I knew you'd make it one day, despite some hairy moments with certain shipping line owners, no names no kit bags but the name of B ending with elverley rings a bell." Day said, nodding to the table full of other Project Managers and a few of the judges.

The bubbly, cigars, and exchanged pleasantries were expended long after most of the party-goers had scoffed the scraps from the buffet and left the makeshift dance area, leaving only John, the McPhee's, Clutterbuck and Day at their table.

"Oh well John Grey! This is your home from home for a few years. I'll arrange some transport to take you to the station for your week's leave. When you come back you'll be able to start on your next project construction and team gathering. I'm off now! Last one out, don't forget to lock the bar up and switch off at the mains." Clutterbuck said yawning, stood up and left the lounge. Day then the McPhee's indicated it was time for them to get turned in, and Day offered to do the honours and lock up.

"See you in the morning Happy! Good night Claire, and your Fergus. Thanks for a brilliant day. I've deposited the winning cheque in the night safe which will be sent along with the results and the good news to Colin and Ben in the morning. They'll be needing that cheque more'n me now they've started phase one of the sister ship to the *Caroline*." John said wearily and started to make his way out.

"Actually John. A third of it belongs to you to set up your operations here. Suggest you see the Auditor about it before you shoot off. See me first before you go though!" McPhee advised and waved John good night.

Chapter XXXVIII

Judgement Day

John came back from his week's leave, to settle down into the rigours of becoming a Project Manager, which to him seemed a bit tame, except for the exams and tests they gave him to see if in fact he really was suited to the position he was accorded and worth the high salary he was to be given.

It wasn't long before they recognised both his capability and his inventive ideas and gave him the go ahead, to get stuck into yet another ship design, then have it drawn by the technical drawing experts before deciding upon its final development.

When the drawings were made to John's satisfaction he decided to take them to the Chief designer and model tester Halford to see if all was okay. He was the one with the final say in any design which was to be recommended for further development by the college.

"Seems okay to me, but you haven't given any indication as to what is being built and who for."

"Sorry Halford, I forgot. As you can see, its fore-end is that of a 6 inch cruiser, with the rear half like a carrier, an assault ship that departs from the current design which stops to flood its stern for the troops to disembark in their landing crafts. Whilst the ship is stopped, waiting to off load the marine's landing craft, she is a virtual sitting duck for any shore bombardments let alone any submarine that may happen to be lurking around. My idea is a cross from watching some cygnets getting off and onto their mother's back whilst she still moved along, and the Norwegian's model of their whale factory ship.

I have a tilted deck going aft to the stern towards a double door at the stern, something like the launch ramp you see at a lifeboat station.

The ship can just steam towards the beach area, then as she turns about, she opens the double doors to let the landing craft launch themselves two by two through them, into the water and away to make their landings. I think of it as a 'fanning out procedure' whilst the ship goes about to come round again to provide a bombardment for the advancing landing forces from the two twin 6 inch for'ard turrets. When ready for the evacuation and for them to pick up the landing crafts again, she can either go astern slowly with her doors open for the landing craft to be driven back on board again. Or, the ship can move slowly ahead still with the doors open so the craft could make it on board as before, as any crippled landing craft could be 'tagged' by a hawser wire thrown to them to be hauled safely aboard. Once all the landing crafts are on board, with the doors shut, she can get well away from the area. This vessel would be capable of carrying a few gunships on the main deck aft of the main superstructure, which is looking something like the flight deck of a carrier to support the landing force, and say maybe 2 more to ferry artillery pieces or supplies to them. It will be able to carry up to 1 battalion of marines plus their landing craft, with them all, baggage and equipment included accommodated below the flight deck as mentioned." he informed, pointing to the various items on the drawings.

"I noticed the vessel has a twin funnels in line abreast instead of line astern of one another. Obviously twin screw?"

"Yes, just like the *SS Canberra* I did my engineering apprenticeship and college course on whilst she was on the stocks in Belfast. She was the first major sized merchant vessel ever to have a twin funnel positioned abreast, mainly thanks to the idea coming from my mother's brother, Fred Crilley."

"Hmm! Okay then, we'll see what the Board of Selectors have to say about it, which includes the Admiral. Make sure you keep it locked up in our vaults in case there's another Pritchard prowling around."

"Yes, and I'll be glad when that situation has been resolved, as it's keeping me from one of my principle tasks, scouting around for a suitable project team, as you already know."

"It's the same for most of us senior staff, according to our legal team now headed by er, er, The Honourable Judge Anderson Q.C. He's the one who apparently spoke to you to give you his card way back before you took off for Canada."

John thought for a moment to recall the name, but couldn't do so.

"Why me of all people?"

"He was one of the passengers on the Admiral's barge when it ran aground in the Solent."

"Ah yes! Now I remember. I can remember the time when I broke Pritchard's model F196 in the test tank under your tutelage if I my memory serves me correctly. And the fact shortly after he joined our project team he pinched my original concept drawing and disappeared, only to find out he had it patented that weekend. Some feat that was, considering it normally takes weeks for the Patents office to investigate a claim, so just who else is in with him and the scam he pulled?"

"Precisely! Which makes me, McPhee and Clutterbuck important witnesses to nail Pritchard down as he's done this trick a few times before."

"It's all been very quiet up to now, perhaps leading up to the finale so to speak. When's the big hearing then?"

"As you know the college is shutting down next week for a week's holiday. As it happens, it is then we'll be up in London. We are all going up together to stay in a nearby hotel overnight, with luck coming back the following day, otherwise we stay until such times as the court makes their decision."

"What are our chances?"

"We can prove Pritchard's theft, but as far as the conceptual design is concerned, it might be difficult to prove in your favour. Anderson will put us right about it all when we meet up with him."

"I hope Pritchard's going to be there!"

"Indeed, he's got to be to defend his claim as will his Admiral Uncle to defend his corner."

"Thanks for the info Halford, I'll get these into the vaults right this minute. See you again later." John concluded, leaving the test tank area.

"Hello John! Off to set the world to rights again?" Day asked with a smile, seeing John about to leave the college for their pending court appearance up in the 'smoke'.

"'Fraid so Happy. Shades of Barbados comes to mind, shame Bruce Larter wasn't here to help me out on the finer things though." John said stoically.

"Yes your friend Bruce was definitely what the RN called a 'lower deck lawyer' and very capable too. But methinks our man Anderson is infinitely more qualified than him to handle what you and the college are about. If I know you John, you'll pose more questions to the prosecution lawyer than he can gain his own answers to, or have time to draw breath, just like you've been doing for the past decade or so. For your own sake curb it, just answer the man accordingly."

"Sorry and all that Happy, but I'll answer his questions with my own, and pose even more, which, according to Bruce will tongue-tie the man and confuse him so much he won't know what day it was. As far as I'm concerned, Pritchard is a rat and a sneak-thief who's done it before. We need others who suffered the same fate as me, to climb aboard our wagon and nail him along with all the others who seem to be part of his scam, his Admiral Uncle included perhaps."

"Just be careful John on that score John, or the panel of judges might think you are only out for revenge for what he did to you and your project team."

"No worries! The next thing he and his Admiral Uncle will know they will find themselves on the other side of the 'Black Stump' eating 'desert oysters' for their supper. Er, that's kangaroo bollocks in case you didn't know, according to my very good

Antipodean friend Aussie Clarke. God and Taraniti bless him.""•

"Hmm! Well anyway John. When you come back I'll be up north in Bonny Scotland. So take care my young friend, and hope to see you again soon." Day said, grasping John's hand, shaking it in farewell.

"You can bet on that my dear old Chief. Mind you, when we do meet up you'd better not be…"

"I know, adrift! And less of the 'old' if you don't mind." Day said with a big grin, watching John board the minibus to take them away.

John walked into the courtroom to find it was just as forbidding a place as he'd previously encountered quite a few times in his past life, yet it somehow seemed quite different from them.

There were several po-faced men dressed in black cloaks, wearing the traditional grey wig which looked like a toupee planked almost haphazardly upon their heads. He imagined these wigs as fuel tanks dispensing the gobbledygook language which only they could understand.

It took several speeches and oratory performances from both of the legal teams, to try to establish between the two opposing sides, just who was the creator of the 'one castle' vessel over 200 ft, leaving John in a quandary as to which one had given an 'Oscar-winning 'performance'.

It finally came down to the simple argument of who owned the initial idea, which put John into the hot seat for an aggressive cross-examinations from Pritchard's team of lawyers.

"Mr Grey, it seems from your records, you are purely and simply a Marine Engineering Officer, albeit with some distinction. This being so, why have you decided to up your

---

• The 'Black Stump' is a revered place which is in fact the remains of a sand encrusted petrified tree some millennia years old, situated in the back of beyond and reputed to be somewhere way out in the middle of the Australian desert. Ask any 'Abbo' who's bound to know where it is, as we don't.

career by stealing the ideas of an established shipbuilder such as my client Mr Pritchard?"

John looked over to see the sneering face of Pritchard, but decided to concentrate on his own questions.

"When I first met Mr Pritchard, it was in the ISDM tank testing area whereby he was testing his very latest model of a ship, deemed to be the best design in the modern world of ship design. So I'll ask Pritchard my own questions…"

"I'm the one asking the questions Grey not you." The bewigged barrister sniped.

"Okay then your very learned person. If Pritchard was testing the model of his very latest ship design, then how come it didn't come in the shape that I had designed in the first place?

Pritchard was invited to join our team as the only ship designer with any sort of experience, so we would be able to construct such a ship as my concept drawings suggested.

It takes an average of 10 weeks for the Patents office to investigate the provenance and idea claimed by the proposer. Given that, how come Pritchard got hold of my initial concept drawing showing a ship in two separate sections, all without the practical ways of building such a vessel, yet had it patented almost overnight?

Who was it who said he had to have it patented in such a manner?

Who is the figurehead behind his somewhat devious existence in the ISDM college, when everybody else has to work long and hard over several years to become even a project team member let alone a project leader?

Pritchard's model F196 turned out to be a total failure in the test tank at the college, simply because he had stolen the original idea from a fellow team member. If he is a genuine ship designer, then how come his version of my model failed miserably in the test tank, i.e. by snapping itself into two pieces, yet my model was able to win the ISDM's yearly competition? Who was it…? " John snapped, but was silenced angrily by the

Judge telling him he'd be held in contempt of court unless he answered only the questions put top him by the prosecutors, he was not to pose his own..

"M'Lud! I will refuse to answer any further questions until such times as Pritchard or his brief answer the ones I've just posed. I have several other leading questions which no doubt my legal brief will put on my behalf. For you to get to the truth of all this M'Lud, it's Pritchard you should be prosecuting not me. He's the one who stole my drawing of a concept ship, showing a ship being built in two sections. If he'd actually devised and built such a ship then it would have had disastrous consequences for all on board, as his model snapped into two separate pieces as per drawings. Which bears out the fact he did build the concept ship as per drawing, and merely welded the two pieces together. My model of the design was actually built on the shores of the Great Lakes, and is still in one piece, as my detailed drawings have proved. Had it been the other way round and I had stolen his design from the very beginning, then it would have been my ship to snap in two not his." John snarled.

His outburst caused such a stir within the courtroom, that the judge slammed his ornate wooden hammer onto its gavel to declare a recess, ordering both briefs to come and see him in his chambers, then demanded that John be taken down to the holding cells until such times as they convene again.

Anderson came storming over to John and told him that he might face imprisonment for his outburst, as he should have been the one to pose such questions in a manner according to court etiquette.

"So be it. I'm not one to pander to the leap-frogging, funny handshakes brigade whilst passing the bar of soap. Pritchard is the guilty one not me." he sniped, as he was led away down into the bowels of the multi storey building.

"The court will reconvene in 2 hours time, so unless you give me your word you will to behave and not utter another word, you'll be staying in the cells until such times as this issue has been resolved. I have many of my own questions to ask Pritchard and his Admiral Uncle which might clear up several mysteries and brown envelope deals they've been doing for the past 5 years. So be off with you and trust me as I am after all a fully fledged QC." Anderson stated flatly.

Clutterbuck and Halford also expressed their disquiet of John's outburst repeating more or less what Anderson had said.

"Aussie was right after all. A lot of bullshit and ego massaging going round, never mind the truth." he muttered to himself, allowing the steward of the court to lock him in a cell that had only a seat for him to use.

"It should be Pritchard here not me officer." he said to the man.

"Actually, we've got bets on Pritchard and his Uncle both ending up here once the judge is finished with them. In the meanwhile I'll get some sandwiches and a cuppa sent down for you."

"How long is this recess?"

"His Lordship's got a lunch date at the Dorchester just down the road from here, which normally takes about 2 hours by the time they've scoffed their £600 a head meal and quaffed their vintage wine costing around £250 a bottle. So he'll be back in his chauffer driven limo in time to wrap things up before he goes out with his mistress for an evening at the opera." the man sighed, leaving John alone in his cell.

"All rise! The Honourable Judge Frizzel is now in court!" the clerk of the court announced, and everybody waited until the judged indicated they may sit down again.

John who been taken back into the court some moments previously saw see the still smirking face of Pritchard looking at him.

McPhee sat next to John this time and whispered to him to take no notice of Pritchard and to calm down.

The prosecution summed up their argument for the plaintiff before the defence team took over the court, asking very pertinent questions that to John, were the same questions he had posed yet put in a cleverly disguised way so the plaintiffs could not bluff their way out of.

Pritchard, still smirking was put onto the 'stand', but after a severe grilling by Anderson the smirk was wiped off his face to be replaced by a look of terror and deep worry lines etched on his forehead. For Anderson had wiped the floor with the plaintiff's arguments, so much so the judge decided to call a halt and to make an easy judgment on this unusual case.

"This is a case of several merits but can be compared to an easy analogy. Two people walking along a beach, when one sees a watch lying in the sand, the other person picks it up to claim it for himself. Who does the watch belong to, the person who first spotted it or the one who actually picked it up? In this case, it appears that whilst Grey spotted the idea it was Pritchard who took it up to have it patented. However, from the history of inventions, the actual concept of Grey's idea is too important for just one person to claim. A classic example of just who was the one to lay claim to the idea of putting a sail on a boat for the winds to push it along. Therefore making the world of shipbuilders and sailors all the better for it, causing them to pursue their improvements to the original concept as the centuries came along. This case being a modern idea that can possibly be accredited to Grey as one of that ilk, but it will remain in the public domain for the many to benefit not the individual. Pritchard's underhand methods of gaining the accolade of an international ship-designer are now at an end. He is to serve a 5 year sentence for the crime of 'industrial espionage' and will no longer be allowed to undertake any future ship designs or the building thereof. His model will be kept in perpetuity at the Greenwich Maritime museum as a sinister reminder of his work.

"Bloody hell! What a load of bullshit as a good friend of mine would say. Pritchard only got 5 years? What about his conniving

Uncle? And what about my conceptual idea?" John asked in an anger aside to Anderson, who was all smiles to everybody in the room.

"Think yourself lucky Grey! Your ship is of a far better design and is safe to operate. I've just received a telegram from the office of my research team. Pritchard had a ship built which was launched three months ago. It sank four days days ago whilst on voyage from Borneo to Japan with only 2 lucky survivors who were fortunately picked up by an American rescue plane two days ago. They tell about the way it sank, which describes exactly what happened to Pritchard's model in the test tank. The after-superstructure sheared off neatly along the join mark with the cargo hold. Also, whoever built the ship to his design will be facing big fines from the Lloyds Insurance investigators, plus millions of pounds in compensation to the families of the men who perished on it. Pritchard will never live this down nor will his Admiral Uncle. He'll be facing the chop and kiss his gold-plated pension goodbye."

Before the judge declared the proceedings over, Anderson asked him if he could make one brief announcement, which the judge agreed to but with annoyance.

"Your honour, learned gentlemen and all attending this court! I have just received a communication from my research team's office concerning this trial." Anderson started, then went on to inform the court about the sinking of Pritchard's ship which had happened in the same manner as the model one did in the test tank. This shock statement caused a deathly hush over the room, and the judge declared that although he had already passed his sentence to Pritchard, it didn't rule out any future proceedings which would inevitably arise.

He turned to Pritchard and told him that he was lucky to escape this trial with 5 years, but could face possible murder charges in respect of designing a ship not suitable for purpose or even seaworthy.

Pritchard went a ghostly white and fainted whilst the Admiral stormed out of the court, vowing to get even on the people he had relied upon over the past two decades.

"You can go back to your college now Grey, vindicated in part inasmuch as Pritchard has been given 5 years in jail. Next time you get a brainwave, keep it to yourself until such times as you can have it validated and verified by those responsible for doing so. Now that we're quits, I bid you goodbye." Anderson said, shaking John's hand.

"I didn't know we were beholden, but thank you anyway." John replied, leaving with the rest of the ISDM team.

"When we get back to the college Grey, get those new design plans underway by the end of the month. It will take time for the dust to settle on this one so it's best you hang your 'gone fishing' sign on your door and go home for a month's leave." Clutterbuck said with a grin as the team made their train journey back to Southampton.

"Ma I'm home!" he called out, and gave his mother a peck on her cheek.

"Glad you're home son. I've got some exciting news to tell you. Norah and Billy have applied to immigrate to Australia and I'll be going with them to help look after the twins for them."

"Oh! That's a sudden move Ma! It's a long way to go only to come back if you don't like the place, big as it is. Has Billy got a job to go to, only you're not allowed to emigrate on the £10 ticket if you don't have a job to go to."

"Billy's been made redundant as an ambulance driver for the Lagan Valley Hospital, but has been offered an ambulance driver's job in Melbourne. Norah will be required to work where she can. The twins will be going to school so I'm going to look after them when Billy and Norah are out working."

"Hmm! It means I'll have no home apart from the college, unless I go over to Birmingham and stay with Nancy and Arthur."

"Yes I suppose so, but then just maybe you'll meet a wee girl and settle down now you've finished with the sea and in a college."

"Me and wee girls don't seem to manage the course, what with one dead, two on the other side of the world, and the fourth got married to her school boyfriend. Oh well Ma! I might just decide to come with you all, for I've got some very dear friends down there I can look up. Let's forget it for now as I'm home for a month's leave. I'll have some breakfast now, maybe go fishing after dinner." he said softly.

THE END. . .

or IS IT?

Author's Note

"His recent month at home seemed to have flown by and when John returned he decided to team up with Klein on a huge project for which both of were needed. It would mean the two of them working in tandem instead of the usual conflict of ideas and protectionism from each individual Project Manager."

This then sets the scene for the final novel in this series. The outline notes for this book, which was due to come out somewhere between books 3 -7, were missing from the start and when found it was too late.

I have decided to use the main theme of the story which will be updated and tagged on the end to complete the 'Adventures of John Grey', which I hope you will still enjoy and appreciate my endeavours of producing an 11 novel series within 5 years.

The title for book 11 is still to be decided but '*The Last Voyage*' or '*The Long March*' are the favourites so far, but whatever you do, DON'T MISS IT!

I have 4 more novels to follow my series:

HMS UNRIVALLED (D20)

Is about a pre WW2 destroyer who's crew, thanks to their tyrannical and very cruel Captain, mutinied and the aftermath that faced them.

MR WALKER

Is about a simple Shepherd boy who, when growing up, was kidnapped by his hated former school bully who forced him to join the Army to fight in France during WW1.

THE WATER NYMPH

Is about the youngest son of a Duke who earns his way as an engineer and boat builder set around the 1900s. It contains an Upstairs Downstairs-style romance, and some daring deeds by the son.

THE BODY HUNTERS
Is about the lives of former pirates and ship-wreckers living on some small yet remote islands who are shunned by the rest of the world.

All published by Guaranteed Books
www.theguaranteedpartnership.com